Dedicated to my beautif
May you grow up to learn
folklore and cul
the struggle and the
and never forget w
or the battles that have be ...ṣ ṃves lost,
so that you and your people may live on.
Life is for the living,
but we must never forget
the honourable dead.

ISBN: 9781521915547

For more information, comments or questions, please visit my
twitter and facebook pages:
https://www.facebook.com/EngliscWarrior/
And don't forget to show your support and hit the 'Like' button.
Thank you.

Author's Note

For centuries, the Roman Empire dominated most of Britain and Europe, yet beyond Rome's vast shadow remained fiercely independent clans, known to the Romans as the Germani. The forests the Germani inhabited was known as Germania, the Land of Spears. The Germani included the Goths, Franks, Burgundians, Vandals, Jutes, Angles (Englisc), Saxons, Frīsians, and many others.

Offa belonged to the same Angles who, fifty years later, would settle Roman Britannia, giving their name to the Kingdom of Ængla land (England). Offa was a real historical character and would become one of the greatest Anglo-Saxon heroes and therefore one of the greatest English heroes to ever live. Ket and Wīg are also real historical characters and their story is based on true events.

Ellen sceal on eorle...
Bravery belongs to a hero...

North Germania 394 A. D.

SWEDELAND

JUTLAND

•Gothenburg

Horsens

Gēatland

Wēland's Cabin

Hornbæk

Grib
Forest

Kolding

Hleidargard

DANELAND

ÆNGLA LAND

Jötunn Forest

Angeln

Schleswig

Hedeby

River Eider

Monster's Gate

War-Beards

Hamburg

VANDALS

River Elba

SAXONY

River Wesser

Offa
Rise of the Englisc Warrior

Second Edition

S. A. Swaffington

"The Langabardi (Long-Beards) are distinguished by the
fewness of their numbers. Ringed round as they are by many
mighty clans, they find safety, not in submission, but in battle
and its perils. After them come the Reudigni (Rondings),
Auiones (Eowan), Angli (Angles/English), Varni (Wærne),
Eudoses (Jutes), Suarines, and Nuithones (Teutons),
well-guarded by rivers and forests. There is nothing
remarkable about these clans, unless it is the common worship
of Nerthuz (Earth Mother). They believe she is interested in
men's affairs and drives amongst them."

Cornelius Tacitus, 1st Century A. D.
Germania

The first reference to the English people 1,000 years before the
Norman Invasion.

Prologue

394 A. D.
Jötunn Forest

An eagle with a wingspan of at least sixteen-feet-across and a
body the size of a horse soared high above the vast, ancient
forest, a forest older than mankind; its long slender wings
resting gracefully on the air, its yellow beak slashing through
the winds. Below, in a small clearing by a rushing brook, two
men were dressed in bear pelts and armed with bows and

arrows, short-swords and axes. 'You're in Troll Country now, lad,' spoke Eadrīc, deep in the heart of the Jötunn Forest, named after the mighty trolls that dwell there, and miles from any settlements. 'Time to hunt.'

'How do you know we're in Troll Country?' the young Randolf asked as the tall, slender trees swayed in the swirling winds above his head.

'Because I'm standing in front of a pile of fresh troll turd,' Eadrīc replied, looking upon the ground, playing with his long grey beard. 'I'll soon prove the bastards are real.'

'How do you know it's troll turd?' Randolf asked, while Eadrīc's dog sniffed at it.

'I've been hunting this forest for twenty years,' Eadrīc replied. 'I've seen many bears and wolves, even lost an ear to a bear, but I've never seen a turd that big. Put your fingers in and tell me what you think.'

Reluctantly, Randolf did as he was told and pushed two fingers inside.

'It's still warm,' spoke Randolf, turning his head in disgust.

'I know that,' spoke Eadrīc. 'I can see the steam coming off it. Smell it, lad.'

Randolf lifted his fingers to his nose.

'It stinks,' Randolf told him, choking on the smell.

'Well, does it belong to a bear or a wolf?' Eadrīc asked, scanning the forest and sniffing at the wind.

'I don't know what a bear or wolf turd smells like,' Randolf replied.

'Neither do I,' Eadrīc added. 'I've never had the pleasure of sniffing their turds.'

'Then why am I smelling it?' Randolf asked.

'I don't know, lad,' Eadrīc answered. 'You were always a strange one.'

'I can't believe you made me do that,' spoke Randolf, getting back to his feet, wiping his hand on his breeches. 'I thought that's how you track game?'

'It's how others track game,' Eadrīc replied. 'I prefer to use dogs. It's less smelly. I used to come out here with two of them, but instead of hunting they spent most of the time sniffing each other's arseholes. So now I just bring the one.'

'Have you truly seen a troll, Eadrīc, or are you making fun of me?' Randolf asked, getting frustrated.

'About fifteen years ago,' spoke Eadrīc, putting his boot up against a fallen tree, 'I was out here with my family, teaching my sons to hunt, when my eldest was snatched and taken high into the trees by an unseen hand. I heard his screams while he was carried away into the forest. I followed the best I could until I lost the trail. I've been looking for him ever since. I made a vow to the Gods that I won't rest until I find whatever took my son and claim its head.'

'What makes you think you'll find whatever took your son?' Randolf asked. 'It was a long time ago.'

'Look at all of these trees,' spoke Eadrīc. 'They haven't blown over with the wind. They have been uprooted by something big, like the day my son was taken. Whatever took that dump is nearby.'

Taking a deep, calming breath, Randolf drew his seax; a two-foot-long traditional short-sword, and took a long hard look into the forest.

'Where's your dog?' Randolf asked.

They both turned their heads and saw the dog staring into the forest, its fur erect; growling at some unseen thing.

'What is it, boy?' Eadrīc asked, looking between the trees, growing nervous. 'What's out there?' The dog continued to growl, revealing his fangs, not taking his eyes from the shadows. 'Get him, boy! Go get him!'

The dog ran between the trees, barking. Eadrīc and Randolf stood anxiously, their eyes fixed on the forest, listening; their hearts hammering inside their chest.

'Do you think there's a troll here?' Randolf asked as the dog disappeared from view.

'Something has spooked him,' Eadrīc answered, preparing his bow.

The dog's bark could be heard echoing into the forest, but then a squeal was heard and the barking stopped.

'What was that?' Randolf asked with a dry mouth.

'It's here,' Eadrīc answered, licking his lips whilst walking further into the forest. 'It's killed my dog. You stay here, in the light. Trolls don't like the light. It turns the bastards to stone.'

Randolf watched as Eadrĭc ran between the trees with his bow, calling his dog. Randolf's heartbeat was frantic and sweat rolled down the back of his neck. He gripped his seax until his knuckles turned white. He could no longer see Eadrĭc, but he could hear him roaring like a bear from beyond the trees, challenging whatever was out there; causing dozens of ravens to flee from the surrounding treetops.

'Run, Randolf!' Eadrĭc yelled from somewhere in the shadows, but then a deadly silence fell over the forest, terrifying Randolf to his bones.

In the corner of his eye, Randolf saw a shadow coming towards him, creeping along one of the uprooted trees. It had a large head and a big thick mane. Its claws were like steel, its fur was as black as coal; its drooling fangs were like long-knives and its eyes were red and glowing. It looked like a wolf, but it was the size of a bear, and it was neither wolf nor bear. The hellish beast leapt from the tree several feet above Randolf's head, with its mouth wide open, and landed upon the young hunter, knocking him to the ground, tearing out his throat and sending his soul to the afterlife.

Chapter One
Hallowed Ground

Wēland's Cabin, Jötunn Forest

Broken light sliced between the branches of the canopy, lighting the way through the deep fairy-haunted forest. Ket and his brother, Wīg, were leading ten youngsters to see the famous Wēland the Smith to begin their training as Wolf-Coats. It was tradition for the clan's noble-born to be taken away from their parents at the age of seven and trained in ancient lore and the ways of the warrior. 'How much further?' Offa asked, walking the steep slope in the gentle rain. 'We've been walking for days.'

'I want to go home and climb back in bed,' the chubby-cheeked Bardawulf added, being careful not to stand inside the ring of mushrooms, known as fairy rings.

'Stop your whining, it's just over this hill,' Ket answered, carrying his boar-crested helm under his arm, allowing the rain to fall into his blonde shaggy locks.

'I'm so hungry I could eat a wolf's heart,' spoke Bardawulf, dragging his tired feet.

'That's why you're a fat swine,' Haakon joked, a brutish lad with long red hair and a cruel freckled face. The others laughed.

'Well, Bardawulf, your training is about to begin,' spoke Wīg. 'Soon you will get your chance.'

'Why couldn't we come on horseback?' Grendel asked, using a stick to knock the head off a flower. 'My feet are aching and I'm tired.'

'Because walking makes you strong,' Ket answered from in front. 'You can't be swinging from your mother's udders for the rest of your life. Why do you think we are here?'

Ket was fifteen-years-old. His brother, Wīg, was fourteen. They were a distant relation to Offa and were descended from Wōden, God of war and poetry. It was Wōden who gave his name to Wōdnesdæg - Wednesday. Ket and Wīg had finished their time in the wild, killing a wolf with their own blade and skinning it to make their coats. They were accompanying the group to Wēland's cabin to offer their support. Some of them were from the Kingdom of Angeln, where Offa's father was King, though most came from the Earldom of Schleswig, where Ket and Wīg's father was Earl. They would each come-of-age by the time they reached their fourteenth birthday, but the path to manhood was long and fraught with danger.

If their will was strong enough they would become Cnihts and later train to become Thegns, the King's highest ranking warriors; but first they had to spend many months in the forest. With only each other for company, the group had to survive wild aurochs, giant snakes, spiders and rats, tuskers, man-eating bears, trolls and dragons, river serpents, sprites, fairies and imps, as well as hunt deer, giant boars and rabid wolves to prove their worth. After which they would go through rigorous training with Wēland, pushing each of them to their limits and separating the would-be-warriors from the future farmers and labourers. Their ultimate test would come when they would step into the pit and stand face to face with the near seven-foot-tall wild cattle called aurochs, weapon and shield in hand. Only then could a Cniht become a Thegn and claim to have paid the price of his birth and shown himself worthy of country and parents.

'Look,' said Wīg, pointing towards two ravens resting under the shelter of the trees. 'Huginn and Muninn are watching us, waiting to send word to the Gods. What will they say of you, I wonder?'

The group passed the two birds, one after the other, and the ravens took little notice, but when Offa passed they turned their heads and watched him closely with their dark piercing eyes. Once at the top of the hill, Offa looked down the other side and saw dark grey smoke rising to the heavens from a small wooden cabin. There were four cabins in total built closely together on a small patch of land, surrounded by dense forest. One of them was being used to house a few domest-icated animals, such as chickens and swine. There was also a small muddy yard where they were to practice with swords, axes and spears. The cackle of birds erupted from the treetops as dozens of ravens began circling the cloudy sky above. After making their way down the other side of the hill, Ket led the group to Wēland's cabin; a cabin shrouded in mystery. Above the threshold was a set of large antlers, at least twelve-feet-across, belonging to a primordial beast that had once walked the Earth.

'Wait there,' spoke Ket, stepping onto the porch. 'And keep your weapons out of view. It's impolite to stand outside a man's home bearing arms. Hælsa!' Ket yelled, knocking on the rattling wooden door. 'Wēland?'

Wēland belonged by birth to the Goth Clan. When he was a younger man, he fought under King Fritigern and was there at the Battle of Adrianople, the largest defeat the Romans have ever known; a battle they brought on themselves. After Adrianople, Wēland grew weary of war and took his wife and child into the forest and settled far from civilisation. There were many sword-smiths in Ængla land, but none could match the skill and grace of Wēland the Smith. They say when Wēland makes his swords, he hides himself away in the forest to not reveal his secrets. They say each cut, each engravement, each decoration, is a powerful spell.

The group heard banging coming from inside the cabin, accompanied by lots of cursing. Then the banging stopped and they heard the sound of heavy footsteps approaching. The old wooden door slowly creaked open on its rusty hinges and a heavily tattooed arm reached out and removed the bearskin that hung over the threshold. A man's face appeared. He was in his early forties and had a long weather-beaten face, with a jagged scar all the way down his left side like something had torn the flesh from his skull. He had long brown hair with streaks of grey, a long nose and moustache, but no beard. He wore a dirty blue linen jerkin with the sleeves rolled up to his elbows and was wiping his hands on a dirty grey cloth. He had runic tattoos up and down his arms and all over his neck.

'Ket and Wīg, what brings you back here so soon?' Wēland asked in a gruff voice. 'I had prayed I had seen the last of you two.'

'Sorry to disappoint,' Ket joked. 'We accompany Offa, the King's son. He has come-of-age and is here to begin his training, if you will have him. The rest of these changelings we found along the way.'

'Ah,' spoke Wēland, taking a long hard look at them. 'Look at those young faces. They're like scared little pups about to wet themselves.' Ket laughed. 'But we will make them strong here. Here, frightened pups become snarling wolves. Well, some of you will. The rest will become carpenters, tanners, milk-maidens, maybe even sheep-lovers.' Many of them laughed. 'That's if you survive!' Many stopped laughing. 'You there,' Wēland pointed at Haakon. 'Can you sew?'

'Sewing is for the womenfolk,' Haakon answered to a bout of laughter.

'After a bear attack, I had to sew my own face back together,' spoke Wēland, pointing to his scar. 'What if it's you out there, bleeding to death, and there are no women around?' Wēland looked at each of them. 'You are all noble-born, but let me assure you, I don't give a damn who your mothers and fathers are. You have been taken away from them for a reason, to escape the comfort of your mothers' loving udders, to train you how to wield a sword, axe and spear. We live in peaceful times, but even in times of peace, young lads and lasses like you should be preparing for war.'

From one of the cabins came Wēland's son and daughter, making their way through the light rain. Both had long blonde hair and bright blue eyes. Wudga was tall and slim and was sixteen-years-old. Ælfwynn was a pretty nine-year-old girl with plaited hair. In their arms were many wooden seaxes and shields that they tossed to the ground.

'I see it in your eyes,' spoke Wēland, 'some of you believe you are born to become heroes, destined to one day sit in Valhalla amongst the Gods. Let me tell you something, young cubs: heroes aren't born, but are forged in the furnace of war, sprouted from a coward's soul. Only where there is fear, can a man truly be brave. Only when he believes in his heart he is fated to lose, to die in battle, yet chooses to fight anyway, to protect his kith and kin, that's what makes a hero. Any one of you is capable of taking the life of another, but it takes someone special to become a hero, to gain the Gods' attention. You are not here to learn how to kill, you already know that; the human body is a weak and fragile thing. You are here to preserve life, to learn how to protect your life and those you care about. Today is the first day of Ēastremōnath, the month we give to Ēostre, Goddess of renewal and rebirth. You are here to be reborn!'

Wēland took a deep breath. 'Beneath your feet is hallowed ground,' Wēland continued. 'No God has ever walked here. No God has ever spoken here. There are no shrines and no offerings, yet this is where cubs become wolves. You are noble-born and you believe the Gods protect you and your family, because that is what your mothers have told you since the day you first came screaming into this cruel world. Let me tell you something: none of you are protected by the Gods. None of you are of worth. I am known throughout the land as a famous swordsman, yet my father was a common craftsman, my mother, a weaver.'

Wēland turned to Ælfwynn. 'My daughter is not noble-born.' Ælfwynn stepped forward and proudly stood by her father's side. 'The day Ælfwynn came into this world, I carved her a wooden seax and as her tiny hand gripped the pommel, I knew she would become one of my greatest warriors. Like her brother, Ælfwynn has trained her entire life and has never spent a moment away from her seax. Now, young cubs, I ask for volunteers. Which one of you is brave enough to challenge my daughter to a duel? Which one of you is stupid enough? Any of you?'

'I am!' spoke a confident Offa, holding his hand up.

'There's always one,' spoke Wēland, while the others laughed, all but Ælfwynn. 'You think you can defeat a girl?'

Everyone was staring at Offa, including Ælfwynn who had yet to speak a word.

'Yes,' Offa answered. 'I think so.'

'Yes?' Wēland asked. 'You sound like a mouse having its nuts tickled with a feather. Raise your chin and answer like you mean it, lad.'

'Yes!' Offa yelled, his eyes fixed on Ælfwynn. 'I can beat her.'

'I was hoping you would say that,' spoke Ælfwynn with a smile, revealing tiny white teeth and dimpled cheeks.

'You think you are a great swordsman?' Wēland asked.

'No,' Offa answered, 'but with your guidance, I will one day become a great warrior and a great king.'

'I can only teach you the way of the warrior,' Wēland replied. 'It is within your own heart whether you will become a great king or not.' Wēland drew Offa's seax from its sheath, a pattern-welded two-foot-long short-sword given to him by his father. 'Choose a wooden seax and shield, young cub. Let's see what you're made of.'

Ket and Wīg began chanting, getting the others involved, whilst forming a circle around them. Offa stepped forward and picked up two seaxes, one in each hand, leaving the shields on the ground.

'This is how I've trained,' spoke Offa. Wēland nodded with approval.

Ælfwynn stood before Offa, her blue eyes burning brightly. In one hand was a wooden seax, in the other was a shield decorated with a snarling wolf. Offa didn't know what looked more fierce, Ælfwynn or the wolf. 'Begin!' Wēland yelled.

With the gentle wind and rain blowing in her face, Ælfwynn stood her ground. Offa ran at her and roared as he leapt into the air, driving his right seax downwards, forcing Ælfwynn to block it with her shield, causing a loud cracking sound. Offa turned around, his long brown hair flicking around the back of his neck, and attacked. Once again Ælfwynn blocked it with her shield. Offa attacked with his left seax, forcing Ælfwynn to parry the blow. Offa followed with his right seax, but Ælf-wynn surprised him by rolling forward and struck him on the back of his leg, knocking him to one knee. If it had been a real sword, Offa would have been maimed for life. Offa rose to his feet and ignored the scarlet welt that had sprang up on his leg. Ælfwynn screamed and ran towards him, forcing Offa to use both seaxes to block her advance, which he did surprisingly well. While Offa was blocking her attack, Ælfwynn took advantage and kicked him hard in the stomach, knocking the breath from his body and knocked him to the mud. Ælfwynn allowed him to gather his wits and get back to his feet.

'She's only a girl, Offa. Come on, you're embarrassing us,' Haakon yelled to the group's joy.

Offa was being humiliated and Wēland noticed he was getting angry. Offa ran at Ælfwynn, but she used his momentum against him, tripping him; once again knocking him to the wet mud. Offa took a breath and rose to his feet. His chest was rising and falling and he was tiring quickly. Ælfwynn stepped closer, and smiled. 'Do you wish to surrender?' she asked with a wide grin. 'Do you want to run back to the King?'

'No! Never!' Offa answered with a snarl.

'Then I must hurt you,' spoke Ælfwynn, her voice cold and cruel.

Ælfwynn ran at Offa, leapt into the air and attempted to strike his arm. As Offa parried the blow, Ælfwynn used her shield to hit him hard in the teeth, knocking him to the ground with a spray of blood. Offa was exhausted and was laid flat on his back, spitting blood. Ælfwynn placed one foot on his chest and the tip of her seax against his throat.

'I am the victor,' she said, looking down into his big brown eyes.

Haakon and the others laughed, all but Bardawulf, who was left wondering what he had got himself into.

'It seems years of training and discipline has triumphed over the noble son of a King,' spoke Wēland. Wēland turned to Freya and Sunna, the only girls in the group, while Bardawulf helped Offa back to his feet. 'Even the smallest of women can triumph over a more powerful enemy, if her mind is sharp enough.' Wēland held up Offa's pattern-welded seax for all to see. 'The seax is an honoured weapon. The Saxons themselves are named after it. It is a symbol of honour and freedom and should be worn with pride. As you have learned here today, the seax doesn't care for nobility. It doesn't answer to the Gods, but to the person holding it. The seax knows no mercy, it has no understanding of human weakness, no understanding of pain and feels no remorse. The seax has no thought, hears no prayers, yet it thirsts for blood and answers only to the skill and grace of the person who wields it. You did well, Offa. In future, I expect a lot more.' Wēland handed Offa his seax and looked him in the eye. 'You fought like a cub today, baring your tiny fangs. For úrum þéode wé weorðaþ wulfas! For our clan we become wolves!'

Chapter Two
Forged

Wēland's Cabin, Jötunn Forest

Offa and the group had spent the night in one of the wooden cabins, sleeping in beds as cold as stone. Each wall was decorated with magnificent antlers, some as long as fifteen-feet-across, fuelling their imaginations. The rain was hitting the thatched roof all night and the trees outside were creaking and blowing against the strong winds. It was a restless night and Offa didn't get much sleep.

The following morning, Wudga woke them up at the break of dawn to begin their training. They were standing outside, in the cold damp air, but they were grateful that the rain had finally stopped. 'Now, until you prove otherwise,' spoke Wēl-and, 'you are all carrion for the wolf and the raven, and I have a higher opinion of what's fallen out of a troll's arse than I do any of you. Is that understood?'

'Yes!' the group yelled with smirks on their faces.

'I am here to teach lazy soft turds like you how to become warriors that your clan can be proud of. This is a place where boys are raised as men, and men are forged into something of worth. Do you wish to become milk-maidens and spend your lives fondling a cow's udders?'

'No!' the group yelled.

'I do!' Grendel shouted to the laughter of the group.

'Grendel, you are clearly inbred, but I like you,' spoke Wēl-and. 'Now, I want you all to take the back of your right hand and place it on the left side of your mouth. Good. Now wipe your mouths. Good. This is you wiping the last of your mother's breast milk from your lips. I don't care if your father is a king or a nobleman, or likes to wear women's clothes; you are all equal in my eyes until you prove yourselves better, or in some cases prove yourselves to be no better than slaves. From now on you have a choice: you can become real men and make your fathers proud, and one day share your beds with real women. Or you can choose to work the fields and make friends with the sheep.'

'Grendel has made his choice,' Haakon joked to yet more laughter. 'The sheep know him well already.'

'Be quiet before you get my boot up your arse,' spoke Wēl-and. 'Now, let me make this clear to all of you: for the next year you will not be able to see your mothers or fathers, brothers or sisters. The person standing beside you is your family now, so look after each other. There will be times when you find it difficult to carry on and feel like giving up. This is normal and natural. But you must carry on. This is how you will grow. This is a piece of steel,' spoke Wēland, holding out a piece of metal ore in one hand. 'When a blacksmith takes a piece of steel like this, he sees the potential in it. Men are not born with claws, scales or sharp fangs, and so we must forge them in fire and craft them in steel. A blacksmith takes something ugly and turns it into something beautiful. He places the steel in the fire and allows it to get hot. He then beats the steel with a hammer, twists it, folds it and hammers it again and again, moulding it into his desired shape, sharpening it, before quenching it in freezing water.' Wēland drew his own seax and handed it to Haakon. 'Pass it around. See the beauty in it, the pattern-welding, the strength. I have beaten the steel into something of worth. It has become something better. It now has a purpose. Do you understand?'

'Yes,' Grendel replied, 'you're going to hit us with a hammer.'

After spending the morning teaching the group how to forage, make spears, bows and arrows, how to fish, hunt and make fires, and how to build shelters, Wēland turned their attention to sparring. Ket and Wīg were sparring with Offa, two against one. Offa hadn't forgotten his embarrassment from the day before, and so he trained harder than everyone else, determined to prove himself. Offa's wooden seax clashed against shield after shield, again and again, echoing into the enchanted forest, until his arms ached, and yet he carried on. As Bardawulf hit the ground face first, courtesy of Haakon's brutal attack, Ket used the distraction to knock Offa to the ground beside him. 'Why aren't you getting mad, Offa?' Ket asked, taunting him, to Haakon's amusement. 'Do you like being the fool?'

Offa rose to his feet, raised his seax and shield and waited for Ket to attack. Ket rushed at Offa, once again knocking him to the ground, to the laughter of those around them.

The laughter caught Wēland's attention. 'I've heard about you, Offa,' spoke Wēland. 'You have the heart of a warrior, but the skill of an inbred troll high on poisonous mushrooms, whilst trying to balance on a three-legged table.' Wēland took a moment to look Offa up and down. 'And with what I've seen so far, I'd say they were right.' Wēland stroked his moustache. 'You need to work on your balance, young cub. You need to stay on your feet and learn to dance around your enemies. Don't stand there and allow them to knock you over like a drunken oar-man.'

'I will do better,' Offa answered, flicking his long hair from his face.

'Ket!' Wēland called. 'Spar with Bardawulf. You can't expect Offa to fight against two of you when he can't even stand against the wind. Offa, spar with Wudga. Wīg, you spar with Grendel.'

Wudga hit Offa hard with his wooden seax, giving him a welt on his arm.

'Pay attention!' Wudga yelled. 'Raise your shield.'

'I prefer to use two seaxes,' Offa answered, rubbing his arm. 'Holding a shield doesn't feel right.'

'A shield covers more of your body,' Wudga told him. 'And you can still use it as a weapon.' Wudga stepped forward and hit Offa hard in the face with his shield, knocking him to the wet mud. 'Like that.'

Tired of being humiliated, Offa rose to his feet and charged at Wudga, but Wudga easily knocked his younger opponent to the ground. Beside him fell Sunna, courtesy of Ælfwynn.

'It seems Sunna likes lying in the dirt,' Haakon joked. 'Maybe her brother, Mōna, wishes to join her?'

'Haakon!' Sunna roared, getting back to her feet, raising her sword and shield. 'Put me on my back then.'

'Ooohh, Sunna wants to fight,' Haakon bellowed to the others. 'She thinks she is one of us.'

The group formed a circle around them, while Wēland looked on with his arms folded. Sunna's bright eyes were fixed on her arrogant opponent, who smirked and boasted to the onlookers. Sunna took a deep breath and struck Haakon's shield. The sound of wood on wood echoed into the forest. They fought back and forth, yet neither of them fought with any real skill. Sunna fought with great determination, but

Haakon's strength got the better of her. Sunna was knocked to the ground several times, yet she kept struggling back to her feet, determined to fight on.

'Those who pit their own strength when fighting a bear are already dead,' spoke Wēland. 'Like a wolf, one must use cunning and seize the opportunity to strike.'

Sunna nodded her head as though she understood. Taking deep breaths, Haakon and Sunna now circled each other. Sunna waited for Haakon to strike, but Haakon was no fool. Seeing Haakon wouldn't strike first, Sunna feigned an attack, forcing Haakon to block, therefore leaving himself vulnerable to Sunna's strike that bounced off Haakon's ribs. Mōna and several others cheered.

'Well done, Sunna,' spoke Wēland. 'When facing a stronger opponent, you must learn to outwit them, like a housewife with her husband.'

'That won't happen again,' spoke Haakon, charging at Sunna, causing them both to trip. Sunna hit the ground hard and Haakon landed on top of her.

'My arm!' Sunna screamed, loud enough to frighten the birds from the treetops. 'I think my arm is broken!'

'Let me see,' spoke Wēland, kneeling beside her. 'You're right, lass, it's snapped like a twig under a fat kid's foot.'

'Aaaahh!' Sunna screamed with frustration, clutching her elbow. 'What does this mean? I want to train.'

'It means you are done, young cub,' Wēland answered softly. 'You need to go home and heal.'

'I can't,' spoke Sunna, wincing in pain. 'I need to be with my brother. We've never been apart. Please!'

Mōna knelt beside his injured twin sister.

'It will be all right,' spoke Mōna. 'I'll be home before you know it.'

'No,' said Sunna with tears in her eyes. 'I can do it. I can heal in the forest. Please don't send me home, Wēland. Please.'

'You can't survive in the wilderness with a broken arm, lass,' Wēland answered. 'You can return next year with your head held high.'

'I can't leave my sister,' spoke Mōna. 'Not when she needs

me the most.'

'You must let her go,' Wēland replied. 'This is a test set by the Gods. This will make you both stronger. Sunna, when you are home and in pain and you feel helpless, take that time to find yourself, retreat into yourself and search your own soul. Only when one knows weakness and suffering, when one is truly alone and takes time out from this world, can one truly listen to their soul. Only then will you know your own strength. Find your self, and I promise you, when you return next year, your arm will be as iron.' Wēland looked up at his son. 'Wudga, take her home.'

'But father, it's a three day trek,' Wudga argued.

'It's a trek you've made a hundred times before,' spoke Wēland. 'And besides, we need more supplies. It is settled. You will leave after your morning meal.'

Offa sat inside the cabin, alongside Ket and Wīg, eating a warm bowl of lumpy, burnt porridge that Ælfwynn had prepared. The rest of the group were also there, filling their stomachs and chatting amongst themselves.

'Will you two be coming with us when we enter the forest tomorrow?' Offa asked his kinsmen.

Ket laughed whilst scraping his bowl clean.

'No, Offa, you're on your own,' Ket answered. 'We've done our time in the forest and returned with our wolf pelts. It's time you wiped your own arse. Those who survived the forest last year will return to continue their training with Wēland. Wīg and I will help spar with them for a few weeks, to keep ourselves out of trouble.'

Wudga stood to his feet, placed his wolf pelt over Sunna's shoulders and picked up his supplies.

'I will see you soon,' spoke Mōna, embracing his sister, being careful not to hurt her arm. 'Tell mother and father I love them.'

'I will,' Sunna replied, her arm secured in a sling. 'Be safe, brother. I know the Gods are with you.' Though she didn't wish to show it, Sunna's eyes were filled with tears.

After saying their farewells, Wudga and Sunna made their

way outside to begin their long trek to Schleswig.

'Make sure you don't come back early, Offa,' spoke Ket, watching as Wudga and Sunna left, 'otherwise you will become an outcast and will never be king. You must keep yourself alive out there. Wēland has shown you how to make a fire, how to kill and flay animals, and how to survive. It's up to you now. You must be strong. You must find a wolf and challenge it, kill it and return wearing its coat. This is your rite-of-passage, nothing else matters. Do you understand?'

'Yes, I understand,' Offa answered.

'If you fail,' Wīg added, 'then your father will have no heir. The King is old. The men of Angeln will be forced to fight to decide the new king. It will be a bloodbath. And the alliance between Angeln and Schleswig will quickly crumble while men scramble for power. You must succeed, Offa. Like a pack of wolves, leadership goes to the strongest, never the weak. This is your chance to prove yourself worthy to your folks and to the Gods. If you want to lead the people, first you must suffer and prove yourself worthy.'

Offa swallowed his food, only now realising how serious it was and the consequences of failing.

'While you're out there, you must make sure you don't allow another to become leader,' spoke Ket, quietly. 'You need to be the strongest of the pack. Don't allow Haakon to lead. There is only one rule out there: survive! You must be ruthless. If you need to, kill anyone who stands in your way, starting with Haakon. I never did like him. You don't know him, but I do. His father is a cruel man and has probably told him the same thing about you. You are the King's only son. Some of them will be out for your blood. And there is no one out there to protect you but yourself. To become leader of the pack, a wolf must kill its competition. This is the law of the forest. It is no different amongst men.'

Offa chewed his food and looked across the room at Haakon, watching him boast about breaking Sunna's arm. Offa's stomach began to twist into knots, and he wondered, if he was left with no choice, would he be capable of taking Haakon's life?

Chapter Three
The Wild Hunt

Wēland's Cabin, Jötunn Forest

The rains slashed down from the heavens, flooding the muddy yard where Offa and the group had trained throughout the day. Offa's wooden seax clashed with Ælfwynn's shield. Offa knocked Grendel to the ground and smashed through the wall of rain as his wooden sword raced towards Haakon's skull. Offa took a punch to the face from Ket, a shield-thrust from Wīg, and yet he stood, finally learning to raise his shield. As night cloaked the realm in darkness and the wolves came out to hunt, Offa fought with Grendel, with Bardawulf, and with Wēland, growing stronger with every stroke of his sword.

***

Jötunn Forest, en route to Schleswig

After Haakon had broken Sunna's arm during training, Wudga, son of Wēland, had been given the task of returning Sunna to her home village, in Schleswig. It was now dark and cold and the two of them were deep in the forest and a long way from home. They had settled down for the night, sharing a small tent made from branches and animal pelts.

'We need to start a fire,' spoke Wudga from inside the tent. 'It's going to be a long cold night.'

'I can't, I'm in too much pain,' Sunna replied. 'Besides, it's raining. The wood will be wet.'

'After a year in this forest, you will learn where to find dry wood. It could be the difference between life and death,' Wudga answered, stepping outside. 'I'll go and look for wood. You stay here.'

'Don't worry, I'm not going anywhere,' Sunna replied, wincing.

The moon was hiding behind the clouds, allowing the blackness to consume the land. Wudga was frightened, yet Wēland had always taught his son to overcome his fear and to challenge himself whenever possible. And so Wudga walked into the forest that night, afraid and alone, yet determined to find dry wood and start a fire. Wudga crouched under the tall swaying trees next to the bracken, while the rain fell upon him, trying not to look into the darkness of the primordial forest. He was brushing away the wet leaves with his hand, when he found several fallen branches that he collected under his arm. Wudga closed his eyes and reached further into the shadows, feeling along the ground with his fingertips for any branches hiding under the layers of wet leaves, when he heard something in the dark.

Wudga felt something was watching him and the hairs on the back of his neck began to stand on end. He stared into the blackness and saw what looked like breath floating on the damp night air in front of him, carrying with it the stench of death. The breath inside his lungs escaped his body when he saw two shining eyes staring at him from the shadows. Remembering his training, his time in the wild, Wudga remained deadly still, except for his right hand that gently reached for his seax. Slowly, the wolf came out of the shadows and stepped into the moonlight, one limb at a time. It was as if the night itself had come to life. Dropping the branches from under his left arm, Wudga drew his weapon with his right hand. Before he could strike, the wolf leapt forward and bit into his right arm with a terrifying snarl. Wudga roared and dropped his seax onto the ground.

'Help, Sunna! Help!' Wudga screamed, hitting the wolf in the face with his left hand.

Wudga could feel the wolf's fangs sinking into his soft flesh, sending a terrible pain throughout his arm. Acting on instinct, Wudga jammed his thumb into its eye and forced it to release him. He then ran as fast as he could towards the tent. 'What's wrong?' Sunna asked, crouching by the open flap.

Wudga's ankle suddenly gave way and he fell face first into the wet mud. He had twisted his ankle and could hear the wolf snarling behind him. Without looking over his shoulder, Wudga rose to his feet and tried running towards Sunna, but his ankle couldn't take his weight, and once again he fell to the ground in agony. The wolf was quickly upon him. Sunna rushed to Wudga's aid and used her seax to slash at the wolf's face, drawing blood, forcing it to release him. Wudga turned his head and saw the madness in the wolf's predatory eyes, while it backed away into the shadows.

'Come on!' Sunna yelled, pulling Wudga to his feet, using her good arm; the other still in its sling.

'I can't walk,' Wudga moaned, terrified of putting weight on his ankle.

'Put your arm around me,' spoke Sunna, helping Wudga to the tent, where they both threw themselves inside and crashed to the ground.

Rolling onto their backs, the two of them stared at the tent's opening. They remained silent, too afraid to move. The only noise they could hear was their own heavy breathing. After a few intense moments and with sweat rolling down his forehead, Wudga gently crawled towards the door that was flapping in the winds. He tried looking through the small gap, but he couldn't see anything. Wudga slowly reached out with a shaking hand, closed the flap and tied it shut.

***

Wēland's Cabin, Jötunn Forest

Offa and the group were outside, practising with sword and shield, under the light of the moon and the ever falling rain. Their hair and clothes were drenched and they longed to be inside, in front of the warm hearth. They were tired, hungry and their arms and legs were weary. 'The rain is coming down hard,' Wēland told them. 'I don't expect you to be afraid of a little rain. The time will come when you will need to fight at night, in the pouring rain, and so you will be out here all night if I wish it.'

'*I think I hate him,*' Grendel whispered, hitting Offa's shield.

Haakon knocked Bardawulf to the ground, knocking the air from his lungs. Bardawulf cried in agony, resting on his hands and knees, the rain pouring down upon him; lightning flashing above his head.

'Get up, Bardawulf!' Wēland yelled. 'You are here to prove yourself a man and become a Thegn your King can be proud of. You can't do that on your hands and knees.' Wēland paced the muddy yard. 'Show promise, and some of you may even become Ealdormen and one day lead the Thegns in battle.'

'I'm exhausted,' Bardawulf complained, now back on his feet. 'When can we eat?'

'You are tired and hungry?' Wēland asked. 'Well how do you think you will feel when you are out there, in the middle of the forest, with no food or shelter? Will you give up? Fight through it, Bardawulf, or go home to your mother's breasts. I won't waste my time with lazy swine. And that goes for the rest of you. These tests are to separate the weak from the strong, the common man from the King's Thegns. As you know, the word *king* comes from the word *kin*. A king is the leader of his kinsmen. It is a king's role to protect his folk and nation, to honour his people, even if that means sacrificing his life on the battlefield. Will you be worthy to fight by your King's side? Now is the time to push yourselves harder than you ever imagined possible. Pain is weakness leaving the body. What separates us from the animals is our desire to better ourselves, to ascend to the heavens. You must push past the pain and carry on. Remember: the Gods are watching!'

Offa watched Haakon and Bardawulf sword-playing, giving Grendel the opportunity to take advantage and hit Offa in the face with his shield. 'Ha! Pay attention,' spoke Grendel as the sky lit up with a flash of light. 'I wouldn't want you to lose any teeth.'

'Don't worry,' Offa answered. 'You won't catch me off-guard again.'

Offa's seax struck Grendel's shield. The sound travelled through the air and into the rain clouds, where it rolled along the dark night sky, rumbling and thundering. Every time their wooden swords clashed, the sky lit up with streaks of terrifying white light, in an amazing display by Thunor, God of thunder and lightning. It was Thunor who gave his name to

Thunoresdæg - Thursday.

'Offa, pair with Haakon,' Wēland yelled over the sound of thunder.

'Why do I have to pair with Offa when he can't even fight a girl?' Haakon asked. 'I can't be responsible for hurting the delicate flower.'

Offa stood ready and was determined to knock the smile from Haakon's face. Offa attacked, yet Haakon easily avoided the blow and struck Offa hard on the back of his head. Offa didn't want to show that he was in pain, so he never made a sound, not a whimper. Haakon wished to humiliate Offa, yet Offa took the opportunity to study Haakon, with the fear they might one day face each other in a fight to the death. Haakon tried taking Offa's head off, but Offa anticipated the move and ducked, kicking Haakon hard in the stomach, knocking him to the ground, like Ælfwynn had done to him the day before.

'Come on, Haakon, you troll humper,' Offa told him. 'I'm ready for you.'

'Oh, really?' Haakon asked, rising to his feet. Haakon charged, forcing Offa to sidestep. Offa turned his body in order to strike Haakon's arm, but Haakon managed to block the attack with his shield, which then cracked in half. It was an incredible display of strength, strength Offa didn't know he had. A flock of ravens flew from the surrounding trees - hundreds of them. Wēland was right, the Gods were watching.

'That's enough for tonight!' Wēland yelled, much to the group's relief. 'This was just a taste of what's to come if you should pass your test. Now go inside and warm your bones.'

The group made their way inside the cabin, where they were to spend their second night, exhausted and soaked to the bone. Wēland followed them inside and started a fire at the hearth. Offa was rubbing his hands together over the hot flames, trying to get warm, when there was a loud crack above their heads, scaring some of them.

'It seems the Gods are awake,' spoke Wēland with a smile, poking the fire. 'Perhaps it is Thunor killing Frost-Giants with his hammer, or maybe Wōden is riding the night sky on a Wild Hunt.'

'What's a Wild Hunt?' Edwin asked. The group gathered around the crackling fire or laid on their beds, lying on their stomachs, resting their chin in their hands, and listened.

'The Wild Hunt,' spoke Wēland, 'is a group of supernatural huntsmen, Wolf-Coats, berserkers and other noble warriors, who have died an honourable death, weapon in hand, dripping with the blood of their enemy. The huntsmen wear the coats of wolves or bears and cover their exposed flesh with black soot. They travel the dark night sky on a chariot, pulled along by black hounds, in mad pursuit of trolls and giants. On the eleventh night of Yule, the day before the Winter Solstice, you can sometimes see Wōden leading the hunt.'

Ælfwynn opened the doors to the cabin and entered with a large pan filled with burnt porridge, while the sky behind her lit up, followed by a loud rumble.

***

Jötunn Forest, en route to Schleswig

Morning had arrived, the rains had finally stopped and an otherworldly mist hid the forest in a milky veil. Wudga and Sunna were making their way to Schleswig, when Wudga stopped to look over his shoulder. The back of his neck was caked in dry blood and his arm was bloody and sore. There, standing on the top of a small hill, its black coat silhouetted against the surrounding mist, stood the injured wolf; watching them.

'Come on, Wudga, we need to leave,' spoke Sunna.

Wudga turned away from the wolf and tried to walk, but his ankle had been badly twisted the night before and he could only manage a gentle limp. With his good arm around Sunna's shoulder, the two of them slowly made their way further into the forest, through the mist, with the hungry wolf ever at their tail.

***

Wēland's Cabin, Jötunn Forest

When Offa and the group stepped outside they were shocked at the thick mist that blotted out the light of the sun. It was as if the clouds had fallen from the sky and it was impossible to see even a few feet in front. The winds were cold and bit against their exposed flesh and the ground was saturated with rain-water from the night before. They were armed with their seaxes and dressed in jerkins and cloaks, ready as they would ever be to go out into the wild, to the untamed forest like their fathers before them.

'You all know why you're here,' spoke Wēland, wrapped in a bear pelt; his breath visible on the cold damp air. 'You are to live in the forest, with no adult supervision, wearing only the clothes on your back. You are to surrender your flesh, your minds and your souls to the forest, and to Wōden, the leader of the Wild Hunt. You are to live like a pack of wolves and join the realm of the dead. You are to hunt wolves and will return to your people on the eleventh night of Yule, during Mothers' Night, when the veil between the living and the dead is thin, wearing your wolf pelts. Then and only then will you be able to return to the realm of the living. This is your rite-of-passage, when you prove yourselves to be something of worth, to be more than a nose picker. Wearing the coat of a wolf slain by your own hand separates the men from the boys, the noble from the common. You are to work together as a team, as a pack of wild dogs, and forge a new brotherhood. A life of shame awaits you if you fail. If you should find gifts lying on the path in front, be sure to thank the imps and land wights with food. But remember, little fledglings: leaving food will be sure to attract unwanted attention. Out there, it's Troll Country, and whatever you do, do not cross paths with one of them.'

'But what should we do if one finds us?' Grendel asked.

'Then you, Grendel, should return to your own kind,' Wēland joked to a bout of laughter.

'Don't worry, if we come across a troll, I'll cut its danglies off and put them in a stew,' Haakon joked to yet more laughter.

'Speaking of food, the bread in your sack is for you to keep,'

Wēland continued. 'Bread is a symbol of life and the home and helps repel the fairy folk.'

'Ooops, is that what that was for?' Grendel asked. 'I've already eaten mine.' The others laughed.

'Pay attention, young cubs,' Wēland continued. 'In your sacks you will find a needle and thread and several other supplies. Each of you will be armed with only your wits, your teeth and the seaxes your fathers gave you. Yet I expect you to make your own spears, bows and arrows, like I've shown you. And remember: unity, teamwork and kinship are key to your survival. You will sleep in the beds you make with your bare hands, catch your own fish and hunt your own food. No boar tastes finer than the one you have hunted and killed with your own two hands. I expect you to have fun, to look after each other, to bond as a family. And don't think about coming back here and stealing from me, otherwise I'll be decorating my walls with your hides. Do you understand?'

'Yes,' they answered.

'I can't hear you!'

'YES!' they yelled.

'Nine of you will enter the forest today as bearns, dressed in sheep clothing,' spoke Wēland. 'I don't expect all of you to return, but those who do will return as young adults, with a wolf pelt on your back. Then and only then will I train you to become warriors. The brightest amongst you will understand, you are not entering the forest to just hunt and kill wolves, but to find yourselves and kill the child within. What you will experience will be physically and mentally draining, but you must remember that you are also on a spiritual journey. You must let the land feed your soul and heal any hurt you carry in your heart. You must let in the darkness, allow it to consume you, but you must make sure you are still able to find the light and return home. There is a danger out there that I haven't mentioned yet. Sometimes a child becomes so consumed by the darkness they are unable to find the light and never return home. Some say they are still out there, living as wolves, wild and hungry for human flesh. So look after each other. Yes, you will suffer and you will struggle, but struggle breeds greatness.

Now run to the trees yonder.' Wēland pointed to the forest. 'And don't come back without your wolf pelts. May Wōden be with you.'

Cold wet mud sprayed up the side of their legs and back as the group ran into the mist, leaving Ket and Wīg behind, howling like a pack of wolves, running into the unknown; none of them having any idea of their fate or the gruesome, dark horrors that awaited.

Chapter Four
Wolves in the Mist

Jötunn Forest

A long penetrating howl echoed between the trees and deep into the mist of the forest. Offa, Freya and Grendel could only see several feet in front of them. They drew their seaxes and looked in every direction. 'We know it's you, Haakon,' Freya yelled into the mist. 'We're not afraid.'

Haakon laughed from behind the trees and carried on howling. They had spent much of the day walking deeper into the forest, none of them having any real idea where they were going.

'Come on out!' Grendel yelled. 'We need to find shelter. We have no time for games.' Yet the howling continued.

'We have spent too long wasting time,' spoke Freya. 'It will be dark soon. Where are we going to sleep?'

'I don't know,' Offa answered, walking beside her. 'But I'm tired and hungry and getting fed up.' Offa and Freya stood still and listened, when they heard a loud scream coming from behind the trees.

'What was that?' Bardawulf asked.

More screaming was heard all around them.

'This way!' Freya yelled, running towards the noise.

'He's killed one. He's killed a beast,' they heard Haakon bellowing.

As Offa ran through the mist, he saw Dunstān kneeling on the ground before him. Dunstān turned his head and looked

Offa in the eye. Dunstān's right cheek was decorated with an arrow, painted in blood.

'I've killed one,' Dunstān told him. 'I've killed it. I am the ripper, tearer, the thing that lurks in the shadows. I am Dunstān, son of Thorne. We are here, in this great forest, to slay that which haunts our nightmares and prove our worth to our peers. Offa, you are the King's only son, your opinion holds worth. Does this count?' Dunstān held out the beast he had killed by its long ears, the beast whose dark red blood now marked his face with the rune of Tīw, God of war. It was a dead rabbit and the group burst with laughter.

'Do you think I can make a coat out of it?' Dunstān asked. 'Maybe a hat? Do you think my father will be proud?'

'I shall name you Dunstān, the slayer of mighty rabbits,' Haakon joked to the laughter of them all. But then an eerie cry pierced the laughter and an old familiar song could be heard all around them, echoing between the trees. It was a sad song, a song as old as the world itself; long drawn-out wailings and half sobs, desperate pleas for food.

***

Jötunn Forest, en route to Schleswig

Sunna walked a step in front of Wudga, while the son of Wēland stretched out his good arm and steadied himself on her shoulder. 'What are we going to do?' Sunna asked. 'We can't go on like this. Your ankle is hurt and my arm is in agony. My hand is starting to feel tingly. Maybe we should turn back and see your father?'

'No,' Wudga answered, limping onwards. 'We've come too far. We need to get you home. I'll be fine. Don't worry about me. Think of something else.'

Wudga slowly limped down the bank of a small river and staggered amongst the rough strewn rocks. The two of them were burdened with food and supplies. They were tired, injured and visibility was poor through the endless mist. Whenever Sunna turned around to face Wudga, the pain and misery he was in was clear to see, and they were still a long way from home. Behind them, through the haze of the mist, the wolf could sometimes be seen, walking with a slight limp. Sunna had injured it the night before, it was no doubt hungry, and it continued to follow them into the mist, ever in their wake. And it was starting to get dark.

***

Jötunn Forest

Niht, the grandmother of Thunor and mother of Day, was riding her great black stallion across the dome of the sky, bringing darkness to the realm and awakening the night-time creatures from their slumber. Offa and the group of hunters were wanting to settle down for the night, but they had built no shelter and had eaten the small amount of food they had brought with them. Their stomachs ached and growled and they were tired and cold. 'We should stay here,' spoke Haakon, taking charge. 'This place is as good as any. I'll start a fire.'

'We'll have to sleep on the ground tonight,' spoke Freya, getting frustrated.

'But it's wet,' spoke Grendel. 'I'm not sleeping on a wet floor. I would expect more for my slave.'

'We have no choice,' Dunstān added, helping Haakon to find dry twigs and leaves from under the foliage.

'I'm scared,' spoke Bardawulf, looking around. 'I don't even like the forest. My father has told me what's out here. I know about the man-eating spiders.'

'Be quiet, Bardawulf,' spoke Offa. 'Don't frighten everyone.'

'Well we should be frightened,' Bardawulf replied. 'We have a lot to be frightened of.'

Haakon and Dunstān managed to get the fire going.

'This should be enough to scare any spiders away,' spoke Haakon. 'For now.'

***

Jötunn Forest, en route to Schleswig

'Is it still out there?' Wudga asked from inside their makeshift tent.

Sunna opened the flap and looked outside. 'I can hear it breathing,' Sunna answered. 'I can see its breath floating on the air.'

'Come back inside,' Wudga told her.

'Do you think there might be more of them?' Sunna asked, nursing her arm.

'Wolves usually hunt in packs,' Wudga answered. 'It's possible it might be an outcast, but I don't know. It's hungry and injured. It knows we're hurting and it's hunting us; both of us.' Wudga took a deep breath. 'Wōden, my lord, I ask that you look out for us this night. May you forgive our weakness and be here with us. It is not my wish to hurt one of your divine creatures. I know the wolf's need to feed is strong. It must kill us in order to survive, our lives to preserve its own. But if need be, I will kill it. I will end its life and force a stick down its throat and one up its arse and hold it over a roaring fire. I will cook and eat its flesh, its life to preserve my own. This is my promise. Test me if you will.'

***

Jötunn Forest

From under the forest canopy, the moon could be seen watching over the land, looking on as the small group of hunters rested on the wet ground, with no shelter but the swaying trees above their heads. Haakon had made a small fire where they were able to warm their hands. Cooking over the fire was a small rabbit that had everyone licking their lips. 'Because you were the one to take this rabbit's life, Dunstān, you should get the greater share,' spoke Offa.

'And who made you leader?' Haakon asked, poking the fire with a stick. 'You can't even beat a girl.'

'It's only fair,' Offa replied.

'Fair?' Haakon asked, rising to his feet. 'There is no fair. Life is what it is. It's a cruel place where only the strong survive.'

'We should have a leader,' spoke Freya. 'We need a leader. We have spent the day fooling around. We have little food, but no drink or shelter. Our kin would be ashamed.'

'And who should lead?' Edwin asked.

'What about Offa?' Bardawulf suggested. 'He is the King's son.'

'Offa?' Haakon asked, surprised. 'Most of us don't even know him. We're not from Angeln. We are from Schleswig. I might not be the son of a King, nor claim to be descended from a God, but I am noble-born and I was born to lead. And Offa won't stand in my way, will you, Offa?'

To Haakon's surprise, Offa stood to his feet, took a deep breath and looked Haakon in the eye. 'I want to lead,' Offa answered nervously. 'I am the King's son.'

'Then let's settle this,' spoke Haakon confidently.

'You're going to fight?' Freya asked. 'We should vote for who we want as leader. There is no need to fight.' Freya tried to stop them, but Haakon pushed her aside and punched Offa hard in the face, knocking him to the ground. While the others looked on, some of them cheering, Offa rose to his feet, roared, and charged at Haakon, shoulder-tackling him into the fire. Haakon's woollen jerkin quickly set alight. Offa was on top of Haakon, hitting him with closed fists and split his bottom lip. Haakon pushed Offa aside, stood back to his feet and tossed his jerkin to the ground. He roared and hit Offa hard on the jaw, knocking him to the dirt. Haakon knelt over Offa and hit him again and again. Offa's face felt like it was being pummelled by a bear.

'That's enough!' Edwin yelled. 'He's had enough!'

'I'm the leader,' Haakon spat, now back on his feet, pointing at his chest. 'I'm in charge!'

A distant howl echoed throughout the forest, but Offa couldn't hear it for the ringing in his ears. On shaking legs, Offa stood back to his feet. 'He's back up,' spoke Grendel in disbelief, watching as Haakon stepped forward and hit Offa again.

'Stay down!' Haakon yelled, spitting blood, but once again Offa stood to his feet and drew his seax.

'He's had enough!' Freya yelled, stepping between them. 'Leave him be, Haakon. Don't you hear them? There are wolves out there. And they can smell your blood!'

Chapter Five
The Great Earl of Schleswig

Schleswig

It is good to be Earl.

Earl Frēawine of Schleswig was descended from the Gods and believed in his heart that he was born to populate the realm of the living with endless children to many beautiful women. For most of his life, Frēawine had known peace and so he had become a man of leisure. He is a man who enjoys his drink, the company of kith and kin, a good fire and the love of many good elven women, not all of them pretty, but Frēawine believes even the ugly ones deserve a little happiness.

It was nearing twilight, the stars were bright and the moon was full and round. The lonely boy in the sky must have looked down upon Schleswig that night with great envy, listening to the drunken laughter of those mortal beings and the distant lament of the wolves in the surrounding forest. Frēawine's teenage sons, Ket and Wīg, were away at Wēland's cabin, giving the Earl time to enjoy himself with the absence of children and the abundance of drunken women. Several women danced wildly around the bonfire, eager to become closer to the Gods, and they don't get much closer to the Gods than spending a night with Earl Frēawine, or so he would tell them. With his long flowing blonde hair, bright blue eyes, muscular frame, good looks and the most well-groomed beard in all the lands, the women of Schleswig adored the handsome thirty-five-year-old. And Frēawine took every opportunity to please his people, as a good Earl should.

Frēawine took down his wolf hood, allowing his hair to flow freely, and put the gilded horn to his lips, gulping down the honeyed mead; no longer caring for the spillage down his magnificent beard. He was heavily drunk and enjoyed standing outside, under the starry night sky, watching the men and women of Schleswig dancing around the blazing fire, while it burned with the bones of sacrificed goats and chickens.

Hoodening is an ancient custom amongst the Angles and involves folks dressing up in animal pelts and carrying the heads of sacrificed animals in a ritual dance. The heads are paraded around the burning fires and wolves are flayed and worn in order to honour the wolf, for wolves are sacred to Wōden. Deer antlers are also worn and are a symbol of wisdom, fertility and strength; a symbol of the forest.

The womenfolk enjoy taking part in the ritualised dancing, often wearing a cloak of falcon feathers, like the one owned by Freya, Goddess of love, beauty, fertility, gold, magic and war. A married woman is expected to keep her hair bound so others will know she is already taken, yet the ritual of dance allows her to let her hair down and enjoy herself. The women looked beautiful that night, dancing with a pole between their thighs, decorated with the skull of a sacrificed horse. Many chose to dance barefoot and bare their beautiful breasts and legs; their flesh as white as ivory, with wolf-cloaked men dancing around them. Frēawine watched them circling the fire, their wolf heads dancing as though they had risen from the dead, while the women danced to the rhythm of the drums. He watched one woman in particular. She was the most beautiful woman he had ever seen and had a face so bright she could dim the stars and a smile that never seemed to sleep. The Goddess, Frīge, must have looked upon her beauty with great envy.

Egwen's face was hidden behind a mask that night and her upper body was covered in long brown feathers, silhouetted against the bright fire behind her. Her legs were bare, except for the short skirt she wore, made from countless strips of leather, revealing her nakedness beneath. At her waist, drawing attention to her most intimate area, the gateway to her womb, was a shining gold disk, representing the sun, the giver of life. It was easy to fall in love with a woman like Egwen. A man couldn't help but admire her, to want to be close to her, to feel her warmth against his skin, to kiss her lips; if only for the briefest of moments.

'Your wife enjoys the company of men. You do not mind?' A woman, not a day over fifty, stood beside the Earl. Her plaited hair was long and grey. Her eyes were bright blue and her lips were red like roses.

'I am just a man of flesh and blood,' Frēawine answered.

'Just a man?' Svanhilda asked, looking up at the Earl. 'I thought you were a God?' She had a cheeky, yet beautiful smile. It was clear to see that Svanhilda had been a beautiful woman in her youth, yet the years had not been unkind. She had a noble face, high cheekbones, a pointed jaw and mesmerizing blue eyes, like deep lakes hiding many secrets. 'I wish my late husband had been more like you,' Svanhilda confessed. 'The fun we might have had.'

'You will never find a man quite like me,' Frēawine answered confidently.

'She is so beautiful,' spoke Svanhilda, watching Egwen dancing around the high flames. 'What I wouldn't give to be so young and beautiful again.'

'You are still quite stunning,' Frēawine told her, looking into her eyes. 'The oldest trees in the forest are always the most beautiful.'

'I've been compared to the Vænír once or twice in my lifetime,' Svanhilda laughed, 'but never to a weathered old tree.'

'I meant no offence,' Frēawine answered. 'I see the look in your eyes, that is where a woman's true beauty lies.'

'I bet you say that to all the women,' spoke Svanhilda. Egwen looked through the dancing flames and saw her husband standing next to Svanhilda. 'What would your pretty wife think of you talking like this to a woman old enough to be your mother?'

'If I know my wife like I think I do,' spoke Frēawine, 'she wouldn't mind at all.'

Svanhilda froze, her heart hammering inside her chest. Frēawine leaned forward and gently lifted Svanhilda's chin, kissed her on the lips and led her into the shadows.

It is good to be Earl.

Frēawine awoke in the mead-hall, naked, half covered with a bear pelt and surrounded by many sleeping women, including Svanhilda and his wife, Egwen. After a stretch and a yawn, Frēawine turned to Egwen and kissed her gently on the shoulder. '*Good morning, my love*,' Egwen whispered, opening her eyes and stretching her arms. 'Did you enjoy last night?'

'Yes,' Frēawine answered. 'Did you?'

'Of course,' Egwen replied with a smile, placing a hand on her husband's leg, 'though a woman's appetite is never truly satisfied.'

'Well it will have to wait,' spoke Frēawine, 'I need to take a leak.' The Earl threw back the covers and made his way outside, still completely naked, where a thick mist clung to the forest. Whilst relieving himself, a young boy approached him from out of the forest; a fisherman's son named Fólki.

'My lord!' Fólki yelled, running towards him, dressed as a Wolf-Coat.

'What?' Frēawine asked. 'Can't you see I'm taking a leak?'

'My lord, I was about to go fishing when I saw something strange,' spoke Fólki. 'I thought it was a serpent coming out of the fjord, but then I realised it was no serpent, but a warship carrying fighting men and women.'

'A warship?' Frēawine asked, shaking himself. 'Did anyone see you or speak to you?'

'No, my lord,' Fólki answered. 'No one saw me. I ran straight here to warn you.'

'How many?'

'Fifteen or so, maybe twenty,' Fólki answered.

'Go into the hall,' Frēawine told him. 'Tell the others. I'll go and see what these rovers want.'

'My lord, you can't go alone,' spoke Fólki. 'You're naked and unarmed. They'll kill you.'

'If I am to die this day,' spoke Frēawine, 'then I will leave this world the same way I came into it - screaming, naked and covered in someone else's blood. Now go and wake the others.' Fólki ran towards the hall. 'Fisherman!'

'Yes, my lord.'

'Tell my wife to fetch my sword and shield.'

'Yes, my lord.'

Frēawine walked anxiously towards the fjord, naked as the day he was born. It was a cold morning, but still, the Earl wasn't a small man. The morning sea fog covered the land in a milky veil, hiding her beauty from the sea rovers who dared come down the fjord uninvited. Frēawine couldn't see far in front and didn't see another soul until reaching the fjord. There were several birds resting on the calm waters and all was quiet. But then Frēawine saw the ship's dragon-headed prow appearing out of the mist like a sea brute come to attack those within range of its gnashing fangs.

Frēawine heard the creaking of the rigging and the wind in the sail. He heard voices travelling on the cool morning breeze, but saw no faces. He looked up at the prow. His heart was thumping and he was nervous, yet excited to see who had visited them. In Schleswig they were used to seeing fishing boats, meeting travellers, traders and storytellers, but never a warship, not for many years. As the mist slowly lifted from the ship, the Earl saw the silhouettes of men and began to feel a great sense of dread.

'Hæl!' came a strange voice from above. Frēawine looked up and saw a man step forward. He put one boot against the side of the ship and looked down upon the naked Earl. The stranger was in his mid-forties and had long grey hair and a long plaited beard. His eyes were a deep shade of blue and he was a handsome man. Frēawine noticed his arms were decorated with gold rings, the sign of a wealthy man. 'Ic eom eorla drihten, beorna bēahgifa - I am the lord of heroes and ring giver. Mín nama is Bēow Shielding, King of the Shielding Clan!' There was a distant rumble of thunder. Looking over the prow of the ship, Bēow Shielding tilted his head and looked down at Earl Frēawine with a confused look in his calculating blue eyes. Frēawine stood naked, looking up at the Danish King's confident smile; his manhood hanging like a war-horse for all to see. 'And who might you be, naked man?' King Bēow asked to the laughter of his crew.

'Frēawine is my name, the Earl of Schleswig,' he answered proudly.

'I'm intrigued by you, Earl Frēawine,' spoke Bēow, playing with his beard. 'You dare greet us naked and unarmed? Do the Gods favour you, I wonder? Are you not afraid?'

'Need I be?' Frēawine asked. 'Do you wish us harm, King Bēow?'

'I haven't decided yet,' Bēow answered, his soul-piercing eyes staring at Frēawine the entire time. 'Like I said, you intrigue me.'

As a cold morning breeze blew against Frēawine's naked flesh, Egwen arrived with a small host of men and women, looking anxious and armed to the teeth. Egwen handed her husband a broadsword and shield. Several of them looked down at Frēawine's manhood and wondered why the Earl was naked. 'Aah, your weapons have arrived, I see,' spoke Bēow, shifting his gaze to Egwen. 'And what is your name, girl?'

'I am Lady Egwen, the wife of the Earl. And I am no girl. What is your purpose here?' Egwen asked, holding her spear-shaft with a firm grip; her green eyes fixed on the Danish King.

'Egwen. What a beautiful name,' Bēow replied, ignoring her question. 'Unfortunately for me, I see you are fully dressed, unlike your husband here.' Bēow grinned. 'To answer your question, my son and I, along with our crew, find ourselves lost at sea. Is it not your custom to invite strangers into your home and offer food and drink and present us with gifts?'

'It is,' Frēawine answered, nodding his head, 'but first I must ask you to leave your weapons here, on your ship. It is against our custom to bring weapons into the hall.'

'Very well,' Bēow responded. 'You seem like good people. We will leave our weapons on our ship. But on one condition.'

'What condition?' Frēawine asked.

'The beautiful Egwen must give me her word that they will be returned to us upon our leaving,' Bēow replied.

'Around here a man's word is much like his manhood,' spoke Frēawine. 'He is nothing without it. I am Earl. I promise you, my word is all you need.'

'Do not be insulted, my friend,' spoke Bēow, 'the word of a woman is far more valuable than that of any man, or so my wife often tells me. Do you not agree?'

Egwen stood tall and looked up at the Danish King, who still leaned over the side of the ship with his boot up.

'In Wōden's name,' spoke Egwen, 'I give you my word: lay down your weapons, and you and your people will not be harmed.'

And so Bēow and his crew left their weapons in their ship that morning and followed the Earl and his beautiful wife into the village, where unfortunate things were to happen.

Chapter Six
The Mead-Hall

Schleswig

Halfdan, son of King Bēow, looked nervous whilst entering Earl Frēawine's mead-hall, as did the rest of the crew, including Halfdan's sons, Heorogār, Hrōthgār and Halga. The dark hall was beautifully decorated with wooden shields, deer antlers and animal pelts. Various weapons and armour, including swords and spears, hung on every wall above the flameless torches that rested in iron brackets. At the far end of the hall was a wooden dais, a raised platform where the Earl would sit upon his rune-decorated gift-stool. The ceiling was high with iron-braced wooden beams supporting the thatched roof, and there were two long wooden tables along each side of the hall. Bēow didn't know what to make of Frēawine or the Englisc folk. He didn't know if he could trust them.

Frēawine gave instructions for his servants to prepare food. In the meantime the Danes gathered around one of the tables, talking amongst themselves, occasionally looking up at the Angles who had started to gather inside the hall in large numbers.

'Frēawine is a handsome man, yes?' Queen Ingebørg asked, wrapping her long hair around her finger. 'His woman, she is pretty, is she not?'

'She seems a fierce one,' spoke Athils. 'I like a fierce woman.'

'She looks like she would tear open your throat and spit down your neck,' Halfdan added.

Ingebørg never took her gaze from her husband, still awaiting his answer.

'She is pretty,' Bēow replied.

'But not as pretty as me?' Ingebørg asked.

'Of course not, my Queen,' Bēow answered wisely. Bēow kissed Ingebørg on the lips. 'Not as pretty as you.'

'What do we do now?' Athils asked, growing impatient. 'I thought we were here to raid them, yet we sit waiting to be fed like dogs wagging our tails?'

'A man cannot fight on an empty stomach,' Bēow answered quietly. 'We will eat and drink and see what these folks have to offer.'

A maid approached the Danes' bench with great unease. Her hands were shaking whilst placing several loaves of bread on the table. The Danes reached for them, tearing the bread apart with their bare hands and ate like hungry men and women do. As Frēawine returned fully dressed from behind a wall, Ingebørg was first to comment.

'A shame,' spoke Ingebørg. 'I was enjoying the view.'

'Well enjoy gazing upon him while you can,' Halfdan told her, stuffing bread into his mouth and getting crumbs in his beard. 'Soon he will be dead. They will all be dead.'

'But not his woman,' spoke Ingebørg, her eyes upon Egwen. 'I like her. She would make an interesting pet.'

More food was placed before them and the Danes ate their fill, yet all the while more Angles entered the hall.

'There are too many,' Bēow told the others. 'We are outnumbered. We must put thoughts of violence aside for now. Let us get to know our hosts a while longer.'

After finishing their toasted bread and honeyed mead, Frēawine raised his voice and demanded the attention of the entire hall.

'Hwæt! Hwæt! Now that you have eaten, I wish to know why

you, King Bēow, have come to my Earldom with so many
fighting men and women?' Frēawine asked. 'Do you wish me
and my people harm?'

The Angles looked at Bēow expectantly, and so Bēow
smiled back at them. 'Like I said, Earl Frēawine, we were lost
at sea,' Bēow answered, remaining in his seat. 'You have
nothing to fear from us, my friend. Like you, we are good
people.' Bēow stood to his feet and turned to Frēawine's wife.
'Egwen, may I say what a beautiful woman you are, my lady,
one of the most beautiful I have seen.'

'Thank you,' Egwen replied, bowing her head.

'My lady, please, will you come and sit by my side so we
may get to know each other?' Bēow asked, now sitting down
and patting the bench beside him. 'There is no need to be
afraid. I mean you no harm.'

There was an awkward tension in the hall, yet Egwen, acting
as a peace-weaver, rose to her feet and looked down at her
husband. With Frēawine's blessing, Egwen made her way
towards the bench and sat by Bēow's side. 'Do not look so
frightened,' spoke Bēow, softly.

'I am not so easily frightened,' Egwen replied.

'You are a beautiful woman,' Bēow told her. 'Is she not?'

Halfdan remained silent, yet Athils was quick to agree, as
did Ingebørg.

'I love the plaits in your hair, my lady Egwen,' Ingebørg told
her, playing with Egwen's long blonde hair.

'Thank you,' Egwen replied. 'You are a beautiful woman
yourself, as many Danish women are.'

Bēow emptied his cup, spilling some in his beard, and rose
to his feet.

'My lord Frēawine, my people and I wish for more of your
delicious honeyed mead,' spoke Bēow. 'We Danes are thirsty
people.'

Later that day, the ancient forest thirst for water and the
heavens opened up, drowning the Earldom of Schleswig and
forced its inhabitants inside the great hall. The Angles had
been feasting and drinking heavily all afternoon, along with

their guests, the Shieldings. Night had now come and cloaked the land in darkness.

'My lord,' spoke Bēow, sitting in Egwen's chair, leaning towards the Earl with a cup of mead in his hand, 'you are a fine host, do you know that? Perhaps the finest in all the lands. I confess, I came here with the intention of raiding you, my good friend, but that thought has since been washed away with many fine draughts of mead.' Bēow looked into Frēawine's eyes. 'I now consider you a brother and hope our two people can continue this friendship for many years, *hiccup*, to come.'

'As do I,' Frēawine answered, his eyes bloodshot from drinking. 'As do I.'

'Tell me, Frēawine, when was the last time you fought a real battle?' Bēow asked, sipping his mead. 'When was the last time you were face to face with a man who wanted to kill you? When was the last time you tasted another man's breath while it escaped his dying body?'

'It has been many years,' Frēawine confessed, before drinking deeply.

'Me, too, my friend,' spoke Bēow, softly. 'Though I fear I may have to raise my sword in battle one more time. You are familiar with the War-Beards and King Frōda?'

'Of course,' Frēawine answered.

'Frōda is an ambitious man. I fear war is looming. When the time comes, can I count on your help?' Bēow asked.

Frēawine sighed deeply and looked into his cup.

'I cannot, my friend,' the Earl replied, shaking his head. 'I'm sorry, but I won't put my people in harm's way. The answer is no.'

Bēow sat back in his chair and finished his drink.

'Your answer disappoints me,' he said.

***

Jötunn Forest

Offa and Bardawulf stayed awake that night, while the others slept on the ground, under the swaying trees; their only shelter.

Every once in a while a faint howl could be heard in the distance, half-drowned out from the slashing rain. 'How are your wounds?' Bardawulf asked, referring to the injuries Offa had received, courtesy of Haakon.

'Sore, but I'll live,' Offa answered, shivering in the cold.

'Fear makes the wolf seem larger than he is,' spoke Bardawulf.

'I'm not afraid of Haakon,' Offa told him firmly.

'There is no shame in being afraid,' spoke Bardawulf. 'I am. Haakon scares me. I don't like the way he looks at me. And the thought of dying out here and ending up as a pile of turd fallen from a wolf's arse terrifies me. My father would be so mad. We are disorganised. We are hungry and thirsty, cold and wet. We still have no shelter and no one to instruct us. We have much to be frightened of.'

***

Jötunn Forest, en route to Schleswig

Throughout the night, the winds were high and the rain was unrelenting. Sunna and Wudga heard the wolf creeping around outside their small tent, yet neither of them were in any condition to go outside and confront it. 'The winds are getting stronger,' spoke Wudga, lying inside the tent.

'We won't blow away, will we?' Sunna asked, lying beside him.

'No, I don't think so,' Wudga answered, though he could hear the trees bending in the fierce winds, 'but we need to get some rest.'

The two of them had settled down for the night. Wudga had fallen asleep, yet Sunna remained awake; her arm was in a great deal of pain and she was worrying about the trees falling on their tent. As Sunna's eyelids began to grow heavy, the two of them were awakened by a terrifying howl.

'The wolf!' Sunna yelled, sitting up, reaching for her weapon.

The entire tent was shaking and the branches that were holding the tent together were being ripped from their holes.

'It's not the wolf,' Wudga told her, 'it's the wind. It's too strong.'

The howling continued all around them and the tent was quickly torn apart. The two of them were forced to climb outside, in the wind and rain, and drag what remained of their tent under the trees to use as a makeshift shelter. They wrapped their tired and aching bodies the best they could with animal pelts, but it did little to stop the wind and rain.

'Frīge, I beg you,' spoke Sunna, 'please help us. We need you. Please help us get home safely.'

The two of them were cursing at the endless rain, yet both were thankful that the wolf had left them alone, for now. Though they were in for a long night.

***

Schleswig

King Bēow Shielding looked across Frēawine's hall, watching as the Angles and Danes laughed, joked and played drunken games. The Earl's wife, Egwen, had spent much of the day alongside Bēow's young bride, Queen Ingebørg. 'Beautiful, are they not?' Bēow asked, referring to their wives, watching as they drank and laughed together.

'Yes they are,' Frēawine answered, nodding his head; his wide eyes fixed on the Danish Queen.

Bēow rose from Egwen's chair and turned to face the Earl.

'I think I shall give my wife a kiss,' said Bēow, 'for I have not kissed her all day.'

Frēawine raised his horn of mead, watching as Bēow sat beside Ingebørg and kissed her passionately on the lips. 'You have mead in your beard, my love,' Ingebørg told her husband with a warm smile, wiping it with her hand.

'You two are getting along, I see,' Bēow said to Egwen.

'Your wife is a charming woman,' the drunken Egwen replied, leaning into Ingebørg and kissed her on the lips.

'You are truly getting along,' Bēow said with a smile, watching as Ingebørg kissed her back.

Remembering his reasons for this voyage, to find adventure and excitement, to refuse to grow old and die in his bed, Bēow decided to take a risk that night. With the drunken Frēawine slouched on his gift-stool, looking on from across the hall, Bēow leaned past Ingebørg and pulled Egwen close to him and kissed her deeply on the lips. To Bēow's surprise, the Earl's wife kissed him back with great affection. With his lips pressed against Egwen's, Bēow turned his head and stared at Frēawine. The Earl sat and watched without saying a word. Frēawine's entire retinue looked on, yet did nothing to stop him; instead they cheered Bēow on, for it was a common sight in Schleswig to see Egwen merry and flirtatious. Bēow smiled at Frēawine, almost laughing. Laughing at him.

While Bēow was kissing the Earl's wife, Earl Frēawine saw the look in the Danes' eyes. It was a look of victory, of arrogance, an almost sinister smile. Egwen had an insatiable appetite for life and all of its pleasures, and Frēawine had always allowed her to have her fun with others, but Bēow saw it as something else. Bēow believed himself to be a god that night, but there was only room for one god in Schleswig and that was Earl Frēawine. Still heavily drunk, and with his gaze upon King Bēow, Frēawine stood to his feet. The entire hall became deadly silent, the only sound coming from the pouring rain crashing down upon the thatched roof. Frēawine stared across the flame-lit hall, seeing the challenge in Bēow's lustful blue eyes. Frēawine saw it on the King's face, Bēow dared Frēawine to do something, to say something. He waited for it. Hungered for it. Frēawine took a deep breath and drew his broadsword.

'Kill them all!' Frēawine yelled, his voice echoing around the drinking hall.

Egwen removed herself from the bench and got behind the hearth-guards. Bēow nodded his head, still looking Frēawine in the eye, before reaching down to reveal his seax that he had hidden inside his boot. The rest of the Danes did likewise. Frēawine left the wooden dais, walked down a couple of steps and headed towards Bēow, when a Dane dared to challenge him. Frēawine's sword felt heavier than usual, yet even in his drunken state the Earl managed to step back onto the dais and kill the Dane without much effort, spraying his wooden table with warm blood.

Several of Frēawine's men had attacked the Danish King, forcing Bēow to take his gaze from Frēawine and defend himself, which he did with great skill and passion. Death-cries soon filled the feasting hall and fresh blood decorated the walls. As Queen Ingebørg joined her husband, Frēawine saw more Danes coming up the wooden stairs, and so he kicked the one at the front, knocking him and his fellow Danes back down the steps. The Earl glanced towards his wife and saw her defending herself, alongside the hearth-troops, screaming; her seax slashing a Dane's throat.

Gathering his wits, Frēawine raised his sword and began killing the Danes on the stairs, one after the other. Then he saw Bēow fighting amongst the crowd. Frēawine stepped over the twitching bodies of the Spear-Danes with the intention of meeting Bēow in battle, but one man stood in his way. Athils was tall and handsome with a long beard and dark blonde hair. He wore a red tunic and brown breeches. Around his arms were several rings of gold, a symbol of courage and honour. He smiled at Frēawine, eager for a fight; eager to find fame by being the one to kill the great Earl of Schleswig. But Frēawine would not have it so.

'Are you ready to greet Wōden?' Athils asked confidently, spittle flying from his lips.

The Earl stepped backwards up the stairs, being careful not to trip on the dead Danes by his feet. He didn't care for Athils, but Frēawine needed to take his life in order to reach King Bēow. Frēawine wasted little time in making the first move and Athils was quick to parry the blow. Still climbing the stairs, Athils used speed and strength to attack, knocking Frēawine backwards. Frēawine steadied himself, while Athils made his way onto the dais. Using both hands, Frēawine raised his sword and tried cutting Athils in half, but Athils stepped out of harm's way and used his much shorter seax to bite Frēawine's arm, causing the Earl to drop his sword. Ignoring the excruciating pain, Frēawine looked into Athils' eyes with utter hatred in his heart. Drawing his smaller seax, Frēawine sidestepped Athils' attack and knocked him several feet back. Frēawine stepped forward and attacked, knowing he must end it quickly in order to reach Bēow, before someone else takes the King's life.

The Earl danced towards Athils and slashed against his chest. As blood splattered up the walls, Frēawine looked into Athils' reddened eyes and saw the pain there. Acting quickly, Frēawine stepped forward and thrust his seax hard, determined to spill Athils' innards all over the wooden floorboards, but Athils managed to grasp Frēawine's wrist. The two men now stood face to face, eye to eye, nose to nose. Frēawine's breathing quickened, his organs boiled beneath his skin and blood poured from his mouth. Frēawine squealed in agony, while Athils retrieved his bloodied seax from the Earl's stomach. Athils looked like a wolf ready to pounce inside a chicken coop. He licked his dry lips, raised his bloodied seax and slashed through the air, cutting Frēawine's beard and slicing the delicate flesh around his throat wide open.

Frēawine became dizzy and dropped his seax on the ground, before crashing to his knees. He tried holding the wound together with his bare hands, but warm blood gushed between his fingers like a river that had burst its bank. Frēawine dropped to the ground, lying in a pool of his own blood, watching as Athils walked away to join his fellow Danes in the fight against the Angles.

Frēawine was shivering uncontrollably and left for dead. He saw his beautiful wife being thrown to the ground by her hair. He wanted to help her, to protect her, but he couldn't move. He could only watch in silence as the world around him crumbled. Egwen was his life, his reason for living; his reason for breath. He loved her more than any poet could describe, yet Frēawine felt himself moving away from her that night like a piece of driftwood on the ocean waves.

With his life-force draining from his mortal body, Frēawine noticed the doors had blown open from the rainstorm outside and the hall began filling with an otherworldly mist. He saw a woman enter the hall, riding a pale white horse and grasping a spear. She was dressed all in white with a long white gown hanging over the horse's ribs. But it was no ordinary horse, for it had far too many legs. The sound of the steed's giant hooves walking over the old wooden floorboards echoed in Frēawine's ears. No one in the hall seemed to notice the enveloping mist that came out of nowhere or the large eight-legged horse walking between them. Frēawine slowly reached for his seax and gently wrapped his fingers around the pommel.

As the smell of blood filled his senses, Frēawine couldn't help but stare at the ghostly figure. Her long white hair was blowing over her shoulder, her pale blue eyes looking into his. Was it a Valkyrie? Was he dying? Would Frēawine leave his wife behind, his precious baby daughter and two sons? What would become of them, he wondered? The last thing Frēawine remembered was the feeling of his own blood warming his dying flesh. He heard feet stamping on wooden floorboards, cups being slammed on top of tables and thousands of men and women chanting his name, over and over. Could it be the din and clamour of Valhalla?

Chapter Seven
Devoured

Jötunn Forest

'I wonder how Sunna fares,' spoke Mōna, spear in hand, walking through the morning mist; following a small river. 'My sister should be home by now.'

'She will be eating a nice bowl of warm porridge without any burnt bits in it,' Offa told him. 'She's probably worrying about you.'

'I'm so hungry,' Haakon complained, dragging his tired feet. 'We need to try and find food today. I've heard stories about a group coming out here and starving. They eventually went mad and began killing each other, picking on the weakest first.' Haakon stared at Bardawulf. 'They would slit throats in the night and feast on human flesh. The forest was so wet they couldn't start a fire, and so they began eating them raw. My father says they are still out here, mad, living as wolves; hunting the next group of unsuspecting fledglings. If we don't find food today, I'm eating Bardawulf. I bet he tastes just like a pig. Oink! Oink!'

'Maybe we should split up,' Freya suggested. 'All the more likely we'll find something to eat.'

'All the more likely we'll become something to eat,' Grendel replied, making some of them laugh.

'Look,' spoke Haakon, 'I'm in charge and I think Freya is right. We should split up. We need shelter, food and water. I'm not sleeping in the rain again. Dunstān, Leofrīc, Bardawulf, come with me. We'll look for food. The rest of you need to build a shelter and try to start a fire. We'll meet by this river later today.'

Haakon led half the group further into the forest, leaving the others behind. Offa and Grendel were gathering wood, while Mōna and Edwin began constructing a shelter. Before entering the forest, Freya had helped Wēland find several hemp plants. Once they had enough they stripped off the leaves and soaked the stems for half a day. After squeezing out the water, Freya helped pulp the stems so the individual strands could peel away, producing long thin fibres. She then spun them like wool over a handful of twigs. Freya now used those fibres to make a bowstring, tying it to a long flexible branch.

'We have a bow,' spoke Freya. 'And this twine can be used for fishing lines and nets. And we can use it to strangle Haakon when he gets back,' she joked.

Though hunger was slowly sapping their strength, the group had worked hard and managed to produce a makeshift shelter and one bow. While Freya began making an arrow, and Edwin tried his best at making a spear, Offa and Grendel decided to go and try their luck at fishing.

***

Jötunn Forest, en route to Schleswig

Injured and tired, Wudga and Sunna continued to make slow

progress. Neither of them had managed to get any sleep the night before. They were weak and tired, cold and hungry, and their clothes were wet and clammy against their flesh. They had lost their food rations when their tent was destroyed. They now had no food, no means of boiling water and were both in great danger. It seemed Wōden was indeed testing them.

'You had to provoke the Gods, didn't you?' Sunna asked, walking in front with Wudga's hand resting on her shoulder for support.

Occasionally Wudga would turn his head and look over his shoulder to see if the wolf was still following them. Neither of them had seen or heard it since the night before.

'Hopefully it's dead,' spoke Wudga. 'It might have died from its injuries by now.'

'Does that mean I'm a Wolf-Coat?' Sunna asked.

'Maybe,' Wudga answered. 'I don't know.'

They walked past rolling hills, before heading back into the forest where the mist still clung to the base of the trees. Under the forest canopy, the ground was soggy, causing their boots to sink into the mud with a squelching sound. Wudga walked in Sunna's footsteps, yet the water squirted from under his feet with every step he took, and the wet mud was reluctant to release its grip. Though visibility was low, Wudga knew where they were and knew they were making poor progress.

'I need to rest,' spoke Wudga, wincing in pain. 'Sit me down here.'

The two of them sat down in the sludge, no longer caring for the wetness or the cold, for they had become numb to it.

'My arm is hurting,' Sunna complained. 'This sling needs tying again.'

'I'll do it in a moment,' spoke Wudga. 'I can't believe I've hurt my ankle out here.'

'I can't believe I've broken my arm,' Sunna complained.

'No wonder the wolf was after us,' Wudga smiled. 'We're easy prey.'

'No,' said Sunna, 'we're not easy prey. We showed the wolf that we were ready for a fight. We hurt him and...'

Suddenly a dark shadow leapt from the bracken without a

sound and sank its fangs into Sunna's throat. Wudga took Sunna's seax from her sheath, but before he could strike, the wolf ran back into the mist and disappeared, leaving Sunna on the ground with blood spurting from her throat.

'Nooooooo!' Wudga cried, trying to stop the bleeding, but it was no use, Sunna was coughing up pints of blood and a crimson river flowed from her throat. 'Don't leave me! Don't leave me here alone. Sunna! Sunna! Noooooooooo!'

Sunna was dead, Wudga was now on his own, and the wolf was still out there, hiding in the shadows, with the taste of human blood in its mouth.

***

Jötunn Forest

Offa's stomach hurt from hunger, yet he couldn't help but laugh as Grendel attempted to fish. Grendel was knee-deep in the river, naked as the day he was born, holding out his line and hook.

'What are you laughing at?' Grendel asked.

'Nothing,' Offa answered, 'just your maggot.'

'It's not a maggot,' Grendel replied. 'It's a worm.'

'I'm not talking about what's on your hook,' Offa laughed, 'but what's dangling above the waterline. I'm waiting for a fish to jump out of the water and take a bite.'

Edwin and the others laughed.

'I've got one,' Mōna yelled, pulling a fish out of the river and dropping it to the ground.

Edwin came from behind Mōna and pushed him in the river, causing a splash. 'Now it's mine,' Edwin said with a laugh, trying not to stand on the fish.

'You will scare the fish away!' Freya yelled, pushing Edwin into the river.

They all laughed and jumped into the water, not caring about the fish or the cold, or the pains in their stomach. They enjoyed the moment, enjoying each other's company, blissfully unaware that Mōna's twin sister was lying in the same forest, in a pool of her own blood; her eyes rolled into the back of her skull.

Chapter Eight
Night of Monsters

Jötunn Forest

With the group divided in two, Haakon led Dunstān, Leofrīc and Bardawulf further into the forest, searching for food, leaving the others behind to build a shelter and try their luck at fishing. Haakon's group had been gone a while, dragging their tired feet through the endless mist. Most of them now walked in a stooped posture, their shoulders forward, their heads farther still; their eyes bent upon the ground. No one was talking and they kept walking mile after mile, into the abyss, until Haakon held up his hand and told them all to stop.

'*I see something*,' Haakon whispered.

Bardawulf looked over Haakon's shoulder and saw what looked like a boar eating something on the ground. Haakon placed his wooden spear that he had made over his right shoulder. He tensed, took a breath and tossed the spear towards the boar. It sailed through the air, managing to hit the unsuspecting animal in its rear. The boar squealed in terror as it rushed through the undergrowth. 'Don't let it get away!' Haakon roared, chasing it between the trees.

Dunstān ran after Haakon, yet Bardawulf and Leofrīc remained behind, dead in their tracks; both dumbfounded at what they saw lying on the ground. Haakon ran after the boar as fast as he could, the branches whipping him in the face for the intrusion. Once the boar was in sight, Dunstān tossed his spear through the air, also sticking in the boar's hairy arse, causing it to squeal in protest. The boar began to tire and Haakon got close enough to use his seax to stab it, before his momentum caused him to tumble to the ground. Running for its life, the boar left a trail of blood in the forest.

'Damn it!' Haakon yelled, stopping to take a breath.

Exhausted, Haakon and Dunstān returned to the others to

find several adult wolves lying on the ground, ripped and torn to shreds. A cold chill crept up Haakon's spine. They all knew something was wrong.

'What could have done this?' Dunstān mumbled.

'Do you think we can skin this one?' Leofrīc asked, crouching beside one of the wolves that was missing a head. 'I think I can make a coat out of it.'

'No,' spoke Dunstān, firmly. 'This is not our tradition. It is not our kill. Something else did this. Something unholy.'

'We are our traditions,' Haakon added, remembering his father's words. 'We are our deeds. Without tradition, without honouring our folk's past, we become vessels for the dark things that lurk the Earth.'

Bardawulf looked unnerved.

'It's getting dark,' spoke Dunstān. 'It shouldn't be going dark this early.'

'It's as if the sun has been swallowed up by the wolf,' Leofrīc added.

'Let's head back to the river and find the others,' spoke Haakon. 'I don't like it here.'

Haakon, Dunstān, Leofrīc and Bardawulf had been travelling for a while, visibility had been poor all day, but now night had come and cloaked the land in darkness. Owls could be heard in the trees above them, hooting their calls - a bad omen. Whilst rushing through the forest they heard a bark from behind them. They all stopped running and turned their heads to listen. 'A dog?' Bardawulf asked. 'People could be nearby.'

'It's not a dog,' Dunstān told him. '*Be quiet.*'

A second bark was heard, followed by a scuffling in the bracken, then a long drawn-out wailing. '*Whatever killed those wolves,*' Haakon whispered, '*I think they are hunting us. I think they're right here, in the shadows.*'

'*Don't say that,*' spoke Bardawulf. '*I want to go home.*'

'*Come on, let's get back to the others,*' spoke Haakon.

Leofrīc and Bardawulf ran through the forest, following Haakon and Dunstān, hoping they knew where they were going. They heard something behind them, getting closer,

barking and howling; tormenting them and terrifying them.
After a race through the blackened forest, the four of them
heard the river nearby and Haakon was first to smell smoke.
Dashing between the trees, they ran to the riverside and
followed it to find the others. Haakon was still at the front,
yelling to the other group.

'Where are you?' Haakon screamed. 'Where are you?'

The unseen beasts were now even closer and louder than
before.

'Wait for me!' Bardawulf yelled from the back. 'Wait!' But
no one waited and the pack were soon at Bardawulf's heel.

'Haakon!' Freya called from somewhere in the smoke fog.
'Over here!'

They rushed towards Freya's voice. Freya's group had
managed to start a fire. Its hot glowing embers filled the night
sky like a thousand tiny stars returning to the heavens, and the
four of them ran towards it as fast as their tired legs could
manage. Bardawulf looked over his shoulder and saw a large
moving blackness right behind him, snapping at his ankles.
Bardawulf had never ran so fast. His chest was in agony and
his legs felt like they were going to buckle at any moment, yet
he pushed himself harder than he ever thought possible. He
had never felt so alive. When Bardawulf looked over his
shoulder for a second time, he saw the beast had gone.

The natural noises of the forest ceased and all became deadly
silent, all but the sound of the group's heavy breathing and the
crackling fire. They huddled together by the hot flames and
could hear a light breathing, almost a growl coming from
somewhere in the dark. They saw the breath of several beasts
floating upwards towards the moon. No one spoke a word, no
one dared make a sound, none but Offa dared to move. With
his flame-lit torch in hand, Offa took a deep breath and stepped
forward, walking several feet into the darkness. He stood his
ground and slowly held the torch out in front of him. Embers
danced on the air around him whilst making their way to the
heavens. What he saw that night sent shivers up his spine. At
least a dozen pair of eyes glowed like fire in the light of the
torch. They were snarling, showing their gleaming white

fangs; their hot breath floating away on the cold crisp air.

'*Don't move,*' Freya whispered. '*Stare back at them. Don't show any fear.*'

'*Look at the size of them,*' spoke Haakon.

After what seemed like an eternity, the ungodly beasts slowly backed away and faded into the blackness.

'What did they want?' Grendel asked.

'To rip out your heart,' Freya replied, 'and pick at your bones.'

'I don't want them to do that,' spoke Grendel, shaking his head.

Offa and the others were grouped together under the shelter they had built, using a simple frame, and sat on a pile of criss-crossed twigs, covered with foliage; the fire blazing before them. Cooking in the flames were several fish they had caught earlier that day. There was enough for everyone. The flames flickered against the surrounding trees, casting frightening shadows all around them, yet the fire was a warm comfort; a shield from what was lurking in the dark.

'Do you think they're gone?' Mōna asked, sinking his teeth into the cooked fish. 'I keep thinking I can hear something.'

'Don't worry,' Offa said with a mouthful of fish. 'Wolves are afraid of fire. We'll be safe. Probably.'

'Offa is right,' Freya added. 'The fire will keep them away tonight, but they'll be back.'

'My uncle is a priest,' spoke Edwin. 'He said wolves are misunderstood. He called them the teachers. We shouldn't judge them by their fearsome appearance, for they are holy beings and are not the monsters they first appear to be. Wolves are the protectors of the forest, keeping man safe from the true horrors that awaits us. When fairies create magical lights to misguide folks through the night-time forest, wolves are the ones who lead them back to safety. It's a good omen to see a wolf before battle. We must remember: everything we love about the dogs back home comes from the wolf. Wolves are shy and they don't hunt people. Wolves don't attack people. There is something out there, something unholy, but they are not wolves.'

'If they're not wolves, then what are they?' Haakon asked.

'I think they're hell hounds!' Edwin replied.

***

Jötunn Forest, en route to Schleswig

It was the morning after Sunna's death and Wudga was resting on the ground with his back against a tree, eating a handful of berries. He had been hopping and dragging his tired and aching body the best he could through the forest. His feet were wet and sore and the bottom of his boots had worn away, revealing holes where his bare flesh now rubbed against the ground. He didn't sleep well the night before, nor had he eaten since Tīwesdæg, the day given to Tīw, God of justice and war. It was now Thunoresdæg and Wudga was weak. He no longer cared for the pain he was in, the damp, or the wetness; his only thought was for food. He was so hungry he felt sick.

As cruel as it may seem, Wudga's grief for Sunna had slowly been replaced by thoughts of the wolf feeding on himself, on his own flesh and bone. Wudga had hoped the wolf might have had its fill of Sunna's flesh and so leave him alone, giving him a chance to find food and a dry spot where he could rest his heavy eyelids.

Wudga sat on the ground with his arms wrapped around his legs, shivering. He had been wet for days. His clothes now clung to his flesh, wrapping him in a cold clammy embrace. His eyelids were heavy and he had thoughts of closing them and never waking up. He didn't know what gave him the strength to carry on, but he somehow managed to get back to his feet and hopped gently onwards, heading towards Schleswig, when through sheer weariness he fell to the ground. He looked up at the ageless sky, staring into the endless grey. He laid there for some time, in a constant battle to keep his eyelids from closing. With great determination, he sat up and felt along the ground, searching for dry moss and wood; anything he could use to start a fire. He had built a heap of moss and twigs, but no matter how hard he tried he couldn't get enough friction to start a fire. He was desperate. Wudga's feet were painful and itchy and hopelessly uncomfortable. He needed to dry them in order to walk the rest of the way to Schleswig.

Out of frustration, Wudga knocked over the heap and cried out in despair. He was ready to give up. He laid down and tried to sob, to give himself a small release, but he couldn't even do that. He took several calming breaths and finally closed his eyes. He didn't care anymore and just wanted to sleep. Wudga was with the Valkyries, riding a pale horse, riding through the vast forest of Ásgard. Upon the horizon he saw Valhalla, the greatest of halls. By the doorway stood a man wearing an eye-patch and a large grey hat. Wudga heard a grunt, followed by a light growl. He opened his eyes and saw the wolf watching him, panting. Unable to walk, Wudga struggled to his knees and took a breath. With clenched fists, he waited. Wudga knew, either he or the wolf was going to die that day, but Wudga wouldn't go down without a fight. His life's candle wouldn't go out so easily. If he was to die that day, he would go out in a blaze of glory, in an inferno, and join his ancestors in the great hall. Though terrified, Wudga was ready.

'Lo there, do I see my mother?' Wudga asked. 'And my sisters and my brothers? Lo there, do I see the line of my people, back to the beginning. Lo, they do call to me. They bid me take my place among them in the hall of Valhalla, where the brave may live forever.'

The wolf stepped forward and fear gripped Wudga's soul. His breathing was heavy and his body trembled, yet he refused to show the fear that coursed through his blood. He lowered his wolf headdress and stared into the wolf's yellow eyes, letting it know that he too was also a monster who hungered for its flesh and thirst for its blood. Wudga was a Wolf-Coat and had killed a wolf before. He revealed his teeth, biting his outstretched tongue, snarling; allowing saliva to drip from his mouth. Yet still the wolf came. Wudga and the wolf stared into each other's souls. Nothing else mattered, nothing else existed, just Wudga and the wolf.

Once again the rains fell from the heavens, hitting thousands of leaves and soaked Wudga to the bone. Then the wolf came at him and leapt upon him with its jaws wide open. Wudga roared with terror, raising his arm. He felt the beast's fangs penetrate the thin layer of fat on his left arm, while his right hand lifted Sunna's seax from off the ground and plunged it deep into the wolf's guts. The wolf was lying on the ground, breathing heavily, its blood seeping into the wet earth. Wudga had won this fight, and so had earned his right to live, to exist. The wolf's soul belonged to Wōden, but its flesh and bone now belonged to Wudga. With a powerful puncture of the heart, Wudga killed the wolf and brought its suffering to an end.

Wudga heaped up the moss and twigs and rubbed the sticks together until a small flame appeared. Gently blowing into it, the fire took hold and he added more twigs and moss. After saying a prayer, he flayed the dead wolf, cutting out a joint, wrapped it in its own fat and used the wolf's hind quarters to make a spit, before roasting it over the fire. Wudga sat under the weeping heavens, wrapped in his new wolf pelt, warming his hands and feet, drinking the wolf's blood and eating the wolf's flesh, defiant of the rain; defiant of death.

***

Jötunn Forest

Offa and Grendel were peeing on the ground.

'What are you doing?' Freya asked, tossing fish bones into the fire.

'We are marking our territory,' Grendel replied. 'We are letting the monsters know this land is ours.'

'Last night we were taken by surprise,' spoke Haakon, addressing the entire group. 'And we became the hunted. Today, to restore order, we must now go on the hunt. We now know what's out there. Today we make our mothers and fathers proud. Gather your weapons and let's find these hell hounds and kill them all!'

Chapter Nine
The Hollow

Jötunn Forest

Armed with their seaxes and makeshift bows and spears,
Haakon led Offa and the others further into the forest, in
search of the hounds. They were cold and frightened, yet they
had eaten plenty of fish the night before, and so hunger was
kept at bay, for now. They had been walking for several miles
when they came across a terrifying tree, one that seemed to be
looking at them. It stood alone and was taller than the rest. It
was thick with many branches that resembled long arms
reaching towards them, waiting for the right moment to snatch
an unsuspecting soul. It seemed as though the top of the tree
touched heaven itself, while its roots remained hidden in the
depths of hell. It was so wide, it would take at least five of
them to form a circle around it, stretching out their arms and
holding hands. Seven feet from the ground there was a large
hollow opening that was both wide and tall and looked like a
mouth with long crooked teeth. Above the mouth was a small
opening, giving it the appearance of an empty eye socket.

'Is it the World Tree?' Grendel asked in awe.

'I'm not going near that thing,' spoke Bardawulf, stopping in
his tracks. 'It looks like a Frost-Giant frozen-in-time.'

'Stop being a coward,' Dunstān snapped, brushing past him.
'It's just a tree.'

'It's not just a tree,' spoke Mōna. 'Look, the branches are
decorated with cloth. I think it's an altar. A shrine to the Gods.'

Edwin crouched and picked up a wooden figure that had
fallen over in the grass.

'What is it?' Leofrīc asked.

'*A figure of Wōden*,' Edwin answered in a light whisper. 'This
tree belongs to Wōden.'

'Help me up,' spoke Dunstān. Haakon used his hands to lift
Dunstān as high as he could, though Dunstān only just
managed to see inside the hollow. With a struggle, Dunstān
climbed inside. 'There's something in here.'

'What is it?' Haakon asked.

'Weapons,' Dunstān answered, crouching inside. 'There are candles and skulls.' Dunstān stood to his feet and held out a skull. 'Look, I think this belongs to a wolf. There are more of them.'

Dunstān held out a staff with a skull attached and passed it down to Haakon.

'I think it's for protection,' spoke Freya. 'The wolf's skull is to ward off unclean spirits.'

'You mean like the hell hounds?' Grendel asked.

'Maybe,' Freya replied.

Dunstān dropped several spears on the ground that he had found inside the hollow.

'I've found some runes scratched into the tree,' spoke Leofrīc from the opposite side of the tree.

'What do they say?' Offa asked.

'*Ellen sceal on eorle*,' spoke Mōna, running his fingertips along the grooves. '*Bravery belongs to a hero*. This is a holy place.'

'Will we be safe here?' Bardawulf asked.

'Safe?' Haakon asked. 'We're not here to be safe. We are the hunters. Only the strong survive in this world. Only the hard. I won't listen to this talk of cowardice. I come from a line of great men, proud warriors, and you will not dampen my fire.'

Offa stepped between Haakon and Bardawulf.

'Leave him alone!' Offa told him.

As the two of them stood face to face, a noise was heard from behind. Haakon and Offa turned their attention to the forest, and to their horror they saw the hell hounds in the distance, standing by the tree-line; snarling. Within a heart-beat, the hounds ran towards them. 'Run!' Freya screamed.

Leofrīc began helping the others climb inside the hollow by giving them a lift. Haakon pushed past Bardawulf and forced his way to the front.

'Hurry!' Dunstān yelled. 'Hurry!'

Offa glanced over his shoulder and was terrified at the sight of the hungry hell hounds racing towards him.

'Come on!' Leofrīc yelled, crouching, holding out his hands, waiting to give Offa a lift.

Offa put his foot into Leofrīc's hands and leapt to safety, being pulled up by Dunstān and Edwin, before falling inside the hollow. Offa got back on his feet and turned around.

'Leofrīc!' Offa screamed. 'Leofrīc!'

Offa and Dunstān held out their hands, trying to pull Leofrīc inside. Leofrīc was jumping up and reaching out, but the hollow was too high. No one could reach him. Offa watched helplessly as the hounds leapt upon Leofrīc, mauling him, biting him and tearing him limb from limb.

'Leofrīc!' Edwin yelled. The group tossed spears at them, screaming and shouting, but it was too late, Leofrīc was dead and his body was devoured before them. Some crouched inside the hollow, covering their ears, ignoring the sounds of the feeding frenzy. Offa and several others looked on, terrified, yet strangely curious. Offa remembered Ket and Wīg's warning: how he should do everything he could to become the leader.

'What do we tell Leofrīc's parents when we return home?' Offa asked, visibly shaking with fear and blood-rush. 'Do we tell them how we hid up a tree and watched as their son was killed and eaten by hounds? Who will be next? Will we hide once again? Are we not here to challenge ourselves? When did the hunters become the hunted? We are shaming our parents, our folks and our ancestors. We need to fight back!'

'Offa's right,' spoke Freya, wiping her tears. 'We must do something. We must fight!'

'You're both right,' spoke Haakon. 'Pass me the bow.'

Grendel handed Haakon a bow and one arrow. Haakon notched the arrow, pulled back the bowstring, aimed and loosed. The arrow sailed through the air, hitting one of the hounds in its hind leg. The hell brute yelped loudly and struggled to stand. The pack seemed confused.

'Hit it again,' Grendel told him.

Once again Haakon released an arrow, this time hitting the same hound in its throat, causing it to fall to the ground. The rest of the pack panicked and fled between the trees. A moment later, seeing they had gone, Haakon bravely climbed down from the hollow.

'What are you doing?' Freya asked. 'It's suicide to go down there.'

'I won't live in fear,' Haakon replied. 'The Gods are watching.' Haakon walked towards the dying hound, keeping his eye on the forest. The hound was lying still, panting, its blood seeping into the soil, watching Haakon as he stood over it. Haakon placed his bow on the ground and drew his seax. 'Whoever sent you here to kill us, tell them Haakon has sent you back.' Haakon cut the hound's throat open and painted his face with its warm blood. He stood back to his feet. 'Wōōōōōōdeeeeen!' Haakon yelled. 'I am worthy!'

'Has he gone mad?' Freya asked from inside the hollow.

Haakon stared into the forest, when a deep, penetrating howl could be heard coming from somewhere in the darkening forest.

'Arm yourselves!' Haakon ordered, the whites of his eyes contrasting against the dark red blood smeared on his face. 'This is what we were born to do. We are to join the Wild Hunt!'

***

Schleswig

Ket, son of Earl Frēawine, was sitting on a fallen tree, deep in the forest, holding his baby sister on his lap. Heaven's light was fading and darkness now crawled along the ground, smothering everything it touched. As Earl Frēawine and the brave village folk who had fought back against the Spear-Danes were burning on the funeral pyres, Ket thought of his mother and father. Athelflæd was looking up at her brother, sucking on her fingers and drooling down her clothes.

'I have brought you to this special place, Athelflæd, to tell you something important,' spoke Ket, gently. 'Our father has been cruelly taken from us. Bad people came to our home and took his life. Now you won't see his face again until he greets you in the afterlife. But I want you to know that our father loved you with all of his heart. As you grow up without him, I will remind you that he was the one who put you in bed at night. He was the one to tell you stories and he was the one who kissed your forehead while you slept.' Ket had tears in his eyes. 'Your father loved you. He loved us all. Family was everything to him. Your smile alone was enough to bring a tear to his eyes, but he is no longer able to hold you in his arms. Our father was a good man and didn't deserve what's happened. He didn't deserve to be murdered. But don't worry, little sister, our father's death won't go unanswered. And no man will ever harm you or any of our kin again, for I will kill them all.'

Athelflæd looked up at Ket, and smiled, though she was too young to understand.

'You, my sister, are loved by all,' Ket continued. 'Wīg and I cherish you. We have loved you and would die for you since before you were born and still growing in our mother's womb, waiting to be greeted by your kin. But soon, Wīg and I will have to leave you for a short time. The same people who killed our father have also taken our mother away. The Danes haven't seen our faces, and so Wīg and I will travel to Daneland and give them false identities, in order to discover the man responsible for our father's death and spill his blood onto the soil. And I vow to the Gods that we will bring our mother home safely, where you will once again suckle at her breast. And one day, when you're older, you will become a fierce shield-maiden, driving your grim spear into the hearts of Danes and feed their guts to the raven and the wolf. Those who have done our family harm will pay the ultimate price for their wrong-doings. Wīg and I will make you proud, and Daneland will flow with the blood of our father's killer. This I promise you. This I swear!'

Whilst sitting in silence, enjoying the calming sounds of the forest, the birds singing, the trees swaying above, Ket heard a scuffling in the bracken behind him. With Athelflæd in one arm, Ket stood to his feet and drew his seax.

'Name yourself!' Ket yelled into the shadows, but there was no reply. He looked past the trees, but saw nothing. With Athelflæd in one arm, he walked further into the forest, slowly; taking one step at a time. 'Hælsa?' he yelled, but still no answer. Fearing for Athelflæd's life, Ket turned to walk home, when he heard a twig snap from behind. He turned around and saw a dark figure standing by a tree. 'Who are you?'

As the figure stepped into the light, Ket saw his face and recognised him. It was Wudga, son of Wēland.

Chapter Ten
Hunter's Moon

Jötunn Forest

Night had fallen and it was a full moon, brightening up the dome of the sky. Leaving the hollow behind, Haakon, Dunstān, Edwin and Mōna were carrying the dead hound through the dark forest, while on their way back to their shelter. To become a Wolf-Coat, Haakon needed to flay the beast and make a coat out of it, but even then he would still need to finish his time in the wild. None of them had eaten properly since the night before and they were tired, weak and had a long walk back to their shelter. Each of them longed to cook the dead hound and feed on its flesh. As Offa followed the others, he looked nervously into the forest and could feel something pulling him, almost whispering to him. 'Do you think they're watching us?' Grendel asked, referring to the hounds.

'Maybe,' Offa answered. 'I don't know.'

'It's a hunter's moon tonight,' spoke Haakon. 'They're out there, somewhere.'

'I hope my sister has arrived home safely,' spoke Mōna, trying to change the subject.

'She will be fine,' spoke Edwin. 'Sunna is travelling in the other direction. And besides, Wudga is with her. It's us I'm worried about. I don't want to end up a pile of turd fallen from the arse of a beast. My father won't be too happy if that's to be my legacy.'

'I need water,' spoke Edwin. 'And food. I'm so hungry.'

'Are we truly going to eat this?' Grendel asked. 'Will we

make the others angry, do you think?'

'You're damned right we're going to eat it,' Haakon answered. 'By eating your kill, you gain the strength of it. And if those fleabags turn up, we'll add more of them to the fire.'

'Good, because I'm starving,' spoke Grendel. 'I could eat a leather shoe right now.'

'Me too,' added Bardawulf. 'I can't wait to sit by the fire, knowing those things are afraid of it, and eat some meat. I'm so hungry I would even eat its dangly.'

It was hard to see whilst walking through the night-time forest, yet Haakon pushed on, bravely leading the way.

'You're quiet tonight, Freya,' spoke Offa.

'This is much harder than I thought,' Freya answered. 'I never imagined one of us might be killed. Leofrīc gave his life for us. I can't stop thinking about it.'

'Can we not talk of death?' Mōna asked. 'Not while those things are out there.'

A noise was heard from somewhere in the shadows.

'Wait!' spoke Haakon. '*Listen*.' They all stopped and listened, but nothing more was heard. 'Come on, let's go before something does show up.'

All of a sudden, a shadow leapt from between the trees and attacked Edwin, biting his hand, before disappearing again. The group panicked. Haakon and Dunstān dropped the dead hound and drew their seaxes. Edwin drew his seax with his good hand, but he was attacked again and dragged to the ground. All he could see were razor-sharp fangs snapping in his face. He tried backing away, but a hound rushed at his throat and sank its fangs into his soft flesh. Haakon and Dunstān stood over Edwin and stabbed the beast in its ribs, again and again, until they were confident it was dead. Offa and the others stared into the blackness, guarding Freya while she knelt beside Edwin. Offa heard Edwin choking on his own blood, but he didn't dare take his eyes from the forest whilst holding his seax in a tight grip.

'*I'm d-d-dying*,' spoke Edwin, in disbelief, struggling to talk, while blood poured from his throat.

'*Yes*,' Freya answered, '*you are going to die*.'

'*I can't... d-die...,*' Edwin told her, clutching his throat, while blood poured between his fingers. '*I c-can't d-die l-like th-this.*'

'*Look at me,*' spoke Freya, placing Edwin's seax in his hand. '*Think brave thoughts. Here, hold your seax. Think of Valhalla. You are not going to die an old man warm in his bed. You are not going to fade into the night. You are going to die having lived. You will die fighting a hell hound.*' Freya smiled. '*How many people can say that? The Gods await you, Edwin. They await you. And they will welcome you as a warrior.*'

'*Do you r-r-really th-think s-so?*' Edwin asked.

'*Yes,*' Freya answered. '*You will die a hero's death. Your clan will be proud of you. And your parents will be proud of you.*'

Freya had brought a smile to Edwin's face, but the smile quickly faded and he closed his eyes for the final time.

'Is he dead?' Bardawulf asked. 'He's dead, isn't he?'

'Yes,' Freya answered. 'He's gone.'

Offa was breathing heavily, listening to the hounds fighting in the shadows.

'We have to leave Edwin here,' spoke Haakon. 'We have to run.'

'What are they doing?' Dunstān asked.

'They're fighting amongst themselves,' Mōna answered.

'What about these dead hounds?' Dunstān asked.

'Leave them!' Haakon snapped. 'We need to get to the shelter.'

'We'll never outrun them,' spoke Grendel as warm tears rolled down his flushed cheeks.

'We don't have to outrun them,' spoke Haakon, rushing towards the shelter, 'we only need to outrun you!'

The group ran as fast as they could, through the forest, desperate to get back to the shelter and start a fire. They ran down a steep slope and some of them tripped in the darkness. Offa rolled alongside Grendel and Bardawulf, yelling for the others to wait, but no one waited for them. It was everyone for themselves. They heard the brutes behind them, growling and barking as they chased them through the forest. After a terrifying run they reached camp and Freya tried to start a fire, using a small gathering of twigs and dry moss.

'Come on!' Dunstān yelled, dropping to his knees, helping.

Though it was dark and they could see very little, they all knew the hounds were right there, all around them.

'Hurry!' Offa told them, standing guard, looking into the abyss, seax in hand; shaking.

'I am! I am!' Freya replied.

A beast howled several feet in front of them. Then out of nowhere Mōna was attacked and one of the hounds sank its fangs into his leg with a terrifying snarl. Screaming, both Haakon and Offa attacked it with their seaxes, forcing it to flee back into the darkness.

'My leg!' Mōna screamed, lying on the ground, writhing in agony. 'My leg!'

Dunstān and Freya managed to make a flame. Blowing gently, Freya brought the fire to life. Haakon lit one of the torches the group had prepared earlier, causing a flash of blinding light. As the fire lit up the surrounding darkness, the hell hounds quietened down and backed away. Mōna was crying and blood was pouring from his torn flesh.

'We have to seal the wound,' spoke Freya.

'No,' said Mōna. 'Please!'

'You'll bleed to death if we do nothing,' Freya told him.

'Bite on this,' spoke Bardawulf, after finding a stick on the ground.

Mōna held the stick in his mouth, while Offa passed Freya a torch.

'Brace yourself,' spoke Freya. 'One, two...'

Freya pressed the flame against Mōna's open wound, causing him to scream. The smell of burning flesh filled the air and Mōna cried so hard he passed out.

'*Have they gone?*' Dunstān asked with his hand gripped around his seax.

Haakon used his torch to light several others and tossed one of them into the forest. It landed on the ground with a burst of light, illuminating the faces of several red-eyed hell brutes. They stared at the group, each with a snarl, almost as if they were challenging them.

'Why won't they leave us alone?' Bardawulf asked from

beside the fire. 'Why won't you leave us alone?!'

'This is their territory,' spoke Offa, calmly. 'To keep it they will kill us all.'

Offa and the others sat around the blazing fire, receiving a small amount of comfort from the warm flames, yet they knew the fire was all that stood before them and the ferocious hell hounds that had already killed two of them. They heard them occasionally scuffling in the bracken and howling to the moon. They knew in their hearts, the love they felt for their families, the grace and nobility within themselves, their thoughts and feelings, the love they have to give to the world, could be torn from them and devoured at any moment.

'How's your leg?' Freya asked.

'Painful,' Mōna replied, 'but I'll live. I hope.'

'That hound liked the way you taste,' Haakon joked. 'He's probably in the shadows, waiting for the rest of you.'

'Were you dropped on your head as a bearn?' Freya asked with a tear in her eye. 'Leofrīc and Edwin are dead. Don't you care? They had brothers and sisters. Mothers and fathers.'

'What's wrong?' Offa asked.

'I lost my mother when I was two-years-old,' Freya replied. 'I don't really remember her, except for the sound of her voice and the way she would say my name. I remember her laughter. She used to hold me and dance with me and laugh in the funniest way. I don't remember her eyes, or her hair, but I do remember her mouth. She was always smiling. And I felt safe with her. I always felt safe with her. I wish she was here now, because I don't feel safe anymore. I'm frightened. I have never been more scared and I don't want to let her down.'

'You haven't let her down,' Offa reassured her. 'She will be proud of you, I know it. You have been the strongest of us. If it wasn't for you, we wouldn't have a shelter.'

Freya looked into Offa's eyes, and smiled.

'These talks of dead mothers are depressing me,' spoke Grendel, poking the fire. 'Can't we talk about something else? And not about being eaten. I want to forget what's out there for a while, just a little while.'

'My sister was out there with those things,' spoke Mōna, wincing in pain, with tears rolling down his cheeks. 'She's dead, isn't she?'

'We don't know that,' spoke Freya, shaking her head.

'Mōna, why don't you tell us the story of creation again?' Dunstān asked. 'It might take our mind from being eaten.'

'I'm not in the mood,' Mōna replied. 'I want to go home.'

The fire crackled and spat.

'Please, Mōna,' spoke Freya, 'we're all scared. It will help remind us that the Gods are out there, watching. We have to be strong for them.'

'Alright, if you wish,' Mōna sighed as fire-shadows illuminated the darkness of his face and the surrounding trees. 'Deep in the forest of Ásgard, Wōden rode his eight-legged steed, Slippery-One, until coming across three mysterious women sitting by a well. They were busy spinning the great web of wyrd. Wyrd is the destiny of all things, a fate that cannot be changed. The first sister gave her name, *Fate*, the second, *Being*, and the third, *Necessity*. The Wyrd Sisters revealed to Wōden the secrets of the distant past, as well as the near future. But Wōden was eager to learn more about the different worlds, and so they sent him to the giant Mimir, who dwelt at the Spring of Wisdom.'

An owl was heard hooting nearby. Haakon stood to his feet and gripped his seax.

'Wōden rode to Mimir,' Mōna continued, 'but the ageing giant wouldn't share his knowledge without a great sacrifice. And so Wōden agreed to sacrifice one eye to the Well of Wisdom. Pleased with this, Mimir allowed Wōden to take a drink from the well, just a sip, but enough for him to finally understand the mysteries of the worlds. Wōden learned there had once been two realms, one of ice, the other of fire; and creation began when these two realms enveloped one another and the giant Aurgelmir was formed.'

The group were listening intently, some of them with glazed eyes.

'On the way back through the forest, Wōden came upon a leafless ash tree, blanketed with snow and ice. It seemed as

though the tree had been there since time first began, frozen
and lifeless. As he passed, the tree reached out to him and
squeezed him in a tight grip. Wōden hung between heaven and
hell for nine days and nights, freezing in the blistering cold
winds. His steed circled around him and his two ravens swirled
above his head, bringing the worlds' thoughts to his ears.
Whilst deep in thought, as snowflakes bit into his flesh, caught
somewhere between life and death, Wōden found the symbols
of life's noblest values. He called these magical symbols runes,
meaning *to whisper*.'

A bat flew above their heads, flying through the smoke and
through the rising embers.

'With his mind teeming with knowledge, Wōden travelled to
the Land of Giants and killed Aurgelmir the Frost-Giant. From
the giant's skull, Wōden made the dome of the sky, placing a
dwarf in each of the four corners - Norþ, Eást, Sūþ and West.
From his blood he made the sea and the lakes. From his flesh
he made the earth. From his bones he made the mountains.
And from his teeth he made the rocks and stones. Pleased with
this, Wōden took Day and his mother, Niht, and placed them
in the sky until Ragnarök, the twilight of the Gods. Day's
stallion is called Shining-Mane and pulls Sunna in a golden
chariot, illuminating Middle-earth and drawing light to mankind and to all living creatures. Niht's stallion is called Frost-
Mane, bringing cold and darkness to the realm; a time when
monsters roam free and the wolves chase Mōna, wishing to
devour him. When the moon is finally eaten, the world will be
plunged into darkness and a new age will begin, a dark age.'

Mōna smiled at the group with the firelight flickering upon
his young handsome face.

'Thanks, now I'm even more scared,' spoke Bardawulf to a
bout of laughter.

But the laughter soon stopped when Mōna was dragged into
the forest by a ravenous hell brute, his screams echoing into
the darkness.

'Mōna!' Freya yelled, standing on her feet, seax in hand,
shaking; tears rolling down her cheeks.

Then the screaming stopped and Mōna was gone. The entire

group were on their feet, weapons drawn. Grendel and Bardawulf were shaking and crying, desperate to escape their nightmare. The group panicked and could hear the pack fighting over Mōna's flesh in a feeding frenzy, until a strange noise was heard and a squeal penetrated the forest, followed by a deathly silence. 'What was that?' Offa asked, trembling; the hairs on the back of his neck standing on end.

A loud thud was heard, followed by the snapping of twigs and the creaking of trees. The hell brutes could be heard barking, their deafening cries echoing around the night-time forest. Then the barking sounded more distant, like they were running away. *'There's something else out there,'* Dunstān whispered, shaking like a leaf, *'and it just scared the hell hounds.'*

The six of them stood behind the fire, listening to the sounds of the forest; staring into the blackness. *'I've just shit myself,'* Grendel confessed.

'Could it be a bear?' Dunstān asked. *'It's got to be a bear, right?'*

Haakon scanned the forest and heard his own heart beating inside his chest. The ground began to shake and the hunters looked beyond the fire and the floating embers and up to the treetops, where they saw something large moving behind them. As dark clouds gathered to block out the light of the moon, it brought with it a deep, terrifying fear that none of them would live to see the rising sun. Then, out of nowhere, one of the hounds flew through the air and landed in the fire, causing an explosion of heat and light. The hound was clearly dead. The group huddled inside the shelter, terrified.

'What's out there?' Offa whispered.

'It's not a bear,' Haakon told them.

'Then what is it?' Offa asked.

'It can't be,' spoke Freya, stepping out of the shelter to take a closer look. *'The legends can't be true.'*

'Come back,' Bardawulf cried, clutching Offa's jerkin.

Freya scanned the forest.

'What is it?' Offa asked.

'My father talked of something living in this forest,' Freya

answered, '*something unholy. He would say...*'

Suddenly Freya was lifted off the ground by an unseen force and disappeared into the night sky, her screams echoing into the forest.

Chapter Eleven
The Monster's Cave

Jötunn Forest

'*What was that?*' Grendel asked from inside the shelter, his face heavily tear-marked.

'*I don't know,*' Offa replied, shaking his head; his eyes wide with terror. '*I don't know.*'

'*Are you sure it wasn't a bear?*' Bardawulf whispered, still holding onto Offa, crying.

'That was no bear,' spoke Haakon.

'Then what was it?' Offa asked. 'What's happening?'

'I've heard folks speak of them in the hall,' Haakon muttered. 'They claimed to have seen two creatures prowling the forest, huge marauders from an unseen world. One of them, they said, looks like a woman; the other, warped in the shape of a man, moves beyond the pale larger than any mortal man.'

Haakon was painting his face with soot from the fire, making sure it was entirely blackened.

'*What are you doing?*' Dunstān asked in a whisper.

'Before battle our ancestors used to paint their faces black to blend into the darkness, to become the night. If we are to find Freya, then we must hide ourselves from unclean spirits and blend into the shadows, like wraiths.'

'*Find her?*' Bardawulf asked. '*She's dead. We're all dead!*'

'What makes you think she will still be alive?' Offa asked, refusing to show his emotions; though his eyes were clearly glazed.

Haakon sighed deeply. 'Because sometimes they keep them as pets,' Haakon answered. 'Some folks have managed to escape them, though their minds were never the same.'

'*I'm not going out there to be eaten*,' spoke Bardawulf. '*I can't go out there. I can't!*'

'We are a team. A family,' spoke Haakon. 'We don't leave our kin behind. If it was you out there, Bardawulf, and there was a chance you were still alive, I would go looking for you.'

'Bardawulf is right,' spoke Dunstān, 'Freya is dead. And I'm not going out there to die with her.'

'I'm frightened too,' Haakon confessed. 'I'm terrified, but I would rather do something than wait here for that thing to come back and take someone else.'

'Haakon is right,' spoke Offa. 'We will die if we stay here. How are we to find her? Do you truly think she could still be alive?'

'A few miles from here,' spoke Haakon, 'a frost-stiffened forest waits and keeps watch above a mere. Those who have dared enter that part of the forest say the water burns at night. On its bank heather refuses to grow, the deer in flight from pursuing hounds would rather turn to face the pack of snapping jaws than go further into that forest. That is no good place. I think that is where we will find her.'

'But that thing might be waiting for us,' spoke Bardawulf. 'Or the hell hounds might sniff us out. We should stay here and find help in the morning.'

'That thing was a monster,' Haakon continued. 'Our folk stories aren't just stories to scare us, but are based on something real.'

'I don't believe in monsters,' spoke Bardawulf.

'By sunrise, you will,' Haakon told him. 'It's been gone awhile now and it's scared away the hounds. Now we make our move, before something gets hungry and comes back for us. Remember why we are here. We're not waiting for someone to rescue us. We are to become the hunters or the hunted, you must make that choice. We are here to claim this forest for ourselves, to rise above all challenges, so we can walk amongst our people with our heads held high.'

'We are all scared,' Offa added, painting his face with soot, 'but Haakon is right. It is better to die this night than sit idle and wait to be struck from this world in the morning. I will go with you, Haakon.'

Haakon nodded his head. 'Who will join us?' Haakon asked. 'Who wants to feed on the hide of a beast tonight?'

'I want to see what its heart looks like,' spoke Dunstān. 'And make a necklace from its teeth.'

'I want to see what its danglies look like and put them in a stew,' spoke Grendel.

'You're strange,' Dunstān told him. 'Very strange.'

'You must come with us,' Haakon told Bardawulf. 'We will protect you.'

Reluctantly, with tears rolling down his flushed cheeks, Bardawulf nodded his head.

'Well I'm not staying here on my own,' Bardawulf mumbled, wiping his nose.

With their bows, seaxes and makeshift spears, the five of them took a deep breath, said a prayer to Wōden and stalked through the night-time forest; trying to find Freya. Their flesh was painted black and they were being as quiet as possible, none of them saying a word. Haakon was at the front, leading them deeper into the forest, when he came upon something lying on the ground, caked in black congealed blood; its entrails covering the ground.

'It smells like my father's feet,' spoke Grendel; his teeth bright against the blackness of his face.

'I think it's one of the hounds we killed,' spoke Haakon, helping to poke it. 'Something has ripped its head off.'

'Where's the rest of it?' Grendel asked.

'*Probably eaten*,' Haakon whispered, raising his finger to his mouth, reminding them to keep quiet. '*Come on, let's find this thing.*'

Freya awoke in the darkness, cold and alone. Her stomach hurt from hunger, but that was the least of her concerns. The first thing she noticed was the smell. The stink of death filled her senses and forced her stomach to heave. She noticed the ground was hard like the floor of a cave. Rising to her feet, she thought she heard a noise. She was listening intently, when she remembered that she had been snatched from the shelter. Then

she heard something moving inside the cave and realised she
wasn't alone after all, causing the hairs on the back of her neck
to stand on end. She heard it breathing. She tried to keep still,
but she couldn't stop herself from shaking. Slowly, Freya drew
her seax and crouched against the wall, trying not to breathe.

Walking through the Jötunn Forest, it began turning cold and
Offa started to feel a great sense of dread. Something deep in
his stomach was telling him to turn around, to not go any
further, yet he carried on following the others. Haakon led the
group forward until seeing the tree he had mentioned earlier,
the one watching over the foul smelling swamp. And there it
was, the cave where the monster was said to dwell. Offa stood
by the side of the swamp, looking into the dark cave entrance,
into the mysterious abyss; wondering what horrors lurked
inside. Haakon planted a spear-butt in the ground.
    '*This is it, the monster's cave,*' spoke Haakon. '*Let's hope
we're not too late.*'
    'Someone needs to go inside,' spoke Dunstān. 'But I can't, it's
too dark. I can't do it. I'm sorry.'
    'I'll do it,' spoke Offa, remembering Ket's advice, to make
sure he became the leader of the group. 'þéodisc mín blód,
wylfen mín sáwol. Native my blood, fierce my soul.'
    The tree above the cave was swaying in the night-time
winds, almost as if it was watching them.
    'You're crazy,' spoke Bardawulf. 'Aren't you afraid?'
    'If you let your fears own you, no one will ever remember
your name,' spoke Offa, drawing his seax.

Freya crouched inside the cave with her back against the wall,
unable to see anything. Whatever had taken her now towered
above her like an old oak tree, grunting and moaning; terrifying her to her bones. She knew she was no match for it, yet she
wouldn't go down without a fight. She gritted her teeth and
raised her seax.
    'What are you?' Freya asked. 'What do you want with me?
Answer me!'

The mysterious beast stepped forward. Freya could taste its foul breath in her mouth. It grasped her suddenly in its claw and lifted her several feet off the ground, squeezing her tightly. Both of her arms were trapped. She wanted to scream, but she was too scared to scream; too scared to breathe. It held her close to its mouth. Freya braced herself. It sniffed at her, at her hair in particular. Freya was frightened and wanted to die, for it to be over, but then she heard voices coming from outside the cave. And the monster heard them, too. It dropped Freya on the ground, turned from her and slowly made its way outside the cave.

Offa took a deep breath and gently stepped into the swamp. It was ice-cold and came up to his waist. 'My nuts!' Offa complained.

The others hid themselves in the bracken, their blackened faces blending into the shadows. Offa was wading through the murky water, making his way towards the cave entrance, which, the closer he got, began to look more like a serpent's mouth.

'Wait!' a voice called from behind.

Offa turned around to see Grendel had joined him, splashing in the swamp. '*Be quiet,*' Offa told him. '*What are you doing?*'

'I can't sit and hide,' spoke Grendel. 'Not with Freya in danger. I think I love her.'

Offa rolled his eyes and the two of them bravely approached the mysterious cave opening, the entrance to the underworld. As they entered, it seemed as if the cave was swallowing them like the Jörmungand, the giant serpent that has the Earth wrapped in its coils, holding in the oceans. Offa and Grendel were wading through the icy water, the noise of their splashing echoed off the cave walls and neither of them could see a thing. They were anxious and their hearts were thumping. They had turned a corner and could no longer see the moonlight outside. The cave had consumed them, numbing their flesh and numbing their souls. Offa felt relieved when he finally climbed out of the water and stood on dry land. They stood there for a moment, soaking wet and shivering, when

Grendel began sniffing the air.

'*Something stinks in here and it isn't me*,' Grendel whispered.

There was dripping wet moss up and down the cave walls and clinging vines hanging from the ceiling, stroking the two of them in the face as they passed. Walking further into the darkness, Offa began to feel an even greater sense of dread.

'*I think we should leave*,' spoke Grendel. '*I'm scared*!'

'*I'm scared, too*,' Offa confessed, '*but we must see if Freya is still alive*.'

Then they heard something, a voice coming from the darkness.

'*Gr... en... del*.'

The hairs on the back of their necks pricked and their hearts skipped a beat. It sounded near-human, but it was no man. Something else was with them that night. Grendel held onto the back of Offa's jerkin and Offa started to see something moving in front of them, something in the shadows. He saw it watching them and could smell its breath floating on the cold crisp air. Offa saw the outline of it. Whatever it was, it was at least twelve-feet-tall.

'*Gr... en... del*,' it whispered again, causing Offa's heart to hammer inside his chest.

'Freya!' Offa yelled, his voice echoing throughout the cave.

Grendel panicked and turned towards the exit, but he slipped and fell into a pile of bones that scattered the ground, causing him to drop his seax.

'Don't leave me!' Grendel begged.

Offa raised his seax to strike at the monster, but it swiped it away with its talon, clawing the flesh from Offa's chest and knocking him to the hard ground. Offa watched in horror as the Death-Shadow slowly moved along the cave walls. Offa froze, unable to move, as a cold shiver crept up his spine. Taking deep breaths, Offa ran his hands along the ground, feeling the bones of children all around him, desperately trying to find his seax in the pitch dark. The monster was sniffing the air, trying to find the two trespassers and gobble them both up. Offa was running his hand along the cold cave floor, when he picked something up that he thought was his seax, but it was another bone.

Grendel saw something moving in front of him and screamed. The monster took hold of him, squeezing him tightly in its death-grip, causing him to spit gouts of blood. Offa heard an horrific cry of joy coming from the monster. Offa had his back against the wall, watching helplessly while it lifted Grendel several feet off the ground. Grendel tried to scream, but his ribs were being crushed and Offa could hear them snapping.

'Grendel!' Offa screamed.

Offa heard Grendel's skull crack between its teeth and his brain slither down the monster's stinking throat.

Freya was shaking with fear, when she heard Offa calling her name, giving her a small sense of hope; hope that was quickly dashed by the sound of Grendel's terrifying, blood-curdling screams. Rather than wait for her own death, she began walking in the direction of the screams. The smell was overwhelming and her entire body was shaking, yet Freya pushed forward, into the darkness.

Offa desperately tried to find his seax. When he found it, the monster dropped what remained of Grendel and turned to him, roaring at him; causing Offa's long shaggy hair to blow over his shoulder and choke him with the scent of rotting flesh. Offa turned and ran as fast as he could, his panicked voice echoing off the cave walls that seemed to be closing in on him. Then, to his horror, he tripped and fell into the water. The bitter cold took his breath away and he swallowed a mouthful of foul, stagnant water. He panicked and was wading through the freezing water, desperately trying to escape the Death-Stalker. He heard it behind him, getting closer and closer, but Offa felt a small sense of relief when he finally passed the corner and saw moonlight at the end of the tunnel. He rushed out of the cave as fast as his tired legs could take him, climbing out of the swamp and back onto dry land.

'Troll! Troll! Troll!' he roared.

Haakon and the others heard his screams and ran into the forest, leaving Offa behind. Offa glanced over his shoulder and saw the hideous troll standing in the swamp, sniffing at the night air, before running into the forest, after Haakon and the others; causing the ground to shake. Offa ran in the opposite direction. His lungs burned, yet he ran as fast as he could until he could no longer breathe. All the while he heard the screams of his friends, their death-cries echoing throughout the forest.

Freya heard the troll outside the cave. It was her chance to escape. She rushed ahead and nearly fell into the water. Wasting no time, she took a deep breath and stepped into the freezing swamp. After turning the corner, she saw moonlight at the end of the tunnel and rushed towards it. With the sound of the others screaming in the forest, Freya left the cave behind, climbed out of the stinking water and rushed into the forest. The screams were echoing all around the forest and Freya couldn't make out where they were coming from, and so she ran as fast as she could towards the trees and kept on running. The branches slapped her in the face, but she didn't stop running until the fear inside her blood had sapped the last of her strength. She rested with her back against a tree and tried catching her breath. '*Freya!*' a voice whispered. It sounded like Dunstān, but it was too dark to see.

'*Where are you?*' Freya asked.

'*Over here,*' Dunstān answered, stepping from behind a tree and into the moonlight.

Freya was relieved to no longer be alone. Dunstān sneaked towards her, being as quiet as possible, when they both heard a loud noise coming from behind Dunstān, like the uprooting of a tree. The troll appeared from out of nowhere and rampaged towards Dunstān, causing the ground to shake like an earthquake. Dunstān ran as fast as he could, screaming, while the troll gained on him. Saliva dripped from the troll's mouth and its eyes widened at seeing its helpless prey running for his life. The unnatural beast held out its enormous twisted claw and snatched Dunstān from off the ground. It squeezed him hard, crushing his ribs and causing dark red blood to pour from his mouth. The troll roared in his face and Dunstān felt his own soul draining from his earthly flesh-shield. The troll then opened its hideous mouth and crunched on Dunstān's skull.

Freya screamed in terror, alerting the troll to her presence. It turned its gruesome head and looked right at her. Unable to outrun it, Freya knew she had but one choice. She gripped her seax tightly and stepped into the moonlight. A twig snapped from within the shadows. Freya turned her head and saw a man wearing a large grey hat, watching her from amongst the trees.

'Wōden!' Freya yelled with tears flowing down her flushed cheeks. 'This night I offer you a feast of blood!'

No longer afraid, no longer caring to live, Freya was free. And for the first time in her young life, she truly felt alive. The troll stepped towards her, its mouth drooling with Dunstān's blood. Freya screamed as loud as possible, not out of fear, but in rage, and ran towards the monster. It dropped what remained of Dunstān's body and charged at her; the ground shaking and thundering. With the grace of a cat, Freya leapt into the air and struck the troll's stomach with her seax, before rolling to the ground. Breathing heavily, she looked over her shoulder, but the troll's scaly hide was too hard to penetrate.

The troll ran at her and took hold of her in its talon, lifting her off the ground. It looked into her eyes like before, but this time Freya saw the anger on its grotesque face. The troll roared at her and squeezed her as hard as it could. Freya could no longer scream and her seax slipped from her grasp and landed on the ground. With blood oozing from her mouth, she looked into the troll's soul-less eyes. She felt her bones breaking and heard them cracking and snapping. She looked inside the troll's mouth. It was a dark, vile, stinking hole, filled with long crooked teeth.

'I hope... I give you... the shits!' Freya spat, whilst being placed inside the mouth of the beast.

Freya heard the sound of her own skull breaking, yet the sound of crunching bones was soon replaced by the sound of a sweet voice calling her name. It was her mother.

Exhausted, Offa stopped to take a breath, when he found a

bear carcass lying on the ground, probably killed by the troll, he thought. Using his seax, he cut open the bear's stomach, ripped out its stinking guts and tossed them into the bracken. He hacked away at the bear's insides until he had enough room to climb inside and hide from the troll. Curling into a ball, Offa sobbed his heart out. He was thinking of Grendel and how he had watched him be eaten, and of Haakon and the others, wondering if any had survived. And where was the troll? Would it be able to find him? What about Freya? Offa cried himself to sleep that night, in that dark stinking corpse.

Chapter Twelve
The Untamed

Jötunn Forest

Offa was asleep, dreaming of being eaten alive, when a noise awoke him. It was still dark and he was still inside the stinking bear carcass, cold and hungry, when he heard grunting and sniffing. The hell hounds had found the bear and were eating it, tearing chunks out of it, causing it to shake. Offa didn't dare move a muscle or make a sound. He held his breath, too terrified to even breathe. All he could do was lie there and listen to the feeding frenzy. He heard panting and whining sounds near his head, while the hounds pulled and ripped at the bear's rotting flesh.

Offa closed his eyes and imagined standing above the bear, looking down upon the carcass, seeing a pile of bones half-buried in the dirt, and the hounds were long gone. He felt safe. He knew time was a fleeting thing and his entire existence was insignificant. The fear coursing through his body at that moment in time meant nothing. He was already dead, his bones burned to ash. He knew his mortal body wasn't going to live for ever, but his soul would shine for eternity. While the hounds ripped and gnawed on the bear's flesh, Offa's pains faded away; his fear vanished and he drifted into a state of altered consciousness.

Offa stood alone, deep in the forest. It was dark, yet the moon could be seen from above the tall swaying trees. A black hell hound, at least fifty-feet-tall, looked over the tops of the trees, its fangs as long as spears, with one brown eye, the other a light shade of blue. Saliva lathered the ground where Offa stood, but he wasn't afraid. Offa knew his soul was made of light and he wasn't afraid to part from his mortal flesh. His body felt as light as a feather. He felt no pain, no fear, only a heightened sense of things - the wind blowing against the trees, the smell on the hound's breath; the Gods watching from beyond the moon. Offa drew his seax and bared his teeth. The giant hound leaned forward, opened its enormous jaws and tried taking Offa in its mouth, but Offa struck at the beast, drawing blood, causing it to turn its head away.

Offa awoke from his dream to the sweet sound of birds singing in the trees above his head. He was still hiding inside the bear carcass. The wounds on his chest, inflicted by the troll, were sore and itchy and were beginning to scab. He listened for a while, making sure the hounds had gone, before opening up the bear's stomach and stretched out one arm, resting his hand on the ground. Gently, Offa crawled from out of the bear, covered in black congealed blood, and scared away the birds that looked on from the treetops. He wandered around the forest for a while, trying to find the others, though he didn't dare shout out their names for fear of the troll.

Bardawulf was sitting by the river, sobbing, when he heard a noise coming from behind. He stood to his feet and turned around. Heading towards him was a dark and terrifying apparition, its white eyes staring at him. Bardawulf held his spear tightly.

'Keep away!' Bardawulf yelled. 'I am a great warrior, the greatest of my kind.'

'Bardawulf, it's me,' spoke the dark figure.

'Offa, you're alive,' Bardawulf replied, wiping away his tears. 'Thank the Gods. I thought you were dead. Where's Grendel?'

Bardawulf's face was still blackened with ash from the night before, though it was now heavily tear-marked.

'Grendel's dead,' Offa answered. 'Where are the others?'

'Dead,' Bardawulf replied.

'How do you know?' Offa asked.

'I was looking for them, when I found parts of them every-where,' spoke Bardawulf. 'There was a pair of legs lying before me with guts spread out all over the ground. When I carried on walking, I found more of them. I think they're all dead.' Barda-wulf looked into Offa's eyes. 'We're in a lot of trouble, aren't we?'

'We can't give up,' Offa answered. 'Some of them might still be alive, too terrified to call for help. Come on, we have to try and find them.'

'You stink,' spoke Bardawulf. 'Why do you smell so bad? What happened to you?'

'I slept inside a bear,' Offa replied. 'A dead one. I need to wash.'

Offa and Bardawulf were by the river. 'What do you think will happen if we can't find food?' Bardawulf asked, while Offa dressed. 'If we're too weak to hunt, we will go home, right?'

'We can't go home,' Offa replied. 'We can't live the rest of our lives as outcasts. We will get through this. We can find food.'

As Offa spoke, Bardawulf looked over Offa's shoulder and stared into the forest like he had seen a ghost. Offa slowly drew his seax, took a breath and turned around. Standing before them was a beautiful giant deer. It stood eight-feet-tall, with long magnificent curved antlers, twelve-feet-across. It was a majestic and beautiful creature with a strong muscular frame and a long grey coat. It was making its way towards the river, when it saw the two of them standing there, and watched them with a curious eye. Offa and Bardawulf remained still, not wanting to frighten it. Bardawulf picked up his spear.

'Let's kill it!' Bardawulf yelled, running towards the giant, screaming; waving his spear in the air.

Offa ran by his side, seax in hand. Though their hearts were racing, the two of them were desperate for food and bravely challenged the enormous primordial beast. The deer stamped its front hoof and lifted its forelegs off the ground, before driving its antlers forward and smashed them into Bardawulf's chest, knocking him to the ground. Offa didn't know if Bardawulf was dead or not. Offa struck the deer's antlers. Fearing it would rise on its hind legs and crush him, Offa dropped his seax and grabbed hold of the deer's antlers. Offa looked into the giant's eyes, when suddenly a spear was pushed into the deer's throat, causing it to cry out in pain. Bardawulf lived, and the two of them used their seaxes to bring the giant to its knees and finally to the ground. The deer was lying on its side, breathing heavily; blood flowing from its open wounds. Offa knelt by its side, looked into its eye and stroked its nose.

'I'm sorry,' Offa whispered, *'but we need to eat. Fare you well in the afterlife.'*

Offa and Bardawulf were sitting on the ground, before a small fire, enjoying a nice meal, courtesy of the deer. After drinking and eating their fill, the two of them rested for a while in the sunshine, with their back to the river; neither of them able to keep their eyes open and neither remembering to discard the deer's remains away from the fire. Offa was drifting in and out of sleep, when he opened his eyes and was startled to see that the two of them were no longer alone. A hell hound stood nearby, watching them. Leaving Bardawulf asleep, Offa slowly rose to his feet. He looked between the trees and saw many more hounds stepping out of the shadows, staring at Offa with curious, blood-lust eyes. Offa reached for his seax and gently drew his weapon.

The largest and most fierce hound stepped towards Offa, while Bardawulf remained asleep. It was the size of a bear and had the blackest coat Offa had ever seen; blacker than a winter's night, with eyes made of fire and fangs like small knives. Offa named him Wulfnoth - the brave wolf. The pack followed their leader and stepped forward, snarling and thirsting for blood.

'Bardawulf!' Offa called. 'Get up!'

Bardawulf opened his eyes and stood to his feet, suddenly

gasping for breath; his chest rising and falling, and drew his seax, leaving the broken spear on the ground.

'What should we do?' Bardawulf asked, his eyes wide with terror.

'Fight,' Offa answered. 'Kill them all!' Smelling fear upon the air, the pack of hell brutes leapt forward and rushed towards the two boys. As the wolves leapt upon them, Offa and Bardawulf jumped into the river. The cold water hit them hard, taking their breath away. They swam down the gentle flowing river as fast as they could, trying not to swallow the ice-cold water, before climbing out the other side. After catching their breath they ran deeper into the forest, leaving the pack of hounds pacing at the far side of the river, still hungry for blood.

'You haven't spoken much today,' Bardawulf said to Offa, resting inside the shelter.

'I'm sad,' Offa replied, sitting on his backside, slicing a branch to a fine point. 'I miss my mother and father.'

'Isn't your mother dead?' Bardawulf asked.

'Yes, and I miss her more everyday,' Offa answered.

'I miss my mother, too,' Bardawulf confessed. 'I can't wait to see her again. Why can't we go back, Offa? We can explain that we have lost the others.'

'No,' Offa replied. 'We must return as warriors or not at all. I won't live my life as an outcast. You know our custom.'

'We can go to Wēland and tell him the others are missing,' spoke Bardawulf. 'Maybe he will help us find them.'

'No,' Offa said again, 'they're all probably dead. We're on our own until we become Wolf-Coats. We must hunt these brutes and kill them all. There is no other choice.'

With a stomach full of deer, Offa and Bardawulf settled down for the night, resting on the ground, inside their shelter. Far above their heads, the stars shone brightly and the ever-watchful moon looked down upon them resting by the fire; a small light flickering in the blackness of the primordial forest. With his seax in his hand, Offa sat awake and watched over

Bardawulf while he slept. Bardawulf was shuffling around and talking in his sleep, clearly having a bad dream. A deep, penetrating howl echoed throughout the forest, waking Bardawulf from his nightmares. 'They're back,' spoke Bardawulf, sitting up.

'They never left,' Offa replied. 'Go back to sleep. I'll stay awake tonight and keep the fire lit.'

A twig snapped from somewhere in the shadows.

'The troll?' Bardawulf asked, rising to his feet.

Offa stood beside him and stared past the flames and into the forest.

'No matter what happens, we must stand and fight,' spoke Offa, quietly. *'If we run, we die.'*

Offa took a deep breath and calmed his trembling hands. From behind the trees, a dark figure appeared. It walked slowly towards them, snapping more twigs as it did so. The two young hunters raised their seaxes and stood their ground. As the mysterious figure came closer they saw it had black flesh and piercing white eyes and teeth.

'I won't run,' Bardawulf whispered. *'I will die fighting, as is the custom of my clan.'*

Offa tightened his grip on his seax and took a deep breath.

'Haakon?' Offa asked, excited and surprised that Haakon was still alive.

Haakon's flesh was covered in black soot and dried blood. He was shivering, weak and tired.

'Where's Dunstān?' Haakon asked, sitting by the fire.

'Dead,' Offa replied. 'It's just the three of us now.'

As the fire illuminated Haakon's face, Offa noticed a large piece of flesh had been torn and was hanging loosely from Haakon's cheek.

'You're hurt,' spoke Offa.

'I know,' Haakon replied, lifting his gaze. 'Do either of you have the needle and thread Wēland gave us?'

Bardawulf reached into his straw sack and found his needle.

'Do you want me to do it?' Bardawulf asked.

'No,' Haakon answered, 'but what choice do I have?'

'I'm sorry about this,' spoke Bardawulf, holding the torn flesh and pressing the bone needle against Haakon's face, piercing deeply, drawing blood, and stitched the torn flesh back together.

Offa held the torch near Haakon's face, to give them light, yet the heat of the flame caused Haakon's wound to burn. Haakon was breathing heavily and winced in pain, while blood and sweat poured down his face and onto his ragged clothes. Bardawulf was concentrating, when once again a howl could be heard in the forest, singing to the boy in the sky, wishing to devour him, but now it was closer and louder than before.

'Tomorrow, when morning comes, we will do what we were born to do,' spoke Haakon, tasting his own blood. 'We will become what we were born to be. We will toss our sheep coats to the ground and we will become wolves!'

It was the morning after Haakon's return and the three survivors awoke in their shelter, cold and hungry. 'Why can't we go home?' Bardawulf asked, lying inside the shelter. 'I'm so tired of this. I didn't sleep well at all. I'm aching everywhere. I want my bed and a warm bowl of porridge. Even Ælfwynn's burnt porridge will do.'

'Stop your bellyaching,' Haakon told him, painting his face with black soot from the dying fire. 'It's at least a four day walk from here. We would never make it. And we would die as cowards. Besides, my father has forbidden me from return-ing before my time is over. He told me to return a man or not at all. He said it's better I end up a pile of wolf turd, than to spend the rest of my life begging for the Earl's scraps. And he's right. I would rather fight and die on this day than live one more as a coward. Are you with me, Offa? Are you prepared to die if need be?'

'I want to live,' Offa answered, painting his face with soot. 'I want to earn the life I have been blessed with, prove my worth to the Gods and pay the price of my birth.' Offa drew his seax. 'Now let's send these ball-lickers back where they came from.'

Haakon led Offa and Bardawulf through the forest, with burning torches in hand, seaxes sheathed at their waist and their faces painted black. They were heading towards the hollow to provide a safe place where they could mount an offensive against the hounds. When walking through the ancient forest they heard a growl coming from behind.

'What was that?' Bardawulf asked, looking into the shadows.

They turned around and to their astonishment there stood an unholy apparition staring at them. It stood on two legs, with the body of a man and the head of a wolf. Remembering Wēland's warning about feral children living in the forest, lost to the darkness and unable to find the light, Haakon drew his seax and gritted his teeth.

'Run to the hollow!' Haakon yelled.

The ghostly figure ran at Haakon, growling and lusting for blood, and knocked him to the ground. Haakon tried to fight back, but he had dropped his seax. The unnatural cretin clawed at Haakon's face, tearing out his stitches, filling Haakon's vision with blood. The stranger from the forest bit Haakon's cheek and ripped off the torn flesh with its teeth. Haakon roared in agony. The feral beast looked down at Haakon, gritting its bloodstained teeth, when its throat was slashed wide open, courtesy of Offa's seax. It released Haakon and fell to the ground, spraying the air with blood. Haakon crawled on his hands and knees, roared in the stranger's face and forced his thumbs into its bloodshot eyes, pushing them into the back of its skull and brought its existence to an end. Haakon laid flat on his back and was breathing heavily.

'Your face,' spoke Offa, shaking and gasping for breath.

Bardawulf helped Haakon to his feet, while Offa turned his head and was sick.

'How bad is it?' Haakon asked, referring to his face.

'It's bad,' Bardawulf replied.

'The hollow is just over yonder,' spoke Haakon. 'I need to rest.'

'Behind you!' spoke Offa, pointing with his bloodied seax.

Haakon and Bardawulf turned around, expecting to see more feral children, but it was something much worse; Wulfnoth, the pack's leader, stood in the shadows, watching. He was smelling the blood in the air, his black fur blending into the forest behind him; his eyes glowing red, and his hot breath floating on the cool morning air. Offa stepped forward.

'No,' spoke Haakon. 'Look, there's more of them.'

More hellish beasts emerged from the shadows, too many for the three of them to have any chance of survival. Wulfnoth growled and snarled, his eyes fixed on Offa in particular.

'What should we do?' Bardawulf asked, shaking.

'Run!' Haakon yelled.

The three of them ran towards the nearby hollow as fast as they could. Haakon was first to reach the ancient tree and, to the other's surprise, he crouched and held out his hands. 'Come on!' he yelled, using his hands to give Offa a lift, allowing him to jump up and pull himself inside. He then did the same for Bardawulf. Offa and Bardawulf turned around and reached down to pull Haakon inside.

'Jump, Haakon!' Offa yelled, leaning over, stretching his arms down. 'Jump! You can do it! Come on!'

Offa and Bardawulf held onto him, trying their best to lift him up, but Haakon couldn't get his footing. Haakon stopped trying to climb, looked up at them and gave the slightest of nods. Haakon knew he couldn't make it inside the hollow without a lift, and so he chose to turn around and drew his seax.

'Wōden!' Haakon roared with blood running down his face. 'I hope you're watching!'

Haakon ran towards the pack, wielding his seax. He ran along a fallen tree, using it to propel himself into the air and strike one of the hounds as it leapt at him; its jaws wide open, trying to bite him in half. As the injured hound crashed to the ground with a spray of blood, Offa and Bardawulf watched in horror, when Haakon turned around to face the rest of the pack. Haakon roared, striking the snarling beasts, drawing blood, but there were too many of them and he was soon dragged to the ground. Haakon felt powerless lying there, no longer able to raise his arms whilst being mauled by strong jaws and razor-sharp teeth. He could smell their foul breath all over him and felt their fangs sinking into his soft flesh, ripping and tearing him apart. But Haakon was beyond pain or fear, or human weakness; he embraced his fate and welcomed death with a smile on his bloodied and torn face.

Chapter Thirteen
The Troll

Jötunn Forest

Offa and Bardawulf remained inside the hollow, looking out, with tears streaming down their flushed cheeks, while Haakon's corpse was devoured before their eyes. Offa notched an arrow he had found and aimed carefully at the hungry brutes, before releasing the bowstring. The arrow sailed through the air and hit one of the hounds in its hind leg, causing it and the entire pack to flee between the trees, leaving Haakon's half-eaten remains on the ground. 'What are we to do?' Bardawulf asked, trying to hold back the tears. 'They won't leave us alone until we're both dead.'

'I wonder,' spoke Offa, staring into the forest, 'who or what has released the hounds from hell's domain? This is a test, Bardawulf. Don't you see? We must never give up. We must never surrender. We must fight until our dying breath!'

A short while later, Offa and Bardawulf climbed down from the hollow and stood over Haakon's remains. 'Wōden, hear my prayer,' spoke Offa. 'I give myself to this forest. I give my flesh and my soul. I surrender myself to you, All-Father. Make me strong and I swear to you: I will hunt these monsters back to their den and I will kill them all. Nothing will stand in my way. And if I should come across the troll that has taken the lives of my friends, I swear to you: I will cut off its big hairy nuts with my seax. This is my promise to you, my lord.' Offa turned to Bardawulf. 'Come on, let's start walking.'

'Where are we going?' Bardawulf asked.

'We will follow their scat until we find their den,' Offa replied.

'Are you mad?' Bardawulf asked. 'They're going to kill us!'

'We are here to hunt and kill a single wolf and wear its coat to prove ourselves as warriors, right?' Offa asked. 'But we are the ones being hunted. If we are to survive, we must kill them all.'

'But they will kill us,' spoke Bardawulf, trembling.

'We all die some time,' Offa replied. 'Cattle die and kinsmen die, yourself too must soon die, but the one thing that will never die, fair fame of one who has earned it. If I am to die this day, I plan on leaving my mark across the face of the beast.'

Offa and Bardawulf had walked many miles in search of the hell hounds' den, but the sun had long-since fled the two wolves chasing her in the sky and it was getting colder with every step they took. The two of them had settled down for the night by a small fire they had built, far from the hollow and their makeshift shelter. Both of them knew what was out there and both were full of dread.

'It's too quiet,' spoke Bardawulf. 'Why is it so quiet? I don't like it here, we are too exposed. Those things might come for us at any moment, or the troll might find us. It could be hunting us right now.'

'Lower your voice, Bardawulf,' spoke Offa, sharpening his seax. 'We have wounded them. They will be frightened and cautious. Keep your nerve. Remember: the Gods are watching.'

A twig snapped from somewhere in the shadows.

'*What was that*?' Bardawulf asked, looking into the dark forest.

They both stood to their feet and listened a moment, before running to a nearby tree and began to climb. Once high in the tree they looked into the shadows and waited. More noises were heard, twigs snapping, small trees being uprooted, grunting. Something had tracked them.

'*Gr... en... del*,' a voice whispered in the darkness.

Offa and Bardawulf clung to the tree, neither daring to breathe, looking beyond the fire and into the shadows. They saw a face appear in the darkness, looking at the fire, but it was not the face of a man. It licked its lips and picked its nose. It was the troll! It waited a moment, before stepping into the firelight and sniffed at the air. Though hidden in the trees, Offa and Bardawulf were nearly face to face with the hideous monster. After sniffing the air, it turned its ugly head and stared into the treetops, where the two boys saw its deformed face for the first time. They saw its misshapen lump of a head, with bits of hair sticking up, its big floppy ears, long snotty nose, crooked teeth, one broken tusk, and its terrifyingly human eyes. With his heart pounding inside his bone-house, Offa slowly drew his seax.

'*No*,' Bardawulf whispered. '*Please*!'

But Offa ignored Bardawulf and quietly walked along the thick branch, being careful not to fall. The troll looked all around, sniffing at the air, grunting, when it turned and saw Offa running towards it in the treetops.

'Noooooooo!' Bardawulf roared.

With seax in hand, Offa leapt into the air, towards the troll, screaming; his voice echoing around the forest. Offa's aim was true and his blade hit the troll on top of its skull. Offa had visions of it splitting the troll's head in two, but its skull was too hard and too thick. Offa fell to the ground and dropped his weapon. Offa ran towards the bracken, fearful of being caught, when the troll snatched him up in its talon and squeezed him tightly. It held him close and looked right at him, breathing on him and terrifying him. The two of them were nose to nose, eye to eye; its breath stinking of rotting flesh. Offa looked into its mouth and feared being eaten alive.

Bardawulf was lying on the ground, when he turned and saw Offa in the troll's clasp. Bardawulf knew this was it, his time to kill the child he once was. He took a breath and prepared the bow and arrow. He drew the bowstring, aimed at the troll, and released. The arrow sailed through the air and hit the troll in its throat, causing it to drop Offa to the ground, but the arrow never penetrated the troll's scaly hide. With a grunt, the Death-Shadow reached out and snatched Bardawulf up. Bardawulf roared in defiance, terrified, yet refusing to cower. Out of desperation to save Bardawulf's life, Offa took a breath, picked up his seax and ran along the ground, towards the troll, and slid between its tree-like legs, reaching up with his seax. The sharp edge of Offa's blade cut away the troll's most delicate parts, its big hairy dangling balls, forcing it to drop Bardawulf and retreat back into the forest and into the darkness.

***

Schleswig

With help from her two sons, Ket and Wīg, Lady Egwen, Earl Frēawine's widow, had escaped the clutches of the Spear-Danes, and together the three of them had rowed throughout the night and arrived in Schleswig early the following morning. Mist had settled on the fjord and it was cold, damp and quiet. Though exhausted, it was beyond words how relieved Egwen was to climb out of the rocking boat and drop to the mud on her hands and knees. She struggled back to her feet and turned to Ket and Wīg.

'Are you coming?' she asked, looking upon her two sons; her heart racing. Ket and Wīg remained sitting in the boat and Egwen saw something in Ket's eyes, something dark. 'Ket? Wīg? We are home now.'

'Athils still lives,' Wīg replied.

'But not for much longer,' Ket added.

Egwen knew there was nothing she could do or say to change their minds.

'Then may Wōden be with you,' Egwen told them.

She stood on the muddy bank and watched as her two sons rowed along the fjord and disappeared into the morning mist. She then turned her thoughts to her daughter, Athelflæd. In what was one of the most important moments of her life, Egwen ran through the mist and across the thick mud, dragging her tired and aching body to the great hall and used her last bit of strength to push open the doors. Egwen saw a small group of maidens sitting by the hearth. And to her relief, the young slave girl, Beadohilde, held baby Athelflæd in her arms. Athelflæd's eyes lit up and her smile widened when she saw her mother standing before her, caked in mud, with tears rolling down her flushed cheeks. Egwen took Athelflæd in her loving arms and held her against her bosom, close to her beating heart. Egwen never said a word, though she thanked the Gods from the bottom of her soul for reuniting her with her only daughter.

Chapter Fourteen
The Cub

Jötunn Forest

Offa and Bardawulf had been walking all morning and had managed to hunt several rabbits. They now continued their long journey through the forest, hoping to track the hounds and kill them all, or die in the attempt. Offa could smell death all around him, when all of a sudden Bardawulf tripped and fell to the ground. When he looked up, he found himself face to face with a set of large teeth belonging to a dead, maggot-infested creature. 'Ahhh!' Bardawulf screamed, resting on his hands and knees, on top of the dead animal, slowly sinking further into the putrid, soft flesh.

'It stinks,' said Offa, waving the flies away.

'Help me!' Bardawulf demanded, desperately trying to climb from the rotting corpse.

'We must be close to their den,' spoke Offa, holding out his hand and pulling Bardawulf to his feet.

After washing themselves in the cold river, Offa saw something in the bracken behind him.

'What is it?' Bardawulf asked, looking over his shoulder.

'*Something is watching us,*' Offa whispered.

'*Don't scare me,*' spoke Bardawulf, his eyes wide with terror.

Offa drew his seax and gently approached the bracken. As he moved the bushes, he was shocked at what he saw looking back at him.

'It's a cub,' spoke Offa. 'Just a harmless cub.'

The cub's fur was as black as a dog's nose, but the most striking thing of all was its eyes. Its left eye was a dark shade of brown, its right was pale blue like the Baltic Sea on a midsummer's day. Offa remembered his dream, when he saw the giant wolf with the different coloured eyes. The cub was watching them, sniffing the air, trying to catch their scent on the gentle breeze. Perhaps it was wondering if Offa and Bardawulf were to be his dinner. Or perhaps they were too big and it wondered if they were meat eaters too, like him.

'It's young,' spoke Bardawulf. 'It must have crawled from its den.'

Offa stepped towards it, being careful not to frighten it away. It looked up at him and growled. Offa reached down to pick it up, but it began kicking its back legs and scratched his chest. Offa held it firmly and could feel its tiny heart beating in his hands. It looked at him and wondered what strange creature he was.

'Ouch, it's bitten my finger,' Offa complained, much to Bardawulf's amusement. The cub's survival instincts were strong. Offa could feel its fangs nibbling at his flesh, drawing blood. 'Aaaahh, get off me,' he yelled, trying to pull his finger free, but the cub stared at him; his fangs embedded in Offa's flesh. It seemed to smile at him, enjoying his agony.

'Kill it before it calls its mother,' said Bardawulf. 'She can't be far away.'

'No,' Offa replied, freeing his finger. 'There is no honour in killing an infant.'

'Well what are we going to do then?' Bardawulf asked.

Before Offa could answer, he saw something in the corner of his eye, causing him to jump out of his skin. The air rushed from his lungs and the hairs on the back of his neck stood on end. A large hell brute with matted black fur blowing in the gentle breeze was watching them from the shadows. It slowly emerged from the darkness and into the light that sliced between the trees, one limb at a time, gently, as though it was afraid of upsetting the hallowed ground. It was Wulfnoth.

Still holding the cub in his arms, Offa forgot to breathe. He looked deep into Wulfnoth's eyes and saw an abyss of terror. It was looking at him, into Offa's terrified and bewildered eyes, studying him. Wulfnoth's body was poised, staying low to the ground, preparing to kill. Every hair on his mane was bristling with rage, all the while showing the two of them his perfectly white fangs that he wished to devour them with.

'What should we do?' Bardawulf asked with a trembling voice.

Finally, Offa's legs awoke and he dropped the cub on the ground, causing it to squeal in protest.

'Run!' Offa screamed.

They heard Wulfnoth behind them as they ran as fast as they could to the nearest tree. Offa stopped his momentum and placed one foot against the tree, before leaping up, grasping whatever branches he could, and began to climb. Offa scratched his chest, stomach and legs against the bark of the tree, using all of his strength to climb. All the while he was having terrifying visions of his ankles getting caught in the jaws of death. Reaching a high point, Offa and Bardawulf sat on a branch and hugged the tree. Offa was struggling for breath and his heart was beating so fast he thought it was going to burst out of his chest like a raging boar charging at a group of hunters. When he looked down, he saw several hounds prancing impatiently around the base of the tree, irritated and hungry. Offa held the hammer that was hanging from his neck, hoping Thunor would come and save them from the jaws of death that lurked below.

Offa wasn't sure how long he and Bardawulf had been up the tree for, when he found the courage to look down for a second time.

'Have they gone?' Bardawulf asked, clinging to the tree, refusing to look himself.

'No,' Offa answered. 'Wulfnoth is still sitting in the shade, watching. Waiting.'

Offa saw the cub fighting with the other infants, biting their tails and hind legs and generally being a nuisance. The two boys looked on curiously, watching them play-fighting, testing each other's courage, chasing each other and biting each other's tails. Offa imagined himself being a wolf, a member of the pack. He wondered how such wild beasts were capable of so much love and affection towards each other. He was fascinated by them, forgetting, of course, that he and Bardawulf were to be their dinner. It was eat or die for the pack. Life was simple.

'The Englisc have gained knowledge from the wolf pack,'

spoke Offa, sitting safely in the tree. 'I've listened to the poets singing of the courage and wisdom that comes from them. Wolves are known to adopt strays and orphaned cubs and raise them as their own, as members of the pack. They always look out for their own kind, a key to their survival. There is much knowledge to be learned from the forest and from all the natural and supernatural beings that dwell here.'

'Thank you, that makes me feel much better about the situation,' Bardawulf replied. 'I'll be sure to learn a lot while they're chewing my face off.'

'The wolf,' Offa continued, 'is mankind's oldest companion and is engraved on war helms, swords and shields. The wolf is a sign of power, loyalty, freedom, wisdom and courage. Our clan have been taught to learn from the wolf, to be like the wolf, proud and noble; to fight as one, as a pack, and never show fear or intimidation in the face of the enemy. Come on, Bardawulf, we will not be intimidated. The Gods are testing us. They are watching. We must climb down and face this challenge with valour in our hearts. This is what we are here for. This is our test. Haakon was right, this is what we were born to do.'

'We're here to face ordinary wolves,' Bardawulf replied, 'not these creatures from hell.'

Offa noticed two ravens watching from an opposite tree. They were large birds with long black beaks and dark, soul-less eyes. It was *Thought* and *Memory*, Wōden's ravens who watch over the land and report to the Lord of Hosts. Offa knew Wōden was watching, and so he looked towards the heavens.

'Wōden, I don't ask for your protection,' spoke a confident Offa. 'I don't need your help. I only ask that you watch.'

Offa took a deep breath and began climbing down the tree, one branch at a time, to face the snarling beasts with honour and courage. He had dropped his bow, but he was still armed with his seax.

'Are you mad?' Bardawulf asked. 'What are you doing?'

'Come on,' Offa told him. 'The wolf won't give us his coat. We must take it!'

Wulfnoth and the hell hounds paced along the ground,

panting in the heat, waiting for Offa and Bardawulf to come down from the safety of the tree, but Offa wouldn't surrender his life easily. If the hounds wanted to feast on Offa's flesh, then they would have to earn it; they would have to bleed for it. Reluctantly, Bardawulf followed Offa down the tree, afraid that he might be left behind.

'This is a bad idea,' spoke Bardawulf. 'A truly bad idea!'

Reaching the bottom, Offa looked at the pack. They were on their feet, growling and snarling, revealing their white fangs down to their dark gums. Offa's heart was beating so fast it was sapping the strength from his arms and legs. He could feel the warm blood under his skin getting hotter and his chest was lifting up and down as his breathing quickened. Sweat rolled down the back of his neck and forehead and his palms were wet and clammy. He stepped forward, giving Bardawulf room to get behind him. There were several large females in the pack, each as beautiful and as deadly as the next. One of them began to approach, slowly and cautiously. Her ears were flat, her head was low to the ground and her narrow eyes were fixed on Offa. She growled and revealed her fangs. Offa and Bardawulf were both trembling.

'*Don't be afraid, girl*,' Offa whispered to the she-wolf. '*I have something for you.*'

The rest of the pack began to gather around, watching with mysterious glowing eyes, whilst panting in the heat.

'*Offa, what are you doing?*' Bardawulf asked. '*They will tear you apart.*'

Wulfnoth challenged the approaching female, growling at her, forcing her to cower. It was the most terrifying sound Offa and Bardawulf had ever heard, frightening them to their bones. Bardawulf whimpered and cried from behind Offa. Once the female had submitted, Wulfnoth turned from her and stared at Offa. With a thumping heart, Offa knelt and reached into his straw sack to reveal a dead rabbit. Still kneeling, Offa held the rabbit towards the black, snarling hound with his left hand. Wulfnoth stood his ground and stared at Offa with saliva dripping from his fangs, unsure what to do. Offa saw the whites of Wulfnoth's eyes and the whites of his teeth.

The cub that Offa had dropped earlier had gathered with his siblings, hiding behind his mother's legs, snarling at Offa and Bardawulf, trying his best to be terrifying. The entire pack gathered around. Wulfnoth was at the front, turning his head, snapping at any that dared step in front of him, causing them to scurry. Wulfnoth's instincts were telling him not to trust Offa, but his hunger, his lust for food, was overwhelming.

After what seemed like an eternity, the snarling hound lowered his head and stepped closer, inch by inch. Offa saw the blood-lust in those hungry eyes that were now fixed on the rabbit. The other members of the pack looked on curiously, licking their chops. Offa's breathing quickened still. Wulfnoth finally came close enough, his eyes glistening in the sunlight that penetrated the forest canopy. He opened his jaws to reveal a mouthful of knife-like fangs. Wulfnoth could have easily attacked Offa and fed him to his pack; his life to preserve theirs.

With his left hand, Offa held out the rabbit, while his right hand was firmly gripped on the pommel of his seax, ready to strike. Wulfnoth crept closer, calm and cautious, his eyes fixed on the dead meat. He took another step forward. Offa could now smell Wulfnoth's foul breath upon him. He was about to strike, when he was startled by someone calling out from behind the trees. Wulfnoth turned around to see who was approaching. The entire pack pricked their ears and listened to the strange, unfamiliar sounds; looking into the shadows. Wulfnoth turned his attention back to Offa, his mane bristling with rage, wrinkling his muzzle; his eyes now completely fixed on the King's son. In a panic, Bardawulf did the unthinkable and ran towards the sound of people.

'Nooooooo!' Offa screamed.

Wulfnoth leapt upon Bardawulf's back, knocking him to the ground; his screams echoing into the forest, causing a flock of ravens to burst from the surrounding trees. Dropping the rabbit, Offa climbed back up the tree. Ket and Wīg appeared from behind the trees. They saw Offa in the tree, before looking down, where they saw the pack of hell brutes all over Bardawulf in a feeding frenzy.

'Run!' Offa yelled. 'Run!'

Offa watched from the safety of the tree, while Ket and Wīg ran past the hounds, threatening them with their seaxes. Wulfnoth was growling and snapping his mighty jaws in Bardawulf's face, spitting saliva all over him. Using both hands, Bardawulf managed to hold the brute back by his mane. Bardawulf was still gripping his seax, but he couldn't hold Wulfnoth back with just one hand whilst striking with the other. Ket and Wīg began climbing, while the excited hounds leapt up at the tree, snapping at their ankles. Bardawulf gave out a chilling scream, screaming for his life, crying for help. Bardawulf wasn't strong enough to hold Wulfnoth back much longer. The big bad wolf was determined, pushing and pushing, using his weight and strength to drive forward, inching closer and closer to Bardawulf's vulnerable face with snapping jaws. After toying with his prey, Wulfnoth pushed forward and sank his dagger-like fangs into Bardawulf's cheek and ripped his flesh from the bone. 'Aaaaaaaaaaahh!' Bardawulf cried.

'What are you doing here?' Offa asked his kinsmen.

'We were rowing in the fjord, when we heard you yelling,' Ket answered.

'What are we going to do?' Wīg asked, holding onto the tree trunk. 'What the hell are we going to do?'

'I don't know,' Ket answered, unable to take his eyes from Bardawulf. '*I don't know*.'

None of them knew what to do. Offa looked down at his friend, watching as Bardawulf cried out, while the hounds tore him apart like starved creatures of the night. Bardawulf's screaming suddenly stopped and the pack devoured his body, tearing off chunks of flesh. The three of them watched from the safety of the trees, while Wulfnoth sniffed around Bardawulf's lifeless body. The she-wolf and several others slowly and cautiously approached Bardawulf's bloody corpse, taking small bites of flesh, while Wulfnoth sought the liver. Offa felt sick to his stomach with shame and guilt, wondering how the Wyrd Sisters would weave their great web and free them from the same fate.

Whilst sitting high in the temples of the Gods, with the leaves flapping in the winds, waiting for a sign from the three sisters, Offa noticed the two ravens were still watching them and was afraid they might report that he was unworthy to one day be chosen by the Valkyries, the Chooses of the Slain, to dine in Valhalla. Offa felt ashamed, hiding like a coward in the tree, watching as Bardawulf was torn to shreds. He took a deep breath, gathered his thoughts and wiped the tears from his eyes. He wouldn't show weakness, not in front of Wōden's ravens. And the three of them wouldn't sit and hide from the hell brutes any longer.

'Are we not Wolf-Coats?' Wīg asked his brother. 'Why are we hiding like gutless cowards?'

The bloodstained hounds had been disturbed and were now circling the bottom of the tree.

'You're right,' spoke Ket, drawing his seax. 'We are Thegns. We belong to the Angle Clan! To Ængla land! We were born to fight! I say we send these arse-licking fiends back to hell!'

Offa didn't say a word and Bardawulf's haunting eyes were still looking at him through the blood-splattered blades of grass. Fear had gripped Offa in a tight embrace, draining his soul, but he was Wōden-born and was determined to prove his worth. With the ravens looking on, the three of them bravely jumped down from the safety of the tree and confronted the blood-hungry pack with weapons drawn and revenge in their hearts. Ket and Wīg seemed fearless, but Offa was young and frightened. He tried holding his seax with a tight grip, but his hands were sweaty and he couldn't stop shaking. Ket took a deep breath, before giving out a war cry; a primal scream that echoed throughout the ancient forest.

Wulfnoth stepped towards them, his eyes glowing like fire; his hackles raised, his fangs revealed. The pack were behind him, supporting their brave leader. Offa's heart was beating faster than a rabbit's at Easter with a blade to its throat. Wulfnoth stepped closer, savouring the moment, staring at them; his fur erect and lusting for the kill. The cub Offa had handled earlier was snarling at him, revealing its bloodstained fangs. The hounds attacked, growling and snarling as they leapt upon the three of them, trying to tear their throats open. Offa was almost numb with terror. Ket and Wīg hacked and slashed at the pack, drawing blood, but the hounds kept circling and coming back for more.

'Come on, Offa, kill them all!' Wīg yelled, trying to encourage his kinsman to join in, while he and Ket attacked with all of their might, spraying the ground with blood.

The pack began to form a circle of death around them. One of the hounds stalked Offa in particular. Offa stepped backwards, one foot at a time, shaking like a leaf, nervously holding out his seax and pointing the sharpened tip toward the beast. Offa could feel the earth beneath his feet and the sweat rolling down his forehead and neck. His skin felt hot and he felt himself panicking. Sensing fear, the hound charged at Offa with a terrifying snarl, throwing its weight forward, opening its jaws as wide as it could and sank its fangs into his arm. It ripped and tore at the soft flesh, forcing Offa to drop his weapon, and dragged him to the ground. Offa felt each fang as they punctured his flesh. He saw nothing but fur and teeth, feeling nothing but a burning pain rushing through his arm. Offa hit the brute with his free hand, but it wouldn't let go. It was trying to pull him across the ground, almost tearing his arm out of the socket. Offa thought he was going to die there and then.

Lying flat on his back, Offa struggled to fight off the savage beast, when he looked up and saw two figures standing above him. Ket and Wīg stepped forward, striking the ferocious hound, again and again, forcing it to release Offa from its powerful jaws. The unholy beast collapsed to the ground and its life-force leaked into the earth. Ket reached out his sweaty palm and helped Offa to his feet. Offa could smell iron, blood and death all over him. The remaining hounds continued stalking them, inching closer and closer, fangs revealed; their eyes glowing red with blood-lust. Offa's arm was burning like fire. He looked down and was horrified to see his arm plastered in blood. He looked at the ground and saw the beast that had bitten him. Its legs were shaking horribly and a thick crimson puddle began to form around it.

'*Offa*,' Ket whispered, slowly stepping backwards.

Offa lifted his gaze and saw Wulfnoth standing before the three of them, his black mane bristling with rage.

'If I am to die,' spoke Ket, 'I will die as a warrior, like my fathers before me.'

'Lo there..., do I see my father?' Wīg asked.

With tears streaming down his cheeks, Offa took a deep breath.

'Lo there..., do I see my mother?' Offa asked.

'And my sisters and my brothers?' Ket asked.

'Lo there..., do I see the line of my people, back to the beginning?' they asked together. 'Lo..., they do call to me. They bid me take my place among them in the halls of Valhalla, where the brave live forever.'

Ket flicked blood from his blade, stepped forward and confronted Wulfnoth, knowing his kinsmen were with him and Valhalla awaited. Wulfnoth and the pack bolted towards the three of them, and they equally ran towards the pack, with seaxes in hand and hate in their hearts. Offa's blood rushed through his body so quickly that his fear melted away like ice in the morning sun. Offa felt intoxicated, possessed by the spirits of his ancestors. With no regard for his own safety, Offa charged at Wulfnoth with the desire to tear open the beast's throat with his bare teeth if need be. Offa no longer cared if his flesh was to be torn from his skull; he only cared to draw blood, to seize his glory and fight until his dying breath, because he was alive and wouldn't go down without a damn good fight. And so Offa fought that day with sword in hand and valour in his heart. And drew blood.

Offa's face was scratched, he was bitten and he bled, but he never gave up. With Wulfnoth on top of him, Offa refused to surrender to the beast. Wulfnoth bit Offa's wrist, forcing him to release his seax, but Offa screamed in defiance and held him back with his mane. Offa fought with every ounce of strength he had. He knew he was no match for Wulfnoth. He knew he would die that day, but he didn't care. Offa could smell Wulfnoth's stinking breath in his face, but he was no longer afraid. Offa was happy to die fighting to the death, tooth and claw.

With strength he didn't know he had, Offa held Wulfnoth back with one hand and reached for his seax with the other. Offa's fingertips touched his weapon, but he couldn't quite grasp it. Wulfnoth's snapping jaws were getting closer and closer. Offa roared whilst desperately trying to retrieve his weapon, when suddenly Wulfnoth yelped and dark red blood poured from between his fangs and fell into Offa's mouth. Offa looked into Wulfnoth's eyes and saw the lights go out. He then tossed Wulfnoth's twitching corpse aside and saw Ket and Wīg standing above him.

'I have never seen such a wolf,' spoke Ket, pulling his seax from the back of Wulfnoth's skull.

'*How did Offa hold it back with one hand*?' Wīg whispered. '*That was inhuman. No man alive could do that.*'

'He is Wōden-born,' Ket answered. 'Offa has a God in him, as do we.'

Offa couldn't stop shaking. After taking several deep breaths, he began to calm down and got to his hands and knees. He saw the remaining hounds lying on the ground, dead, with Wulfnoth and the she-wolf lying amongst them. Then Offa heard a small whimper and saw the cub sniffing at the lifeless bodies of his mother and father, lying motionless on the ground. The cub cried by his mother's side, licking her wounds, trying to wake her up, but she couldn't wake. She would never wake again. Offa picked the cub up and joined his kinsmen as they ran towards their boat, leaving Bardawulf's corpse behind for the birds and the beasts.

Chapter Fifteen
Fall From Grace

Jötunn Forest, en route to Daneland

After the death of Bardawulf, Ket and Wīg led Offa to their boat that rested on the shore. They had told Offa what had happened to their father and how they had visited Daneland under false identities, in order to discover their father's killer and free their mother, Egwen, from slavery. After taking their mother home and reuniting her with Athelflæd, they were now returning to Daneland to kill Athils, their father's killer, and they were taking Offa with them.

Offa placed the cub inside the boat and helped push it into the water, before jumping inside. He knew he had to finish his rite-of-passage, but Earl Frēawine was his blood and Offa felt it was more honourable to help avenge his kinsman's murder than to finish his time in the wild. The three of them took it in turns rowing up the fjord and out to sea. Offa didn't say much that day. He sat quietly and listened to the oars crashing into the Baltic Sea and the endless waves splashing against the hull, his mind some-place else. The cub sat under the bench with his tail tucked between his legs, not daring to move or make a sound.

'You should throw that fleabag overboard,' spoke Ket. 'It will only bring you trouble.'

'No,' Offa replied. 'I want to keep him and train him.'

'A wolf belongs amongst its own kind,' spoke Ket. 'It's unnatural and cruel for a living creature to dwell amongst its natural predators. To be away from your own kind can drain one's soul and leave nothing but an empty shell.'

'I will take good care of him,' Offa replied. 'I will give him a good life.'

'Well he's your responsibility,' spoke Ket.

'What is small and helpless today, may grow large and fierce tomorrow,' Wīg added. 'He may not seem it now, but he's dangerous. But if you treat him well, with love and respect, he may be the best friend you will ever have.'

'Or,' spoke Ket, 'he may one day tear out your throat when you least expect it.'

Leaving their boat on the sandy beach of Daneland, an anxious and excitable Ket led his two kinsman into the forest. Offa was holding the cub in his arms. It wriggled and scratched whilst trying to escape. A short while later, Ket recognised where they were.

'I think this is the trail,' spoke Ket, quietly. 'This is where

Athils brought us hunting. He comes this way by himself, following the same game trail. Hopefully we haven't missed him.'

They walked along a game trail for several miles, surrounded by dense forest on either side. Offa was feeling hungry and dry-mouthed and was thinking of Grendel, Haakon, Bardawulf and the poor cub who had lost his entire family. Offa knew what it was like to lose a mother at a young age. Everything the cub had ever known, every bit of warmth and pleasure, every bit of its understanding of the world, had come from its mother and the pack. And now they were gone forever.

'Come on, Offa, make haste,' Wīg told him, looking over his shoulder. 'We don't want to miss him. He should be here somewhere. Somewhere in this forest is the man who murdered our father and raped our mother. I can smell him on the wind. Athils is here somewhere, I know it.'

Later, the three of them had stopped to rest on the familiar path and waited for Athils to show himself. With Ket's attention fixed on the path ahead, Offa knelt on one knee and tried playing with the cub. Every time Offa attempted to scratch under his chin, the cub tried to bite Offa's hand. Offa found it amusing until the moment the cub managed to catch his finger in its mouth and drew blood.

'Ouch,' Offa complained, 'it's bitten me.'

'*Be quiet,*' spoke Ket. '*There's movement ahead.*'

A large shadow appeared on the trail, causing Offa's heart to skip beats. The shadow came closer and stepped into the light. It was the figure of a man. The hilt of his sword gave a flash of light.

'*Athils,*' Wīg whispered, staying out of sight. '*He's here.*'

'*Get down and hide,*' Ket told them, drawing his seax. '*And calm down, brother. I'm going to kill him. You don't need to worry about anything.*'

Offa held a hand above his eyes to stop the sun's bright glare and watched Athils walking towards them, still oblivious to their presence. Athils was wearing a white under-tunic with the sleeves rolled up to his elbows. Over his back was a wooden shield and hanging from his waist was a sheathed broadsword.

Ket and Wīg, fifteen and fourteen-years-old, armed with only their seaxes, with no armour or shield, were about to challenge him. Ket and Wīg bravely stood to their feet and stepped onto the trail, in plain view of the approaching Dane. Athils spotted them standing there, seaxes in hand and darkness upon their youthful faces. He stopped walking and assessed the situation. He took a deep breath and drew his sword. All Offa could do was keep out of the way and watch. In his arms was the cub, still trying to break free, unaware that his fate was being woven with that of mankind.

Ket and Wīg anxiously approached the man who had murdered their father and raped their mother. They had visited Daneland with false identities and had befriended Athils, to learn of his routes and patterns, but now they had every intention of butchering him like a pig at the winter slaughter. With the cub held tightly, Offa made his way through the bracken, trying to get a closer look, keeping out of view. If Ket and Wīg were to be slain, then Offa didn't want to be next.

'Evarīc, Erwīg, we meet again,' spoke Athils with a smile, using the names they had given to hide their true identities. 'Or should I call you Ket and Wīg? I was just thinking about the two of you and what you did to rescue your mother. What great courage that must have taken, what nerves of steel you two must have. Your mother, Egwen, must be proud. In these changing times, we Danes would welcome two young warriors such as you. Your names are spoken with honour amongst my people.'

Ket removed the hair from his innocent-looking blue eyes and Offa saw the anger and frustration upon his kinsman's cold expression.

'Before you die,' spoke Ket, 'I want you to know something. The day we found you hunting in this forest, it was Halfdan who told us where to find you. He wanted us to murder you and dump your rotting corpse in the forest, so Halfdan would be free to end his father's life and rule in his stead, without you getting in the way. That is what your friend thinks of you.'

Ket paused to allow Athils to digest the news.

'Well,' Athils replied, 'that doesn't surprise me. Halfdan has always been jealous of my good looks. Halfdan and I are as brothers. And like brothers, we sometimes fight to get what we want. Let me assure you, lads: after I've finished with the two of you, Halfdan will get exactly what he deserves, don't you worry about that.'

Athils scratched his bearded chin, his wolfish eyes going from one brother to the next. The cub moaned and struggled to free itself from Offa's grip. Athils heard it and turned his head to scan the forest, where he saw Offa hiding in the bracken. Athils stared at him, looking into his eyes, smiling.

'You killed our father!' Ket yelled, regaining Athils' attention. 'He wasn't perfect, but he was a good man and a good father.'

'So, lads, you have come for your wergild?' Athils asked, nodding his head.

'No! We're not interested in your blood-money,' Ket replied. 'We want your stinking head!'

The smell of rank marshes and swamps filled the air and ravens could be heard squawking in the surrounding trees. Athils took off a gold ring from around his arm and tossed it onto the muddy trail as compensation for the losses he had inflicted.

'Take the wergild, lads,' spoke Athils. 'I say this, not out of fear, but pity for your youthfulness. I don't wish you to waste such promising young talents on a premature thirst for glory. Put your weapons away and join me. And I promise you weapons, women, riches and the glory young nobles such as yourselves hunger for. We will return to the hall and wait for the right moment to strike at Halfdan, and then we will rule this island together. What do you say?'

'The only glory I'm after,' Ket replied, 'is the glory of avenging my father's death and honouring my family's good name. Now stop wasting my time and prepare to dine with the Gods.' Athils stared into Ket's eyes, but Ket showed no fear and stood his ground. Ket was dressed as a Wolf-Coat, choosing to cover his blonde hair with his wolf hood. He turned to Wīg. 'This bastard is going to bleed!'

A flock of ravens flew from the treetops. 'Maybe you should

wipe your mother's milk from his mouth and have your little brother help you in your quest for vengeance,' Athils told the blood-hungry Ket. 'Then the two of you can die together and I can boast of killing an entire family.'

'No!' Ket snapped. 'I will fight you alone, as is custom. There is no honour in beating you two on one.'

'How noble of you,' spoke Athils, nodding his head, seemingly impressed. 'Very well, as you wish.'

Sunna hid herself behind darkening clouds. Athils stepped forward and tossed his shield to the ground. It would be dishonourable for one man to have an advantage over his opponent. In the Germanic world, the honour of one's family and one's people comes before the safety of one's self. The two brave warriors, Ket and Athils, opposed each other with deadly weapons in hand and bad intentions on their mind. Above their heads there was a light thunder and raindrops began to fall from the heavens. Ket made the first move and stepped forward, wielding his seax, trying to catch Athils off-guard, but Athils stepped out of harm's way and knocked Ket to the ground. Ket was furious. He stood back to his feet and spat on the ground. Athils laughed, wielding his broadsword in a show of skill and confidence. Ket ran and slashed through the air, trying to cut the Dane's arm off, but Athils used Ket's own enthusiasm against him, once again knocking him to the ground.

'Get up, lad, you're making this too easy,' the Dane yelled, while Ket was lying on the ground, trying to catch his breath.

A nervous Wīg looked on from the pathway and Offa looked on from the surrounding bushes, holding Thunor's hammer in his hand. Offa's arm and chest was sore and the cub once again squirmed in his arms, determined to break free. With blood dripping down his face, Ket rose to his feet and paced around.

'You killed my father!' Ket had tears in his eyes, pointing his weapon at Athils. 'You have brought shame to my people..., to my family! Now I'm going to make you pay for what you have done!'

Ket ran at Athils, feigning an attack, throwing Athils off-guard, before cutting him across his inner-thigh. Athils roared in pain, before his anger turned to laughter.

'Your mother scratched me harder than that,' Athils laughed.

Ket ran at the weakened Athils, screaming for blood, but Athils managed to knock Ket to the ground, blowing a dust cloud into the air. Athils saw Ket had dropped his seax and so he kicked it away. Athils stepped forward, his shadow slowly creeping over the dirt path, and kicked Ket hard in the ribs. Ket winced in agony whilst trying to protect himself with his arms. With Ket lying on the ground, struggling to breathe, Athils turned his back on him and looked at Wīg.

'Listen to me..., Wīg,' spoke Athils, breathing heavily. 'I will defeat... and kill... your brother..., and when I do..., you will be bound... by honour... to avenge his death. Then you too... will die... by my sword... like a little, squealing pig. Draw your weapon... and give you... and your brother... a fighting chance to live.'

Wīg glanced towards the bushes and looked into Offa's terrified eyes. Offa wanted to tell his kinsman to stay back, but the words wouldn't come out. Wīg stood there, shaking with fear and rage, his shaggy blonde hair falling into his eyes, and drew his seax. Wīg took a deep breath and took slow steps towards the man who had beaten his brother, killed his father and raped his mother.

While Athils had his back to him, Ket quietly rose to his feet and took a deep breath. Ket's back was covered in dry leaves and his legs were trembling. He leaned over and picked his seax from off the trail. Wīg bravely stood his ground and prepared to fight. Ket now stood behind Athils like a shadow of death, seax in hand, hungry for vengeance. Ket's eyes had changed. He looked at Athils with a primal stare, with an urge to kill. With a flash of light gleaming from his blade, Ket screamed as his seax ripped through the Dane's white under-tunic and tore open the flesh on his back. Athils cried out whilst arching backwards. Offa saw the pain rush upon Athils' face and heard the sound of his torment echoing throughout the forest.

Like a wolf, Wīg smelled blood and stepped forward, screaming, and thrust his naked blade deep into the Dane's unprotected stomach. Athils' bloodshot eyes bulged and blood poured from his mouth and stomach. He crashed to his knees, dropping his sword; the sharp tip cutting into the earth. The rain continued falling from the sky, the birds were singing and the trees danced in the wind. Athils remained on his knees, frothing at the mouth, unable to move. Ket took deep breaths, stalking Athils like a wolf before a wounded animal. Wīg stood still, unsure what to do. Athils spat gouts of blood, trying to hold the wound on his stomach closed, all the while glaring up at Ket, but there was no remorse in Ket's eyes. Without speaking a word, Ket sheathed his seax and retrieved Athils' broadsword from off the beaten trail.

'Your father d-d-died... as a w-w-warrior,' spoke Athils, coughing and choking. *'Allow me... the s-s-same... h-h-honour.'*

Ket pointed Athils' own sword at him. 'You killed our father!' Ket roared. 'You raped our mother! You deserve to go to hell for what you have done!'

Ket's breathing quickened. With the rain gently falling from the heavens and Sunna still hiding behind the rain clouds, Ket gripped the Dane's broadsword with two hands and raised it above his head. Raindrops rolled along the sharp edge. Screaming, Ket cut through the air, slicing raindrops in two, and slashed Athils across his stomach, splitting him wide open like a freshly slaughtered boar. Blood, guts and intestines spewed out onto the leaf-littered ground like wriggling eels. Athils cried in agony, perhaps from the pain, or perhaps from being denied his sword in his final moments.

'That was for my father!' Ket told him, tossing Athils' sword to the ground. Athils desperately tried to reach it, stretching out his arm and fingertips, but Ket would never allow his father's killer to go to Valhalla. Once again, Ket drew his bloodied seax, stood behind Athils and placed the sharp tip against Athils' under-tunic, cutting it to reveal the white flesh beneath. Offa looked on silently, too afraid to make a sound. While Athils cried in despair, Ket's blade slowly bit into his soft flesh, drawing blood, and scraped his blade down Athils' spine. 'This is for my mother!'

Ket grunted, spat and cursed as he cut through flesh and bone, splitting Athils' back wide open to reveal the red flesh beneath, which resembled a rack of lamb. Ket cut away the ribs from the spine, one at a time, cracking and snapping, before tearing out his bloody lungs past the bones, giving the appearance of an eagle spreading its bloodstained wings, in what is called a blood-eagle. Athils was dead and his flesh now belonged to the wolves and the ravens, his soul a gift for Hel, guardian of the underworld. Using the blood on his hands, Ket marked his face with the rune of Tīw, God of Justice, and looked up into the heavens.

'Aaaaaaaaahh!!!!' Ket roared, his primal scream echoing throughout the forest. 'Father......., we have avenged thee!'

The fight with Athils wasn't a fair fight, it was an ambush of two against one. It was murder, and there is no honour in murder. Offa's kinsmen had brought shame upon the Englisc folk and shame upon Offa's father. After arriving in Angeln, the three of them went to the mead-hall to inform King Wǣrmund of Athils' death.

'You know our customs,' the King said to Ket and Wīg, sitting upon his gift-stool, before the entire hall. 'It is a disgrace for two warriors to fight a lone man. But, given the circumstances, and taking in account your youth, I believe the Gods will forgive you, as should I. As should we all. You have freed your mother from the Danes and avenged your father's death. You have earned an old man's respect and therefore your names will be for ever praised in this hall.'

Many cheered the King's words, including their mother, Egwen, who stood listening with Athelflæd in her arms. The King then turned to Offa. 'Offa, my son, you have returned to this hall before Mothers' Night and without wearing a wolf-cloak, telling tales of hell hounds and trolls. You have shamed us, Offa. You have shamed me.'

'I'm sorry, father,' spoke Offa, while the folks in the hall listened on. 'I thought it more honourable to help my kinsmen avenge their father's death than to finish my time in the wild.'

'Nevertheless, Offa,' spoke his father, 'you cannot be king

now. You can never be king.' Wærmund lowered his gaze, refusing to look his son in the eye. 'You must leave us tonight. Tonight we mourn the deaths of the children we have lost. You shouldn't be here.'

Offa turned to look at the folks in the hall. Some of them were the parents of those who had died in the forest. Offa sighed deeply and lowered his head whilst making his way outside, closing the door behind him. He entered his dwelling and saw the cub resting under his bed, its black nose peeking from the shadows.

'All of my friends are dead,' Offa told the cub, with a heavy heart. 'I have brought shame to my people and shame to my father. Ket and Wīg have broken our laws and killed a man, without honour. I fear there is only one way to clear the good name of the Englisc folk. Me þæt wyrd gewæf ond gewyrht forgeaf. For me fate wove this, gave this to do.'

The cub was snarling at Offa, growling from under the bed, its fangs revealed; its eyes glowing in the dark.

Chapter Sixteen
The Changeling

Hamburg

Clouds of thunder had gathered in the dark grey skies and countless ravens circled high above the battlefield, swooping to the ground to feed off the dead. Flies feasted as swine rotted in the marsh, a foul stench; a gift to Seaxnēat. Brave men and women fought honourably, with courage in their hearts. Strength met with cunning. Shield clashed with spear. Steel met with flesh and bone. Bone-protectors and skin-shields were smashed and torn. And seaxes and spears glutted and gorged on human flesh.

'Seaxnēat!' spoke Mōdthryth, loud and clear, so the heavens could hear her. She stood above her fallen victim, her feather-crested swan-helm rested upon her head and she was armed with two seaxes, one in each hand. 'This man is a great warrior and has fought well. I now offer his soul to you, Furious One.

May you in your wisdom continue to guide our weapons in battle and grant my people victory.'

Mōdthryth's beautiful face was hidden beneath a crimson mask and her long plaited hair was dark with blood. Without mercy, she slashed the Mofding's throat wide open, using both blades, spraying herself with blood. Mōdthryth had become a favourite amongst the Valkyries - warrior-maidens from beyond the grave; the choosers of the slain. They are present on every battlefield, choosing who is worthy to die and be taken to Wōden's feast-hall, Valhalla. Sometimes the Valkyries choose to fight in the battles themselves by possessing the female spectators. The women would become enraged and pick up their ash-spears and charge into battle, possessed and fearless; feasting on blood and bone. Mōdthryth had come to know the Valkyries well.

The long-limbed Mōdthryth ran into battle and tossed one of her bloodstained seaxes through the air, embedding it in a man's chest, killing him instantly. After pulling the weapon free, she rushed to her father's side and killed everyone in her way, cutting open their skin-shields and freeing their souls from their flesh-bound vessels. It wasn't long before the remaining Mofdings were cut down in battle or fled into the surrounding forest. Ēadgils, King of the invading Mire-Dwellers, tossed his wolf headdress to the ground to reveal an aged face, hardened by years of war and conquest, and a long grey beard that dripped with blood. He looked across the blood-slake field and saw Wīdsīth approaching.

'What now, my lord?' Wīdsīth asked, flicking blood from his rune-decorated blade.

King Ēadgils took a deep breath and looked into the forest.

'Now we head north,' the King answered as rain fell onto his face and beard, washing away the blood of the slain. 'Earl Frēawine is dead. The Mofdings are conquered. Now we head north. Now we take Schleswig!'

The war between the Mire-Dwellers and the Mofdings had raged for many months and hundreds had died. It was Mōdthryth who had provoked it. Princess Mōdthryth had done many wrongdoings in her young life. If any mortal being, other than her kin, dared look her in the face, if an eye not her lord's stared at her, the outcome was sealed; he was kept bound by shackles and tortured until his soul fled from the world of the living. The King of the Mofdings had dared to propose marriage between his eldest son and the Princess. Mōdthryth refused the proposal and instead took the young man's life, for no ordinary man, not even a Prince, was worthy of calling her wife. Only a god amongst men would do.

***

Jötunn Forest

After witnessing the death of Athils at the hands of Ket and Wīg, Offa returned to Angeln before his time in the wild had passed and without wearing a wolf coat, and so he had failed to complete his rite-of-passage. As a result, Offa had brought shame upon himself and shame upon his father. Folks now believed Offa was a changeling, the offspring of a troll or fairy, swapped at birth with the King's true son. Offa dealt with the shame of it by hiding himself away, spending more time with the cub, deep in the forest; a forest teeming with dangers and many restless spirits. It had been a week since Athils' death and Offa had barely spoken a word since.

Offa and the cub had been travelling for several days and were now deep in the forest, lying inside a small make-shift tent. Though he feared the troll was still out there, Offa was looking for Bardawulf's body, to bring him home, so he could have a funeral and his kin could say their farewells. He felt he owed him that, despite the dangers. Offa wasn't sleeping well and was tossing and turning all night, caught somewhere between waking and dreaming. The cries of Leofrīc, Edwin and Grendel, the vision of Haakon being pulled apart by the pack, the terrifying troll, the screams of Bardawulf, the look in Ket and Wīg's eyes, Athils being split open, Offa slashing the wild boy's throat open, flashed in his mind, haunting him. He awoke in a cold sweat, with the cub lying beside him, shaking his back legs and whining in his sleep.

As the sun gently warmed the land and burned away the cold morning mist that covered the ground in a milky veil, Offa and the cub made their way further into the forest. Offa hadn't eaten that morning and his stomach growled like he had swallowed a bear. He saw the cub sniffing at the cool breeze, perhaps trying to track his family. Offa wondered if the cub knew of death? His mother had brought him and his siblings dead meat from the forest, but did he understand the meat was once alive, free to roam the land; its heart once beating inside its chest? Offa felt bad for him. The first time the cub had come in contact with humans, he witnessed his entire pack being slaughtered. Now he was in the middle of the forest with only a human for company.

Much of the day had passed, when the cub found his pack lying on the ground with black congealed blood oozing from every orifice; their tongues ripped from their mouths and their eyes plucked from their skulls. He was sniffing and licking them, but they didn't respond. The cub began to whine and sob, yet still they didn't move. The scent of rotting flesh filled Offa's senses and brought tears to his eyes. He looked along the ground where he saw a human hand through the green blades of grass. His stomach began to twist and his heart skipped a beat. He was nervous, yet strangely curious. Offa walked over to the body and wiped his eyes, unable to stop the flow of tears that blurred his vision. The creatures of the forest had enjoyed a feast. Offa's stomach wrenched and he heaved and heaved, yet nothing came out.

The cub followed him and started to sniff at the body. To Offa's surprise, the cub began to chew on what remained of Bardawulf's putrid flesh. Offa watched him pull and tug, trying to put some meat into his hungry stomach. Offa growled at him like his mother would, to teach him what was acceptable and what was not. Bardawulf was Offa's friend, but he had to ask himself: did the cub know right from wrong? It was one animal eating the flesh of another, in order to preserve its own life, a reminder of how cruel the world can be; a reminder of the struggle for existence that all animals share in their blood. Who was Offa to deny the cub his feed? He didn't know right from wrong, only what was natural and unnatural. He was an animal and obeyed the laws of nature. It was natural for him to eat the flesh of a dead animal, human or otherwise, and so Offa allowed him to have his fill. That was his first mistake with the cub.

After the cub had eaten, Offa drew his seax and with great sadness began cutting the remains of Bardawulf's body into smaller pieces and placed them in his sack, before making the long journey home, with the little cub hobbling behind, struggling to keep up. By the time they arrived in Angeln, Sunna was low in the sky, orange and red as if the wolves had caught her and she was bleeding into the clouds. Offa entered the village and saw horse stables in the distance and dozens of homes made with daub and wattle, with thatched roofs; many with stacks of firewood and hay piled outside. Folks were gathering by the outdoor bonfires, bringing light to the village; their voices and laughter mingled with the usual sound of dogs barking, folks shouting, children playing and babies crying.

Offa saw roaming hens, swine rolling in the dirt and sheep in the distance, lying alongside the cows. He heard the villagers calling each other, making their way back from the fields and the forest, carrying their tools. He witnessed two men working on a deer carcass that was tied to a tree. One man held it still while the other skinned it. Warriors who had finished training for the day were starting to gather inside the hall. Some of the Cnihts continued training a while longer, their wooden swords and shields clanged, clattered and clashed together, echoing into the forest.

With the cub under his arm and the sack of bones in his other hand, Offa made his way to his dwelling, yet as he ran the cub began to slip from his grasp. Offa tried holding onto him, but he wriggled and scratched his way free and fell to the ground. Offa tried scooping him up, but the cub turned and bit his hand. There were several people going about their business.

'Is that a wolf?' one of the onlookers asked.

'It is,' spoke another.

'What's wrong with his eyes?' a woman asked.

'He's a bit too small for a coat, I think,' one man joked,

followed by a bout of laughter.

The cub stood on the ground, hackles raised, overwhelmed by the attention. One child tried patting him on the head, but the cub warned her, growling and snarling.

'Go away, you filthy animal. Be away with you,' one man yelled, striking the defenceless cub with a stick.

The cub didn't know what to do and cowered whilst being hit over and over. Offa wanted to shout, to tell him to stop, but the words wouldn't come out, and so he kicked the man hard in the nuts. As he crouched in pain, roaring in agony, the cub ran away and disappeared through the crowd of onlookers. The man tried to grasp Offa by his arm, but he pulled away and ran after the cub as fast as he could. The cub had spotted one of the hunting dogs and had instinctively ran after it, perhaps mistaking it for a member of his pack. The dog looked like him, yet the cub would soon learn how different they truly were.

Offa watched the cub running towards the dog, beaming with excitement. It was a hunting dog with a shiny black and grey coat. It was leashed by its owner, a short, heavy-built man by the name of Hothbrodd. Nature had been cruel to Hothbrodd. He had been born with a deformed face and a lazy eye, with overgrown eyebrows resting above like two giant caterpillars. He had a large nose, with nostrils as wide as a war-horse, a scruffy, unkempt beard and his teeth were crooked and over-sized like that of a troll. Many believed Hothbrodd was a changeling, switched at birth by the fairy folk. The world had been cruel to Hothbrodd, and in return, Hothbrodd had learned to be cruel back, taking his frustrations out on his dogs. He had learned to master them, to demand their obedience, otherwise he would beat them within an inch of their lives. He was a cruel man with a cruel heart.

Hothbrodd's dogs were killers, allowed to do what comes natural, to obey the strongest of the pack; in this case Hothbrodd, and give chase to weaker things and kill them. The cub playfully ran and jumped at Hothbrodd's dog, hoping to unite with his own kind, but the cub would learn a valuable lesson. The dog may have once been bred from the wolves that first betrayed their natural instincts and left the forest to sit by the warm fires of man, but the dog had long since sold its soul and swore no allegiance to their own kind. The cub jumped at the dog, squealing with joy and excitement, wanting to play, but the dog turned its head to the side and raised its hackles. Within a heartbeat, there was a flash of teeth, followed by a horrible cry. The dog was all over the vulnerable cub, mauling him, trying to take his young life away.

Hothbrodd yanked the leash as hard as he could, forcing his dog away from the squealing cub. Offa rushed to the cub's aid and saw blood dripping down the side of his head. The cub held up his paw and sobbed his little heart out. The dog was still barking wildly. Offa knew he had to act quickly to gain the cub's trust, hoping he would see Offa as the leader of his pack. Offa stood in front of the dog, with his back to the cub, shaking, holding out his seax. The dog snapped its jaws, barked and snarled; saliva dripping from its fangs. The hairs on the back of Offa's neck stood on end, his heart thumped and sweat rolled down his forehead and neck. He looked into the dog's eyes and saw no mercy there. He was frightened, yet he remained strong. Like a wolf, Offa growled at the dog, revealing his teeth, holding his seax tightly in his sweating palm. The dog continued barking, jumping forward, twisting its body in the air, trying to break free of its master's hold.

'One day, one of my dogs is going to kill that fleabag,' spoke Hothbrodd, struggling to hold his dog. 'You had better keep it away, or else he'll have him. He'll eat him for supper, he will. Gobble him all up, tooth and claw. He's a killer, this one. Half dog, half wolf, he is. Tor he's called.' Hothbrodd smiled. 'I've warned you, laddy. Remember that! I warned you!'

Offa remained silent, with the cub standing behind him, growling.

Chapter Seventeen
The New Earl of Schleswig

Schleswig

After the death of Earl Frēawine, King Wǣrmund raised Ket to
the rank of his father. As the new Earl, Ket thought life would
be good and did not imagine himself to be in constant demand
by the folks of Schleswig, baring their grievances in public.
Ket was expected to solve each and every problem that was
presented to him. Ket was a warrior, domestic disputes were
beneath him.

'My lord, Penda has bedded my wife... and my sister. I
demand justice,' spoke a common man by the name of Æthelwalh, glancing over his shoulder to his embarrassed wife, who
stood with her hood up, covering her shame.

There were many murmurs amongst the gathered crowd.

'Is this true?' Ket asked, resting comfortably upon what was
once his father's gift-stool.

'Yes, my lord,' Penda answered, while the crowd listened. 'It
is true.'

'His wife... and his sister?' Ket asked, rubbing his chin.
Penda nodded his head. 'And they were both willing?'

'Yes, my lord,' Penda answered proudly, his gaze moving to
Æthelwalh, then to Æthelwalh's blushing wife. 'Very much so.'

There was laughter in the crowd.

'Well, Penda, I am therefore forced to sentence you to join
my hearth-troops and become one of my Thegns. What do you
say to that?' Ket asked.

'I am honoured, my lord,' Penda replied. 'I won't let you
down.'

'I believe you, Penda,' spoke Ket. 'You have proven yourself
to be a far greater man than Æthelwalh here. Æthelwalh thinks
it is appropriate to bother his Earl with such personal matters,
instead of dealing with his own problems like a man.' Ket
turned to the accuser. 'Clearly, you are not up to the task of
pleasing your wife, Æthelwalh. I believe Penda has done your
wife and sister a service. I think you should thank him.' More

laughter. 'Now return to your farmstead and feel free to leave your beautiful wife behind, where I guarantee she will be in good company amongst my men and I.' Æthelwalh's blushing wife glanced at Ket with a smile. 'Now go, Æthelwalh. I am sure the sheep will keep you company tonight.'

The folks in the hall laughed while Æthelwalh left in shame, grasping his wife by the arm and dragging her away, before slamming the door behind them.

Egwen joined her two sons at the table, alongside Penda, the newest member of Ket's hearth-troops. A beautiful hawk gripped Ket's hand with its sharp talons. Its eyes were covered, and so it rested comfortably and silently.

'The hawk is a great hunter,' spoke Ket. 'A man can learn a lot from a predator such as this. When allowed to fly freely, you must take the time to watch as it stalks its prey so grace-fully, so beautifully, before making the inevitable kill; the strong devouring the weak.' Ket smiled whilst admiring the beauty of the bird. 'I am the new Earl, but I won't sit idle while my body grows soft. I will remain strong, focused and always poised for the kill. On the morrow, we go on the hunt.'

'I'll look forward to it, my lord,' spoke Penda.

'You talk of hunting, yet we should be discussing plans to defend ourselves from raiders,' spoke Egwen to her eldest son. 'We should be building ditches and forts and ships to defend our waters.'

'Nonsense,' Ket replied. 'What we need is more men like Penda here.' Penda raised his cup. 'We spend our youth training for war, yet most of us have never known bloodshed, not until our beloved Earl was taken from us so cruelly. What we need is a war we can win. Maybe we should attack one of the lesser clans to sharpen our skills and harden those of weak stomach. What do you think, Penda?'

'I think it's a fine idea, my lord,' Penda replied.

'Make war on our neighbours?' Egwen asked. 'Are you mad? We should be making allies, not enemies. We need to send word to your kinsman, King Wærmund. We should seek his advice.'

'No!' Ket snapped. 'We don't need outside help. Wīg and I killed Athils and freed you from the Danes, without aid. We only need rely on ourselves.'

'I think our mother is right,' Wīg added. 'We should ask Wǽrmund for help. He is a good man. He has made you Earl. What harm can it do, brother?'

'What we need is a show of strength,' Ket answered, slamming his cup onto the table, spilling his drink. 'Asking for help is a sign of weakness. I will hear no more on the subject of King Wǽrmund.'

The doors to the hall opened, flooding the room with daylight, and in came one of Ket's hearth-troops.

'My lord,' spoke the guard, 'the noble-born Wulfhere of the Mire-Dwellers is here to break words with you.'

'The Mire-Dwellers?' Ket asked, turning to his brother.

'Saxons, from the south of the Eider,' Wīg answered. 'What are they doing this far north?'

'Show him in,' Ket told the guard with a wave of his hand. 'This should be interesting.'

The Saxons' ambassador entered the hall and approached the Earl's table. He wore an impressive wolf headdress, making him appear taller than he was. After respectfully removing his headdress, the ambassador broke his silence.

'Wæs þū, Eorle Ket, hāl. My name is Wulfhere, son of King Ēadgils. It pains my people to hear of your loss, my lord,' he said, referring to Ket's father. 'My father, King Ēadgils, sends his deepest condolences.'

Wulfhere was in his mid-twenties. He had a long moustache and no beard. His hair was styled in the Swabian knot, swept back off his face and combed diagonally across the crown, then twisted into a knot above his right ear. He had shrewd eyes and a tight mouth.

'Thank you, your words are kind, but I am eager to find out your purpose here?' Ket asked abruptly. 'It's not often we are blessed with the presence of a Saxon.'

'Then I will get to the point, my lord,' spoke Wulfhere, stepping forward. 'My father, King Ēadgils, has sent me here to seek tribute.'

'Tribute?' Wīg asked with a frown.

'My clan, the Mire-Dwellers, have defeated the Mofdings and have settled their lands,' Wulfhere replied. 'We are now neighbours. My father is an ambitious man, my lord, and sits upon a throne of skulls, belonging to our old enemies. To keep the peace and to stop us from conquering your lands and making slaves of you, he asks for payment.'

'I wish I could give you what you ask for,' spoke Ket with a deep sigh. 'I really do. Life would be so much easier for my people, but you see, I long to drink in Valhalla and I cannot achieve that by submitting to your father's will. To give your King what he wants is to dampen the fire of the Englisc folk. Little ones would grow up in a world that despises them, that teaches them they have no worth. They will become soft and weak and willingly accept foreign men as their masters. We are the Englisc, born to fight, and we will submit to no man! I am descended from Wōden, the Lord of Hosts, God of war! I do not fear war, nor death. I embrace it. I welcome it. Life would be a dull thing if we all lived in fear and tucked our tails between our legs every time we are threatened. A man cannot achieve greatness if he does not know struggle. Leave now, Wulfhere, while I'm in a fair mood. And tell your King that I don't take kindly to threats, nor do I tremble easily. Tell him he can expect a visit from my new ambassador, Penda, very soon, demanding compensation for this insult.'

Penda looked nervous, yet didn't dare say a word.

'This is an outrage,' spoke Wulfhere, raising his voice. 'My father will not be pleased with this. Perhaps he will be forced to add your skull to decorate his throne, Earl Ket.'

In a show of disrespect, the Saxon turned his back to Ket and, with his headdress under his arm, began to make his way towards the doors. Ket stood to his feet and drew his seax. Before anyone could stop him, Ket, son of Frēawine, tossed his seax through the air, embedding it deep in Wulfhere's back. The Saxon Prince crashed to the ground, knocking dust into the air and spilling blood onto the wooden floorboards.

'Brother, what have you done?' Wīg asked, rising to his feet; his face flushed with anger. 'You have just started a war!'

'No!' Ket replied. 'The Saxons started this war. I just struck the first blow.' Ket walked over to Wulfhere and knelt by his side. Wulfhere was squirming and wincing whilst trying to crawl away, scraping his fingernails across the floorboards. With gritted teeth, Ket took hold of his knotted hair, pulled it back and placed his cold steel seax against Wulfhere's throat. 'Perhaps your father will enjoy your skull for his throne, what do you think, Saxon?'

'*He w-will... k-k-kill you... all... f-for... th-th-this,*' Wulfhere stuttered, coughing up gouts of blood.

'*I welcome his attempt,*' Ket whispered, splitting Wulfhere's throat wide open. Blood gushed from the wound, staining the wooden floorboards. With great effort, Ket separated Wulfhere's head from his neck and placed it inside his headdress, before handing it to Penda. 'Make sure King Ēadgils receives this gift to add to his collection. Tell him: I'll look forward to meeting him in person.'

Penda nodded his head, not daring to refuse. Ket looked across the hall to see his mother and brother staring at him in disbelief.

'What have you done?' Egwen asked.

Chapter Eighteen
Fenris Wulf

Jötunn Forest

A new day had dawned and Sunna illuminated the realm of Middle-earth, bringing light to mankind and to all living creatures. Offa and the cub had ventured far into the untamed forest. The cub had recovered well from Tor's unprovoked attack on him several days earlier, yet he still walked with a slight limp. Offa often caught him whimpering, staring into the forest, not looking at the trees or between them, but looking through them, as if he was looking for something. He was only a cub, but could the memory of countless generations running through his veins be telling him something? Was something whispering to him, calling him?

Several days earlier, Bardawulf's remains were burned upon the funeral pyre in a great ceremony, but Offa was not welcomed to attend. To take his mind from it, Offa was thinking of a name for the cub. He stood next to one of the trees and watched the cub stalking an unsuspecting squirrel as it ran from one place to the next. The squirrel held a nut in its forelimbs, preparing to take it back to its den, but then it heard something, or it thought it heard something. Neither Offa nor the cub had made a sound, yet the squirrel seemed to know something was wrong. Sensing the squirrel was about to leave, the cub rushed forward, jumped over a small branch that had fallen to the ground and leapt towards it. Fearing for its life, the squirrel dropped the nut and scurried up the nearest tree. The cub had leapt with all of his might, but had gained nothing for his efforts. All he received was a face full of dirt and a wound to his pride, only to be made worse by being forced to watch the squirrel taunting him from the safety of the treetops. The cub wasn't amused and turned away in a sulk.

Offa and the cub walked through the forest, surrounded by countless ravens that watched from the treetops, whispering secrets to each other, and Offa wondered if the cub saw and heard the same as he did. Could he see the different colours and shapes of the forest, the blue in the sky, the different shades of white and grey in the clouds? Did he listen to the songs of the birds? What was going through his young mind? Offa was fascinated by him. The cub sat in the grass, licking his wounds, when Offa picked up a stick and tossed it as far as he could, expecting him to give chase, but the cub watched as it fell to the ground and looked at Offa with a confused expression. Offa often mistook him for a domesticated dog, something which seemed to annoy him.

Offa decided to take the cub hunting. He pressed himself against a tree that creaked and swayed in the wind and smelled of old damp wood. Offa saw several rabbits nearby, oblivious to the cub watching from the shadows. No one had taught the cub how to hunt, it came natural to him; it was in his blood. His hungry eyes fixed on one rabbit in particular, but the cub was young and impatient and couldn't wait any longer. He took several steps forward, keeping his body low to the ground, and stopped. He watched for a moment, before taking more steps. He was now close enough, his muscles tensed, his eyes focused and he pounced, leaping upon the unsuspecting rabbits with a primal need to kill.

Offa watched as the rabbits scattered into the bracken, trying to escape the jaws of death, but the rabbit the cub had focused on didn't stand a chance. It was younger and smaller than the rest and didn't know what to do. It didn't know what was happening. The cub leapt upon it without mercy, closed his jaws around its throat and tried choking the life out of it. Offa heard the rabbit crying like a small child, before its neck snapped, followed by a deathly silence; only to be broken by the sound of countless ravens squawking as they fled the tree-tops. The cub was successful and the rabbit's legs dangled from his mouth.

The cub was lying on the ground, ripping at the rabbit's fur, trying to get at the soft flesh beneath, swallowing as much meat as possible with every mouthful. Offa stepped from behind the tree and walked towards him. He wanted to pat him on his head, to congratulate him on his successful hunt, but the cub watched him suspiciously and his bloodied muzzle creased with every step Offa took. Offa decided to stay back and not risk the cub fleeing into the forest, afraid he might take his meal away. Offa admired him. He was so young, yet so brave and fierce. Offa found the urge to howl like a wolf, and so he cupped his hands together and howled into the bright blue sky. The cub turned his head and stared at Offa as though he had spoken his language. Offa thought the cub saw something in him that day, something that reminded him of his pack. Offa howled for a long time, trying to get the cub to imitate him, but he made no effort; he was enjoying his meal and barely made a noise all day.

Offa watched the cub ripping and tearing at the rabbit's flesh, when he began to think of a name to call him. Offa decided to name him Fenris Wulf, after the wolf that grew so big and deadly even the Gods feared him and wanted him bound.

Guided by the wisdom of Wōden, the dwarves of Ásgard forged a chain for him made from the secret things of the world - the roots of a mountain, the noise of a moving cat and the breath of a fish. It was only a thin chain, yet not even the strength of Thunor could break it. Fenris wouldn't allow the chain to be put on him unless one of the Gods placed a hand between his jaws as a hostage. In the end, only Tīw volunteered, and so Fenris was bound and the Gods all laughed, all except Tīw who lost a hand. The Englisc have since given the day Tīwesdæg in honour of Tīw, God of battle, courage and justice; his symbol is the spear.

Sunna hid herself behind the trees, darkness began to fall over the land and the goose-pimples on Offa's arms pricked. Offa and the cub were making their way home, trudging through the familiar forest. Offa was cold, tired and hungry. He stopped occasionally and turned around to make sure Fenris was still following him. Offa would sometimes see him looking over his shoulder, staring into the forest as if he was looking for something, or was listening to something; something calling him - something he didn't yet understand. A couple of miles from the village, as the forest darkened and the birds returned to roost, silhouetted across the brazen sky, Offa heard the sound of dogs barking in the distance. He turned around to see Fenris had stopped and was twitching his nose whilst sniffing at the wind.

Offa knew people could be nearby, so close to the village, and many had hunting dogs. Offa called Fenris to him, patting his legs, but the cub stared into the forest, ears pricked, listening to the sound of the dogs as they came closer. Then they appeared, charging down the hillside, Tor and the rest of the pack. Fearing for the cub's life, Offa tried picking him up, but Fenris backed away and revealed his fangs. Tor now stood before Offa, poised and ready to strike. Offa's heart thumped and his body stiffened. Tor's eyes were dark and without mercy or reason, his fangs were large and sharp; and saliva dripped from his bloodstained mouth. The rest of the pack were behind him, dirty and bloody from a day's hunting. Offa drew his seax and slowly backed away, stepping closer to Fenris. Fenris stood behind Offa and snarled at Tor and the pack.

With blood-thirsty eyes, Tor stepped forward and could smell Offa's fear oozing from every pore. Offa heard Hothbrodd calling his dogs from the top of the hill, but they were too focused on the hunt to pay attention. Tor snarled at Offa, took a step forward and attacked, knocking him to the ground. Offa laid flat on his back, holding Tor above him, fearing for his life; his stinking fangs snapping in his face, his putrid breath all over him. Offa instinctively grabbed hold of Tor's mane and tried to hold him back with all the strength he had in his scrawny little arms, all the while having flashbacks of Bardawulf and the hell hounds. The other dogs were barking wildly, not knowing whether to attack or not. Offa still held his seax in his right hand, but he couldn't hold Tor back with just his left whilst thrusting the blade into his neck. Offa needed the Gods. He needed someone. Anyone! Then Offa heard a terrible, bone-chilling growl. It was Fenris.

Fenris charged at Tor and bit him on his muzzle, ripping at his whiskers. Tor left Offa alone and jumped at Fenris, knocking him to the ground. The pack went wild. Some joined Tor in his attack on Fenris, while the others did the unthinkable. In a frenzied moment of madness, the pack had forgotten the bond between man and dog, an unbreakable pact made between man and beast, to protect each other, to be companions; friends until death. They attacked Offa and ripped into his flesh like half-starved creatures from hell. He struggled helplessly on the ground, being mauled by the pack, feeling their fangs sinking into his soft flesh.

'What in the name of Tīw's missing hand are you doing here, laddy?' a voice yelled. Offa looked up and saw a short stature of a man leaning over him with a hideous face. It was Hothbrodd. He had pulled his dogs away. 'Are you trying to get me hanged, laddy?' he yelled, reaching out, pulling Offa to his feet. The dogs were barking wildly behind him.

Offa pulled himself free from Hothbrodd's grip and took a step back. Blood dripped down his arms and legs and his throat was wet and stinging. Offa didn't know if it was blood or saliva, nor did he care; Fenris was his only concern. Hothbrodd had leashed Tor, and the rest of the pack had submitted to their master, cowering beneath his wooden club. Offa saw a mess of black fur lying on the ground, in a pool of blood, and feared the worse. He stepped closer and was relieved to see the cub's ribs moving up and down. Fenris was still breathing and a kindle of hope sparked in Offa's chest. Offa crouched beside him and ran his hand through his fur, slowly and gently, feeling his tiny ribs. Fenris' eyes opened and he creased his muzzle to reveal his bloodstained fangs. Offa knew then that he would live and that it wasn't the end for Fenris Wulf, for his life as a predator had only just begun!

Chapter Nineteen
Wrath of the Saxons

Angeln

Fenris had recovered from Tor's attack on him several weeks earlier, and soon everyone came to know him. Fenris was the one who stole their meat and fish, the one always in trouble and the one who always received the sticks and stones. Fenris had made no friends, human or otherwise, and was often attacked by the other dogs. Fenris longed for the comfort of the pack, yet they never welcomed him as one of their own.

Offa was walking through the village, following Fenris while he sniffed around, when one of the dogs saw him and gave chase. At least four or five others followed. Fenris ran for his life, running in and out of folk's homes, weaving through the many different obstacles, knocking over wood piles and carts of hay, fruits and vegetables; causing all sorts of commotion. By the time Offa caught up with him, he saw someone had cornered Fenris, with the pack behind him, barking and snarling at the terrified cub. Fenris never barked in return. He just stood there with his mane bristling, baring his fangs to the roots.

The dog that had originally given chase stood by its owner's side, holding his paw up, whimpering. The man picked up a stick and struck Fenris as hard as he could. Fenris stood his ground and growled at him. The man raised the stick once again and struck, but this time Fenris caught it in his jaws and held onto it with a vicious snarl. After the man became distracted by Offa's presence, Fenris saw an opportunity to strike back. He released the stick and sank his fangs into his attacker's foot. The man screamed and yelled at Fenris, once again punishing him with the stick, beating him on top of his skull, again and again; encouraging the other dogs to attack. A small crowd had gathered to watch.

'Out of the way!' someone yelled, knocking Offa to one side, away from the fighting dogs. It was Offa's kinsman, Hemming.

Hemming kicked one of the dogs hard in the ribs, causing it to squeal and cower beneath its owner's legs. Its owner turned around in a rage, ready to strike, only to humble himself when he realised who he was talking to.

'My lord, I-I…' He never finished his sentence. Hemming squeezed his fist and punched him hard on the nose, knocking him into several baskets, spilling apples on the ground.

'Does it make you feel like a big man, striking small animals and young children?' Hemming asked with a red face. The man didn't dare say another word. He rose to his feet, wiped the blood from his face and left with his tail between his legs, taking his dogs with him. Offa knelt on one knee and checked on Fenris. 'You had better sort that mutt out,' spoke Hemming, looking down at the snarling cub, 'or one day it's going to hurt you. He's dangerous, Offa. He needs putting back out into the forest, where he belongs.'

Fenris was Offa's only friend and he was worried that one day someone would hurt him. He tried tying him up during the daytime to keep him out of trouble, but Fenris would bite through his ropes and wander wherever he liked. To avoid him stealing, Offa began to steal for him. He would often take meat from the hunters without their permission and sometimes he would sneak out at night and steal the farmer's chickens, giving Fenris a juicy meal in the morning. The villagers knew it was Offa, but he was the King's son, and so they chose to deal with the situation themselves by punishing Fenris. Offa was young and didn't understand that his actions were causing them both to become further alienated.

One day, while resting inside his dwelling, Offa knelt on one knee and tried hand-feeding Fenris with a piece of raw meat. At first, Fenris seemed hesitant and distrusting, for no animal other than his mother had brought him meat before. He sat on the ground and watched Offa with a curious eye, his head tilted to one side, staring at him. Looking into his noble eyes, Offa was reminded that the creature before him was a wild animal, a killer. But he was young and Offa believed he could be the one to tame the beast within Fenris, a task set by the Gods.

Fenris stared at Offa whilst licking his chops, eyeing the dead meat in his hand. He was a scrawny-looking thing with ribs poking through his dirty black coat. He whimpered, jerking his neck forward, wanting to take the meat from Offa's hand, but the memory of his mother and father and their ancestors before them, and the fear they all shared of humans, was strong in him. The cub sat still, ears pricked, eyes fixed, giving the odd whimper. Offa would usually toss the meat to him and keep his distance while he ate, but this time Offa wanted Fenris to approach him and gain his trust. Offa remained still, while Fenris took a step closer. Fenris looked at Offa suspiciously, before taking another step. Finally, Fenris reached up and took the meat from Offa's hand, before running to the other side of the room and swallowed it as fast as he could.

Offa was the only one who loved him, yet Fenris didn't seem to know love. As time passed, he had forgotten his mother and father and the comfort of the pack. He knew only hardship, violence and mistrust. Offa's hand was always warm and gentle to him, yet Fenris always remained wary. A hand to Fenris was something to be frightened of. Over time, Offa gave Fenris meat by hand, and he would take it, yet he always took it with caution and mistrust.

***

The River Eider

Like beasts from the abyss, dozens crawled out of the dark grey waters of the river Eider, making their way through the forest and headed towards Schleswig.

A hooded woman stood alone, the rain showering her through the forest canopy. She was picking fruits from the trees, blissfully unaware that creatures of darkness stalked her from the shadows. Each had a skeletal face with elongated jaws and large fangs, with dark, empty black holes where eyes had once looked out into the world. Armed with an axe, one of them, half man, half wolf, ran ahead of the others, growling and snarling, determined to rob the young woman of her life.

Hearing something behind her, she turned around and screamed, dropping her basket of fruit, and ran for her life. She ran so fast she tripped in the bracken and fell into a muddy puddle. Looking over her shoulder, she saw the blood-thirsty beast was upon her. They were face to face, eye to eye; its stinking breath all over her. Blood dripped from its mouth and its eyes were wide and bloodshot. It cried out, but it wasn't the harrowing cry of a beast, but the death-cry of a mortal man.

The woman was no peasant girl, but a free woman and was armed with a seax. Somehow she had managed to hold out her weapon and thrust it deep into the wolf-man's guts. As his soul drained from his bone-house, she yanked the blade free, allowing him to slump to the ground, before rising to her feet. After taking a deep breath, she looked into the forest and saw dozens more of the fearsome creatures slowly emerging from the shadows; a clan of werewolves, frothing at the mouth. With a firm grip on her seax, she ran as fast as she could and headed towards Schleswig.

***

Schleswig

Earl Ket was sitting inside the smoky hall, having his hair braided by a buxom wench, when his brother entered the hall alongside several fighting men, including Fólki. Each of them seemed anxious as they slowly walked towards the Earl. Seeing something was on Wīg's mind, Ket waved the woman away.

'Brother, come and drink with me,' spoke Ket from upon the dais. 'You look like you have the world on your shoulders. What is on your mind, brother?'

Wīg stepped forward, leaving Fólki and the group standing restlessly in the hall.

'Brother, I feel I need to speak with you on behalf of the men,' spoke Wīg, softly.

'Then speak,' said Ket. 'What's the meaning of this?'

'Against our wishes, you have provoked a war with the Saxons,' spoke Wīg. 'You have refused to ask our kinsman, King Wærmund, for help. Time and again, you have ignored the words of our own mother, a beloved member of the Witan, as well as the rest of the council. It pains me to say so, brother, but we believe, for the sake of peace, we should pacify the Saxons by compensating Wulfhere's death and offer a humble apology to King Ēadgils.'

'A humble apology?' Ket asked, rubbing his chin. 'You mean that I, the Earl, should apologise to the Saxons?' Ket stood to his feet. 'Wulfhere was the one making threats, not me. Let me make this clear to you, brother: I apologise to no man. You say I have provoked a war, but are we not warriors? Do you know another path to Valhalla, other than an honourable death in battle? Surely you can see the Gods favour the man who dares stand up to his neighbours and refuse to show weakness, even when his strength has waned.' Ket walked down the wooden steps and addressed the rest of the men. 'Wulfhere came to our home and threatened us, threatening to take everything we have, everything our father's have fought for, and so I took his life. Only the strong survive in this world. I ask you: are we not strong? Are we not favoured by the Gods? Will you join me in battle, my brothers, as we face each and every enemy at our door? Will the Gods take notice of you? Will they favour you, as they have me? Will you now join me in glory, to be truly by my side, as you once stood by my father's, and have your names on the lips of the Gods? You, Fólki. Your father was killed by Danes. Did I not avenge his death?'

'Yes,' Fólki answered with glazed eyes, nodding his head.

'And you,' Ket asked, pointing to another. 'Have I not avenged your brother's death, after the Danes raided this very hall?'

'Aye,' the man answered. 'I am with you, my lord.'

'And you, Fólki?' Ket asked. 'Are you with me, brother?'

'I am with you,' Fólki answered, which was then echoed by several others.

'And what about you, Wīg?' Ket asked, looking his brother in the eye. 'Will you join me, brother? Will you stand by my side like you did when we avenged our mother and father?'

After a tense moment, Wīg sighed deeply and nodded his head.

'I am with you,' Wīg replied, much to Ket's relief.

Ket pulled him close and held him in a tight embrace.

'*You are my brother,*' Ket whispered in his ear. '*We are stronger together.*' Ket turned to the rest of the men. 'A drink!' he yelled, welcoming them to his table.

Fólki and the others walked the steps and took a seat, when suddenly the doors to the hall opened and in came Ulfina, struggling to breathe. Wīg approached his lover and grasped her tightly.

'Take a breath,' Wīg told her. 'What's wrong?'

'Men... in... the... forest,' Ulfina replied. 'They've followed me!'

Wīg gritted his teeth, drew his seax and made his way outside, followed by Ket and the others. Leaving the hall behind them, they witnessed the entire village under-attack by men dressed in wolf headdresses. Like rats they had swarmed the village, murdering all who stood in their way.

'Kill them all!' Ket yelled, drawing his seax. One of the raiders had killed a woman and now stalked her defenceless child. Ket ran towards him and rammed his seax into the base of his spine. Though he was dressed as a monster, he screamed like a man and he bled like one and died like one. 'Hide!' Ket yelled to the terrified child.

Ket turned around in time to see one of the wolf-men stalking him. He had an axe in hand and tried caving Ket's skull in, but Ket managed to hold the Saxon's wrist with one hand and used the other to slide his seax into his stomach. As his eyes bulged in disbclief, Ket head-butted him, knocking the headdress from his head and allowed him to fall to the ground in a pool of his own innards. Ket's blood was boiling with rage and he became consumed with an urge to kill every last one of them. He went on a rampage, killing one after the other, slaying without mercy; leaving fallen bodies, limbs and sprays of blood in his wake.

Wīg and Ulfina fought side by side against Princess Mōdthryth and her brother, Meaca; their seaxes singing as they cut through the air. As Wīg and Meaca exchanged blows, Mōdthryth slashed across Ulfina's face, drawing blood, and knocked her to the ground. Mōdthryth tried slashing across Ulfina's throat, but Wīg blocked her attack. He looked into Mōdthryth's eyes and saw her long dark hair turn white, her eyes roll into the back of her head and her face age a thousand years. She was possessed by the Valkyries, if only for a moment. Seeing his friends in trouble, Fólki leapt between them and knocked Mōdthryth and Meaca to the ground with a spray of blood.

'Get her out of here!' Fólki yelled to Wīg.

Ulfina was badly injured and Wīg didn't hesitate to take her away from the fighting. Whilst helping Ulfina across the yard, Wīg looked back and saw Fólki on his knees, defenceless, while Mōdthryth and Meaca stood over him, stabbing him in his stomach, one after the other. To finish him off and send his soul rushing to the afterlife, Mōdthryth used her two seaxes to slash Fólki's throat open, painting her face red with blood.

Ket and his men fought hard against the Saxons, but they had been caught off-guard and the people of Schleswig were soon overwhelmed. Ket ran towards one of the attackers and leapt into the air, determined to pierce his flesh from behind, but the Saxon turned around and side-stepped, knocking Ket to the ground. The Saxon stood above Ket and raised his axe high above his headdress. Ket closed his eyes and gritted his teeth.

He thought his time had come. Suddenly Ket's face was covered in warm blood, his lips were split wide open and a razor-sharp spear-tip chipped his front tooth. He opened his eyes to find the Saxon kneeling before him with a spear pushed through the back of his head, out through his mouth and into Ket's own. As the spear was retrieved and the Saxon dropped to the ground, Ket saw a woman sitting upon a great steed. It was his mother, Egwen. Behind her was an army of horse-Thegns. Amongst them was their kinsman, King Wærmund.

'You have betrayed me,' Ket told her, rising to his feet, spitting blood. 'I forbid you from involving Wærmund.'

'You may be Earl, but I am still your mother,' Egwen replied, while her horse circled around, whinnying, puffing out warm air through its flaring nostrils. 'Your father and I ruled this Earldom long before you were born. I know what's best. From now on you will listen to your mother!'

Egwen kicked her heels, rode towards King Wærmund and continued to slay the Mire-Dwellers from above, showering the earth with Saxon blood.

Chapter Twenty
Predators

Angeln

Fenris had grown well and had learned to tolerate Offa, yet he remained wild at heart. When he was large enough, Offa started to give him live chickens. He enjoyed watching him play with them, teasing them with his huge paws, studying them, before devouring them. As the weeks and months passed, Offa spent most of his time away from the village, allowing Fenris to hunt whatever he could find. Offa wanted him to learn how to fend for himself, because he knew the day would come when Fenris would get into trouble and be banished from the village. He needed to learn how to live as the Gods intended, as a free spirit; as a predator. As time passed, Offa and Fenris saw less and less of Hothbrodd and his pack of dogs, but there were other dogs in the village and none of them took a liking to the cub and attacked him at every opportunity. Fenris had been excluded from the pack, he was like them, yet different. He had a different smell about him. He was faster and more intelligent. With each day, Fenris learned to be more cunning and learned to attack them one at a time.

Osgār was one of the few dogs Fenris feared. He was a bully and terrorized the cub at every opportunity, often sending him scurrying to safety. Osgār belonged to one of the farmers. When allowed to roam freely in the village, Osgār led his pack against Fenris, and so the cub learned to be fast on his feet. He was swift and was able to flee the pack, but Fenris also learned how to fight. It was Fenris' natural instinct to defend himself and this he did with great ferocity. When the pack ran after him, sometimes one of them would find itself ahead of the others, only to discover the cub could turn and attack without warning and tear his pursuer limb from limb. He would pounce on them without so much as a snarl and tear open their throats with one bite. After the attack, Fenris would run into the forest and disappear between the trees before the rest of the pack could catch him.

As winter approached, the land became cold and grey and the trees were lifeless like gravemarkers striking out from the ground. It was a time when the heavens opened and the Gods punished the village with floods and disease, destroying many homes and ending many lives. No prayers, no charms, no sacrifices seemed to appease them, yet folks still gave what little they had, asking the Gods for mercy. In the meantime Fenris had grown strong. He wasn't yet full-grown, but he was now as large, if not larger, than most of the dogs in the village. Osgār had continued his wicked ways, making Fenris' life a misery, attacking him at every opportunity. Perhaps he was jealous of Fenris' superiority over him. Fenris was faster, stronger, cleverer and had become more ferocious than nature ever intended him to be. The dog had been bred from the wolf, to work for man as an obedient slave. Dogs were not bred for intelligence, only to work, and they paid for that dearly with Fenris.

Fenris was a wolf amongst dogs, superior in every way to the mongrel breeds, just as nature intended. Over time they learned not to wander from the safety of the pack, for Fenris had grown both in body and in confidence. With the exception of Osgār, who had grown formidable, the other dogs became afraid to leave the pack, for Fenris was out there somewhere, waiting. Fenris was like them, yet different, and his differences were about to manifest themselves in the most horrible and violent way.

Offa awoke to the sound of rain hitting the thatched roof and the sound of Fenris' paws scratching at the door. He sat up and wiped his eyes, before dragging himself out of bed. He sheathed his seax, picked up his small hunting-bow and opened the door. Fenris shot through the door and out into the pouring rain. Offa knew he was up to something, and so he covered his head and followed Fenris through the village. Fenris was soaking wet whilst confidently making his way past Hothbrodd's penned dogs. He snarled at Tor, never forgetting the attack on him several months earlier. Hothbrodd was down the pathway, preparing his dogs for the day's hunt. He never said a word as Offa and Fenris past in the slashing rain. Folks moved from Fenris' path while he made his way towards the open gates and strutted his way out of the village. Folks were afraid of Fenris, many stayed clear of him, just as they stayed clear of Offa. Offa had become the changeling with the strange wolf-dog, a dishonoured outcast.

Fenris ran into the forest, hoping to disappear into the wilderness. Offa ran after him as fast as he could, while the rain hit him hard in the face. Offa called out whilst holding onto a tree, trying to catch his breath, but Fenris never listened. Offa had tried to tame the young hound, but the more he tried, the more defiant Fenris became. The more Offa tried wiping the memory of his forefathers, the more Fenris rebelled. Fenris was a free spirit and had no master. Offa ran further into the forest, calling him, until finally he saw Fenris in the distance, crouching on top of a slope, waiting. Offa had no idea that he was about to witness the most spectacular display of courage, cunning and wrath that he would ever bare witness to.

Offa heard dogs barking in the distance and, after several moments, the pack came into view, chasing a giant deer, unknowingly heading straight into the path of Fenris, who laid in wait. The deer was eight-feet-tall with long curved antlers, twelve-feet-across. It was a majestic and beautiful creature with a strong muscular frame and a long grey coat. It looked spectacular, running through the forest with the rain slashing from the heavens above and a pack of barking dogs at its tail. The deer ran towards the top of the hill and leapt over the edge. It soared through the air gracefully, crashing through the falling rain, high above Fenris' head, its giant antlers sitting proudly on its crown, landing safely a quarter way down the slope; its hooves sinking into the wet mud. Fenris didn't move an inch, ignoring his wild instincts to chase the weaker animal; instead choosing to wreak vengeance upon all those that had rejected him.

Going against all that was natural, Fenris leapt from his crouched position and placed himself before the pack of dogs; all of them excited by the chase and hungry for blood. Fenris stood proud, his fierce eyes wide open; his mane bristling with rage. Fenris growled at their leader, challenging him. Osgār had forgotten all about the deer now that his eyes had fixed on Fenris. The two predators, both soaking wet, leapt forward and went straight for the kill. The other dogs jumped and danced around them as they wrestled, trying to take bites out of Fenris. Mercy and fair-play didn't exist to the primordial being, it was master or be mastered, the law of the forest; and Fenris obeyed.

Osgār jumped on top of Fenris and used his bodyweight to drive him to the ground, but Fenris was strong and refused to be bullied. The other dogs snapped at Fenris' hind legs, causing him to retaliate by snapping back at them, giving Osgār the advantage. While Fenris was distracted, Osgār jumped towards him, but Fenris twisted his entire body and kept low to the ground. Before Offa could blink, Fenris opened his jaws and ripped at Osgār's unprotected throat, biting his jugular and ragged his tormentor left and right; tearing him wide open with a terrifying shriek.

The other dogs barked and whined, not knowing what to do. Offa heard a man shouting from over the hilltop. Fenris turned his head to listen, his muzzle stained red. Then the dogs jumped him. They were all about him and upon him, working as a pack. But Fenris was a born fighter and managed to wound many of them with quick bites to their legs. Fenris circled them, picking his moments, trying to knock them off their feet, one at a time, before ripping and tearing at their underbellies with quick attacks.

Offa witnessed the ferocity of Fenris' attack as he fought the entire pack by himself, but their numbers were too great. He was overwhelmed by them, but still, Fenris fought on, never surrendering; refusing to show even a single moment of weakness. Offa didn't care about his own safety, Fenris needed him, and so he ran up the hill and began firing arrows at the pack. He managed to hit one or two, but it made little difference, the pack were rabid, ripping and tearing at Fenris' soft flesh. The dogs' owners waved sticks in the air, yelling for their dogs to release Fenris from their savage jaws. Offa didn't know why they were helping. Fenris had caused a lot of trouble for them, stealing their game and attacking their dogs, but he was grateful they were there and managed to pull back most of them. Yet some of them held onto Fenris' throat, refusing to let go, determined to make the kill.

One of the men had to prise his own dog's jaw open with his bare hands to get it to release him. It sat on the ground, wagging its tail, waiting for approval from its master for capturing the game, but the approval never came. The second man whipped his dogs with a stick before they finally released Fenris from their unforgiving jaws. After tethering the dogs, the first man knelt in the sludge and checked Fenris' injuries. Fenris was breathing heavily and his matted fur was covered in dark red blood.

'I don't reckon he'll make it, son,' he told Offa as raindrops rolled down his beard. 'He's tough, I know that, but I've never seen a dog recover from something like this before. I'm sorry, son. I'll see to it you are fairly compensated. You will be able to choose from any one of my dogs to claim as your own. All of them are great hunters. Or I can see that you get the first pick of the next litter, after my bitch has had her pups.'

Fenris' entire body was soaked with saliva, blood and rain. He laid silently on the ground, stubbornly refusing to give out so much as a whimper. Offa knelt beside him, ignoring the man's offer and placed his hand on top of Fenris' head. Fenris had never allowed Offa to touch his head before, but now he was helpless and even managed to surprise him by wagging his tail for the first time. Offa's heart was breaking to see him that way. Fenris had always been strong, a fighter; a survivor. Offa had never seen anything break his spirit before. Offa looked up when he heard yet more dogs rampaging through the forest. And to his horror, Tor was at the front, leading the pack towards Fenris, who still laid on the ground, in a puddle of his own gore, bleeding into the earth. Offa stood before Fenris and guarded him with his seax, while rainwater slowly dripped from the tip. Tor stood opposite, with the wild-eyed pack behind him. Offa bared his teeth and growled like a wolf.

It seemed as though the forest was closing in on him, threatening to consume Offa's soul. Darkness had enveloped all around and the two men had disappeared. All Offa could see was Tor and the pack of dogs, wishing to devour his flesh and bone. Offa's senses were heightened and he saw every detail in Tor's bristling, black and grey mane; his shoulder muscles tensing as each hair stiffened with rage. Offa saw the colour in Tor's dark, blood-lust eyes, his pupils dilating as he prepared his mind and body for the kill. He could see Tor's whiskers curling, taste his rancid breath and see the saliva in his mouth glistening as it dripped from his knife-like fangs. His bark was deafening and Offa could smell the wolf in him, the primordial being, older than time. He could taste copper and blood as the rain fell from the skies. Offa felt something burning inside of him, wanting release. The hairs on the back of his neck pricked, his heart thumped and he screamed. For the first time in his young life, Offa heard Nerthuz calling his name. The Earth Mother was screaming at him. And the beast within was about to be unleashed!

Chapter Twenty One
The Calling

396 A. D.
Two Years Later
Jötunn Forest

Two summers had passed since Offa stood above Tor, under
the slashing rain, his seax dripping with blood; Tor's lifeless
body lying by his feet. Offa hadn't spoken to another soul
since. As time passed, he became more withdrawn, choosing to
spend most of his time in the forest, away from the crowds and
the talk of war. Offa no longer enjoyed the company of his
own kind, preferring to be outside, under the watchful eye of
the sun, or sitting under a tree, listening as the rain fell from
the heavens; lost somewhere between fantasy and reality.

Offa watched as the rain fell from the sky and rolled down
the bark of a tree, each droplet running through the rough
ridges; the greens and browns of the tree illuminating through
the water. Offa began to see the world around him differently.
It was alive and vibrant. He listened to the sound of running
water, watching as the snow-white clouds slowly drifted by
and listened to the sweet sound of birds singing their ancient
songs. The forest was pulsing with energy, with living
creatures, plants and animals. Bright colours flooded through
the canopy, floating on the warm air. Offa watched as
raindrops rolled from the tips of leaves and fell to the ground,
seeping into the earth, nourishing the roots of the tree.

Offa noticed the trees that spent most of the day in the shade
were smaller than those that grew in the light. He believed the
same was true for people. One must always seek the light in
order to grow, otherwise remain stunted like a bent-over tree,
forever in the shadow of others. He noticed the way the
flowers leaned towards the sun, growing more beautiful in her
light, attracting more bees and wasps which helped pollinate
them. Offa started to see things through fresh eyes and felt
more connected to the forest, to everything; to all things
strange and wonderful.

In the summer, Offa watched eagles stalking the bright blue skies, before swooping to the ground, snatching mice and small birds in their talons to take back to their hungry offspring. Offa watched the strong devouring the weak. He saw a beautiful, yet cruel world where only the strong and the cunning survive. He saw a world made by Wōden, watching him in the clouds, leading the Wild Hunt, chasing trolls and giants. In the thunder he heard Thunor beating his hammer, and with the warmth of the sun he felt Ing's embrace.

Offa often returned to Wēland's cabin and watched the youngsters training from the shadows, the sound of swords and shields echoing into the forest. Sometimes the Cnihts would notice him and mock him, but usually they left him alone, for he was a shadow, a passing cloud. Offa would sit in the trees, watching as the Cnihts stalked below on a hunt. He wanted to join them, but he hadn't earned his Wolf-Coat, and so wasn't considered worthy. Occasionally Offa would sit quietly at the back of the hall and listen to the poets sing of the glorious deeds of his ancestors. He took comfort in the tales of heroism, almost feeling each slash of the sword while the poets describe the blade slicing through the air, through flesh, blood and bone.

For a long time, Offa found it hard to eat in front of others. He was hungry and wanted to eat, but the thought of food would turn his stomach. Only late at night, long after everyone else had taken to their beds and he was sure no one would talk to him, would he be able to eat and keep it down. Offa's father had tried everything to help cure him of his sickness. Osthryth, the leader of the wise women, had gathered healing herbs, brewed potions for him to drink and spoke many incantations. The wise women, known as wicces, help protect the divine springs and hallowed groves from troublesome fairies, goblins, imps and unclean spirits. They use magic to protect women during pregnancy and to invoke the spirits of their ancestors and the Goddess, Frīge, to help bless the new ones amongst the clan. The wicces are loved by the people and often cast healing spells and use their vast knowledge of plants and herbs to cure sickness and deliver newborns. Osthryth offered many sacrifices to the Gods, but nothing she did gave Offa back his voice.

Offa was nine-years-old, the son of a King, he should have become a warrior, a leader of men, but he had spent most of his childhood in the forest with Fenris; away from his own kind and missed out on his training. Offa was thought by many to be a dumb mute, an idiot; a cruel joke by the Gods. Offa was a lost soul and had become angry with the world and angry with himself. He asked the Gods: 'Why aren't I like everyone else? What is wrong with me? Why can't I speak to people? Would they listen if I did? Would they understand? Why can't I find my self? Who am I? I don't want to be me anymore. I hate who I have become. Do you know me? Does anyone know me? Should I end it all here and now? Will anyone notice? Will anyone care? Do you hear me? Does anyone hear me? Is anyone there?'

***

North of Hedeby

Darkness slowly crept over the frozen forest, a chill filled the night-time air and the moon shone brightly, lighting up the ancient land like a giant candle in the sky, awakening the trolls from their daily slumber. After riding through the snow-blanketed forest, Offa jumped down from his steed, tossed a dead deer to the ground and pulled the horse to the river's edge. The shallow river reflected the moonlight from beyond the tall, swaying, snow-clad trees.

Brogan was a beautiful white stallion with a long flowing mane, bright blue eyes, eight strong legs and a big bushy tail. He was a descendant of Slippery-One, Wōden's eight-legged steed. He would often flirt with the female horses, running around the fields, throwing his white mane back, with a twinkle in his eye and his ugly thing hanging out. Brogan was full of life and was very intelligent and playful. Whenever he saw Offa walking towards him on the cold winter mornings, he would gallop towards him from across the farmstead. They would often go out into the forest together, riding over streams, across rivers and around lakes, over hills and through the fens and valleys, making their way to Hedeby to see the wolf pack.

While Brogan dipped his enormous tongue in the river, Offa turned his attention to the pitch-dark forest. Most people are afraid of the dark, afraid of the natural and supernatural creatures which dwell there, but Offa wasn't most people. He often left presents for the land wights and had become friends with the wolves, the protectors of the forest. Offa cupped his hands together and howled at the moon. As his voice echoed into the forest, he heard a response. The wolves were howling back. It didn't take long before the howling stopped and the natural noises in the forest fell silent, all but the sound of running water washing over the smooth stones that rested on the riverbed. Offa looked into the forest, into the shadows, between the dark swaying trees, and saw little lights begin to appear like flashing stars. The wolves were coming closer.

Brogan became agitated at the sight of the wolves slowly emerging from the depths of the forest, one limb at a time. The pack were now in open view and Offa's heart began to pound. Brogan walked closer towards him, stamping the ground with his front hoof, neighing continuously. He had seen the wolves many times before, yet he remained by Offa's side, always there to protect him and offer a ride to safety. As the largest male, whom Offa had named One-Ear, came closer, Offa did what any submissive wolf would do and backed away from the deer, keeping his head down and avoided eye contact. It was always a frightening experience to be so close to a wild wolf. Offa knew One-Ear could turn on him in a heartbeat and tear him limb from limb.

Brogan stood still, blowing warm air through his flaring nostrils, watching closely. One-Ear was sniffing Offa's long hair and grunted whilst licking his face, his way of showing affection. Offa could smell his wolfish breath on him and hoped he hadn't been licking his nuts. Offa stayed perfectly still until One-Ear felt comfortable enough to take the deer and drag it across the snow and into the forest. One-Ear and the female began feasting on the carcass, while the younger members of the pack looked on, waiting for their share of the flesh. Offa reached for the dead rabbits that he had concealed in his sack and tossed them towards the rest of the pack.

Brogan rubbed his nose against Offa's cheek, neighing, trying to get his attention, and so Offa pulled out a couple of apples for him. He seemed to smile as his crooked teeth bit into them, chomping them down whilst flapping his big bushy tail. Offa watched the young wolves as they fought over the rabbits. Two of them shared one in their jaws, before pulling it apart. When Offa turned to look the other way, a cold chill crept up his spine. A black shadow slowly and silently emerged from the forest. Offa saw no features, no shape, only a blackness; an apparition of some-kind. A single blue eye could be seen glowing in the shadows. It was Fenris!

After Tor's attack on Fenris two years earlier, Offa spent many weeks tending to his wounds. He kept him away from the village, where he was safe from hunters and their dogs. Offa often sang to him, howling as loud as he could, trying to speak his language, but Fenris never howled back; he just looked at Offa like he was an idiot. For a while, Offa hunted for him, bringing back rabbits and birds until he was strong enough to hunt for himself. Still, no matter how much food Offa brought him, Fenris never again wagged his tail or allowed him to pat his head. The wolf refused to be tamed.

Fenris was now an adult and had grown to the size of a bear. He had been banned from the village after his attack on the hunting dogs two years before, but that never kept him away. Sometimes folks would tell stories about him sneaking into the village at night, stealing fish, meat, anything he could get; dogs, cats, chickens, sheep, it didn't matter to Fenris. No one could catch him. He was faster than any spear or arrow, faster than any dog and he always outsmarted the hunters who set traps for him in the forest. He would eat the unlucky animal that got caught in his place, chewing at the ropes, before devouring the maimed creature. Sometimes Offa heard him at night, howling to the moon, mocking the hunters while they slept in their beds.

As time passed, folks came to call Fenris the Black Shuck and were afraid to enter the forest alone. To some, seeing Fenris became an omen of death, for he seemed to be no longer living, nor dead, but something in between. Fenris had marked out a territory for himself around the Kingdom of Angeln. Offa had never seen him that far south before, in the wolf pack's territory, near Hedeby. Fenris had now matured and Offa knew there would be trouble. Fenris walked slowly towards Offa with a confidence unlike any other animal. Offa had tried to tame the wolf, but Fenris had an untameable spirit. He was ferocious and destroyed all living things; nothing was safe in his path, especially other dogs or wolves.

Fenris placed his enormous front paws on a felled tree and lifted himself up. He looked strong, proud and noble, and the scars on his face revealed his struggle for life; for existence. Fenris' expression revealed the wisdom he had gained during his life, a lonely life; a life away from the pack, away from his own kind. He knew the wolves were there, but he showed little concern, for he knew no fear and had long forgotten the terror he once felt for Tor and Osgār when he was a cub. He had since become the master of his own destiny, fearing no natural or supernatural creature, not the Gods themselves.

Brogan had always been jealous of Fenris and would often compete for Offa's affection whenever he was around, and that night was no exception. Offa was trying to get Fenris to come to him, when Brogan began grunting and rubbing his enormous head on him. Offa lowered himself to the ground, showing Fenris he wasn't a threat, but Fenris wasn't interested in Offa and looked past him, into the darkened forest. Offa turned his head to see what he was looking at, when he saw moving shadows all around them. One moment they were there, the next they were gone. Offa heard their cries and whimpers all around. One moment they were behind him, the next they were somewhere in front. Brogan started showing signs of further unrest and Offa knew it was time to leave and return home.

Offa was about to mount Brogan when he heard a vicious snarl coming from behind. The hairs on the back of his neck pricked, fear crept up his spine and his heart was beating like a

cornered animal. Offa turned around and there he witnessed
Fenris growling, revealing his fangs to the pack. Offa mounted
Brogan and saw One-Ear approaching Fenris with his hackles
raised, his eyes wide and focused; saliva dripping from his
snarling jaws. The wolves looked at Fenris with excitement,
not a playful excitement, but the same way they would look
upon a cornered deer. Offa watched as the she-wolf and One-
Ear led the pack towards Fenris, taking one step at a time,
slowly and cautiously. Fenris growled and snarled, revealing
his white fangs to their dark roots. The pack nervously waited
for the attack to begin.

Fenris stood proud, showing no weakness, only aggression.
The male walked around him on his left-side, the female on the
right, while the rest of the pack gathered around, blocking any
escape. One-Ear stepped closer, showing his bravery to the
pack, snapping at Fenris. Suddenly Fenris leapt upon One-Ear
and bit him on his muzzle. The female jumped at Fenris from
behind, snapping at his hind legs. Fenris turned around and
snapped at her, before turning back to face One-Ear. One-Ear
charged at Fenris, biting him on his shoulder, knocking him to
the ground and tried ripping his throat out, but Fenris was fast
and rolled back to his feet. The two males wrestled each other,
while the pack watched, snapping and snarling, waiting for
their chance to attack.

Offa was shaking with blood-rush and fear while Fenris had
One-Ear pinned down by his throat. The female attacked,
snapping her powerful jaws around Fenris' throat, taking
advantage of his vulnerability. Fenris had no choice but to
release One-Ear and defend himself. The she-wolf had a tight
grip. An ordinary wolf would have been choked to death, but
Fenris' mane was so thick that it was hard for her to choke
him. Fenris was too big and too powerful and managed to
throw his weight left and right, using all of his strength to
throw her off. Now free, Fenris turned to the rest of the pack,
warning them to keep their distance, before walking up to the
dazed female, growling at her; warning her. But the she-wolf
refused to be intimidated, she couldn't afford to be, she had
cubs to protect. One-Ear rose to his feet, bloody and beaten,

and tried attacking Fenris from behind, but Fenris turned and leapt upon him, jaws wide open, fangs revealed and ripped his throat out. One-Ear was dead.

Fenris had fought his way into the pack and had won his rightful place as their leader. The she-wolf stood her ground, as did Fenris, both assessing the situation. Offa watched from on top of Brogan, when Fenris did the unthinkable and stalked the helpless cubs, ripping them limb from limb, ending One-Ear's bloodline forever. Fenris had no desire for friends, no desire for offspring; no desire to hear cries and whimpers of a litter, yet he had surrendered to the forest and answered his calling. As the weeks and months passed, Offa searched for Fenris and the wolf pack, but he never found them, not a trace. Yet the day would come when Offa and Fenris would meet again, face to face, eye to eye; Fenris' hot breath all over him, fangs revealed.

Chapter Twenty Two
The Fall of Schleswig

Schleswig

Lady Egwen stood tall under the falling rain, looking as beautiful as an elf-woman. There was a large gathering of Angles around her, including King Wærmund, Hemming and a small army of Thegns from Angeln. Also by her side were her two sons, Ket and Wīg, as well as Wīg's wife, Ulfina, now heavy with child. Kneeling before Egwen, with his arms tied behind his back and Egwen's seax held under his chin, was a captured Saxon.

'Wōden, I offer you this sacrifice in good faith,' spoke Egwen as snow fell in her long golden hair. 'Accept this offering, this great warrior of the Mire-Dwellers. Drink his blood, feast on his flesh and bone and decorate your all-seeing throne with his hide. With this sacrifice, I ask you, Lord of Hosts, King of Kings, grant the noble Englisc folk with victory against the Saxons. Give us the strength we need to carry on and end this blood-feud once and for all.'

Egwen cut the Saxon's throat from ear to ear, choking him on his own blood. As he dropped to the ground, his blood soaking into the soil, Egwen placed her hand upon his wound and smeared her beautiful face with warm blood, in preparation for battle. The war between the Angles and Saxons had raged for two years and both sides had fought valiantly. King Ēadgils, keen to avenge his son's murder at the hands of Ket, had amassed a great Saxon army that included the Mire-Dwellers and the Swǣfe. Nothing upon this Earth was going to stand in his way of vengeance.

Flies swarmed around dead, putrid flesh, brains hung from open skulls, blood and rain saturated the slick ground and black blood oozed from twitching corpses. The Saxons had descended upon Schleswig with great force and overwhelming numbers. Countless Angles lay dead, brave men and women who had died a noble death. Egwen was riding a great war-horse, slaying one Saxon after another, when she was attacked and dragged to the ground by two men, knocking the breath from her lungs. They dragged her away from the fighting and tossed her to the ground. One man held her while another forced himself on top of her. She screamed and clawed, determined to fight back. Egwen looked into the eyes of her attacker, seeing the hate there, when his long hair was pulled back and his throat was slit, spraying Egwen's face with warm blood. As he fell, Egwen saw that it was the slave girl, Beado-hilde, who had saved her. Beadohilde then struck the second attacker from this world and helped Egwen to her feet. The two women now fought side by side, killing everyone in their path.

'You surprise me,' spoke Egwen, her eyes shining bright through her crimson mask.

'I surprise myself,' Beadohilde replied, slashing a throat wide open.

Mōdthryth then appeared from the warring crowd, her feather-crested swan-helm rested upon her head and she was armed with two seaxes, one in each hand. She ran at the two women, crashing through the rain, screaming. Beadohilde raised the bloodied seax she had taken from a fallen warrior and the three women fought blow for blow, and the sparks from their swords flickered like the flames of the Valkyries. Mōdthryth deflected a blow from Beadohilde, before kicking Egwen hard in the stomach, knocking her to the ground. Beadohilde tried cutting down Mōdthryth's ribs, but the Saxon Princess parried the blow and slashed against Beadohilde's throat, slicing through her delicate skin, but not enough to mortally wound her.

Mōdthryth was distracted long enough for Egwen to attempt to slash her throat, but a horse-Thegn charged between them and knocked both Egwen and Beadohilde to the ground and trampled over Beadohilde's legs. While the horse panicked, Egwen took advantage of the distraction and dragged Beado- hilde from the field of battle and out of harm's way.

Past the warring crowd, King Wǣrmund sat upon his great steed and saw King Ēadgils barking out orders, his cloak blowing in the wind; his wolf headdress sitting proudly upon his head. The Englisc King gripped his seax and rode towards his rival. Ēadgils saw Wǣrmund's horse rampaging towards him, kicking up turf. Both King Ēadgils and his son ran towards them, yelling, frightening Wǣrmund's horse and forced it onto its hind legs. Whilst kicking its front legs in the air, Ēadgils and Meaca thrust their bloodied spears into the horse's chest, causing Wǣrmund's beloved steed to crash to the ground, with the King beside it. King Wǣrmund lifted his gaze and was kicked in the face by the horse's back leg, knocking him unconscious. The Englisc lost that day and the Earldom of Schleswig had fallen to the Mire-Dwellers.

Chapter Twenty Three
Yuletide

399 A. D.
Four Years Later
Angeln

It had been six years since Ket and Wīg avenged their father's death, and ever since the Englisc have been mocked by their neighbouring clans, accusing them of cowardice and dishonour. For six long years, Offa had carried the shame of his people with him. After defeating the Englisc, King Ēadgils placed his infamous throne of skulls where Frēawine's gift-stool once sat, an act which did not sit well with Ket and Wīg, who were now forced to reside north, in Angeln. After being knocked unconscious by his own horse, King Wǣrmund had lost his eyesight in both eyes and, as time passed, many Thegns chose to abandon Angeln and joined the Saxons, in return for riches and glory; bringing the Englisc further shame and embarrassment. As a result, the loss of Schleswig to the Mire-Dwellers came to be accepted as fate.

In his arrogance, the Saxon King decided King Wǣrmund was too weak to rule Angeln. Because Offa hadn't spoken in public for many years, nor had he finished his time in the wild, he was also deemed weak and unworthy to rule in his father's stead. It wasn't always given that the son of a king would follow in his father's footsteps. Like a pack of wolves, leader-ship goes to the strongest. Nature does not forgive the weak. And so, King Ēadgils requested that King Wǣrmund abdicate his position and surrender Angeln to the Mire-Dwellers. The Saxons' ambassador informed the Englisc that they would be allowed to remain in Angeln and work the land, as long as they agreed to pay King Ēadgils' demands, which included a monthly tribute. Though blind and feeble, King Wǣrmund was a proud man and their request was denied. And so, as the Winter Solstice approached, King Ēadgils once again sent his ambassador to Angeln.

Yule is a magical time for the Englisc folk and lasts for twelve days and nights, ending at the Winter Solstice, the shortest day and longest night of the year, when the veil between the living and the dead is thinnest and spirits cross the threshold to torment the living. During the twelve days, Wōden can sometimes be heard leading the Wild Hunt, pulled along on a sleigh by black hounds, in pursuit of trolls and giants. To hide from unclean spirits, Englisc children dress in traditional costumes and wear animal masks - foxes, wolves, birds and bears, and go wassailing, where they visit folk's homes and sing in return for a drink from the wassail bowl. Yule is the most important event of the year, a time for feasting and fellowship, gift-giving and toasting. The first toast is to Wōden, God of death and poetry, the second is to Ing to bring back the sun, the third is to the king, wishing him good health and hæl. Memorial toasts are then made in memory of departed kinsmen.

Yule is a time when the sun leaves the realm of the living, allowing darkness and ice to cover the land, killing plants and crops, and folks run low on food supplies to feed their livestock. Only a small number of animals can be fed and taken care of through the long winter months, the remainder are then sacrificed to the Gods; a kindness, to save them from starvation and disease. The day before the Winter Solstice is named Mothers' Night, a time when the Englisc honour the Goddesses to bring peace and protection to their kith and kin, and when sons and daughters return from the dead, dressed as Wolf-Coats and Swan-Maidens, to the embrace of their mothers and fathers.

As the Winter Solstice approaches, a boar is chosen and sacrificed to Ing, God of peace and agriculture, in the hope he will bring back the sun. Trees are also decorated with stars to represent the sun's return. Candles and bonfires from the sacrificed animals are lit to brighten up the dome of the sky, in defiance of the dark winter and to represent life triumphing over death. Yule is a terrifying time when the Englisc decorate their homes with magic to protect themselves from the dark things that roam the forest. Mistletoe, ivy and holly do not die, even when the tree itself appears to be dead. They live between the world of the living and the dead, and so are used to protect folk's homes, the communal hall and the surrounding forest. Gifts are left under trees for the land wights, the spirits that help protect the forest.

One cold winter night as the snow fell and blanketed the Kingdom of Angeln, Offa took his steed, Brogan, to the stables, where he noticed the white dragon banner of the Englisc lying in the mud, trodden on and soiled by the horses.

After brushing Brogan's coat, Offa walked outside, embracing winter's bitter kiss, when he heard the sound of sleigh-bells approaching. Offa's heart thumped when he looked along the pathways that were lit with candles and small bonfires, hoping to see Wōden leading the Wild Hunt, but what he saw was a large sleigh being pulled along by two giant goats the size of bulls. The surrounding trees were decorated with red ribbons, ivy, holly and mistletoe. Suddenly a cold gush of wind blew out the candles, sending a cold chill up Offa's spine.

Riding the sleigh was a giant figure in the shape of a man, silhouetted against the night-time fog, with two giant curved goat horns on his head. The apparition stared at Offa from behind a mask made from a goat pelt, his breath visible on the cold crisp air, before stepping down from the sleigh; the snow crunching beneath his heavy boots. Behind the mysterious figure were no less than eleven warriors making their way towards the stables. Snowflakes floated down from the heavens, swirling above their heads, melting as they fell upon the flickering torches. Some of the visitors held the banner of the raven, the emblem of the Mire-Dwellers. One man got down from his horse and approached Offa.

'Here, lad, feed and water my steed,' spoke the stranger, mistaking Offa for the stable boy. 'Look after him, or I'll come back for you and offer your soul to unclean spirits and your flesh to the wolves.'

Offa took the horse's reins without saying a word. He noticed the one who had rode in the sleigh stood head and shoulders above the rest. His entire body was draped with several giant goat pelts and his fellow companions seemed unnerved to be standing so close to him. After leaving their horses and goats with Offa, the Mire-Dwellers made their way towards the hall. Once he had taken the animals safely inside the stable, which was decorated with protection spells, Offa followed the Saxons to the hall to listen in to their negotiations with his father. Offa opened the doors and ducked as he passed beneath the mistle-toe and the enormous deer antlers that marked the threshold.

The mead-hall is a safe-house for warriors and kings and a place for the community to come together and celebrate events such as Yule and Easter. It is a place for ritualised drinking and feasting, for sharing gifts and for speeches and oaths to be made; a place to experience Frith. Frith is to grow up amongst your own people, drink and feast with your own kind, to hear your native tongue spoken and to listen to the sagas of your ancestors. Frith is to know who you are and where you come from. It is the peace of mind in knowing that your people will continue long after you have left this realm, a need embedded deep within the hearts and minds of the Englisc folk. The hall is a sacred place where friendships are forged and bonded with drink and dance, a peaceful, magical place that offers protection from the cruelty of the outside world.

The flame-lit hall was beautifully decorated with giant antlers, boughs of holly, ivy, red ribbons, wreaths and mistletoe. There were many wood carvings of past battles, gilded horns, animal pelts and various weapons and armour, including swords and spears, hanging on every wall above the flaming torches that rested in their iron brackets, glittering in the firelight. There was a blazing hearth-fire in the centre with an old blackened cooking pot suspended above it and a Yule Log feeding the flames. The Yule Log had been cut down on the first day of Yule and was brought into the hall after its branches had been removed to make the protective wreaths. The hearth-fire was lit using a piece of wood from the previous year's Yule Log. The Yule Log symbolises the end of darkness and the coming of light and is slowly fed into the flames over twelve days and nights. After the Winter Solstice the tree's ashes are spread onto the farmers' fields to assure new crops in the coming year.

The smoke from the fire coiled to the hole in the roof like a dark spirit summoned by a priest. The hall smelled like fresh mead and mulled apple cider, candle-smoke and freshly roasted goat, spit over a roaring log-fire. There were two long wooden tables along each side of the hall, where folks had gathered with their children, many of which were dressed in traditional Yule costumes. A fair maiden sat playing a lyre, strumming over the chords, while folks waited for the formalities to begin. The ceiling was high, with iron-braced wooden beams supporting the thatched roof. Each beam was decorated with animals and serpents that came alive as the flames danced in the background. At the far end of the hall was a raised table where King Wǣrmund sat upon his rune-decorated gift-stool. He was accompanied by Ket and Wīg, Egwen and their six-year-old sister, Athelflæd, who was wearing a fox mask. Behind Egwen, bearing a long pink scar across her throat, stood the freed slave, Beadohilde; now Egwen's bodyguard.

Ket and Wīg had been married to their respective wives for several years. One year earlier, Ket's wife had tragically died during childbirth, taking their child with her to the afterlife. Ket had never been the same since. Some say the fire in his belly had been extinguished along with the bright flame of his beloved wife. Yet Wīg had been more fortunate. His wife, Ulfina, had given him a son, Giwis; and they were hoping for the blessing of many more children to come.

The Saxons had gathered on the mead-bench, where a servant poured Meaca a cup of mulled cider. Meaca was the son of King Ēadgils and was a proven warrior of great worth. Offa leaned against the wall and studied him closely. Meaca was in his early twenties and was tall and thin, yet strong and athletic. He had a long pointed nose, a thin moustache and narrow brown eyes, with dark hair that was tied in the Swabian knot.

Sitting on Meaca's left-hand side was his greatest warrior, the giant in the goat mask, Krampus. Some say Krampus had left the Goths in search of wealth and fame amongst other clans, including the Romans, but it was with the Mire-Dwellers where he found it. Some say he was skilled in magic and often spoke with Thunor, the thunder God, who also rode a sleigh pulled along by giant goats. Krampus was a frightening figure with a strong presence and had clearly unnerved the Englisc sitting inside the hall that night. On Meaca's right-hand side, a place of honour, was his sister, Princess Mōdthryth.

After the Saxons had eaten and drank their fill, their ambassador, Wīdsīth, stood to his feet and made his formal greetings. Wīdsīth was forty-years-old and belonged by birth to the Mire-Dwellers, yet he had spent most of his life amongst the Goths. Firelight flashed in folk's eyes and the music stopped playing while the Witan, the council of elders, listened carefully to what Wīdsīth had to say. First, he raised a toast to King Wǣrmund, wishing him grace and good health.

'Wæs þū, Cyning Wǣrmund, hāl. My name is Wīdsīth and I represent the Mire-Dwellers.' Wīdsīth took a sip from his cup in honour of the King, as did the rest of the hall; all but Krampus. Second, he turned his attention to the Englisc Witan. 'I thank you for your hospitality, your food and fine ale, but as you know, I do not come with good tidings. I come to Angeln, along with the noble Meaca and Princess Mōdthryth, to speak on behalf of King Ēadgils. It is the King's wish that this war between the Angles and Saxons comes to an end. Forgive me, King Wǣrmund, but we understand you have lost your eye-sight and we hear rumours that your only son is a mute, a childling who has yet to become a man in the eyes of his peers. And so King Ēadgils asks that you peacefully surrender Angeln to him, an act to save many valuable lives; both Angles and Saxons alike.' There were many murmurs amongst the Englisc. 'Surrender to King Ēadgils, a fine and noble leader, offer him tribute for the harm your people have caused, and I assure you, upon your abdication, the Englisc will be left in peace and be free to work the land, as they do now.'

Offa squeezed his fists in anger and the smoke from the candle in the wall bracket by his head was offending his throat.

'And if we refuse to bow to King Ēadgils' demands?' Ket asked.

'Then the Gods shall decide,' Mōdthryth answered, rising to her feet. 'If you refuse the King's offer, then my father will be forced to make a formal challenge and your fate will be decided in the ancient ways of our people. This war will finally come to an end with a duel, where you will pit your chosen warrior to do battle to the death against our greatest and most honourable Thegn, Krampus. And may the Gods decide the victor.'

Offa turned towards Krampus, his long hair falling into his eyes. In the glory days of Angeln the hall would have roared with proud warriors putting their names forward, yet no one spoke. The shame of the Englisc lingered in the hall that night like a bad smell. Meaca smiled, allowing his sister to sit back down while he stood to his feet and walked over to where Ket and Wīg sat beside King Wærmund. The cooking pot had bubbled over and spilled into the fire, causing a loud popping noise and began filling the crowded hall with smoke.

'Ket, I believe you are the one who killed my older brother, Wulfhere?' Meaca asked from across the table. 'My brother came to you, seeking peace, and you answered by killing him and took his head, before having it so cruelly delivered to my father. Is this true?'

All eyes now fell on Ket. Offa noticed the rage in Mōdthryth's steel-grey eyes.

'It is true,' Ket answered coldly, nodding his head.

'And why did you kill my brother?' Meaca asked.

'He insulted me,' Ket answered. 'So I took his head.'

Mōdthryth once again rose to her feet and drew her weapon, as did Egwen and Beadohilde. The three women met each other's gaze.

'Wait!' Wīdsīth yelled. 'There is no need for violence.'

Mōdthryth sighed deeply and placed her seax back in its sheath. Egwen and Beadohilde did likewise. Reluctantly, the three women sat back down, though their eyes remained fixed on each other.

'Such brave words,' spoke Meaca, his gaze moving to Wīg. 'Such a shame to lose a brother. It would be a shame if I was forced to continue this blood-feud, for where would it end?' Meaca smiled at Wīg, yet Wīg remained silent and unflinching. 'Now, Ket, my father and I are willing to forgive our grievance against you, to see past your crimes, if you and your people are willing to submit to the King's rule.' Meaca paced before the King's table and looked at the young Athelflæd in particular. 'One thing Wīdsīth has forgotten to mention: if you refuse to submit to my father's will and instead choose to fight, and lose, then we will be forced to secure the peace by taking child hostages, as is custom amongst our people.'

Egwen stood back to her feet and drew her seax. 'If you ever look at my daughter again, I will pluck out your eyes and ram them down your throat myself! Do you understand me?' Egwen asked, the smoke from the hearth creeping around her.

Ignoring Egwen's warning, Meaca turned away and addressed the entire hall. 'If you don't accept either offer, to fight or to yield,' spoke Meaca, 'then my father and I will descend upon Angeln with a great army and we will take your lands by force. Is this what you want?'

The Englisc knew the Saxons were more than capable of putting together a mighty army the likes of which Ængla land had never witnessed before, but still, King Wærmund showed his courage.

'On behalf of the proud folks of Angeln, I refuse King Ēadgils' offer,' answered King Wærmund with grit in his dry old voice. 'Damn you!' The blind and aged King stood to his feet and slammed his fists onto the table. 'We are the Englisc! We yield to no one. Nor does any man enter our lands and demand anything of us. In the name of freedom, the Englisc will fight down to the last man, woman and boy. We will not live in shame. The good folks of Ængla land would rather die with honour, than live as slaves to foreigners.' The men and women in the hall muttered in agreement. 'But it need not come to that,' the King added, much to the surprise of Ket and Wīg. 'I won't hear anymore young Angles losing their lives in order to defend the old and the damned. And so, I, King Wær-mund, challenge your father, King Ēadgils, to a duel. And may the winner be the one to end this war once and for all. And you tell your father: though I have lived many moons and I have lost my eyesight, I still have the blood of a God running through these old veins.'

'No!' Meaca replied, throwing his cup onto the table. 'My father is a proud warrior, descended from Seaxnēat himself,' he said, pacing around. 'He will not tarnish his good name and reputation to fight a blind old man. He would never live with the shame of it. I refuse to relay the insult.' Meaca looked across at the Witan and the people of Angeln. Their grim faces revealed their displeasure for the Saxons. 'You will yield to my father, or you will elect a chosen warrior to do battle with

Krampus on the island known as Monster's Gate. Make your decision, you have seven nights.'

There was a moment of silence in the hall, anger surged through Offa's veins and his blood boiled beneath his skin. He was furious at the thought of any mortal man making such demands on his father. What gave Ēadgils the right? Why weren't folks standing up and letting their voices be heard? Why hadn't there been a call-to-arms? What were folks so afraid of?

'Then I shall meet Krampus in seven moons,' Ket yelled, rising to his feet. 'And in victory, may the Englisc forgive me for the shame I have brought to these noble people.'

Krampus stood to his feet and looked across the hall at Ket, his piercing blue eyes staring from beyond his mask. Many gasped at his enormous size.

'Seven nights,' spoke Krampus with the most blood-curdling, inhuman voice, 'until I serve you to the Gods. May they smile upon your bloodied corpse and feast on your flesh and bone.'

Ket grinned and looked ready to fight there and then, though his legs were trembling.

'Then it is settled,' spoke Wīdsīth, trying to keep the peace. 'You fight at the Winter Solstice, at Monster's Gate.'

The Saxons turned to leave and began to make their way towards the wooden doors. Offa had been silent for six years, but something had awoken inside of him, something that had been lying dormant for too long. Offa had always been a loner, an outcast, different; yet the one thing he had always acknowledged and took great pride in was his ancestry. In a strange and confusing world, the one thing he understood was his people. As he looked around the hall that night, he saw the Englisc had forgotten who they were and who they had always been, for the Englisc are a noble race; a race of heroes. Enough was enough! The Saxons were about to leave and Offa couldn't hold his tongue any longer. Finally the Gods had relieved him of his cowardice.

'HALT!!!!!!!!'

The noise echoed throughout the long-hall, silence crept in, the Gods held their breath, and the entire hall stared at Offa.

Chapter Twenty Four
A Hero Rises

Angeln

Meaca stood by the iron-braced door, with Mōdthryth, Krampus and Wīdsīth by his side. Offa stepped away from the wall and walked towards the Saxon Prince, his eyes locked onto his. Both Angles and Saxons looked on with their hands gripped tightly around their spear-shafts.

'Tell your King that I accept your offer,' spoke Offa, so everyone in the smoky hall could hear him clearly. Offa turned to face Krampus. 'And I will face Krampus in seven nights.'

The Saxons looked at Offa in disbelief, as did the rest of the hall. Krampus stood beside his lord and looked at Offa from behind his mask, causing Offa's legs to tremble.

'Who is this young warrior who speaks for the Englisc?' King Wǣrmund demanded from across the hall. 'For I do not know his voice.'

'Your son, my lord,' Wīg answered. 'Offa has spoken.'

'Nonsense! Do not mock me,' the King admonished him.

'I do not mock you, my lord,' Wīg replied. 'Offa has broken his silence. The Gods are with us!'

'This changeling is your son?' Meaca asked, not taking his eyes from Offa. Krampus stared into Offa's soul, yet Offa refused to show how frightened he was. A wolf does not show fear. 'So, you are the King's son,' Meaca continued. 'And what are you going to do?' Meaca stepped forward. 'You are but a child. A pup. A big pup, I see, but a pup nonetheless. Krampus will snap your neck like a twig.' Meaca turned to address the Englisc Witan, giving Offa space to breathe. 'There is no honour to be had here. This child has no worth and is only fit to clean up after Krampus' goats.'

The Saxons laughed, though Krampus remained silent. A bone cracked as Offa stretched his neck and began to pace around the hall, where a thick veil of smoke now lingered, and raised his voice.

'I am Offa, son of King Wǣrmund, son of Wihtlæg, son of
Wōden. And with the Gods beside me, I will fight for the
freedom of my people. I will give my blood and I will take the
blood of others. I will give my life and I will take the lives of
others. I will fight for what belongs to the Englisc folk, our
ancient lands that sweat with the blood of our kith and kin.
This land wasn't given to us, we the Englisc made it our own,
with our sweat, our blood, our sacrifice. We created it, it is
ours, and it is not for the taking. And I will prove my worth by
spilling giant's blood onto the ice at Monster's Gate. Win or
lose, I will end our shame.'

There were many murmurs in the hall.

'If Offa loses at Monster's Gate,' spoke Egwen, taking charge
of the situation, 'then King Ēadgils will rule over the Englisc
and we will submit to his will. And there will be no reper-
cussions. And if Offa wins, then there will be no revenge-
killings, no blood-feud between us, and Offa will rule over the
Saxons. And when he comes of age, to secure the peace
between our two great people, Princess Mōdthryth will act as a
frithuwebbe, a peace-weaver, and marry Offa, putting this feud
behind us, once and for all.'

Meaca laughed at the thought.

'If by some miracle Offa wins,' spoke Mōdthryth, 'then he
will truly be blessed by the Gods, and so I will marry him.
Though I do not think it likely. Gǣþa ā wyrd swā hīo scel. Fate
goes where fate must.' Mōdthryth turned to face Offa. 'If there
is only you who has the courage to challenge Krampus, then
the men of Angeln will know the spear of a conqueror.'

'And as for your women...,' spoke Meaca.

Offa saw red and rushed at Meaca before he could finish his
sentence, knocking him to the ground and tried strangling the
life out of him. The entire hall became berserk and the Angles
and Saxons began fighting there and then. Krampus grabbed
hold of Offa, pulling him from Meaca and tossed him across
the hall like he was a small child. Offa got back to his feet and
drew his seax, but his father's men took hold of him and held
him back. Offa was kicking and yelling, trying to break free;
screaming for blood. Meaca rose to his feet and stood by

Krampus' side, when they were attacked from behind.

Offa looked across the hall and saw his father and Athelflæd were protected by the hearth-troops, who escorted them outside. Offa witnessed Ket and Wīg climbing over the King's table in mad pursuit of Saxon blood. Ket leapt from the table with his sword held high above his head, and struck, cutting through the smoke that filled the feasting-hall and through a warrior's skull. Wīg's sword found its way through a warrior's ribcage, pinning him to a support beam. He screamed in the Saxon's face, placed his boot on his chest and pulled his sword free, spraying the air with dark red blood.

A Saxon ran towards the doors, fleeing for his life, but he was soon impaled on an Englisc spear that ripped through his soft stomach. As Hemming retrieved the spear, the Saxon's guts fell out of his flesh-shield and spilled onto the wooden floorboards. Chaos erupted and swords sang the gruesome song of death. Everything became a blur, a mix of yelling and screaming, and blood-mist sprayed the air Offa breathed. Offa saw Ket slash a man's throat open whilst being cut across his left arm. Wīg rammed the edge of his shield into the throat of a Saxon, before thrusting his seax into his mouth, splitting his teeth.

Egwen and Beadohilde roared like Valkyries, battling against the fierce Mōdthryth. Offa saw dark figures in the shapes of men and women, blood-drunk as they took each other's lives. He heard the sound of flesh being sliced open, bones breaking and the screams of dying men and wailing women as many turned to flee the hall. Offa looked across the hall and was horrified to see his kinsman, Wīg, sword-bitten and lying in a pool of his own gore. A badly injured Ket stood over him, protecting him from enemy spears, killing all who dared step too close. Ket's left arm was limp, though his right remained strong.

'Let go of me!' Offa screamed, struggling to free himself from his father's guards.

The shame of the Englisc was all too clear to see. Many had lost their lives during the years they had been at war with the Saxons, King Wǣrmund had been insulted, many had died from disease and many more lost their lives that night. Ket and Wīg had brought the Englisc great shame by killing Athils, two against one. It was clear to all that the Gods had forsaken them. Offa then felt an overwhelming urge to balance the scale.

'Let go of me!' Offa yelled to his father's guards. 'Meaca!... Krampus!... I want you both! I want you both!!!'

The doors to the hall swung open from the howling night-time winds, the flaming torches on the walls flickered, winter chilled everyone to the bone, and the men and women in the hall shivered as the hairs on the back of their necks stood on end. Wolves could be heard outside, in the surrounding snow-clad forest, singing to the moon, waiting for their chance to devour him.

Meaca, Mōdthryth, Krampus, Wīdsīth and the remaining Saxons had grouped together behind an upturned table and were surrounded by many angry warriors, led by Egwen and Hemming. The Saxons held their ground well. Wīg was lying on the floorboards, spitting blood, struggling to breathe, whilst being comforted by his brother, Ket, who had dropped his seax beside him. The flesh on Ket's face had been badly slashed and blood flowed down his face, along with many tears.

'Don't die on me,' Ket begged. 'Don't you die on me, brother. Not like this! Not like this!'

Seeing her son lying on the ground, in a pool of his own blood, Egwen turned from the Saxons and rushed to kneel by his side.

'No, Wīg! Not my son! *Not my son!*'

'*It hurts so much,*' spoke Wīg, coughing up blood.

'I'm here,' spoke Egwen, gently caressing her son's cheek. '*I'm here.*'

'*My wife,*' Wīg whispered with tears rolling down his cheeks. '*My son. Tell them I love them.*'

'I will,' spoke Egwen. 'I will.'

King Wǣrmund's men finally released Offa from their grip, while the entire hall listened on.

'*Look after them, m-make s-sure they are w-well,*' Wīg begged.

'*You have my word,*' Egwen whispered with a smile. '*I promise.*'

'You're not going anywhere,' spoke Ket, comforting his brother with his good arm. 'You can't leave us.'

Wīg was shaking and struggled to breathe, while Egwen placed his sword in his shaking hand.

'*I'm r-ready,*' spoke Wīg with blood and saliva dripping from his mouth, holding the sword with a gentle grip, securing his place of honour in the afterlife. '*The Valkyries are w-waiting f-for m-me. I s-see th-them. It's j-just my t-t-time. It's just m-m-my t-t-time.*'

'*You have made me proud,*' Egwen whispered, kissing his forehead, before looking into her son's eyes. '*I am proud to call you my son.*'

Wīg turned to face Ket.

'*I shall s-see y-you in V-Valhalla, b-b-brother,*' spoke Wīg, '*for this is n-n-not our f-f-farewell.*'

'Wīg!' Offa yelled with tears flowing down his cheeks. '*I'm sorry.*'

'*No, I'm s-s-sorry, Offa,*' Wīg replied. '*We sh-should not have t-t-taken you with us t-to s-seek r-revenge. It's our f-fault you are n-not a Wolf-Coat. Everything is our f-f-fault.*'

Offa heard the air escape Wīg's lungs and saw his eyes roll into the back of his head. Wīg had left this realm, leaving his mother and brother, a wife and young son behind in the realm of the living. Ket took a deep breath and looked across at those who had taken his brother's life. Consumed with grief, he picked up his seax and rose to his feet. Ket roared a deafening cry and headed towards the Saxons, determined to kill them all.

'No!' Egwen yelled, holding Ket back by his one good arm. 'Killing our guests will only bring us further shame.'

'I must avenge my brother's death,' Ket told her, his arm and cheek bleeding profusely.

'Haven't the Gods punished us enough?' she asked, still holding his arm. 'We must not invoke their wrath further still. Think of Athelflæd. King Ēadgils will retaliate if we kill his son and daughter this way. How many more must die? How many? Don't you understand, we must satisfy the Gods. This war must come to an end as agreed. Honour is everything!' Egwen released Ket's arm and turned to face the Saxons. 'In seven days, on the twelfth night of Yule, at the Winter Solstice, you shall have your fight at Monster's Gate. Win or lose, this war comes to an end.'

Meaca nodded his head from behind the barricade.

'The King's son has challenged myself and Krampus to a fight. Am I to accept this as your final decision?' Meaca asked.

'No!' Ket yelled, full of rage. 'I will be the one...'

'You are badly injured,' Egwen interrupted. 'Offa is the King's son. He has made the challenge, and so we must accept it.' Egwen faced the Saxons. 'Drop your weapons and you may leave here tonight with your lives intact.'

'You are a strong, honourable woman,' spoke Mōdthryth, looking Egwen in the eye. 'If only there were more like you.' Mōdthryth turned to face Offa. 'You are a brave cub, Offa. The Gods will honour your death.'

Mōdthryth was first to drop her weapons onto the wooden floorboards. Reluctantly, the remaining Saxons did likewise, in an act of defeat, as is custom.

'Leave now,' Egwen told them, 'there is no more need for words. Leave us in our grief.'

Sweat poured down Offa's forehead while he watched the Saxons leave. Krampus ducked his head beneath the threshold and met Offa's gaze before entering the cold outside.

'I must avenge my brother's death,' Ket told his mother with tears in his bloodshot eyes.

'You killed your brother!' Egwen yelled, slapping Ket hard across his face. 'Do you know what you have done? You provoked this war. If we lose this fight, then we will all be killed or enslaved. If Offa loses, then I will kill you myself for what you have done. Then I will be forced to take your sister's life and then my own, because I would rather we die with honour than live with the shame of slavery.'

Chapter Twenty Five
Stedefæst

Angeln

King Wǣrmund closed Wīg's eyes and kissed him gently on the forehead, before the priests carried his body away to be bathed. The old King was tall and thin, his grey beard fell to his chest, the lines on his face were deep from many winters burden and tears welled in his pale white eyes. The King turned to Offa and stroked both of his cheeks with his giant cold hands.

'Why, my son, why have you not spoken in all these years? Did I not show you my love? Was I a terrible father?' the King asked solemnly, while the rest of the hall listened.

'My silence represents the shame I feel inside my soul,' Offa confessed with glazed eyes. 'I have witnessed the death of my friends, yet I did little to help. I was there when Ket and Wīg killed Athils without honour. I have since become consumed with shame. This is why I must now fight, to restore the pride of our people and to redeem my self.'

'Why have you agreed to fight King Ēadgils' finest warriors, when you have no training?' Ælfgār asked, the leader of the hearth-troops, wiping blood from his spear-tip. 'Are you suddenly possessed by Thunor or are you completely mad?'

'To restore the balance,' Offa replied, 'and to restore honour to the Englisc folk. Our people lost our grace, our favour with the Gods, when two Angles took the life of a lone warrior. Now one of those men, my kinsman, has paid with his life; the other is badly injured. I am the King's son: to restore our dignity, I alone must fight two men. It is my duty. Whether I live or die does not matter, only that I fight with honour.'

'But, my lord, you're not ready,' Ælfgār protested. 'You will surely lose and bring shame upon us all,' he said, turning to the Witan, seeking their agreement.

'It is better to die for something, than live for nothing,' Offa answered.

'You are brave, Offa,' spoke Ælfgār, 'but you are young and

unschooled, undisciplined and unwise. You're not ready. We need a warrior, not a boy-child who wishes to emulate his ancestors. Angeln depends upon it. My King,' Ælfgār turned to King Wǣrmund, 'you must not allow this to happen. Your son will bring destruction to our people, to Ængla land. The Saxons will ruin us and the Englisc will become no more than a slave race.'

There was a lot of talk in the hall, a lot of mixed emotions.

'Silence!' Hemming yelled with a powerful voice.

King Wǣrmund thanked Hemming for calming folks down, before turning to Offa.

'Offa, my brave, brave son, tell me you can do this, that you can win this fight,' spoke the King. 'How is it you are strong enough? Wise enough? Can you handle a sword with grace? Have the Gods revealed themselves to you, asking you to defend the Englisc folk in our time of need?'

'Of course they haven't,' spoke an irritated Ælfgār. 'I'm sorry, my King, but Offa is without honour and does not wear the wolf coat.'

Offa took a deep breath, raised his voice and unlocked this word-hoard:

'My strength comes from Wōden, whose blood runs through my veins. My wisdom comes from the forest, for I have watched the wolves of Ængla land and studied their ways. My bravery comes from the sagas I hear of my ancestors. My skills come from hunting and watching Wēland teach the Cnihts how to fight with spear and seax. I have drank the blood of the wolf. I am Wōden-born. And above all, I am a proud Angle. I know the history of my people..., I would see that we have a future.'

The folks in the hall didn't know what to make of him.

'Fine words, my lad,' spoke Hemming, slapping Offa hard on the back, nearly knocking him over. 'Fine words.'

'It worries me,' spoke Ket, softly, 'to think I could lose a second brother, but perhaps the Gods favour you, Offa. Maybe you possess something the rest of us do not. Perhaps you are the one to end this curse, to redeem my wrongdoings and pay for all of our mistakes. Perhaps you are the one to remind us the ways of our people, for we have lost ourselves. My mother is right, the Gods have forsaken us. That much is clear. Help us, Offa. Kill them both!'

'Listen to me, Offa, my son,' spoke the blind old King, his pale white eyes piercing deep within Offa's soul, 'you will avenge Wīg's death and you will end this curse. You are the great-grandson of Wōden. You are a God! And I feel it in my bones, you will be victorious.'

His father's words warmed Offa's soul.

'Then we had better begin your training, my lad,' spoke Hemming, 'for we have seven days and seven nights. A Kingdom depends on it.'

The King laughed.

'My son needs a weapon.' Wǣrmund turned to Hemming and grasped his arm. 'Did you hear that? My son needs a weapon. A sword and shield.' The King laughed again. '*Stedefæst!...* *Stedefæst*! Praise the Gods! Get my lad *Stedefæst*!!!!'

That night, King Wǣrmund sat on the edge of Offa's bed and woke him from his dreams. Lying on the bed was a heavy object, wrapped in a blue cloth.

'I've been saving this for you, my son, long before you were born,' spoke the King. 'For many years I longed to have a son, yet the Gods refused to answer my prayers. That was until I met your mother. Soon after we were married, your mother's womb swelled with life, and I knew, deep in my soul, that I loved you with all of my heart. I had dreamt of this day, when *Stedefæst* would be unearthed and presented to you, my son.' The King carefully unwrapped the gift, being careful not to cut himself on the sharp edge, and presented Offa with his ancestral sword. 'Take it. *Stedefæst* now belongs to you.'

Offa reached out and took the seax. It was heavier than he imagined.

'*Stedefæst* is the sword of Ængla land,' his father continued, 'the bringer of fame and glory. It has drank the blood of many great warriors and shone like the fire of the Valkyries across many battlefields.' The King placed one hand on the weapon, feeling every curve and engraving. '*Stedefæst* is a three-foot-long seax, a one-handed, silver-gilded long-knife with a single-edged blade, sharp enough to penetrate the hide of a troll. It was forged with fire and magical spells by powerful dwarves, deep beneath the mountains of Ásgard. The handle is made from the ribs of a slain dragon, the blade from the splinters of Thunor's hammer. Notice how the pommel and hilt is beautifully decorated with the Jörmungand, eternally coiled around the bone handle. The blade itself is carved with magical runes, encoded with the language of the Gods, spelling the words: Stedefæst.'

Offa admired the beauty of the sword.

'Wōden passed *Stedefæst* down to his son, Wihtlæg, and my father passed it to me, but I would never use the sword in battle, for fear of its magic. One night, when I was young, I witnessed a dragon soaring through the dark night sky, in a blaze of light and cloaked in flame. The dragon was once a man, cursed to become a serpent for all time, forever stalked by fame-hunting heroes. The dragon was seeking-out buried hoards of treasure that lay hidden in underground caves. After witnessing the dragon crash deep into the earth, I waited many winters for it to leave its darkened lair, before taking the dwarf-wrought sword, hiding it deep underground, where no man dared to tread. This was when I was young and unwise. I have since lived a long healthy life, but now war has come to our land, and so *Stedefæst* has been unearthed and the future of the Englisc race now rests in your hands.'

Chapter Twenty Six
Sacrifice

Angeln

The bright bride of the heavens had long since fled the wolves in her golden chariot. Her brother, Mōna, now rode the dark night sky, fleeing the pack, while the entire Kingdom of Angeln came to show their respects to Wīg and to those who had lost their lives during the Saxons' visit. A pyre had been built by the edge of the forest, decorated with swords, shields, spears, boar-crested helms and white dragon banners that blew fiercely in the cold winter winds.

Folks watched with sorrow in their hearts as Wīg and the other brave men and women were laid to rest upon the wooden planks. King Wǣrmund placed Wīg's sword in his hands, snapped in two to be forged again in Valhalla. Snow had been falling all day and throughout the night, continuing to settle over the cold, dark land, resting upon the shoulders of the mourners. Offa stood in silence, wrapped in his fur coat, shaking the cold from his bones. He looked at Ulfina, Wīg's grieving widow, and felt her pain as she struggled to hold back the floods of grief. Giwis, Wīg's young son, stood by his mother's side.

Osthryth, the leading wicce, made her way through the crowd. Osthryth was an old woman with long white hair that fell loosely below her waist like the tail of a white stallion and was clothed in a long grey wolf pelt. She had a hunched back, skeletal frame and wore an old face with many winters burden. Her eyes were a deep shade of blue and her face had lines as deep as sword cuts.

'A man's blood is like a river,' spoke Osthryth, 'if it is too protected, surrounded by many barriers, then it becomes trapped like a swamp. It will become stagnant and void of natural life. A man should not be afraid to bleed. A man's life-force should be free like a river, flowing through the forests of this world and out into the vast, open sea. Just as the ocean is the final destination of all rivers, Valhalla is the destination of the brave soul. The loss of a little blood is good for a man, it reminds him of his own mortality. Those who protect their life-force too much, protect nothing at all, for a life too protected is a life not worth protecting. Wīg knew this well, for the words of our Lord Wōden were known to him.'

Offa saw the pink scar on Ket's cheek and the pain and heartache in his eyes. Ulfina kept her head low, hiding her own scars and sorrows under her blue hood. The Englisc don't like to make a spectacle of their funerals. When they have heaped up the pyre, only a man's weapons and sometimes his horse are cast into the flames. The tomb is a raised mound of turf. They disdain to show honour by raising monuments of stone; these, they think, lie heavy on the dead. Weeping and wailing are soon over - sorrow and mourning linger. It is thought honourable for women to mourn and for men to remember.

'Wīg was a great warrior,' Osthryth continued, 'a fearless follower of Wōden. He possessed the greatest qualities a mortal man can achieve in this life, the qualities of the wolf; the primal spirit of the forest. Unlike a man, who is naturally flawed in his ways, a wolf can never weave a lie. The wolf knows only truth, discipline, order and duty. And above all, the wolf knows loyalty to his pack, his kith and kin.' Offa looked at his father and it pained him to see his saddened eyes. 'These are qualities that every free-born man and woman should possess. Learn them well, teach your children, your friends and your neighbours.' Folks watched with heartache while Osthryth set the funeral pyre alight, the flames burning so hot the Gods themselves could feel the heat. 'Hæl to thee, brave Wīg. May the Valkyries take your soul over the rainbow bridge and deliver you to Valhalla, the home of the brave.'

Staring into the fire, the winter wind gently cooling his face from the heat of flames, Offa watched as his kinsman's flesh was devoured by hungry fire-spirits, thinking of what was to come. Would he be lying on the funeral pyre in the nights to come? The thought turned his guts to water. Hemming raised his voice and announced food and drink was available in the mead-hall, where toasts and speeches were to be made in honour of Wīg and those who had lost their lives against the Saxons. Egwen and Beadohilde accompanied the King to the hall, leaving Ulfina to speak with Offa.

'Wīg often spoke of you,' Ulfina said to Offa. 'He was worried about your silence and had always felt a great deal of shame with his involvement in Athils' death. I know my husband will be proud of you, Offa. He will be watching you. Honour him. That is all I ask. *Honour him.*'

'The Kingdom has become stagnant,' Ket added, while Ulfina was escorted to the hall. 'We have known peace for such a time that we have forgotten what it is to live, what is needed to survive. The Englisc have forgotten that peace in Ængla land is always paid for with Englisc blood. Osthryth is right, Offa, the loss of a little blood is good for a man. After the death of my wife and my unborn child, something died within me, but watching my brother's flesh melt from his bones has awakened my fighting spirit. Now I want blood! I only wish my arm was strong again and I could trade places with you.'

Offa looked into Ket's eyes and knew he was speaking from the heart. Offa turned to look into the fire, watching as Wīg's mortal flesh was devoured, and saw himself lying there amongst the flames.

'I'm afraid,' spoke Offa. 'My stomach is twisted in elf-knots and my legs are weak. I am afraid to die.'

'You must let fear fade away,' Ket told him. 'You cannot escape wyrd. Death comes to us all, but few ever have the chance to live forever. Fear is for cowards, a valiant soul bravely accepts what the Fates have woven for him on the battlefield. I am injured. I can never fight again. I can never win glory before death and the Gods will never hear my name echo in the hallowed halls of Ásgard. But you, Offa, you have been given the chance for immortality. Show your courage and loyalty to the Angelcynn, to the Gods, and you will live forever.' Ket looked back into the flames, watching Wīg's body as it departed from this world and moved onto the next. 'You must avenge him.'

Hemming approached Offa and Ket from behind.

'I applaud you, Offa,' spoke Hemming, 'you stand up for the Englisc at a time when most folks turn the other cheek. You are a credit to your father and to your people, but heed my words: you are unschooled in the art of swordsmanship. You have never felt the touch of a naked blade upon your flesh, or I dare say the touch of a woman. To speak freely, you are but a child, undisciplined in combat and unwise, more likely to wet yourself than bring glory to our people.' Hemming grasped Offa's arm and stared into his eyes. 'I long for glory. Allow me to take your place and I will honour the Englisc with a graceful victory. A victory the Gods themselves shall sing of.'

'No,' Offa replied, looking back into the flames. 'I am the King's son. For too long I have remained silent while my people have suffered, but now the time has come for me to stand up and have my voice heard. But it's not my words that folks will remember. I will speak with action. *Stedefæst* will have the final word. If not, and I fail to bring our people honour, then hell may claim me and I will embrace my fate.'

Later, after the toasts had finished, King Wærmund, with the help of Egwen and Beadohilde, led the people outside, back into the cold winter night. The stars shone brightly in the vast open sky and the entire village seemed to glow from the settled snow that had enveloped the land. Offa stood in the courtyard, upon a wooden dais, snowflakes biting at his flesh. He was nervous whilst standing before countless people, both nobles and common folk; all still in mourning. He saw the desperation in folk's eyes and the hopeless expressions upon their grim faces. He longed for the warmth of the hearth-fire, when he looked up and saw Ælfgār bringing Brogan towards him.

Offa refused to show emotion whilst taking the leather reins from Ælfgār's cold hands. Brogan brushed his enormous head against Offa and his breath seemed to freeze on the cold night air. Offa looked into Brogan's bright blue eyes and felt his sorrow, for they both knew what must happen. Sacrifice means *to make sacred*. Offa loved Brogan and now he had to sacrifice him to the Gods before blessing himself and his weapons with his blood, his essence. Offa needed Brogan's life-blood to awaken the Gods, in the hope they would bring him battle-grace against the Saxons. Offa rested his head against Brogan's and drew *Stedefæst*.

'*I'm sorry, Brogan*,' Offa whispered. '*Please forgive me. I am doing this because I love you, because you mean the world to me. May you fare well in the afterlife and know that I will see you again. I love you so much, you are my only friend.*' Offa looked into the crowd and saw Ket and Hemming standing beside Ulfina, each with hope in their eyes. He placed the sharpened edge of *Stedefæst* against Brogan's throat and looked up into the heavens. Snowflakes melted as they landed upon his cheek. Brogan began to panic and tried to pull away. 'Wōōōōōden!!' Offa screamed with tears in his eyes. 'Kinsman!

Accept this noble horse, this blood-offering, my friend, into your Kingdom. Give me the strength I need to save my people. And I swear to you, for the sake of my people, I will struggle and fight! And never lose courage! And never surrender! Weriað ðæt Angelcynn!'

Offa thrust *Stedefæst* deep into Brogan's throat, splitting him wide open, spilling blood all over himself. Offa hoped he understood. Could a horse understand such things? Brogan's life-force soaked through Offa's fur coat and stained his soul for all time, shattering Offa's heart like a wooden shield breaking into a thousand pieces under the weight of a warrior's axe. The crowd looked on silently, many with tears in their eyes, while Brogan fell to the wooden planks; his hind legs still kicking. Offa crouched and kissed his friend goodbye. As Brogan closed his noble blue eyes for the final time, Offa's stomach twisted in agony and he was overcome with grief and sorrow; and sobbed his heart out. He had sacrificed his only friend to awaken the Gods and save his people from a terrible fate, a fate worse than death, and he hated every moment of it. He placed a hand on Brogan's wound, feeling the warmth of his blood as it escaped his mortal body. Offa rose to his feet and smeared the sacred blood onto his face, warming his skin. He then addressed the people.

'I am Offa, son of King Wærmund,' Offa yelled. 'Though you don't know me and I don't know you, we share a common bond. We are tied by blood, by common ancestors. I may not be a wise man, but I see what beautiful people the Englisc are. And I will honour you. And I will fight for you, for your children, for their children, and for every member of our race yet born, until my dying breath!' Many in the crowd cheered when Offa raised his seax in the air, drenched in sacrificial blood. 'Weriað ðæt Angelcynn! Weriað ðæt Angelcynn!' Offa yelled those words with great pride. 'Defend the Englisc folk!'

Chapter Twenty Seven
The Howling

Angeln

It was the break of dawn, the cocks were crowing and the snow-clad village began to thaw. Offa sat alone inside his father's hall, while the serfs prepared the slaughtered boar that had been roasting throughout the night. He looked at the floorboards, at the bloodstained spot where Wīg had taken his last breath, thinking of the fight to come. Offa's stomach turned whilst imagining what it would be like to be cut with a cold steel edge. The thought of the blade slicing open his warm flesh sent shivers up his spine. He was feeling nervous and sick, wondering how his death would unfold, wondering what horrors awaited him after his life-thread was severed by the three spinners of fate.

The doors to the hall swung open and Sunna's warm light flooded into the timbered room, bringing the darkened hall to life. Ket and Hemming entered and their shadows danced along the walls like spirits from another world. They were accompanied by King Wǣrmund and Ælfgār. As they made themselves comfortable on the mead-bench they were joined by several maidens, who placed food and drinks on the table.

'Offa, you must eat,' spoke Ælfgār, while a serf filled his cup. 'You have a long journey ahead. The snow is deep at this time of year. No horses can travel through such weather.' He took a sip of water. 'You need to make it on foot. A day's journey to Wēland will take you at least two days and two nights in the snow. Maybe three on foot. Your training must begin as soon as possible. You will need your strength.'

'Ælfgār is right,' Hemming added, placing toasted bread in his mouth. 'Every moment will count. Make sure you listen to what Wēland has to say and heed his instruction.'

'What if I'm to lose?' Offa asked, poking his food. 'What if I die?'

'Then we shall fight!' Hemming stabbed his seax into the wooden table. 'We will kill them all, or die in the attempt, with swords in hand and flesh in our teeth.'

After the death of his mother and father, when Hemming was young, he went to live with his kinsman, King Wǣrmund, and the King had raised him as a son. Hemming was now in his late twenties and had a large gut from drinking too much mead and was starting to go bald. If he had been born a generation earlier, he would have no doubt become a feared Wolf-Coat, but that was not his fate. He had been born during a time of peace, and so he never got to fulfil his dream of becoming a great warrior and dying gloriously in battle. Hemming now spent his days trading with the surrounding earldoms, telling stories and sharing riddles.

'Offa, my son, if you are to lose this fight, then it is the will of the Gods, and we will honour our agreement with the Saxons.' The King turned to Hemming. 'And I would hope, dear Hemming, that you would take no action to further anger the Gods.' He turned back to Offa. 'A warrior should not go into battle being afraid to die. He should go into battle hoping for a beautiful death, in a blaze of glory, sword in hand, dripping with the blood of his enemy. If he truly wishes for this, then it is he who will live and prosper, and it will be his enemy that shall be left to the beasts of battle.'

'Your father is right, Offa,' spoke Hemming. 'You don't get to live as long as we have without attaining great wisdom, or at least how to appreciate a good pot of mead. Speaking of which, where's the wench with the big udders to fill my cup?'

The doors to the hall opened and in came Ulfina and her young son, Giwis. Ulfina removed her hood and gave curtsies to the men at the table. She then turned to Offa.

'My lord,' she removed her catskin gloves, 'I fear I will not see you again before the Winter Solstice. My son asks for an audience with his kinsman.'

Offa paused for a moment until Hemming nudged him, reminding him of his manners.

'Of course,' Offa mumbled, rising to his feet, standing awkwardly.

'Are you the one who is going to avenge my father?' Giwis asked with confidence.

'I will try,' Offa answered with a lump in his throat. 'I will try.'

'Thank you,' said Giwis. 'I will sacrifice a goat for you.'

In Englisc culture, a man must avenge the death of his kinsman or be forever shamed. As Giwis was too young to wield a weapon, it was left to one of his kinsmen to exact revenge on his behalf. Offa carried a heavy burden. After their morning meal, Ket and Hemming accompanied Offa outside the hall, where water dripped from the icicles hanging from the frozen deer horn gables above the hall doors. As the droplets fell to the ground, Offa caught a glimpse of the snow-clad village illuminating through the water.

'It's cold today,' spoke Ket, shaking the chill from his bones. 'We had better get wrapped up. There's nothing worse than travelling in winter, but at least the snow might keep the wolves at bay.'

'Wolves thrive in winter,' spoke Offa. 'They have thick coats and webbed feet. It's us I'm worried about.'

'I think I preferred your last speech,' Ket replied. 'It was more inspiring.'

Offa wrapped his fur coat around himself, trying to keep warm, when the doors to the hall opened and out came Hemming, blowing warm air into his calloused hands.

'Come on, lads, let's get going,' spoke Hemming, rubbing his hands together. 'The days are short and the nights are long. I don't want to spend longer than I have to out there. Meet me with your things at Hothbrodd's dwelling. Make haste.'

'Hothbrodd?' Offa asked, while Hemming made his way to the village; the trodden ice crunching beneath his boots.

'He's bringing his mutts with us,' Ket answered, 'to carry some of our supplies and help frighten the wolves and drive away unclean spirits.'

Offa and Ket gathered their things and followed Hemming through the village. Hothbrodd lived in a wooden house on the outskirts of the village. He had surrounded his home with a fence to keep his dogs in and keep strangers out. Hothbrodd never liked Offa, nor anyone else for that matter, and he had never forgiven him for killing Tor several years earlier. Now at

Hothbrodd's fence, Offa began to feel uneasy. There was a
small gap between the fence panels and Offa saw some of
Hothbrodd's dogs jumping at Hemming while he made his way
towards Hothbrodd's door, yet one of them ran up to the fence
and barked at Offa and Ket. Ket backed away from the fence,
but Offa reached through the panels and patted him on the
head. He saw his tail wagging and knew he was no threat,
regardless of his aggressive appearance. It was a young pup,
mostly black with a tanned muzzle and mane, and big brown
eyes.

'He's just a pup,' spoke Offa. 'He won't hurt you.' Offa looked
at the house and saw Hemming enter. As the door closed
behind him, the rest of the dogs ran towards Offa and Ket and
jumped up at the fence. Offa noticed the pup with the golden
mane moving out of their way. 'He's an outcast. Look at the
way he's watching the others. He's probably been attacked
before.' Offa pointed towards the biggest dog. 'I think he's the
leader. Look how he's pushing the others out of his way. Half
wolf, I think. Look, did you see? The others are afraid of him.'

'I don't like dogs,' Ket muttered. 'I don't trust anything that
licks their own nuts. And I don't like Hothbrodd either. I don't
trust him.'

'He probably does lick his own nuts,' Offa mumbled.

Offa saw Hemming leave the house with a man by his side
and walked the icy pathway. Hothbrodd wasn't as tall as
Hemming, but he was an intimidating figure and sent a cold
chill up Offa's spine.

'Come,' spoke Ket, leading Offa to the gate. As they got
closer, Offa noticed Hothbrodd had gained weight and his hair
had turned grey over the years. 'He looks annoyed with you,'
Ket told Offa. 'It's your fault he's got to leave the comfort of
his home and take us to the middle of nowhere, in the dead of
winter. He's risking his life and that of his mutts for you.'

Hothbrodd called his dogs and began to leash them together.
The pack leader was barking and still trying to jump at Offa
and Ket. Hothbrodd struggled to leash him. The other dogs
allowed Hothbrodd to leash them without much of a struggle,
except for the pup, Golden-Mane. Golden-Mane didn't trust

Hothbrodd and he certainly didn't want to be leashed so close to the other dogs, especially the half wolf. After the dogs were leashed, Hothbrodd took Offa's things from his cold hands and tied them to his dogs.

'*Don't think I've forgotten*,' Hothbrodd whispered. '*You owe me a debt, laddy, and I plan on collecting*.' Offa didn't say a word in return. The moment Hothbrodd turned away, Offa touched his sheath to make sure *Stedefæst* was still there. 'Let's make haste!' Hothbrodd yelled. 'The wolves will be resting. Now we move!'

Hothbrodd was a man who wasn't afraid of the elements and was wise to the great power of the Earth Mother. He understood how Nerthuz laughed at the futility of life and the struggle for existence. Hothbrodd dared to challenge her, yet showed her the respect she deserved.

The group had been travelling for a day, their legs were tired, their feet were throbbing and their stomachs growled with hunger. Offa's cheeks were numb from the cold winds, his fingers felt frostbitten and the cold gnawed at his toes as his feet sank into the deep snow with every step he took. It had been dark for a while and there was a vast silence over the ancient land. It seemed lifeless, without movement or struggle. The land was neither happy nor sad. It was the winter forest, frozen-hearted, raw and unpredictable. This must be what hell is like, Offa thought, passing through the frost-stiffened forest; his thoughts far removed from the fight to come and the training beforehand. All he could think about was the forest as it slowly closed in on him. He felt a strange comfort in it. As they ventured on, the group began to feel something watching them, yet they saw nothing; no living thing. The dogs could sense it too.

Bæda, the half wolf, was at the front of the pack, leading the way through the thick snow. Bæda showed the same qualities as Tor - he was a vicious, nasty dog that bullied the weaker members of the pack. None of the other dogs had the fight in them to stand up to Bæda, except for the newest member of the pack, Golden-Mane. Offa overheard Hothbrodd speaking to

Hemming about him as they trudged through the deep snow.

'Bæda had taken a dislike to Golden-Mane from the moment they first laid eyes on each other,' spoke Hothbrodd. 'Every time my back is turned they're at each other's throats. The one on the right is called Loki. The one there with the black coat is called Sköll. He's a fat, lazy swine and has never made a kill in his life.' Hemming laughed. 'The one on the left is called Hoder. He's always pissing himself, he is. Those two there are brothers, yet they're always fighting each other. They have torn chunks out of each other and out of Hoder too, poor bastard. Good hunters though.' The group listened to Hothbrodd whilst watching the dogs trotting along in front. 'But none are greater than Bæda for hunting. A natural born killer, he is. He's been in some spectacular fights and got the scars to prove it. I've thrown him in the pit with some nasty ones. He's a mean old bastard.'

'What about him…, Golden-Mane?' Ket asked.

'Hmmm, there's something special about Golden-Mane,' Hothbrodd answered. 'I knew that the moment I first laid my good eye on him. He's a warrior and clever too. He'll make a good dog when I break him in. He needs to be taught a lesson though. He needs to know who's boss.'

Darkness had long settled over the forest, it was bitterly cold and the land was covered with snow. The trees looked as solid as ice, like old Frost-Giants frozen-in-time. The group had gathered around a small camp-fire. The wooden log was burning brightly, casting shadows over the silent trees.

'The fire is like a spell, consuming the life-force of what was once a living thing, born of the earth,' spoke Hothbrodd, sitting around the fire, eating and drinking, while shadows danced upon his bearded face. 'Though dead, the tree still possesses its soul, refusing to surrender the life it once held. Its energy is now being released by the magic of the burning flame, yellow, orange and red, flicking like the tongue of a serpent. The same happens to the human body. A corpse refuses to release the soul. The body needs to burn and be consumed by hungry fire-spirits to be freed from its earthly flesh-shield.'

Offa was staring into the flames.

'Offa, what are you thinking, my lad, what's going through that mind of yours?' Hemming asked.

'Nothing,' Offa answered, poking the fire, refusing to engage in conversation and reveal his inner-thoughts.

'That's the problem with the youth today,' spoke Hothbrodd, stirring his porridge over the flames. 'You tell them something interesting and their brain falls asleep. If I had my way, each and every one of them, noble or otherwise, would get a good hiding. They spend their youth hardening their bodies, practising with spear and shield, dancing amongst threatening spears to the applause of their kin, killing wolves, bears and aurochs. Yet when it comes to a conversation they lose their tongue like frightened babes.'

'You dare disrespect the King's son?' Ket asked. 'Offa is here, in the middle of nowhere, to fight for us…, for you, you ignorant bastard.'

For a moment, Offa thought Ket was talking about someone else. He wasn't used to folks standing up for him or speaking kindly on his behalf. Hothbrodd stared at Ket from across the flames and reached for his seax. Like a cat drawing its claws, Hemming drew his weapon and held it to Hothbrodd's throat.

'Back off or I'll cut you from ear to ear,' spoke Hemming, calmly; his blade cutting into Hothbrodd's throat.

Hothbrodd took a deep breath and removed his hand from his weapon. In turn, Hemming gently lowered his seax.

'Yes, Offa, you're a brave lad,' spoke Hothbrodd, softly, stirring his porridge. 'I remember the day you stood before my dog, Tor, wild-eyed and crazed, stabbing him over and over, like you were possessed.' Hemming and Ket turned to stare at Offa. 'But you're a fool for accepting this fight. And your father is an even greater fool for agreeing to it.'

The mention of Offa's father angered him. Offa reached towards his sheath and rose to his feet, *Stedefæst* in hand, pointing the tip at Hothbrodd.

'That's enough!' Hemming yelled, his voice echoing into the wolf-haunted forest.

Taking a deep breath, Offa reluctantly placed *Stedefæst* in its sheath and sat back down.

'*You owe me a dog, laddy*,' Hothbrodd muttered under his breath, stirring his porridge.

'Is it true, you killed his dog?' Ket asked, the corner of his mouth creasing with the promise of a smile.

Offa remained silent and stared into the dancing flames.

'Tor was his name,' spoke Hothbrodd with great sadness. 'I loved that dog.'

Ket and Hemming leaned back and burst with laughter.

'What else don't we know about you, lad?' Hemming asked, still chuckling.

Hothbrodd stared at Offa from across the flames. 'If it wasn't for your father, I would have killed you many years ago,' Hothbrodd warned.

'Why don't you both settle this with something simple, like an arm-wrestle, or tug-o-war?' Hemming asked.

'Yes,' spoke Ket, 'you can both hold a rope over the fire. The first one to get thrown into the flames loses. If Offa loses, then he owes Hothbrodd a dog. If Hothbrodd loses, then he gets nothing but a singed arse.'

'Sounds good to me,' Hemming laughed, slapping himself on the knee.

'Then it's settled,' spoke Ket. 'I'll get the rope.'

Offa's boots were firm on the ground and his grip was tight. He composed himself, looking through the flames, waiting to take the strain. Both Ket and Hemming were on their feet. The dogs were leashed, yet barked wildly with excitement. Hothbrodd was a short man with a heavy build and stood low to the ground. Offa thought Hothbrodd would pull him into the fire, but he was determined to make it as difficult as possible for him. Hothbrodd tossed a goatskin to the ground and used his sleeve to wipe drops of ale from his unkempt beard.

'Get ready to burn, laddy. I can almost smell your flesh cooking and my dogs are still hungry,' spoke Hothbrodd with a crooked smile.

'On the count of three,' spoke Ket. 'One…, two…, three!'

Offa pulled as hard as he could, but Hothbrodd was strong and didn't budge an inch.

'Come on, Offa, you can do it!' Ket yelled. 'Put your back into it!'

Offa's teeth were clenched shut, his arms were outstretched and his shoulders, forearms and fingers were hurting. He was struggling to breathe and the rope was burning through his palms. Offa was young, but he was large for his age and was much stronger than he looked. Hothbrodd was pulling as hard as he could, keeping his body low to the ground, using his small frame to his advantage. Offa was much taller and found it difficult to balance. Ket and Hemming were laughing whilst passing a goatskin between them. Offa pulled and pulled. He was a boy of no worth. Hothbrodd was an outsider. They were two outcasts from the village, but in that moment, deep in the forest, beneath the frozen Frost-Giants, looking into the dancing spirits of death, they were two warriors, standing eye to eye, neither willing nor able to back down in front of their peers.

Ket and Hemming were cheering and the dogs continued to bark. Ket poured ale onto the fire, causing an explosion of heat. Offa looked through the hot flames and saw the look in Hothbrodd's eyes. He was breathing heavily, his teeth were clenched and his reddened face became enveloped by the heavy flesh around his neck. Hothbrodd was pulling as hard as he could, trying to pull Offa into the fire-spirits that danced impatiently, waiting to devour him. Offa held the rope tightly, ignoring the excruciating pain as it cut through his burning flesh, drawing blood. Offa balanced himself well, took deep breaths and pulled as hard as he could. Hothbrodd was yelling at him, trying to frighten him, but something had come over Offa and he no longer felt frightened. He no longer felt weak. He felt strong. And he remembered he was Wōden-born!

'Come on, Offa!' screamed an excited Ket. 'You can do it!'

Offa began to move one hand past the other, in rapid succession, forcing Hothbrodd to step forward, towards the flames; one foot at a time. The dogs were jumping around, going crazy, trying to bite free from their tethers. Offa's hands were burning, not from the fire, but from the rope cutting through his soft palms like razorblades. He was in agony, yet he held strong, determined to pull Hothbrodd into the flames.

'That's it, Offa, you're doing it!' Hemming yelled. 'I can't believe it, you're doing it.'

Offa held his breath and, with one last tug of the rope, he pulled Hothbrodd into the flames. Ket and Hemming were laughing while Hothbrodd ran around the camp, screaming like a little girl, before throwing himself to the ground, rubbing his backside into the cold, wet snow. Even Offa managed to smile.

'I don't believe it, did I just see a smile?' Ket asked, putting his arm around Offa's neck. 'There's hope for you yet.'

Hemming held out his hand and helped Hothbrodd to his feet. Offa braced himself, waiting for Hothbrodd to attack, but to his surprise Hothbrodd laughed.

'Well done, laddy,' spoke Hothbrodd, patting Offa on the back. 'Well done.'

Hothbrodd had a sip of ale and walked over to his dogs. They were barking wildly and wagging their tails. There was a moment of bliss between the group. Hothbrodd was fussing his dogs, Ket and Hemming were drinking and cheering, and Offa was feeling quite proud of himself. But the moment quickly passed when they heard an eerie cry coming from the shadows.

'My dogs are getting unsettled,' spoke Hothbrodd, staring into the forest, which seemed to glow blue from the snow and ice and the silver moonlight shining through the tops of the trees. 'These dogs are wise. They know what lurks in this forest.'

'How many do you think are out there?' Hemming asked.

'I don't know,' Hothbrodd answered. 'Based on the carcasses we've seen, I reckon a dozen. Maybe more. I can't be sure.' The fire crackled and a log fell apart with a spitting sound. 'Let's get some rest, we've a long day on the morrow. Wolves don't attack folks. Only in the stories. My dogs will look after us. We better get some sleep.'

'Toss more kindling on the fire, Offa, that will keep them away,' spoke Ket.

After feeding the fire more wood, the four of them settled down for the night, covering themselves with animal pelts and listening to the mournful cries of the wolves in the distance.

'I can tell you a story of a wolf and a dog,' spoke Hothbrodd, lying on his side, staring into the hot flames. 'The Romans have a giant breed of dog called a Molossus. They introduced them to a place called Rottweil, deep in the Black Forest. The local clan bred them with their own working dogs and called them Rottweilers. I remember when I first laid eyes on one. He was big and strong and had a head like a rock, yet he was a timid young thing. He was excited when they threw him into the pit, wagging his tail, looking up at folks as they gathered around. I felt bad for him. He was an admirable dog, a good dog; I knew he was no match for my half wolf. The Rottweiler didn't have it in him..., *or so I thought*. Folks saw his enormous size and bet on the Rottweiler to win.'

The group rested in silence, listening to every word, forgetting for a moment about the wolves in the surrounding forest.

'I bet everything I had on Bæda to win,' Hothbrodd continued. 'I opened the gate, took off his leash and released him into the pit. The pit stank of blood and death, sending Bæda mad with blood-lust. The moment he saw the Rottweiler, Bæda ran at him. The poor dog didn't know what hit him. Bæda went for his throat, trying to make the kill. The crowd was cheering for blood and the Rottweiler was squealing like a newborn pup. Bæda was trying to force him to the ground, but the Rottweiler was as strong as a bull. Bæda was ripping and tearing at him. Everyone was shouting at the Rottweiler to fight back, waving their arms and yelling, but the pup was terrified and didn't know what to do. He looked around, trying to find his owner, hoping someone would help him, but no help came.'

Offa saw Hothbrodd's breath as fire-shadows danced upon his deformed face.

'The Rottweiler knew he was on his own. It was time to fight or die. I saw it in his eyes..., *he knew*! That's when I saw the change in him. The Rottweiler turned from a scared young pup to what nature intended him to be, a killer. He began to fight back! He stopped crying and whimpering and used his weight and strength to squash Bæda beneath him. Bæda couldn't breathe and was forced to release the pup and retreat. The pup's owner was cheering, ordering him to attack, but the Rottweiler wasn't listening; he was in a world of his own, caught somewhere between life and death.'

The fire crackled and spat, and the dogs' eyes glowed in the firelight, listening to the faint hunger-cries in the surrounding forest.

'The Rottweiler fought his heart out and charged forward, biting Bæda's leg. I thought he was going to tear it off, but he released him and Bæda went for the Rottweiler's throat. Blood was drawn, but the brave pup wouldn't surrender to death so easily. The crowd was yelling, encouraging the Rottweiler to fight back, but they had placed their bets on the wrong dog. Bæda had proven it wasn't the size of the dog in the fight, but size of the fight in the dog. Bæda ripped at his throat, finally tearing the cub wide open. I rushed into the pit and forced Bæda to release him. The pup was lying there, in a pool of his own blood. He looked up at me, thrashing out his last moments of life, and I felt for him. I felt his pain and suffering. I knew then that it was wrong what we had done. His owner turned away in disgust, leaving him there to die in the pit, alone. The pup wasn't a good fighter, but he was a warrior. He fought to the death and never surrendered, not for a moment. He earned my respect that day. The poor bastard deserved better. I have never been to a pit since.'

Offa saw the flames reflected in Hothbrodd's glazed eyes.

'The pup didn't die in a farmer's field after being worked to death,' Hothbrodd continued. 'He died having truly lived, if only for a moment. Of all the dogs I've seen in the pits, the Rottweiler is the one I will always remember. Not for his size, but for his heart.' Hothbrodd looked at Offa from across the flames. 'For the beast I saw awaken in him!'

Offa rested his head, took a deep breath and looked up at the stars. They looked like countless wolf eyes in the night-time sky, looking down upon them, waiting to devour them in their sleep. Offa listened to the wolves in the forest, howling their hunger-cries, and thought of Fenris. Where was he? Was he still alive? Offa hadn't seen Fenris since he was two-years-old, when he ran away with the wolf pack, four years earlier. Offa spent years looking for him, refusing to give up hope, refusing to believe he wouldn't see him again. And he was right, for Fenris still stalked the forests of Ængla land. And he was mad with hunger!

Chapter Twenty Eight
The Primordial Beast

Jötunn Forest

It was morning and Hothbrodd was first to wake from his slumber. The air was damp and cold, and the land was frozen and covered in deep snow. After his dogs had risen from their holes and shook off last night's snow, they began to fight over a few scraps of food, and Hothbrodd was forced to use his stick to separate them. Golden-Mane laid on the ground, beside the others, giving Hothbrodd a light growl. After eating their morning meal, the group continued trudging through the snow-clad forest, making their way to Wēland's cabin.

The snow continued falling all day and the ancient forest started to have a strange effect on the dogs, and on Golden-Mane in particular. Golden-Mane was young and hadn't been out in the wilderness for long periods of time before. The forest had a strange aura about it, mystical, magical and myst-erious. It took Golden-Mane back to a time when the world was still young and primitive law, the law of the forest, was all there was; dog eat dog, kill or be killed, and the sad song of the primordial beasts could be heard, defiant of death itself. The beast was strong in Golden-Mane. The more they travelled, the stronger it grew. Offa watched as Bæda bullied the other members of the pack and noticed how Golden-Mane refused to cower to him or surrender his ration of food. Golden -Mane tried to keep away from him, but Bæda never missed an opportunity to reveal his fangs to the young pup.

Whilst walking through the deep snow, struggling with every step, the dogs sensed something was watching them and began barking into the old enchanted forest. The group looked between the trees, but nothing seemed to be there. Perhaps it was a sprite or a fairy, or maybe the troll was stalking them, Offa wondered, but they saw nothing. Later, as darkness slowly fell over the frozen landscape, strange noises could be heard behind them, from somewhere in the shadows. First, an eerie cry was heard, and the dogs all stopped to turn around; some of them whimpering. Bæda and Golden-Mane were trying to break free from their leash to confront their unseen pursuers. Then a second cry was heard, sending Bæda and Golden-Mane into a frenzy.

'We need shelter,' spoke Hemming. 'I don't want to be dinner to the beast tonight.'

They were all tired and in need of rest.

'My eyes are heavy,' Ket complained, trudging over the flattened snow, behind Hothbrodd and his dogs.

'We'll make camp soon,' spoke Hothbrodd, trying to control his dogs. 'There's a cave up yonder.'

The group made camp inside the cave entrance, with the fire protected from the wind on three sides. Snowflakes fell from the dark night sky, melting as they blew into the hot flames. Frosted cobwebs floated on the cold air above and icicles hung from the cave ceiling like half-forged swords. Hothbrodd fed his dogs and they each swallowed it down as fast as possible.

The group had been settled for a while, making small talk and preparing to sleep. Every now and then they could hear the wolf pack howling in the distance like starved creatures of the night, causing a stir amongst the dogs. Bæda and Golden-Mane had to be separated as neither could tolerate the other. It made no difference that they shared common ancestors, or the fact there were great and terrifying beasts out there, waiting to make a meal out of them both. As the night progressed and the dogs had finally settled, things began to happen around the dying camp-fire. Golden-Mane was lying on the ground, away from the other dogs, resting his head on his forepaws. His ears were pricked as he looked into the darkness of the forest, giving a quiet snarl; almost a ghostly whisper of a threat. Hot embers floated above his head, his hackles raised and he slowly lifted himself from off the ground. Hothbrodd had been mumbling in his sleep, but he opened his eyes when he heard Golden-Mane growling at some unseen thing in the shadows.

'*There's something here*,' Hothbrodd whispered, rising to his feet.

The four of them were soon on their feet, weapons in hand. The forest seemed to be asleep, but then an eerie cry pierced the silence and an old familiar song could be heard echoing between the frosted trees. It was a sad song, as old as the world itself; long drawn-out wailings and half-sobs, desperate pleas for food.

'I've seen one,' spoke Ket, notching an arrow and drawing back his bow. He aimed, but there was nothing to be seen. They were surrounded by trees and dancing shadows, while the fire crackled and spat.

'Get the firelight out of your eyes,' spoke Hemming. 'Focus. There, did you see that one?'

Offa looked into the forest and saw shadows rushing around, before disappearing between the trees. One moment they were there, the next they were gone. The dogs clustered together by the fire, crying and whimpering. Only Golden-Mane and Bæda were showing signs of aggression.

'We need more wood for the fire,' spoke Ket. 'It will die soon and then they will come for us, you'll see.'

Golden-Mane and Bæda were leashed by Offa and Hothbrodd, yet continued barking, eager to attack what was out there and defend the territory. Only the forest wasn't their territory. Their ancestors had abandoned it countless generations ago. The forest belonged to the wolves. Then Bæda did something Hothbrodd had never heard him do before. He sat on the ground, raised his muzzle and howled at the moon like his wolf ancestors before him. As the group listened to Bæda's sad lament, calling to the forest, the forest soon answered, and the wolves began to howl back.

'We need to keep this fire lit,' spoke Hemming, growing anxious.

Later, as the fire began to die out, the blue glow of the frozen forest seemed to get brighter and the group started to see members of the wolf pack stalking them from the shadows.

One in particular approached them.

'I'm going to kill it,' spoke Ket, aiming with his bow.

'No, wait!' spoke Hothbrodd, raising his hand. 'She's female.'

Offa was still holding Golden-Mane by his leash, when the female came close enough for him to see that it was the she-wolf. Offa looked behind her, to the left of her, to the right. Was he there? Could he still be alive after all these years? Taking Golden-Mane with him, Offa walked into the cave and looked for his rations of food. If Fenris was there, then Offa wanted to see him and he knew how driven he was with food. Many winters had passed since Offa last laid eyes on Fenris, but he was still his friend.

With the smouldering fire behind him, Offa's shadow moved along the cave walls, blending into the darkness. He held Golden-Mane tightly, using his free hand to search through his rations, when he heard Hothbrodd yelling. Ket had released some of the dogs without Hothbrodd's consent, and the impor-tance of nobility was quickly forgotten amid the rush and panic. Hothbrodd yelled at Ket, before chasing after his dogs, being pulled along by Bæda. Golden-Mane was trying to chase after them, but Offa had a strong grip and Golden-Mane wasn't going anywhere. Within moments, Hothbrodd had disappeared into the forest and Offa heard his dogs crying and whimpering from somewhere in the shadows.

'He's going to get himself killed,' spoke Hemming.

'Crazy fool,' Ket added.

'And you!' spoke Hemming, pointing his finger. 'You shouldn't have let his dogs loose. What were you thinking?'

'I am an Ealdorman,' spoke Ket. 'I did what I thought best.'

'Your title means nothing out here,' Hemming replied. 'Those wolves will eat you alive and feed your scraps to their young.'

'There's nothing we can do now,' Ket added. 'We just have to wait until Hothbrodd returns. If he returns.'

No one had heard the wolf pack for a while, yet no one wanted to leave the cave to find suitable wood for the dying fire.

'How long has it been?' Hemming asked.

'I don't know,' Ket answered, rubbing his hands together over what remained of the fire. 'Too long.'

'I think it's safe to say Hothbrodd won't be taking us the rest of the way,' spoke Hemming with a heavy heart. 'Ket and I have been there many times before. I'm sure if we put our minds to the task, we'll be able to remember the way. Isn't that right, Ket?'

'Yes,' Ket answered. 'Though we have never travelled during wintertime before. Wēland only teaches in the summer. We're hoping he'll make an exception for you, Offa. We should be there tomorrow, before nightfall. Tomorrow will be a long day. We should all get some rest.'

The three of them were lying inside the cave entrance, by the smouldering fire, trying to get some much needed sleep. Golden-Mane was laid beside Offa, keeping him warm.

'What do you think has happened to Hothbrodd?' Offa asked, looking up at the cave wall, watching how it glistened from the melted ice-water running through the crevices.

'He's ran away with the fairies,' Hemming joked.

'A wolf is probably lying over him right now, picking his teeth with Hothbrodd's ribs,' spoke Ket. 'Now go to sleep, Offa, and stop asking stupid questions.'

'Stupid dogs!' spoke Hothbrodd, holding Bæda on a leash, deep in the forest; tracking the rest of his dogs. 'Where are they, Bæda?' Hothbrodd had followed their tracks, but the snow had been falling for a while and the tracks had since disappeared. Bæda was sniffing the air, trying to catch a scent on the icy breeze. 'It's cold, Bæda. Maybe we should turn back. What do you say, boy?' Hothbrodd turned around, but Bæda had seen something in the shadows and pulled away, breaking free from Hothbrodd's grip; the leash trailing behind him, and disappeared between the trees. 'Bæda, no!' Hothbrodd yelled, running after him, following his tracks in the snow.

Hothbrodd had been looking for Bæda for a while and was struggling for breath, when he came across something in the forest. It was a giant deer, standing ten-feet-tall with long curved antlers, fourteen-feet-across. Hothbrodd had never seen one so large. The deer saw him too and watched him carefully. Hothbrodd slowly stepped towards it, trying not to frighten it; the ice-encrusted snow crunching beneath his boots.

'*It's alright, boy, I won't hurt you,*' spoke Hothbrodd, reaching out his hand.

The deer had never laid eyes on man before and was curious about the strange creature that walked on two legs. Hothbrodd knew the deer could kill him with one kick or thrust with its enormous antlers, but he saw the kindness in its eyes and felt it was a gentle soul. Though Hothbrodd was deformed and unpleasant to look upon, the deer saw past his appearance and saw only the soul that dwelt within. It lowered its giant head and puffed out warm air through its flaring nostrils. Hothbrodd reached up and stroked the gentle giant on its snout.

'*It's nice to meet you,*' spoke Hothbrodd, looking into its big brown eyes. '*Though I don't suppose you've seen any of my dogs or you would have fled far from here.*'

The deer was breathing heavily, soothing the exhausted Hothbrodd, allowing him to forget about his dogs and the wolf pack; if only for a moment, but then he saw something strange. A mysterious blue light had appeared in the forest, flickering like a tiny torch. Hothbrodd had heard of mysterious tiny lights called hobby lanterns or fairy lights. It is said the fairies draw folks away from the safe paths and lead them into danger by encouraging them to follow the light.

Hothbrodd wasn't a fool and knew they were malevolent fairies playing tricks on him, but what choice did he have? Hothbrodd decided to approach the light, and, as he did so, the light disappeared before reappearing further into the forest. Hothbrodd continued to follow the lights, travelling away from the deer and far from the cave; all the while calling Bæda's name. Hothbrodd had been following the lights for a while, when finally the last light blew out and he heard laughter, like that of a small child. And there, to his joy, cowering between the trees, was Bæda, growling into the forest at some unseen thing.

'What is it, boy?' Hothbrodd asked anxiously. Bæda looked at Hothbrodd, but then turned back to stare into the forest, at something behind the trees. Hothbrodd had never seen Bæda frightened of anything before. Hothbrodd looked into the shadows, his heart hammering inside his chest, sweat dripping down his back, when he saw a large figure in the shape of a man standing behind the trees. He looked closer and realised that its legs were half as long as the tree trunk. He looked up into the branches and nearly jumped out of his skin when he saw a hideous face looking back at him, its stinking breath floating on the cold crisp air.

'*Gr... en... del*,' it whispered.

'You're even uglier than I am,' spoke Hothbrodd, drawing his seax. 'Come then! Come getteth some!'

Offa tried sleeping, but he couldn't get comfortable on the cold, hard ground. The fur covers made him too hot, yet he was too cold without them. He laid there half the night, thinking of Hothbrodd's fate. Golden-Mane was kicking his legs and whining in his sleep. Offa looked outside the cave, noticing the silver moonlight and the snowflakes that were gently falling over the frozen landscape. Offa rose to his feet, being careful not to disturb Ket and Hemming, who both snored like pigs. Golden-Mane had also awoken, and so the two of them walked outside and relieved themselves in the snow. Afterwards, Offa yawned and stretched his arms. Golden-Mane stood beside him, wagging his tail.

'*It's alright, boy*,' Offa whispered, '*if Hothbrodd is dead, I'll look after you. I promise.*'

Offa turned to go back inside the cave, being careful not to stand in the yellow snow, when he heard something from beyond the trees. Golden-Mane heard it too. His hackles raised and he stared into the forest, giving a light growl. Offa's heart was racing, yet he stood silently and listened, staring into the trees, when he felt a presence behind him.

'What is it, lad?' Hemming asked from behind, causing Offa to jump with fright.

'*There's something out there*,' Offa answered. '*Listen.*'

'I don't hear anything,' Hemming yawned. 'Go back to sleep.'

'There..., did you hear that?' Offa asked.

'Yes, I heard it,' Hemming replied. 'It can't be. It sounds like Hothbrodd's half-breed.'

Golden-Mane began barking, and there, between the trees, silhouetted against the snow and ice, was the figure of a man. In front of him was a dark shadow jumping forward on four legs.

'Hothbrodd?' Offa yelled, thrilled he was still alive.

'Well who do you think it's going to be out here in the middle of nowhere?' Hothbrodd asked. As he got closer and his face became visible under the moonlight, Offa noticed his hair and beard was white with snow and his face was pale and frost-bitten. 'Awful weather. I need to warm my hands by the fire.' Hothbrodd looked into the cave. 'What happened to the fire?'

'It died,' Ket replied.

'Nobles! Can't wipe your own arses,' Hothbrodd joked.

'Good to see you're still alive,' spoke Hemming, patting Hothbrodd on the back.

Bæda tried rushing at Golden-Mane, but Hothbrodd yanked him back by his leash.

'Down, boy!' Hothbrodd yelled.

Golden-Mane came alive with aggression, his mane bristled and his fangs were revealed.

'It's alright, boy, calm down,' Offa told him, patting Golden-Mane on the head.

'That pup has taken a liking to you,' spoke Hothbrodd. 'Tell you what, Offa, he's yours. He is your responsibility now.'

'Truly?' Offa asked, pleasantly surprised. 'Are you sure?'

'On one condition,' Hothbrodd added. 'If you die at Monster's Gate, then he comes back to me. Understand?'

'I understand,' Offa answered, fussing Golden-Mane.

'Good, now keep him away from Bæda,' spoke Hothbrodd. 'The last thing I need right now is these two at each other's throats.'

'What happened out there?' Ket asked. 'We thought the wolves would have shit you out by now.'

'I don't know,' Hothbrodd answered, struggling to keep warm inside the cave, blowing warm air into his ice-bitten hands, his thoughts adrift.

'What is it?' Offa asked. 'You saw something out there, didn't you?'

'I don't know what I saw,' Hothbrodd answered, staring at the ground, 'but I don't want to ever see it again.'

The following morning as Sunna's warm light slowly crept along the ground, threatening to thaw the ice-encrusted snow, Offa awoke to find himself face to face with a stinking hell brute. His heart seemed to stop and his body froze. Golden-Mane and Bæda were sleeping, tethered at the back of the cave, their ropes secured under rocks, to keep them away from each other. Ket, Hemming and Hothbrodd were dead to the world, still recovering from the long night before. The beast was black and grey, showing its age, and its breath stank like a dead animal. Both of its ears had been torn off and its muzzle had been slashed open countless times, leaving many scars. Its left eye was milky white, the other was the colour of the summer sky. It stared at Offa, smelling his fear. Offa remained lying down, not daring to move. Looking upon the beast, Offa felt a strange sense of familiarity. It was Fenris! But he was old now and wasn't the same cub Offa had known as a child. Fenris was a spirit of the forest, fully grown and mad with hunger. Offa was petrified and couldn't have moved even if he had dared to try.

Fenris turned away from Offa and began sniffing around the burned-out camp-fire, ignoring the three sleeping men. Offa noticed Fenris wasn't alone. There was a pack of wolves with him, trying to get at their rations, including young cubs that were experiencing their first winter. As Offa looked past Fenris' huge stature, he saw the she-wolf approaching the cave. Offa remained still, waiting for them to finish their rations and leave, but then the she-wolf walked over to Ket and began searching him for food, sniffing all about him, whining and crying. Golden-Mane and Bæda awoke from their slumber and began barking from the back of the cave, the noise echoing off the walls.

Ket opened his eyes and found himself face to face with a wolf frothing at the mouth. He jumped back in shock and screamed out loud, frightening the pack. Fearing for their young, the wolves' curiosity turned to aggression. Hemming and Hothbrodd rose to their feet and drew their weapons. The pack began creeping towards the cave entrance, wide-eyed and snarling. Hothbrodd slowly stepped backwards and made his way further into the cave, towards Bæda.

'*What are you doing?*' Hemming asked quietly, trying to keep as still as possible, holding out his seax.

Hothbrodd pushed a rock to one side and released Bæda from his tether. Immediately, Bæda ran at Fenris, but both Fenris and the she-wolf attacked Bæda, while the rest of the pack continued to approach.

'What do we do?' Offa asked, drawing *Stedefæst*.

'Kill them all!' Ket yelled, stepping forward, striking one of the wolves.

Offa had flashbacks to when he was younger, watching as the pack killed Edwin, Leofrīc, Mōna and Bardawulf. Not this time, he thought. Offa screamed with rage, wielding *Stedefæst* through the cold winter air, slashing across a wolf's face, slicing through its whiskers and cutting a fang in half. It yelped and backed away, while the rest of the pack leapt upon the group in a mad frenzy. Golden-Mane was still at the back of the cave, trying to bite through his tether. Offa tried to prevent the wolves from passing him, but there were too many of them. Four managed to pass and headed straight for the defenceless pup. Whilst fighting off the pack, Offa glanced over his shoulder and saw Golden-Mane had become tangled with his tether. The pack was all about him and upon him. Golden-Mane's cries scorned Offa's ears and added to the rage that he now unleashed upon the pack.

Ket, Hemming and Hothbrodd were still fighting off the rest of the pack, while Bæda and Fenris were tearing each other to shreds. Offa noticed the she-wolf lying on the ground, dead. Bæda was on top of Fenris, using his weight to force him to the ground, trying to tear his throat out, but Fenris managed to twist himself free. Snow and ice sprayed the cool air as fangs clashed with fangs and muzzles and ears dripped with gore. Bæda rushed towards Fenris' throat, but Fenris shifted his weight and charged at Bæda, crashing into his shoulder, knocking him to the ground. Bæda rolled out of harm's way and tried attacking again, but Fenris drew back his head and curved in from the side, sinking his fangs into Bæda's soft throat, puncturing a hole in his flesh and pinned him to the ground. Bæda had all the savagery of his wolf ancestors, but all the weaknesses of his mongrel father; he was no match for the wolf. Fenris ripped Bæda's throat out and brought his life to a bloody end.

After Fenris had dropped Bæda's lifeless body to the ground, he turned to Offa, foaming at the mouth; bloodied saliva dripping from his fangs, and stepped forward. His eyes were bulging, his scarred muzzle was wet and bloodied, and his mane bristled with rage. Fenris seemed to have forgotten who Offa was and forgotten the years they had spent together, just the two of them. Fenris had forgotten how they used to sleep in the same room and how Offa used to protect him from Tor. He had forgotten everything. Offa had tried to tame him, but had failed. Fenris remained true to himself, true to his nature; true to what was real, and refused to live under the thrall of man. Fenris was hungry and Offa was meat to him, just another animal to eat. That was primitive law, kill or be killed, eat or be eaten; life was simple for the wolf, unburdened by moral dilemmas.

Fenris took a second step forward, terrifying Offa to his bones, challenging Offa to a fight as if he was a true wolf. Offa's mind flashed back to the time when he sat by Fenris in the forest, teaching him how to howl. Offa wanted Fenris to see him as a friend, the leader of his pack, but now Fenris saw him as nothing more than a threat. Offa trembled whilst stepping backwards, making his way into the cave. Fenris' mane bristled with rage, his muscles tensed and his fangs were revealed to their bloodied roots. Fenris was almost upon him, snarling and lusting for blood. Offa heard his companions yelling and cursing behind him, fighting off the pack. He thought his time had come, when the Fates would cut his life-thread and leave him as carrion for the birds and the beasts, but then Golden-Mane leapt between Offa and Fenris as if back from the dead.

Golden-Mane's coat was wet and covered in dark red gore, his mane bristled, his muscles tensed and he snarled at Fenris, warning him. Golden-Mane had been torn to shreds by the pack, but he yet lived, and the primordial beast raged within him like an inferno. Ket, Hemming and Hothbrodd had slain most of the pack, causing many to retreat. They noticed Fenris stalking Offa and rushed to help. Fenris thought better than to stay and fight a battle he couldn't win, and so he led the remaining members of his pack into the forest and disappeared between the snow-clad trees, leaving the dead members of their pack behind. Golden-Mane stopped barking and seemed dazed and confused. Offa watched as he stumbled along the ground and collapsed into the snow.

'Golden-Mane!' Offa yelled, running towards him, while the others looked on. Offa knelt over him and placed a hand on his ribs. 'Come on, boy, you're alright. You'll live.' Golden-Mane remained lying down, panting heavily, wagging his tail. Offa stroked the top of his head. 'Come on, boy, get up. We've won. We did it.' Tears streamed down Offa's cheeks. 'You saved my life! You can have all of my rations, if you will just get up!'

'Leave him be,' spoke Hothbrodd, gently. 'Let him rest, laddy. Let him rest.'

'No!' Offa snapped. 'He's not going to die. He's too young to die.'

'Dying isn't about young or old,' Hothbrodd answered. 'Death comes to us all. Some die young, some die old, but it's the ones who make their life mean something that gives their life purpose. A mere existence is for the damned, something I know all too well. Golden-Mane refused to live a life of simple existence. He chose to fight. In his sacrifice, he gave his life meaning and purpose. He saved you, Offa. Now you're in his debt. Make your life mean something in return. Now end his pain, laddy. You owe him that much.'

With *Stedefæst* in hand, Offa looked down at Golden-Mane and saw the pain in his big brown eyes. For a moment, Offa saw his eight-legged steed looking back at him. The pain he felt when he cut Brogan's throat was too much to endure for a second time.

'I can't do it,' spoke Offa. '*I'm sorry.*'

'Move aside,' Hothbrodd told him, kneeling down, stroking Golden-Mane's head. 'May the Gods acknowledge your bravery, young pup. May they welcome you into the afterlife.' Hothbrodd's eyes were full of tears. 'May you and Bæda howl into the night sky as brothers.' Tears rolled down Offa's face, while Hothbrodd held a knife to Golden-Mane's throat. 'Goodbye, brave pup. I'll miss you.'

Golden-Mane yelped and kicked his legs, but then silence. Stillness. Golden-Mane was dead. Offa stared into the forest, angry and upset, and stabbed his seax into a tree. He remained silent for most of the day, not speaking a word, yet he was screaming on the inside.

Chapter Twenty Nine
Return to Wēland's Cabin

Wēland's Cabin, Jötunn Forest

It was still light by the time the group arrived at Wēland's cabin, deep in the winter forest. It was a cold day, yet Sunna shone brightly above the forest canopy, illuminating the frozen landscape. Offa, Ket, Hemming and Hothbrodd had come a long way. They were tired and hungry and covered in cuts and bruises. Offa had blisters on his feet and fingertips, and his toes felt frost-bitten. He looked past the snow-covered trees and down the sloping hill where Wēland's cabin stood in a small clearing. Offa noticed one of the cabins, the one he had once stayed in, had collapsed under the weight of the snow. He paused to take a breath, remembering his first time there, the cold air filling his aching lungs; the laughter of ghosts ringing in his ears.

'This way, my lad,' spoke Hemming.

Loud bangs were coming from the workshop and dark smoke coiled to the heavens from a hole in the roof. The famous blacksmith was hard at work. After Hemming had knocked on the door, the noises stopped and the door opened, creaking on its iron hinges.

'Guests?' Wēland asked, surprised to see them. 'At this time of year? You must be raving mad.' Offa noticed he had aged a great deal since they first met six years earlier.

'It's good to see you too, old friend,' Hemming replied. 'Though I wasn't expected to be greeted with a weapon in your hand.'

'This.' Wēland held up a half-forged sword. 'This is a request from King Siegmund of the Nibelungs. Have you heard of him? I call the sword *Gram*.'

'Of course,' Hemming answered. 'I've heard their clan mentioned once or twice.'

'Come, you had better follow me,' spoke Wēland, leaving the sword on the workbench. 'It's freezing, you will catch your death out here.'

Wēland led them to the main cabin. The porch had a bench on it and there were many footprints on the wooden floor-boards, made of dirt and trodden snow. The group followed Wēland inside, where Wudga rose from his chair to greet them.

'Welcome,' spoke Wudga, shaking their hands and embracing Ket as a brother.

There was also a young woman with long blonde hair, dressed in a long-sleeved kirtle and breeches, sitting in a rune-decorated chair by the hearth-fire. Inside the fire was a Yule Log that would burn until the Winter Solstice. She watched them with great interest as they walked into the open space and made their way towards the fire to warm their hands.

'You all remember my daughter, Ælfwynn?' Wēland asked.

Ælfwynn rose to her feet and tossed her long blonde hair over her shoulder. Offa had long forgotten about Ælfwynn, the girl who had once humiliated him in a duel, six years earlier. Her skin was as white as freshly fallen snow, her eyes were as blue as a summer sky, her nose was button-like; and her smile caused Offa's heart to skip beats. There was no doubt about it in Offa's mind, Ælfwynn was ælfsciene - elf-beautiful. She smiled at him, causing warm blood to rush to his face.

'Welcome back, Offa,' spoke Ælfwynn. 'I never thought I would see you again. They say you are a mute, is this true?'

'I only speak when there is something worth saying,' Offa replied.

'Well answered,' spoke Ælfwynn with a smile, revealing her dimpled cheeks.

Ælfwynn noticed her father staring at her, and so she left the room with the promise of food and drink for their guests.

'Make yourselves at home,' spoke Wēland, 'you've had a long journey.' Offa was happy to sit down by the fire and rest his tired legs, when he noticed Wēland looking at him. 'I've seen you from time to time, Offa, watching me train the young Cnihts. Watching them living as werewolves, something you yourself never managed to achieve.' Offa sat in silence, once again reminded of his shame. 'It is never too late to achieve honour in one's life, young cub. While there is breath in your lungs and desire in your heart, you can do the unthinkable. A man must never give up on himself. The Gods don't judge a man by how far he falls in life, but how he gets back to his feet.'

'I thought our fate is already set?' Ket asked.

'True,' Wēland replied, 'but if the Fates had given you a poor existence, say perhaps you were born a slave, wouldn't you do all you could to defy them?'

'Yes, I would,' Ket replied, nodding. 'I would kill my masters and forge my own destiny.'

'But how would you know that wasn't to be your fate all along?' Wēland asked.

'I don't know,' Ket answered. 'I suppose it's impossible to know.'

'We should all try to live the best life we can and do some good in this world,' spoke Wēland. 'One is never too old or too weak to change their life.'

'That is why we are here,' Hemming added. 'Offa seeks your help.'

After Ket and Hemming had finished telling Wēland everything that had happened between the Angles and Saxons and the challenge Offa had made, Ælfwynn returned with food and drinks. Offa was so hungry he could have eaten a horse. He reached for some bread.

'Not you, young cub. If you want my help, then you need to come with me,' spoke Wēland, leading Offa outside. Once again the snow began to fall and an icy wind blew in Offa's face. He was cold and hungry and longed to be inside with the others, in front of the roaring firc. 'So, you have agreed to fight the Saxons,' spoke Wēland with his back against the wind. 'That is either very brave or very stupid. Perhaps both. I can't say I'm surprised though. You have a fire burning within your chest, Offa. You have a sense of destiny about you. Any fool can see that. Finally, after all of these wasted years, you have discovered something greater than yourself; something worth fighting for. A noble cause, indeed. I admire that.' Wēland pointed to the heavens. 'Wōden will admire that. Let me see your weapon.'

Offa drew *Stedefæst* and handed it to Wēland.

'Ah, a beauty,' spoke Wēland. 'The craftsmanship is extraordinary. Forged by dwarves they say. Owned by Wōden himself, before being passed to his earthly son. And now it is passed to you. Let me tell you something, young cub: I will agree to teach you, to train you the best I can in the short time we have, but I'll tell you what I tell all the cubs who come here to learn. I don't care who your father is or what God you have in your bloodline, your hide belongs to me now. You will do what I tell you, when I tell you, and you will do it without complaint. Do you understand?'

'Yes,' Offa answered, nodding his head and rubbing his hands up and down his arms.

'Now I know circumstances are different with you. You never did earn a wolf coat and you have missed out on your training. You are a failure, an embarrassment to your father and an embarrassment to your people. Yet for some reason you now feel ready to rise and become a man. And I have only a few days to train you. And you're not fighting one, but two men. One, the son of a King; the other, their greatest warrior. Let me tell you something about Meaca and Krampus. At the age of twelve, Meaca was to stand before his people and face his older brother in a fight to the death. The two of them had been close, but each was a threat on the path to their father's throne, a gift-stool built of flesh and bone. When the night came and hundreds of folks had gathered to watch the spectacle, Meaca appeared before the crowd, holding up his brother's decapitated head. Before the fight was to take place, Meaca had crept into his brother's dwelling, stabbed him through the heart and took his head. Afterwards, Meaca's father named him leader of the hearth-troops.'

Wēland spat into the snow and wiped his mouth on his sleeve.

'Krampus has a reputation well-earned. Born amongst the Goths, he was only a lad when he witnessed his parents slaughtered by the Huns. The Goths turned to the Romans for help, but they were betrayed, starved and humiliated. The Goths were so hungry that Krampus was sold to the Romans in exchange for a dead dog, but Krampus had a reputation for violence and his life as a common slave was short-lived. At the age of nine, he killed his masters in cold blood. Upon his capture, he was beaten almost to the point of death, but one man saw the spark in his eyes and saved his life. Soon after, he was sold into a gladiator school. Krampus proved to be the best, growing up in a world of violence, slaying great warriors, giants and strange beasts from the darkest shadows of the Empire. They say every life he took consumed a part of his soul until there was nothing left.

'The day finally came when Krampus bought his freedom and joined the Germanic auxiliaries who fought on behalf of Rome. During the Roman civil wars, Krampus' army was sent to battle by their Roman commander. Krampus and the clans of Germania, more beasts than men, charged into the opposing Roman army, annihilating all who stood before them. Upon victory, Krampus and the blood-drunk warriors by his side turned their attention towards their Roman commanders. In a mad frenzy they charged the Roman centuries, who had stood idly by, watching as brave Saxons and Goths fell at the hands of the enemy. It was a massacre. Roman corpses were stripped naked and hung from trees, their weapons and armour burned. The leader of the Saxons was no other than Meaca, son of King Ēadgils. They have both built their reputations on the corpses of others and now they want to throw your lifeless body onto the pile of broken bones. I'm going to be honest with you, young cub: there is only one way you are going to walk away from this fight without being greeted by one of Wōden's maidens.'

Wēland spat into the snow and handed him *Stedefæst*.

'You must enter the fight as a wraith, as Death itself. You must learn to give up your humanity, your soul. You must be born again, like when you were thrust from your mother's womb, kicking and screaming, full of life, covered in blood and gore, ready to take on the world as new. You must give yourself entirely to Wōden and become your other self, the beast within; the beast that has always been there, bubbling at the surface, waiting to be freed from its fetters. When you first entered the forest, alongside Haakon and the others, you joined the army of the dead, but you never left the forest. Your soul is still trapped between the realm of the living and the realm of the dead. You must embrace what you are. That which is not living cannot be killed and must not fear death. If you fight as a lad, you will die. If you fight as a swordsman, you will die. But if you are fearless and embrace the wolf and fight as the undead, then, Wōden willing, you might be the last man standing.'

After re-entering the cabin, Ælfwynn greeted Offa with food, water and a beautiful smile.

'Thank you,' spoke Offa, taking the plate from her hands. Ælfwynn smiled as she walked away.

Ket, Hemming and Hothbrodd were enjoying their food and drink, eating like a pack of stray dogs. Offa was sitting by the fire, beside Hothbrodd on the hard wooden floor, watching the Yule Log burning in the flames, when Wēland entered the room.

'Eat hearty, young cub, and pray to Wōden,' spoke Wēland, 'for tonight your training shall begin.'

Ælfwynn had prepared bread and cheese, a true delight for a hungry stomach. Offa knew his training would be hard, and so he ate as much as possible, savouring every mouthful.

'I'm sorry to hear of your brother,' Ælfwynn said to Ket, placing food on the table. 'Wīg was a good man and a good warrior.' Ælfwynn paused for a moment. Offa looked up at her and noticed her glazed eyes. 'He was my friend,' she said with great sadness. 'I will miss him.'

Ket lifted his head and forced a weak smile out of politeness.

'I remember when he first came here,' spoke Wēland, leaning against the wall, 'a young lad full of life, eager to learn and impress his older brother. He was a skilled fighter and will be missed.'

With full stomachs, Offa, Ket, Hemming and Hothbrodd settled down in front of the fire to get some much needed sleep. It had been a long day. Offa was tossing and turning, trying to get comfortable on the hard wooden floor, listening to Hemming and Hothbrodd snoring and farting. He had finally fallen asleep and was dreaming about flying through the clouds on a winged serpent, before crashing through the trees on his way back down to the ground. Once he hit the ground and realised he wasn't hurt, that's when he opened his eyes to find Wēland standing over him, in the pitch dark.

'Come, young cub,' spoke Wēland, throwing off his covers. 'Time to get up. Fate waits for no man.' It was early in the morning, or late at night, Offa wasn't sure which. He wrapped himself in his coat, stretched his arms and made his way outside. It was still dark and the snow continued to fall over the silent land. Winter held the forest in a tight grip, trying to freeze the life out of all living things. Wēland was wrapped in a bear pelt, his breath freezing on the cold night air. 'Take your coat off, lad,' Wēland ordered.

'But I'll freeze to death out here,' Offa complained, shivering.

'Listen to me, young cub, you are going to be fighting two

men at Monster's Gate,' spoke Wēland. 'You need to be able to move like the wind. You must learn to dance, to be faster than your enemy, or you will catch your death, that's for certain. Now take your coat off. It won't protect you in battle. Saxon swords will cut through it like a pack of wolves on a deer carcass.' Reluctantly, Offa removed his coat and dropped it to the snow. He now stood in the dead of winter, late at night, in the middle of the forest, wearing nothing but a sleeveless jerkin and breeches. He was shivering uncontrollably and found it hard to breathe. 'Learn to embrace the cold, young cub. Don't fight it. The cold is the enemy of the Saxons. An enemy of your enemy is a friend.'

'I'll t-t-try,' Offa mumbled through chattering teeth.

'The Saxons will be wearing large fur coats,' Wēland continued. 'They will be slow and restricted, yet you will be fast and unfazed by the winter cold.' Wēland took a good look at him. 'You're a big lad. Strong, I see. You will have as much grace and skill as a blind one-legged troll, whose mother was also his sister and whose father was also his brother, but we can use that to our advantage. The Saxons will expect you to fight like a trained warrior and will be thrown off their game when they see you don't fight as expected, but remain raw and unpredictable, like a wounded animal. Now, what has been your first lesson, young cub?' Offa was shivering beyond control and his back ached from tensing. He was still trying to figure out if what Wēland had said was possible, could someone's mother also be his sister, and his father be his brother? 'Find your tongue!' Wēland demanded.

'T-t-to e-embrace th-the c-c-cold,' Offa answered.

'Good, you understand,' spoke Wēland. 'You're a quick learner and aren't as dim-witted as they say you are. Now, I want you to go over to the barn there and find the axe. Then I want you to go into the forest and bring back as much fire-wood as you can before the sun rises and my roosters awake. And make sure it's dry. Wet wood is about as useful as a blunt sword.'

Wēland picked Offa's coat from off the ground, and smiled. He looked quite pleased with himself, leaving Offa in the cold, alone. Offa was standing in the snow, almost frozen to his bones. He looked through the giant snowflakes as they fell from the night-time sky, looking deep into the mysterious forest, knowing Fenris was still out there somewhere, waiting in the shadows.

Chapter Thirty
Wolfsangle

Wēland's Cabin, Jötunn Forest

After a long cold night, Offa awoke to the smell of frying swine flesh floating throughout the cabin and the sound of crowing cockerels scaring away the malevolent fairies. Ket and Hemming were eating their morning meal and Hothbrodd was sitting in front of the fire, pushing the Yule Log further into the flames, still brooding over his dogs.

'Eat well, my lad,' spoke Hemming, gesturing to Offa's plate. 'Wēland is going to break you today. He will break you down, before building you back up again.'

'Thank you,' Offa replied, 'that's just what I want to hear the first thing in the morning.'

Offa was exhausted and needed to go outside to relieve himself in the snow. He was putting his coat on, when Wēland grunted from the other side of the room. With a sulk, Offa tossed his coat to Hemming and wore only his sleeveless jerkin. After relieving himself outside, in the morning mist, Offa noticed Ælfwynn smiling at him whilst walking past the workshop with a live chicken in her arms. Offa felt humiliated standing there with his manhood in hand, and so he quickly rushed back inside.

'Take a seat, Offa,' spoke Wudga. 'Eat your fill. It's going to be a long day for you.'

'Though not so much for us,' Hemming laughed, looking quite proud of himself, stuffing more food into his mouth.

Offa took a seat next to Hothbrodd, who stank like a wet dog, and never spoke a word.

'I'm sorry for your dogs,' spoke Offa, softly.

The others looked on quietly, while Hothbrodd poked at his food.

'Don't worry about your dogs,' spoke Hemming. 'They were fighting dogs. They only had one destination.'

'Yes, doggie Valhalla,' said Ket, adding humour to the table.

'Doghalla!' Hemming yelled, bringing a smile to Hothbrodd's disgruntled face.

'I bet they're all gnawing bones and sniffing each other's arses in the afterlife,' Ket joked.

Moments later, after Wēland and Wudga made their way outside, Hemming took the opportunity to ask Offa about Ælfwynn.

'So, my lad, what do you think of Wēland's young lass? She's about your age and unmarried.'

'I've seen the way she looks at you,' Ket laughed, but Offa never said a word. He had always felt uncomfortable around the fairer sex.

Wēland re-entered the cabin. 'Your training is about to begin.'

Offa stood outside, in the deep snow, dressed in his sleeveless jerkin and breeches, with *Stedefæst* secured in its sheath. Wēland was dressed in a bear pelt and Ælfwynn was wrapped in a long red cloak, complete with hood. The land was cold and a thick mist clung to the forest, allowing them to see only a few feet in front of them. Wēland nodded at his daughter. She then walked over to Offa with a chicken held close to her chest. She looked him in the eye and gently reached out, drawing *Stedefæst* from its sheath, sighing as she did so. Offa's heart was racing. Ælfwynn held the chicken tightly and raised the pointed tip of *Stedefæst* to its throat.

'For your blood, I thank thee, young chicken,' spoke Ælfwynn. 'I now give your life-force to the All-Father, Wōden, God of death and fury. I give your bones to the earth and your flesh to Nerthuz, mother of men.'

Offa watched as Ælfwynn sliced the sharpened edge of *Stedefæst* against the chicken's throat, allowing its blood to flow into a bucket of black paint. She then passed *Stedefæst* to her father and mixed the blood and paint together with a stick, before asking Offa to reveal his bare chest. Offa did as he was told, dropping his jerkin to the ground.

'Do you know what a wolfsangle is, young cub?' Wēland asked, wiping the chicken's blood from *Stedefæst* with a cloth.

'Yes,' Offa answered. 'It is a runic symbol that represents the wolf trap.'

'More than that, the wolfsangle is a powerful ancient rune, passed down from Wōden to his greatest priests and most dedicated warriors,' spoke Wēland. 'It is the symbol of primitive law, of the archaic origins of man and beast. It is the symbol of the werewolf, one of Wōden's most powerful and revered warriors. A werewolf is a man so in touch with nature, with the Gods and the Earth Mother, that he can call upon the wolf to enter his skin-shield and possess every part of his being, transforming him from a flawed, imperfect warrior, to becoming something greater; something primordial. A werewolf is a magical creature, an almost unstoppable predator, with heightened hearing, smell, vision, speed, agility, strength and courage. He is fearless and ferocious, unkind to his enemies and unforgiving, yet he is not a beast of darkness. A werewolf knows kinship, love and loyalty and does all he can to protect his pack. Are you now ready to have the wolfsangle revealed to you?'

'Yes,' Offa answered, nodding his head, shivering.

'I can't hear you!'

'YES!'

'Are you prepared to give your flesh to the forest and your soul to our lord, Wōden?' Wēland asked.

'YES!'

'Then it shall be revealed to you,' spoke Ælfwynn, stepping forward, painting Offa's chest. 'I mark thee, Offa, son of King Wǣrmund, with the wolfsangle, the mark of the werewolf.'

Wēland handed Offa *Stedefæst* and a wooden shield that had been painted black. Both father and daughter turned around and walked back inside the cabin, leaving Offa alone, in the fog. The winter wind was hissing in his ears and he heard howling all around him, echoing into the snow-clad forest. Offa was nervous and didn't know what to expect. He held his bone-protector close to his body, learning to shield himself from the bitter winds, whilst holding *Stedefæst* in his other hand. He looked over the rim of his shield and scanned the surrounding forest, trying to see through the mist. The howls were getting closer. Offa heard the sound of footsteps crunching in the snow and movement all around him, coming from different directions; though he had yet to see anything. He wielded *Stedefæst* as hard as he could, the blade sang as it cut through the cold winter air.

Offa paused for a moment and listened again. He heard something. He looked up and gasped when he saw many shadows stalking him from beyond the trees. At least half-a-dozen wolves slowly revealed themselves through the fog of the falling snow, and Offa soon realised these were no ordinary wolves. They were werewolves, wild men who lived in the forest, hunted as a pack and were each marked with the wolfs-angle. They ate only meat and slept in caves to escape the elements. They weren't men, nor were they wolves, but something in between; something otherworldly. Their leader stopped and stared at Offa, sniffing at the air, trying to catch his scent on the wind. To Offa's surprise, he then stood on two legs like a man and stepped forward. Offa couldn't see his face through his wolf pelt and so his features remained a mystery.

The rest of the pack began to gather around, crawling on their bare hands and feet, growling and snarling. None of them showed any signs of discomfort in the cold. The wolf-man stood face to face with Offa, staring at him from behind his mask, his head tilted to one side; his long hair hanging loose. Offa stood his ground. His heart was thumping and his legs trembled. After the pack's leader had judged Offa's worth, he removed a part of his wolf pelt to reveal a sword and shield. Offa knew what was to happen and had forgotten about the cold and the howling winter winds and focused solely on the stranger who stood menacingly before him.

The wild-man raised his chin, stuck his nose in the air and howled, but this was no mournful lament, but the noise a wolf makes before a feeding frenzy. For a moment Offa lost himself. The howl was a calling to him, taking him back to the time he spent with Fenris, teaching him how to howl. It took him further back, to a time when the worlds were young and man had yet to step foot upon the soil of Middle-earth, to a time of beasts, when the primordial song echoed throughout the forest.

Suddenly the wolf-man charged at Offa with a harrowing snarl. Offa held up his shield to take the blow, but his opponent was strong, far stronger than an ordinary man. The impact sent shock-waves through Offa's left arm and chest, causing him to stumble backwards. The pack began jumping and dancing all around them, growling and snarling. Offa managed to keep his balance. He stepped forward, wielding *Stedefæst* towards the wolf-man's skull with one hand, while holding his shield in the other. The man from the forest parried the blow whilst grunting like an animal. He rushed at Offa, hitting his shield so hard it knocked him to the ground. Offa was lying flat on his back, in the snow; the cold seeping into his skin. He looked up at the sky, watching as the snowflakes floated and danced on the air; he saw blues, whites and purples.

The pack pounced on Offa, sinking their hard teeth into his arms and legs. He could feel them all over him, biting into his flesh, pulling his hair and shredding his jerkin apart with their teeth. Offa saw black fur, black expressionless wolf masks, teeth and blood. He had dropped his sword and shield and was kicking his legs and waving his arms, trying to throw them off. One of them sank its teeth into Offa's throat. He tried calling for help, but he couldn't make a sound.

As Offa laid there, being eaten alive by the pack, a strange feeling fell over him. His heartbeat was rapid and he felt his skin burning from the cold snow. Looking up at the falling snowflakes, Offa felt alive. He knew then what Hothbrodd had talked about, when he told him the story of the Rottweiler and how he burst into a violent rage when his life was threatened. As Offa faced certain death, lying in the snow and ice, he remembered the wolfsangle painted on his chest and then something strange happened. Offa sprang back to life as if back from the dead. He had somehow called upon the wolf, and the primordial beast within him awoke, stripping him of fear and human weakness. It wasn't something he thought about or believed in, it just happened.

Offa used his legs to shake one of them off, then kneed another in the head, before kicking two others in the face. He jerked his entire body, trying to wriggle free from their grip, but they were still biting his arms and throat. Offa managed to wrap a leg around a werewolf's throat, the one that was biting his left arm, and forced it to the ground, trying to crush its windpipe with his thigh muscles. He then used his left hand to jam a thumb into the wolf's eye that was biting into his right arm, forcing it to release him and back away. One of them still held Offa down by sinking its teeth into his throat. Offa then used his fingers to pull open the werewolf's mouth, wrenching its jaw wide open, forcing it to release him. Suddenly Offa was free and reached for his seax that rested in the snow. He stood to his feet, breathing heavily, and pointed *Stedefæst* at them, daring any to step closer. The pack surrounded him, still on their hands and feet, snapping and snarling; all except the wolf-man who still stood on two legs, watching.

'Wyrd oft neroð unfægne eorl þonne his ellen dēah,' spoke the stranger in a hideous voice. 'The Wyrd Sisters, those weavers of fate, often save an undoomed hero as long as his courage is good.'

Offa said nothing in return and remained standing his ground, trying to catch his breath. The wolf-man turned to leave and Offa watched as the pack followed him, crawling away into the fog and disappeared back into the forest.

Later that day, after Ælfwynn had nursed Offa's superficial wounds and stitched his clothing the best she could, Wudga informed him that his training would continue shortly. Offa walked back outside, into the falling snow, using his shield to protect himself from the winter winds. Ælfwynn had joined them and was wrapped in her rose-red cloak, with the hood covering her long braided hair. Both Wēland and Ælfwynn carried a sword and shield.

'Earlier today,' spoke Wēland, 'you were attacked by a pack of werewolves. They sank their fangs into your flesh and began to devour you. Yet here you stand, stronger. You were afraid, yet you overcame your fear and rose to the challenge. You learned valuable lessons. Fear is your friend. Fear is what makes you strong. Use it well. Your enemies will try to intimidate you. They will scream at you. They will make the blood flowing through your veins ripple from the sound, making your muscles weak and your legs tremble. You will learn to embrace fear, absorb it into your inner being and turn it into aggression. The more your enemies try to intimidate you, the more ferocious you will become. Do you understand?'

'I understand,' Offa answered, nodding his head.

'Today you learned the importance of balance,' Wēland continued. 'You lost your feet and the pack devoured you, just as your opponents will at Monster's Gate.' Both Wēland and Ælfwynn began to walk circles around him, crunching through the snow; their eyes fixed on him. 'You must remain on your feet at all times, young cub, or you will die. Every action has a reaction. You are big and strong, but don't be a fool. Don't try to take their blows on your shield and expect to keep your footing. Learn to take the impact. Move your legs. Take a step back as they strike your shield and be aware of your surroundings at all times. Do not trip on anything and don't ever lose your balance.'

Wēland walked behind Offa, while Ælfwynn stepped in front. Offa couldn't take his eyes from her. Wēland was talking, but his words became a blur. Ælfwynn's beauty was too much. Offa was under her spell. Ælfwynn had been blessed by Frīge with charm, charisma and elf-beauty. Her golden hair blew in the wind and her deep blue eyes were fixed on Offa like a cat before devouring a helpless mouse. She was so beautiful, so delicate, yet so deadly. Suddenly a bright light flashed in Offa's eyes and a bolt of lightning travelled to the back of his skull.

'I told you to pay attention!' Ælfwynn yelled after punching Offa hard in the face. 'Pay attention or *die*,' she said with sorrow in her sweet voice.

'You will be fighting two men,' Wēland continued, now walking in front. 'You must not let either one out of your sight for a moment, or they will have your leg off.'

Ælfwynn tried stepping behind him, but Offa was taking small steps back, keeping them both in view. Suddenly Ælfwynn screamed like a Valkyrie and the two of them, father and daughter, charged at Offa with their shields, trying to knock him off-balance. Offa took a step back, placed his weight on his back leg and took the impact. He stumbled backwards, before throwing his weight forward, using his shield to knock Ælfwynn into the snow. Wēland was also knocked back several feet. Ælfwynn rose to her feet as quick as a cat and ran at Offa, changing direction, forcing him to twist his body to meet her advance. She jumped at him and tried to strike, but Offa's shield caught her attack. Offa tried pushing her away with the heel of his boot, but she grabbed his foot and threw his weight to the side, crouched and placed her seax between his legs.

'These belong to me now,' she whispered.

The three of them fought long and hard, practising in the wind and snow, long after Sunna had fled the wolves chasing her across the heavens. It was cold and dark and the silver moonlight gleamed from their swords as they clashed. Wēland taught Offa how to control the ebb and flow of battle and how to manoeuvre his opponents to expose their weaknesses, before striking. Training was intense, yet Offa no longer felt the winter cold biting at his flesh. He was fast and manoeuvred well, despite the cold. Offa had spent many years watching the Cnihts practice sword-play at Wēland's cabin and had learned a great deal, but watching and doing are two completely different things, and Offa was having a lesson he would never forget. Wēland and Ælfwynn spent most of the night teaching Offa his flaws, then showing him how to correct himself. Though he learned a great deal, being shown just how terrible he really was worried him.

Offa was taught how to hold his shield correctly whilst holding his seax in his right hand. Wēland had explained that a sword is more effective when it's held with two hands, but the shield was necessary to take the initial blows, which would be faster and harder than later ones, when his opponents will begin to tire. Offa was taught how to parry blows, search for weaknesses, how to use a broadsword and shield, and how to use a seax in close combat, as well as defend himself without a shield and attack at the same time. He was taught how to hold an enemy's shield with both hands, charging his opponent backwards, to throw him off-guard, before freeing his right hand and using his seax to stab the back of his opponent's head or neck.

Wēland and Ælfwynn attacked Offa at the same time, conditioning him to think fast and act without too much thought. Offa was taught to attack toes, feet, ankles, shins, knees, thighs, stomachs, chests, arms, elbows, fingers, shoulders, ears, eyes, nose, mouth, throat, skull, and to not be afraid to slice off a bollock or two. Spending years in the forest had kept Offa fit, strong and naturally hardened, but nothing had prepared him for Wēland's training.

Offa had nearly broken his arm. His ribs were bruised and all of his knuckles on his left hand, as well as his left elbow, had been battered with unrelenting blows. He was forced to swing a sword that was too heavy for him in order to build confidence and strong arms. They say through intense training a young warrior could develop one arm longer than the other. Offa thought it was an exaggeration, but he was now convinced. Offa's training was tough, but as he grew stronger, his weapons became lighter and he learned how to use *Stedefæst* with a little grace. Wēland and Ælfwynn worked long into the night with him, exhausting him, testing him, pushing him, and forging him into something of worth; into the warrior he needed to become.

Chapter Thirty One
Most Primal

Wēland's Cabin, Jötunn Forest

The Yule Log burned brightly in the hearth-fire and the smell of cooked rabbit and vegetables floated throughout the cabin, reminding Offa of Angeln. Ket, Hemming and Hothbrodd had been drinking mulled apple cider all night and spirits were high. Offa sat by the fire, warming his hands over the hot flames, watching Wēland join the others in a game of Tæfl. Offa had never learned how to play, and so he stayed by the fire and watched from a distance. Ælfwynn joined them and helped herself to the bread she had baked fresh that morning. Ket and Hemming were sharing jokes and trying to figure out each other's word games.

'I am all alone,' spoke Ket, 'wounded by iron and scarred by swords and fire. Often I see battle, yet I am fearless as I face the enemy. I don't expect retirement from warfare until my body is completely broken. I am often knocked about and sword-bitten. Hard edged things made by the blacksmith's hammer attack me with hatred in their hearts, yet I am innocent in all things. I have never been able to find a wicca or wicce who could make me feel better. Instead, the sword gashes all over my body grow larger with each day and night.'

'A shield!' Hemming yelled, slamming his cup onto the table, spilling his cider. 'That's the best you've got?' He laughed. 'I have a good one for you. I am a wondrous creature for women in expectation, a service for neighbours. I harm none of the villages, except my slayer alone. My stem is erect. I stand up in bed, hairy somewhere down below. A comely peasant's daughter grips at me, attacks me in my redness, plunders my head, confines me in a stronghold, feels my encounter directly; woman with braided hair. Wet be that eye.'

They all laughed, spitting food and drink over the table, ruining the remaining bread, trying to guess the answer to the riddle.

'I have no idea,' spoke Ælfwynn, failing to hide her amusement.

They all had a good laugh, all except Hothbrodd.

'The answer is an onion, my dear,' answered Hemming.

'How we laugh and joke,' spoke Hothbrodd, 'but this time of year is no laughing matter. Yule is much more than jokes by the fire, singing and honeyed treats. Yule is the celebration of one cycle coming to an end and the start of another. It will soon be the Winter Solstice, the longest and coldest of nights, when the veil between the realm of the living and the dead is thinnest and it is possible to communicate with our ancestors. Through a child's eyes, mistletoe, holly, ivy and wreaths are pretty decorations, but they are a protection from what is outside, hiding in the forest. Yule is a time when unspeakable beasts cross into the world of the living and Wōden rides the night sky on his chariot, pulled along by black hounds on one of his Wild Hunts, looking for monsters to kill. Listen carefully and you can hear the voices of ghosts, goblins and werewolves screaming in the winter winds and storms. The Night of the Dead approaches and we are in the middle of the forest, a forest teeming with blood-thirsty creatures and restless spirits. Yule is a time to fear!'

While her father and his guests drank and played Tæfl, Offa and Ælfwynn left the cabin and made their way into the forest, where icicles as long as swords hung beneath stiff branches. The forest was beautiful at night, ice-clad and mysterious. Moonlight shone down from above, lighting their path to the lake, and the stars were flickering like candles in the wind. The frozen lake remained unbroken as though it had been there since before the time of man. Fallen branches were trapped in the solid ice and life was nowhere to be found.

'Isn't it wonderful, Offa?' Ælfwynn asked with a smile. 'Even at night, the forest is enchanting, calling you, whispering your name on the cold winds; the moon watching over us and the stars telling us tales of heroes and monsters. Everything is frozen, like a cocoon waiting to burst into life.'

'I have spent most of my life in this forest,' spoke Offa, look-ing across the frozen lake. 'I have seen many things, many shapes and colours, but nothing attracts me more than when the land is frozen and the trees seem blue under the glow of the moonlight. I like to feel the cold air in my lungs, to see the ice sparkle and my breath floating on the cold damp air. I love the forest. It's the place I feel most alive.'

'Look,' spoke Ælfwynn, pointing to a small flame that had appeared over the frozen lake.

'A fairy light,' Offa told her. 'No good thing has ever come from following mysterious lights at night.'

'Come, Offa,' Ælfwynn said, reaching out to him. 'I'm intrigued.'

'Are you mad?' Offa asked.

'It will be safe,' Ælfwynn reassured him. 'Probably.'

Offa trusted her judgement, and so the two of them walked together hand in hand, stepping delicately over the frozen lake, following the mysterious light. She held onto Offa tightly, fearing she might slip on the smooth ice. They both knew if they were to fall in, neither one would be able to make it back to Wēland's cabin alive. Offa's boots were heavy as they crossed, taking one step at a time. The wind was cold and hissed in their ears and their lips were dry as they walked across, being careful of where they placed their feet. As they approached the flickering blue light, it disappeared, only to reappear further across the lake.

'Nearly halfway,' spoke Ælfwynn. 'Don't worry, we're going to make it.'

Offa heard the ice rumbling beneath their feet like a brewing storm. His confidence began to betray him and he started to panic.

'Let's hurry,' he said, looking down at the ice, where little trapped pockets of air ran under their feet, trapped by the ice, before shooting out of sight. 'The ice is thinning!'

'This was a bad idea,' spoke Ælfwynn, walking faster. 'We need to get off this ice. Now!'

The light had disappeared and the lake began groaning beneath them like an angry bear woken up during winter. Small cracks were forming at their feet, travelling like a thunderbolt under the ice.

'Run!' Offa yelled, letting go of Ælfwynn's hand. 'Run!'

The two of them ran for their lives, struggling with every step over the frozen lake. Ælfwynn was in front and Offa saw her red cloak trailing on the ice behind her, when he slipped and crashed to his knees. He got back to his feet without Ælfwynn realising he had fallen. Ælfwynn reached the far side, threw herself into the soft snow and looked over her shoulder.

'Come on, Offa!' she roared. The ice was breaking at his feet. With one big leap, Offa threw himself to the side of Ælfwynn, where they both laid in the deep snow and tried catching their breath. Offa laid there for a moment, in the moon-flooded land, looking up at the stars, thinking about what could have been, when Ælfwynn started to laugh.

'You're mad,' Offa told her.

'We all need a little madness sometimes,' Ælfwynn replied with a smile, 'a reminder that we're still alive.' Offa turned on his side and looked into her eyes. He had never seen anything more beautiful. She stared back at him. 'You know, Offa, you're kind of good looking. Have you ever been with a woman?' Offa's heart began thumping and he didn't know what to say. Ælfwynn was a Swan-Maiden and had sworn her vows to Wōden, to be his wife and his instrument of death. No man could touch the naked flesh of a Swan-Maiden and live to tell of it. Ælfwynn rolled onto her stomach and stared at Offa, looking deep into his soul. 'My flesh belongs to the Gods, Offa..., *dare you defy them?*'

Ælfwynn was an enchantress and Offa was drawn to her like a moth to a flame. He longed for her touch, to smell her hair, to kiss her skin. She stroked his face with her hand, it was soft and sent lightning throughout his body. Offa was nervous and pulled away.

'*I'm sorry,*' he whispered.

'Don't be afraid,' spoke Ælfwynn, touching his arm. 'A warrior shouldn't go into battle having never felt the touch of a woman.' She gazed into his eyes and could feel his breath upon her face. '*A warrior should go into battle with the scent of a woman all over him.*'

Ælfwynn leaned forward and kissed Offa on the lips, blissfully unaware of the danger that slowly approached, creeping over the ice-encrusted snow, hunting in deadly silence. Offa heard a moan, almost a whimper of excitement, followed by an horrifying growl. Ælfwynn turned from Offa and screamed. Offa rose to his feet and drew *Stedefæst*. He turned around, with his back to the lake, and there, standing before them, was a fiend of darkness. Fenris had returned!

Ælfwynn stood beside Offa, while the pack slowly closed in, their eyes glowing in the dark; their fangs dripping with saliva. The wolves had no choice, there was no malice or cunning, no thought for consequence. They needed meat to survive. Offa and Ælfwynn were meat. It was primitive law. At the front of the pack stood Fenris, savage and wild, frothing at the mouth, half mad with hunger. His blind eye shone milky-white and his blue eye turned red with blood-lust. The hairs on the back of Offa's neck stood on end and his arms and legs trembled. *Stedefæst* gleamed under the moonlight, its sharp edge pointed at Fenris. Fenris stood his ground, his mane bristling with rage.

Offa loved Fenris. Offa was the only one who fed Fenris and gave him a home when no one else would. It pained him to now stand before his friend, holding out the dwarf-wrought sword. Fenris stepped towards Offa with a terrifying snarl. Offa saw it in his eyes, Fenris no longer knew who Offa was. In a strange way, it was a comfort for Offa, for he could never have harmed Fenris or been the one to strike him down, but the young boy and the wolf cub who met in the forest all those years before no longer existed. Their friendship had disappeared like a rain-cloud on a summer's day. Offa had to protect Ælfwynn now.

The lake behind them creaked and groaned. Ælfwynn gripped Offa's arm, sinking her fingernails into his flesh. Behind Fenris was the rest of the pack, their eyes glowing like red-hot coals; their warm breath visible on the cold air, waiting for the feeding frenzy to begin. Offa's knees were weak, his palms were sweaty and his shoulders were heavy. With *Stedefæst* in hand, Offa was no longer afraid. There was no time to be scared, no time to panic, no time for human weakness. It was primitive law, kill or be killed. Darkness surrounded Offa. Surrounded them both. Offa's heart pumped warm blood into his arms and legs, his muscles tensed, his eyes remained focused; his mind sharp. He looked Fenris in the eye.

'Come on!' Offa roared, his voice echoing between the frozen trees, carried by the howling winds.

Fenris leapt forward, all teeth and muscle, and sank his fangs deep into Offa's flesh, clenching his enormous jaws around

Offa's badly scarred forearm, causing him to drop *Stedefæst*. The impact knocked Ælfwynn into the snow. Offa screamed, but it wasn't a fearful scream, but a primal scream. A roar! Offa came alive. He used his left hand to hold the top of Fenris' skull and pushed his thumb into his blind eye, forcing Fenris to release him.

'Kill them all!' Ælfwynn screamed, rising to her feet, attacking the rest of the pack.

Blood sprayed into the snow and ice as Ælfwynn screamed like a Valkyrie, mad with fury, and chased the remaining wolves, causing them to scatter; terrified at her harrowing scream. Yet more terrifying was the sound of the wounded wolf crying at her feet.

With Offa's seax resting on the ground, Fenris ran towards Offa and leapt at him, knocking him to the ground and attempted to tear his throat out. Offa used both hands to hold Fenris back by his thick mane. Fenris' jaws snapped in Offa's face, threatening to tear his flesh from the bone. Offa could smell Fenris' stinking breath. Offa knew in his heart, if he was to die, then he would go down fighting and earn his place in Valhalla, amongst his ancestors. Offa roared in defiance and used every bit of strength he had to roll over and place himself on top of Fenris. Still holding his mane, Offa pulled Fenris up and stood to his feet. Fenris was so large, his hind legs still touched the ground. Fenris shook his body, trying to break free, but Offa was strong and began to squeeze around Fenris' throat; all the while screaming his lungs out. Tears flowed down Offa's face and his blood was boiling, causing his skin to sweat. His organs felt as if they were being cooked on the inside and everything became a blur.

Offa screamed and saw nothing but fur, bloodshot eyes, snarling teeth and blood. As the blur started to come back into focus, Offa realised he was down on the blood-splattered ground, on his hands and knees, resting in the pink snow, kneeling beside Fenris. Fenris was lying on the ground, in a pool of his own blood, covered in gaping wounds. His legs were twitching, yet his eyes had rolled into the back of his skull. Fenris was dead! In Offa's hand was *Stedefæst*, dripping with warm blood. He didn't even remember picking it up. Offa watched as the blood rolled from the tip of his seax and melted the snow.

Ælfwynn crouched beside Offa and placed a hand on his shoulder. They were both shaking with blood-rush and a single tear rolled down Offa's cheek. Without saying a word, Ælfwynn wiped the tear with her hand. Offa raised his head and looked her in the eye. She had blood splattered across her face, her blonde hair was blowing gently over her shoulder; her mouth glistened with sparkling teeth and her lips were red and inviting. Offa felt a stir deep within his inner being, a primordial calling. His heart thumped when Ælfwynn leaned towards him and kissed him on the lips.

Offa was trembling, and so Ælfwynn rose to her feet and wrapped her cloak around him and held him close. Offa rested his head against her stomach and closed his eyes. He felt her stomach rising and falling as she breathed and could hear her heart thumping. It was a strange experience for Offa to place his head so close to a young woman's womb, a magical, wondrous place, where life is conceived and nurtured. To Offa, Ælfwynn was a goddess as all women are. That night they laid together in the cold, their bodies entwined, surrounded by dead wolves; both covered in blood and gore. They used each other's bodies to come alive, to be as one in a primitive act of nature, defiant of the Gods.

Fenris had given his life for his pack. There was no right or wrong in what he did. Fenris owed Offa no allegiance. He was loyal to his own kind and Offa respected him for that. Offa had always believed the Gods had set him the task of taming the wolf, but that night he realised that it was the wolf who had been sent to teach him the way of the wolf, to show him the beast within himself, to prepare him for what was to come. Offa was ready!

Chapter Thirty Two
The Winter Solstice

Wēland's Cabin, Jötunn Forest

It was the twelfth day of Yule, the morning of the Winter Solstice, and Offa awoke to the sound of cockerels outside and the scent of apple cider wafting through the cabin. Later that day, himself, Ket, Hemming and Hothbrodd were to travel south, on foot, in order to meet with his father's men, by the river Eider, where an old warship waited to take them to Monster's Gate. Offa made his way outside, where Wēland stood beside Wudga, Ælfwynn, Ket, Hemming and Hothbrodd. On the ground beside them was a wild boar, its legs tied together with rope.

'Hæl Ing, Lord of the fields!' spoke Wēland, looking up into the heavens. 'We hæl you with this sacrifice, this great Yule Boar, that we now give to thee, Ing, God of light.' Wēland slashed the boar's throat wide open and showered the earth with its blood. 'O Golden One, bringer of light, on this sacred day, on the Winter Solstice, we beg you: bring back the sun, the giver of life. Free us from the darkness of winter and allow us the joys of summer once again.'

After the Yule Boar was taken inside the cabin and placed over the hearth to cook, Offa joined Ket, Wēland and Wudga outside for his final lesson. The winter air was cold and the ground was covered with a blanket of freshly fallen snow. The three men attacked, forcing Offa to use his seax and shield to protect himself against their blows, which came fast and hard. Offa blocked Ket's first attack with his shield, parried Wudga's strike with *Stedefæst*, leaving himself vulnerable to Wēland's shield-thrust. Offa was winded and both Ket and Wudga took advantage, knocking him to the ground with shield-thrusts of their own. Hothbrodd was watching from the porch. Offa couldn't tell what he was thinking, nor did he care. Offa's mind was some-place else. He was thinking about Fenris and how he had taken his life, and of Ælfwynn, and how they had laid together the night before.

'On your feet!' Wēland yelled. 'Stay focused. Forget about your wolf. Today is about your people. Now let's continue.'

Offa stood back to his feet, but he couldn't stop thinking about Ælfwynn. Did she love him? Did she love him as he loved her? Ket attacked again, but Offa parried the blow and kicked Ket in the stomach, knocking him on his backside. While Ket was lying in the snow, winded, Wudga attacked from Offa's left, forcing Offa to turn and block with his shield, knocking Wudga back, causing him to stumble through the snow. Wēland seemed impressed with Offa's progress. They had been practising all morning, fighting on an empty stomach, when Ælfwynn walked onto the porch and announced the Yule Boar would soon be ready. Offa looked up at her, their eyes met and she smiled. Hothbrodd, who had been sitting on the porch, was first to go inside, following the scent of Ælfwynn's cooking. The group sat around the wooden table while Ælfwynn presented Offa with a meal large enough to feed two men. Offa noticed an extra place had been prepared at the table.

'With this sacrifice, we hæl Ing, God of light and destroyer of darkness,' spoke Wēland, lifting his cup of cider. 'And we thank the boar for its flesh that will now nourish our bodies and give us the strength we need for the day ahead. Hæl Ing!'

'Hæl Ing!' they echoed, before drinking from their cups.

'The Englisc folk have a long tradition of hunting wild boars to prove their worth as warriors and to provide food for the clan at special occasions,' spoke Wēland, wiping his moustache on his sleeve, 'but no meal is more sacred than the one before you. Today we prepare a feast for the dead and invite our ancestors to join us, to eat and drink beside us. Welcome!' Wēland raised his cup once again. 'Wæs hæl!'

'Drinc hæl,' they echoed.

This was Offa's final meal before the fight at Monster's Gate. He didn't wish to offend Ælfwynn, but he was too nervous to eat and his stomach was twisted in elf-knots, worrying of the fight to come. He sat quietly at the table, playing with his food.

'You should eat something, my lad,' Hemming told him from across the table with grease dripping down his beard. 'You need your strength. We have a long journey ahead.'

'You must learn to overcome fear, young cub,' spoke Wēland. 'No man should go into battle on an empty stomach, not if he is to walk away with his life. Boars represent fertility and strength, ferocity and fearlessness. This is why warriors use the boar to decorate the crest of their helms. Warriors eat the boar to possess these noble qualities, to give them the strength they need for the battles ahead. Now eat up, Offa, a Kingdom depends on you.'

Later that morning, after forcing himself to eat all of his food, hoping to possess the qualities of the wild boar, Ælfwynn began redressing Offa's wound, made by Fenris the night before. After wrapping his forearm in bandages, she painted Offa's face with black soot from the hearth and painted wolfsangle runes across his stomach and chest, casting a powerful spell. The black soot was intended to intimidate his opponents and hide Offa from unclean spirits. Offa laced his boots and was given a blackened shield by Wēland, as well as the newly whetted *Stedefæst*. Wēland handed it to him with great care as if he feared cutting himself on the sacred blade. To Offa's surprise, Wēland then revealed a magnificent broadsword that gleamed in the firelight.

'This is my own sword,' spoke Wēland, 'one I forged myself. I used this sword during the Battle of Adrianople, when my people defeated the mighty Romans. It means a lot to me. A sword is forged by magic and flame and is a special gift from a man to his chosen warrior, and from father to son. Carrying a sword is a token of honour and should be cherished like the one you hold dearest to your heart.' Offa glanced at Ælfwynn. 'It is not about life or death for a swordsman, but about honour and dishonour; about going to Valhalla or the frozen waste-lands of hell. The value of a sword is incalculable. The stored up history of the blade is what gives it its power. Every warrior who has wielded it in battle, every oath sworn on its naked edge, every feud it has settled, has contributed to the tale of the sword. But the sword does not represent war, young Cniht, but peace. The sword must only be used to protect, it is not to be used for selfish deeds. I now give this sword to you, Offa. I know it is in safe hands.'

'Thank you,' Offa replied, taking the sword and placing it in its sealskin-lined scabbard. 'I will take great care of it.'

Ket, Hemming and Hothbrodd entered the cabin and surprised Offa with a second unexpected gift.

'For you, brave Cniht,' spoke Wēland with a smile as Ket presented Offa with a new wolf coat and hood. 'After all these years, Offa, you have finally earned your wolf coat. May the Gods take notice, for you have now become a warrior, the warrior you were always destined to become. This will make your father a proud man.'

Offa had tears in his eyes.

'Offa, you now wear the coat of Fenris,' spoke Ælfwynn, dressing him, 'but not in an act of victory over the wolf, but out of respect, to honour the wolf; to be like the wolf and all of his virtues.' Offa nodded, letting her know that he understood. Fenris' head and jaw covered the top of Offa's head, his fangs dug into his forehead and his tail and hind legs hung down his back. Ælfwynn looked into Offa's eyes, and smiled, whilst tying Fenris' forelegs over his chest. 'The wolf you know as Fenris will now guide you on your quest to save your people. He will be with you. Fenris will show you the way.'

'Thank you,' spoke Offa, softly. 'I won't forget this.'

'You are most welcome,' Wēland replied. 'It was slow coming, but your journey to manhood is now complete. I have no doubt, Wōden is by your side.'

Later that day, as snowflakes slowly fell from the frozen skies and the bitter winds rushed at his face, Offa was outside, alongside Wēland and the others. They were standing in front of a large fire, watching as the hot flames consumed Fenris' flesh and bones. The heat of the fire was burning Offa's cheek and the brightness of its flames hurt his eyes, yet nothing compared to the pain he felt on the inside, for his heart had been broken. Fenris was Offa's best friend, his only friend. Even though Fenris hadn't loved Offa the same, Offa was loyal to Fenris until the end, and it pained Offa greatly to know that it was his hand that was forced to take Fenris' life.

'Fenris Wulf was the leader of the wolf pack,' spoke Wēland.

'It was his destiny to one day be defeated and fall by the feet of another. That is the way of the forest. Like a warrior, death is not the end for Fenris. His soul will live on, and one day he will ride the night sky on a Wild Hunt. But on this day, Fenris' soul is here, with us. With Offa.'

Offa was dressed in the coat of Fenris, watching with a heavy heart while his bones turned to ash, yet Offa was comforted in the knowledge that Fenris would always be with him. Offa and Fenris were now as one, man and wolf, bonded in life and death. Offa wore Fenris' pelt with the utmost respect, embracing the courageous spirit of the primordial beast, like his ancestors before him.

'You were right, Hothbrodd,' Wēland continued. 'Yule is a time to fear, yet it is not about death. It is not about dying. Yuletide is a celebration of light triumphing over darkness, of life triumphing over death. You cannot die, Offa, because you are already dead. You are light trapped within an earthly vessel. Your soul will live on. Do not be afraid of being freed from your vessel and ascend to the heavens. You must surrender your soul and sacrifice your flesh and bone to the Gods. You need to fight, not as a boy, nor a man, but as a wolf; as a spirit of light, no longer afraid of pain and suffering, no longer afraid of being parted from your mortal flesh. You must give yourself to Wōden and ascend to another place, to live between worlds, stripped of human weakness. Do not fear your consciousness leaving your body, fight with every part of your being; honour your people, and you will triumph!'

'I can't express my gratitude for all you have done for him,' spoke Hemming, shaking Wēland's hand. 'Thank you.'

'You are most welcome,' Wēland replied.

'Thank you,' Offa added as hot tears rolled down his flushed cheeks. 'I will not let you down.'

'I know you won't,' Wēland replied. 'I know you won't.'

Offa turned to face Ælfwynn, the enchantress who had taken his boyhood in her stride, and saw the sorrow in her eyes. They embraced each other tightly, knowing it could be the last time they would ever lay eyes on each other again, and a great sadness overwhelmed them both.

'Gescildan sē Angelcynn,' Ælfwynn demanded. 'Save the Angle kin.'

'Fight well, young Cniht,' spoke Wēland, shaking Offa's hand. 'No matter the outcome, honour your people. Fight with your heart and soul. That is all a man can do.'

After saying their farewells, Hothbrodd led Offa, Ket and Hemming back into the winter forest and began their long journey to Monster's Gate.

Offa, Ket, Hemming and Hothbrodd had been travelling all evening, through the forest, making their way to meet the King's men. It hadn't snowed for a while, yet the land remained frozen and silent, trapped somewhere between life and death. Before reaching the river, the group was surprised to come across four men waiting patiently at the bottom of a hill, eating, drinking and swapping stories. There were several horses tethered nearby, exhausted from the difficult trek in the deep winter snow. Offa and the others crouched behind the cover of the trees and watched them from the top of the hill.

'*Who are they?*' Hothbrodd asked. '*Are they the King's men?*'

'*I can't be sure,*' Hemming replied. '*They might be Saxons. What do you think, Ket, do you recognise any of them?*'

'*We're too far away,*' Ket replied. '*I can't see their faces.*'

'*They have enough horses for us all,*' Offa whispered. '*They must be my father's men.*'

'*But we agreed to meet by the river,*' spoke Hemming. '*Something is wrong here.*'

As Hemming spoke, the group heard a twig snap behind them, but before they could turn around, Offa felt a cold metal point poking hard into his back.

'On your knees! All of you!' spoke a familiar voice from behind. The four men were decoys and they had just been ambushed by four other men. 'Hands on your head!'

'Ælfgār, you spineless bastard!' spoke Ket through gritted teeth. 'Tell your man to take his blade out of my back, before I turn around and shove it where the sun doesn't shine.'

'You're in no position to make threats,' Ælfgār told him, the leader of King Wǣrmund's hearth-troops.

'What is this?' Hemming asked, kneeling in the muddied snow with his hands on top of his head. 'The King trusted you.'

'Wǣrmund is a fool,' Ælfgār snapped. 'And now he expects this bearn to fight on behalf of Angeln? This child will fall at Monster's Gate and the whole of Ængla land will fall thereafter. If Wǣrmund has his way, my lands, my family, my wife and children, will be killed by Saxons, or worse, be kept as serfs. And why? For the honour of King Wǣrmund? Wǣrmund should have died many years ago, in a pool of his own blood. He should have died a proud man, a proud and noble death befitting a King. Yet he lives and he will drag the rest of us down beside him.'

Offa was furious to hear such disrespect towards his father.

'The King has been good to you and your family,' spoke Hemming. 'This is how you repay him, with treachery?'

'You still don't understand, do you?' Ælfgār asked. 'Yes, Wǣrmund has been good to me and mine. And yes, I owe him a great deal, but this is not about me, nor is it about the King. The existence of the Englisc race is at stake. Proud Angles won't sit idly by and witness their beloved Fatherland be destroyed due to the arrogance of their leaders.' The blade in Offa's back was sharp. 'But if King Wǣrmund's line is no more, if neither Offa nor any of you makes it to Monster's Gate, then there is no need for anyone to fight two against one and dishonour the Englisc with defeat. The fight won't happen. The Englisc army will go to Monster's Gate and we will kill the Saxons without pity or remorse.'

'I see,' spoke Ket with disgust. 'And Angeln will be in need of a new king.'

'And who better to turn to than the leader of the hearth-troops?' Ælfgār asked, receiving a laugh from his companions.

'We trusted you,' spoke Hemming. 'You have let your people down.'

One of Ælfgār's men hit Hemming hard in the back of his head, causing him to fall into the snow.

'Ængla land needs a leader,' Ælfgār replied, 'a man of action, not an old fool or a young lad who wants to play with swords. Offa will be the death of us all.' Ælfgār kicked Offa in the back. 'Well come on, lad, speak up.' His blade was pressed into the centre of Offa's spine, causing him to arch backwards in agony. 'Have you nothing to say? Is it your wish to die for the Englisc, Offa, to have us all destroyed after you fall? Don't you want to live? Why is it you fight, lad?' Ælfgār kicked Offa again, knocking him onto his hands and knees. 'Why, I asked? I want to know.'

Offa rested his hands in the snow, relieving the tension in his shoulders and took a deep breath.

'Who would want to live in a place not worth dying for?' Offa answered.

'Fine choice of words, lad,' spoke Ælfgār with a laugh. 'Well if it's your wish to die, then you're in the right place.' He spat. 'Any last words?'

Offa paused for a moment, his heart thumping wildly.

'My seax,' Offa answered. 'Allow me my seax.'

'At least allow the lad to hold his ancestral sword while you murder him in cold blood,' Hemming demanded, still on his knees with his hands on his head. 'Let him die like a man. As a warrior.'

'Why would I want to do that?' Ælfgār demanded. 'I don't want to see this changeling in the afterlife. Hell can have him for all I care.'

'What harm can it do?' asked one of Ælfgār's men. 'The lad has done no wrong. He has shown courage. Let him die as a warrior.'

The other men seemed to agree.

'Very well,' spoke Ælfgār. 'Take your seax out of your sheath. Slowly!' Offa glanced at Hemming. Ælfgār's blade poked further into Offa's back. 'This sword will slice your spine in two before you could even think about turning around.' With sweat rolling down his forehead, Offa reached for *Stedefæst*, wrapped his cold fingers around the pommel and gently drew the sword from its sheath. Ælfgār looked over Offa's shoulder. '*Stedefæst*! That will make for good trade with the War-Beards once your flesh has been eaten by the wolves. Now hold it tightly, lad, and close your eyes. Let's get this done.'

Offa didn't know what to do, his entire body was shaking and his heart was beating uncontrollably, like it was about to burst inside his ribcage. On his knees, with his hands on top of his head, Offa was in no position to mount an offence, but he couldn't die like that, not without a struggle, not without a fight! He was worth more than that. Suddenly Offa threw himself forward, into the snow. The cold hit his face like a fist. He desperately reached for his shield, which rested in the snow, before turning his body around, lying flat on his back, and held the shield in front of him. Ælfgār stood over Offa, his beard blowing wildly; his face hidden under the darkness of his hood. He raised his sword in the air and struck, hitting Offa's shield. Offa felt the impact vibrating through the shield as Ælfgār's sword scratched the black paint. Offa didn't know what to do. He saw Ælfgār's boots from under his shield. *Cut his ankles*, he thought, but Offa froze like a wild animal finally surrendering to winter's cruel touch.

Offa closed his eyes and waited to be struck from this world, when he heard a strange noise. He moved his shield to the side and saw Ælfgār standing before him with an arm wrapped around his bearded throat, choking the life out of him; almost lifting him off the ground. Ælfgār's face was red, his bloodshot eyes were bulging from his sockets and he was shaking violently. Offa looked into his eyes and saw it on his face: Ælfgār almost expected Offa to help him. Offa watched in shock as Ælfgār's attacker reached for his jaw and with one strong pull, Ælfgār's neck snapped like a twig and his limp body dropped to the ground. Offa looked up at Ælfgār's killer. It was Hothbrodd.

'You owe me, laddy,' spoke Hothbrodd with a smile.

Offa nodded his head before he noticed Hothbrodd's clothes were soaked in blood. While Ælfgār's men were distracted, Offa's three companions had managed to fight back. Ælfgār and his men now laid on the ground, bleeding into the snow, waiting to be eaten by the birds and the beasts. Offa took a breath of relief.

'The decoys,' spoke Ket, wiping his seax on one of their twitching corpses. Offa turned around to see four men running up the hill with weapons drawn. 'No mercy, men. No mercy.'

Ket turned to his kinsman. 'Now is the time, Offa. Now is the time!'

Ket was right, now was the time. Offa had to fight. No more hiding behind shields, no excuses, no fear. Ket and Hemming picked up their attackers' shields and joined Offa as he ran down the hill, yelling and screaming. Offa and Ket were in front, with Hemming on their tail, leaving Hothbrodd behind to nurse his wound. Running down the hill, with the cold wind in his face and fury in his heart, Offa felt alive. The four decoys were running up the hill, roaring; their long beards and hair blowing on the cold winter wind. Ket was faster than Offa and was first to come to blows. He leapt into the air with all the grace of a leaping cat, pouncing upon its helpless prey. Ket's sword came down hard, slicing through the warrior's cowhide helm and splitting his skull wide open. The previous injuries he had gained the night his brother died did nothing to calm his fury.

The next two attackers ran up the hill, side by side. Offa lifted his shield and charged at one of them, knocking him back down the hill. His partner wielded his sword towards Offa's head, but Offa was quick in seeing the threat and kicked him hard in the stomach, sending him flying back down the hill after his companion. Ket was in a rage and struck the fourth attacker with a mighty blow, almost decapitating him. Hemming charged passed Offa like a berserker, running down the hill after the remaining two. He killed one with his axe, leaving himself momentarily vulnerable, allowing the other to attack. Hemming's arm was bleeding heavily. It was a mighty cut, but the brave warrior didn't give a damn. Hemming yelled at his attacker, spitting and cursing, his tongue hanging out like a hell brute. The two men began circling each other like rabid dogs thrown into a fighting pit. Hemming looked possessed, yet his opponent looked calm and calculating. Offa's instinct was to help his kinsman, but he knew all too well the rules of combat. Hemming had made the challenge, and so he would fight his own battle.

Hemming held his axe in the same arm that had been cut, but it didn't seem to affect him; he didn't care. Hemming attacked, his axe biting into his opponent's shield. His opponent out-manoeuvred him, trying to chop Hemming's leg from the knee, but Hemming moved fast for a large man and avoided the blow. Hemming turned on his opponent, using his shield to knock Ælfgār's man several feet back. Hemming roared like a bear and charged forward, swinging a great axe with two hands, forcing the blade down upon the startled enemy's skull. Offa turned away and was sick. He had seen death before, but it was never something he was comfortable with.

'It's alright, lad,' spoke Hothbrodd, limping behind him, 'get it all out.'

Offa looked up and wiped his mouth. 'Your injury?' he asked.

'Just a scratch. I'll live. It takes more than that to kill old Hothbrodd.'

After hiding the bodies from the pathway, the four of them took the horses and made their way towards the ship that was to take them to Monster's Gate. Together they bolted through the snow-clad forest, showering the ground with shards of broken ice, while avoiding the overhanging branches that were filled with heavy snow. The wind was in their eyes, snowflakes spiralled in the cold air and they fought for breath as they raced towards the river Eider, where King Wærmund's men awaited.

'Remember, Offa,' spoke Ket, riding beside him, 'if anyone asks: we never saw Ælfgār or his men. We were attacked by outlaws and took their horses. It's best not to stir up any trouble with the army. Leave the talking to Hemming and I.'

'I didn't talk for four years,' Offa replied. 'I think I can manage it.'

As they approached the river, Offa's heart began thumping. He saw hundreds of men preparing for war, carrying spears and shields, decorated with dragons and ravens, wolves and bears, aurochs, eagles and deer; their iron-tipped spears glistening in the sunlight. Many wore boar-crested helms with long black bristles, and there were many horse-Thegns sitting proudly upon the backs of their war-steeds, holding the white dragon banner of the Englisc folk. Offa got a lump in his throat when he saw the old warship that was to take him to Monster's

Gate, its dragon-headed prow nodding as the ship's belly
rocked in the serpent-infested river and its white dragon-
decorated sail catching the wind. Egwen, dressed in full battle-
gear, greeted them warmly, before taking them to see King
Wærmund. Offa's father looked older than he remembered.

'Greetings. I trust you are well, Offa?'

'Yes, father,' Offa replied.

'Offa has done you proud, my King,' spoke Hemming.
'Wēland has taught him well. It gives me great pleasure to
inform you that your son, Offa, now wears the honoured wolf
coat.'

'How is this possible?' the King asked as tears welled in his
pale white eyes.

'Offa was attacked by Fenris and his pack of rabid wolves,'
Ket answered. 'Offa was forced to kill Fenris and now wears
his coat.'

'Ha! I never lost faith in you, my son,' spoke King Wærmund, trembling in the cold. 'I knew you were special, Offa. I
knew from the moment you were born, twice the size of
an ordinary babe, that you were destined for something greater
than I could possibly fathom.' The blind King smiled whilst
feeling the top of Fenris' head. 'The Gods have tested you.
They sent Fenris after you, yet here you stand, stronger!
Tonight, Offa, you meet your destiny and the future of the
Englisc race rests in your hands. I know the Gods are with you
and you shall be victorious!'

'How you remind me of my dear Wīg,' spoke Egwen, stroking Offa's cheek with the palm of her hand. 'You have a good
heart. Don't let anyone take that away from you. But you have
a great challenge ahead. You must leave your kindness behind
and embrace your destiny. And if there is a wolf in you, be
sure to unleash it.' Egwen leaned forward and kissed Offa on
the cheek. Offa felt she had just kissed him farewell.

With the weight of the world on his young shoulders, Offa
stood by the river Eider and looked upon the red-eyed, dragon-
prowed war-ship. The ship was over ninety-feet-long and
fourteen-feet-across. Walking the wooden gangplank, Offa's
stomach twisted with every step. The ship was filled with

fighting men, waiting for instructions to take them downriver. Offa saw their breath on the cold damp air and the look of war in their fierce eyes. Many looked at Offa with great admiration as he passed. Offa dusted off the snow and sat down on one of the cold, wet benches. He heard the creaking of the rigging and looked up at the red sail that was beautifully woven with the pattern of a two-legged white dragon with outstretched, bat-like wings; the dragon wanting to take to the sky in open flight. Offa saw his father being helped up the gangplank by Ket and Hemming, and so he moved further along the bench to make room for his kinsmen to sit. Offa noticed there was a rune carved into the back of the bench in front.

'I want to thank you, my son,' spoke King Wǣrmund. 'By being here, you have redeemed me in more ways than you could ever fathom. You see, Offa, I am a man who has lived a selfish life. I have grown old and weak, while men far greater than I have perished honourably. I have shamed myself by growing old, allowing myself to wither beyond what is natural. Valhalla is full of young men, it is no place for the old. Yet, if I could go back and start again, I would do things differently. I would prove my worth in battle and I would have many healthy children to many beautiful women. And I would have died alongside my brothers on the battlefield.' The King had tears in his eyes. 'A man should not live his dreams through his son. I am a coward. I have brought shame upon you and for that I am deeply sorry. I have been a poor father, but I want you to know that I am proud of you, Offa. You make me proud to call you my son. Your act of courage will be remembered forever and I applaud you. In the eyes of the Gods, glory is everlasting.'

The ship's commander gave the order and the oar-men began pulling their heavy oars to their chests and the old wave-cutter groaned as it slowly made its way over the dark water and headed towards Monster's Gate, the gateway to hell. Ket and Hemming sat in silence while Offa stared at the rune carved into the bench in front. It was the wolfsangle, the sign of the werewolf.

The surrounding area was frozen and covered in a misty veil

blown in by the ocean breeze. The river was calm and murky, silver shone from the surface like flashes of a thousand swords, and the smell of rank marshes filled the damp air. Offa watched as snowflakes gently fell from the frozen skies, floating and dancing upon the air. He saw blues, whites and purples as they made their way down to the earth to rest upon the oarmen, biting as they came in contact with their exposed flesh. There were many horse-Thegns trotting alongside the river's edge, with many more on foot, most with their heads low as they made the long journey through the harsh winter weather; travelling to an uncertain future.

The ship passed several small towns, where the people came to watch the spectacle. Offa saw the worried faces of ordinary men and women standing by the riverbanks. They were poor people and it pained Offa to look at them. There were many children there, some running around and playing in the snow, some sitting upon the shoulders of their fathers, happy, not quite understanding what was happening, just excited to be there. Offa saw one woman in particular standing beside her husband, with snow in her long braided hair. With one hand on her swollen womb, she never took her eyes from Offa. It was as if she was looking through an open door, seeing his soul. These were the people Offa was fighting for.

As the ship sailed further downriver, the towns became a fading memory and the surrounding forest felt like it was closing in on them. The trees seemed lifeless, almost disappearing under the crushing weight of the winter snow. Many branches hung in their way, some reaching into the ship as if trying to snatch their souls from the realm of the living. On the bank of the river, Offa saw a lone wolf watching them as the ship passed by. Snowflakes continued falling from the heavens and the winter wind was cold and biting at Offa's ears. Countless ravens had gathered in the trees to watch the spectacle and the Gods listened as one man yelled from under his boar-crested helm, 'We're here!'

Chapter Thirty Three
The Fight at Monster's Gate

River Eider, Monster's Gate, disputed territory between the
Angles and Saxons

It was the Winter Solstice, the Night of the Dead. The skies
were cold and grey, mist shrouded the island and snowflakes
fell from the heavens above. The colour seemed to be drained
from Middle-earth as if the Goddess of the underworld walked
amongst the living. Both banks of the river Eider were
crowded with hundreds of warriors and common folks, some
holding the white dragon banner of the Englisc, while many
held the raven banner of the Saxons. King Ēadgils of the Mire-
Dwellers was there to watch, sitting upon his throne, over-
looking the heads of his war-band as they chanted their war-
songs and pointed their spears to the heavens. By the King's
side was his daughter, Princess Mōdthryth. All were there to
witness a new beginning, because either way, the fate of two
clans would be revealed.

From out of the mist, a dragon's head appeared on the river,
unnerving many onlookers. As the mist lifted, a great warship
could be seen, carrying an army of men; its red sail blowing in
the wind, the white dragon displayed for all to see. Offa was
sitting on the bench beside his father, listening to the harrowing sound of Saxon drums echoing into the forest. Wǣrmund
placed a hand upon Offa's shoulder.

'Be strong, my son,' spoke the King. 'And may the Gods
bless you for your selflessness. It is better to live one day as a
god, than a lifetime as a sheep. Wyrd oft neroð unfægne eorl
þonne his ellen dēah.'

'Fight true, brother,' spoke Ket. 'A wolf shows no fear. Only
his fangs are to be shown.'

Ket, Egwen, Hemming and Hothbrodd gave Offa words of
encouragement, before helping the King down the gangplank
and took him to the old wooden bridge that stood high above
the river. Offa wasn't a fool. He knew the reason his father
wanted to be on the bridge was to throw himself off if Offa

was to lose and bring shame upon him and the Englisc folk. The ship's commander gave the order and the ship turned towards Monster's Gate. Offa felt as sick as a dog. He stared into the murky waters that splashed against the hull and saw his dark reflection staring back at him. It was a face he didn't recognise. As Offa stared into his own soul, bubbles began to rise from the bottom of the river and Offa saw a scaly, elongated body break the surface of the water and brush against the hull, before disappearing again under the water.

'Die well, brave Offa,' spoke the ship's commander as the ship came to a stop and the gangplank was lowered to the island.

Offa took a deep breath and his legs felt heavy as he walked down the gangplank, his heart beating to the sound of enemy drums. Offa's boots seemed to disappear as he paced the snow. There was a dead tree in the centre of the island, with a raven sitting on the top branch, squawking as it watched Offa with its dark, soul-less eyes. Offa drew the sword Wēland had given him and wrapped his cold fingers around the pommel with a tight grip. His time to fight had finally come and he didn't have to wait long for his opponents to arrive.

A cold chill crept up Offa's spine when he saw a small boat appear out of the mist. It was carrying four men, two were the oar-men, one was Meaca; the other was Krampus. Offa stood still, like a spectre, his face completely black, wearing the coat of Fenris; staring at them, showing no expression - revealing nothing. As the boat reached the island, the two warriors jumped into the snow and raised their seaxes to salute their King, who looked on from across the river. The Saxons cheered loud enough to awaken the dead. Offa stared at them and took a deep breath. The boat turned around and left the three of them alone to face their fate.

Krampus' face remained a mystery and was covered with a mask made from a goat pelt. Adorned upon his head were two large curved goat horns and his broad shoulders were draped with several goat pelts. At his waist was a sheathed broad-sword and seax. In his left hand was a wooden shield. Like Offa, Meaca was dressed as a Wolf-Coat and wore a bristled, boar-crested iron helm, complete with nose and cheek-guards. He was also armed with a broadsword, a seax and a decorated shield. They looked at Offa the same way a pack of hungry wolves looks upon a wounded animal. Offa stood with sword in hand, his skin painted black like the warriors of old, his face as dark as coal; his eyes as white as snow, and his back draped with the coat of Fenris. He looked like a fiend from the under-world, come to take the damned to hell.

'After we've finished with you,' spoke Meaca, turning to face Offa's father, 'and your twitching corpse lies bleeding into the snow, it looks like the old King will throw himself off the bridge. He would rather feed himself to the monsters that lurk at the bottom of the river, than live with the shame his only son is about to bring upon him.'

Offa showed no emotion, even though his guts were churn-ing on the inside. He stood in complete silence, gripping his sword in his sweating palm. After seeing a flock of ravens fly from the safety of the treetops, a sign of impending danger, the hairs on the back of Offa's neck pricked, when he noticed an eerie presence watching the three of them from across the river. It was the figure of a woman draped in a long white gown, which rested on the ice-encrusted snow. She stood perfectly still, seemingly unaffected by the blistering cold winds, not taking her eyes from them. No one else seemed to be able to see her and a cold shiver slowly crept up Offa's spine. Was it a Valkyrie, Offa wondered? Had she come to claim his restless soul?

'What are you staring at? Have you gone mad?' Meaca asked. 'You are a fool for not accepting my father's offer. Now you are going to die on this sacred day, beneath my stinking feet, like so many before you. But you won't die quickly. I'm going to humiliate you first in front of your father and your wretched people. I'm going to have fun with you, take a little piece of you here and there. Have you any last words, changeling?'

'You are both going to die!' Offa replied, coldly.

Offa had been taunted for the last six years, but enough was enough. Destiny had finally caught up with him and the spirit of his ancestors had entered his flesh-shield. It was now time to fight. Not just for himself, but for his father, his people, for Ængla land; for blood, honour and glory. Offa used his broadsword to draw a line in the snow and ice, daring his opponents to cross the boundary and test their battle-luck against the Wōden-born.

Krampus stepped forward and a hue of colours shone from his blade. Offa held his broadsword and shield close to his body like Wēland had taught him and remained as still as a corpse lying inside a burial mound. He could taste metal in his mouth and the smell of fresh wolf pelt filled his senses. His heart raced and his arms felt heavy and weak. He remembered Wēland's words: to embrace the cold, to embrace fear; to use fear to his advantage and turn it into aggression. Krampus roared and charged forward, thrashing his broadsword towards Offa's skull. Offa heard the giant's blade singing as it cut through the cold winter air, forcing Offa to take a step back, where he fell over the tree roots that reached out of the snow like withered arms from a rotting corpse, reaching from the underworld. Meaca roared to the crowd, raising his sword and shield, before looking down at Offa.

'Get up!' spoke Meaca. 'Don't make Krampus look like a child murderer. Get up and fight!'

Offa tried getting back to his feet, when Krampus ran at him and kicked him hard in the ribs, knocking the air from his lungs. Offa couldn't breathe. Finally, Krampus stepped back and allowed Offa to struggle back to his feet. Once Offa was upright, he tried catching his breath, when he noticed the Valkyrie still watching from across the river. With the battle-fury of a berserker, Offa charged and leapt through the air, using his shield to knock Krampus backwards. Their wooden shields clashed, sending shock-waves through Offa's arms and chest, yet both of them were still on their feet. Offa stepped forward, wielding his broadsword and struck Krampus' shield, smashing it into a thousand splinters. For the first time the crowd of Angles cheered, but Krampus was no ordinary warrior.

Krampus surprised Offa by smashing him hard in the face with the iron spiked-boss that had been a part of his shield.

Krampus held onto the boss by its iron handle, the part he used to hold the shield. The Saxons were applauding their chosen warrior, while Meaca saluted his father. Blood poured from Offa's cheekbone, his legs felt as weak as a newly born calf, his ribs were sore and his face was hurting, but he tried to ignore his aches and pains and the warm blood that trickled down his burning cheek. It was a cold and bitter day. Offa saw his own breath on the damp air, but he was thankful for the cold, for it helped numb the pain.

Offa stood opposite Krampus and their eyes were fixed on each other like two male wolves clashing before the pack. Offa's heart was racing and his face felt like it had been pressed against a roaring flame. He untied his leather straps, tossed his shield to the snow and pulled his wolf hood over his head to hide the innocence of his youthful complexion; allowing Krampus to see only the wolf that stared back at him.

'What are you doing?' Meaca asked, looking on.

'The honour of my people… is at… stake,' Offa replied, breathing heavily; glaring at him from under his wolf hood. 'Krampus has no shield…, so neither… will I. We will fight… as equals.'

Krampus stared at Offa, refusing to blink; refusing to show even a moment of weakness. Offa was frightened to his bones and the fear coursing through his veins was sapping the strength from his arms and legs. Krampus stepped forward and roared, forcing Offa to react and slash the giant across his mask. Krampus stared at Offa in disbelief, his blue eyes bulging from beyond his mask. To Offa's surprise, Krampus raised his arm and gently removed his mask and horns to reveal a big bushy beard, a badly burnt face and a bloody gash under his left eye. Krampus touched the cut and stared at the blood that dripped from his fingers. He then shifted his gaze and cast his steely eyes towards Offa.

Krampus once again charged at Offa, wielding his sword. Offa had no shield to protect himself with and his body was too big to move out of the way. Krampus hacked and slashed in Offa's direction. Offa was stepping backwards, trying to avoid each blow, but it was no use; the sharp edge of Krampus' famous blade sliced the delicate skin on Offa's right arm and down the right-hand-side of his ribs. Warm blood rushed to the surface of his skin and dripped from the open wounds. Offa thought he was about to die, yet he somehow managed to avoid getting hit again and retaliated by swinging his broadsword, smashing it into Krampus' own. Sparks showered them both as steel clashed with steel and their swords broke into fragments. The impact sent shock-waves throughout Offa's upper body, forcing him to release the damaged sword. In the blink of an eye, Offa drew his seax, and the future of the Englisc race rested delicately on the sharpened edge of *Stedefæst*.

Offa's right arm and ribs were bleeding and mixed with the black soot that Ælfwynn had covered his body and face with. His wounds stung as if they were on fire, yet Offa remained silent, refusing to show weakness. Krampus drew his seax. The big Goth was intimidating and his stinking breath was visible on the damp air. The Valkyrie continued watching the spectacle, deciding which one of them was worthy to take with her to Valhalla. Offa stood his ground, remembering Wēland's teaching, and searched for his enemy's weaknesses. Offa believed Krampus' weakness was obvious: he was overconfident.

The raven watching from the dead tree squawked loudly, before turning to preen its black feathers. Offa glanced at Meaca, who looked on with a smile on his face. Offa looked back at Krampus, who stood fiercely in the snow, with the wind at his back, staring at him; his long dark hair blowing in the wind. Krampus stepped forward and tried taking Offa's head off, forcing Offa to parry the blow and attack, but Krampus was fast and avoided the blow. The giant rushed at Offa again, cutting through the air, but Offa stepped out of harm's way, remembering the importance of balance.

With a grunt, Krampus attacked and forced Offa to go on the defence, giving him no time to attack, therefore no chance of victory. Krampus' sword whistled as it cut through the air, keeping Offa on his heels, not giving him chance to compose himself or allow him to catch his breath. Offa had to hold his ground and strike, but Krampus had him on the retreat, forcing him backwards. He was cutting horizontally, then vertically, top to bottom, left to right. Offa waited for a mistake, but none came. Krampus gritted his teeth and his eyes bulged as he roared, his sword-edge travelling towards Offa's unprotected skull at lightning speeds. Offa tensed his body and stepped to the side, before arching backwards, managing to avoid the deadly blow. This was it, Offa's chance to attack.

Offa kicked the back of Krampus' leg and forced him to one knee. The onlookers gasped. Offa screamed out loud and tried slashing the back of Krampus' head, but Krampus turned and instinctively put up his shield-hand. But Krampus had no shield to protect himself with and the blade cut through some of his fingers. Offa stared for a moment, almost forgetting himself. Small droplets of blood rolled from the tip of *Stedefæst* and into the snow, one drop at a time. Still on one knee, Krampus looked at his deformed hand, watching in disbelief as blood squirted from his butchered fingers. Offa didn't know what to do. Was it honourable to strike an unarmed man, he asked himself? He didn't have time to think. Suddenly a blinding light flashed in Offa's head and he found himself falling to the ground. He looked up to see Meaca standing over him.

Krampus held his seax in his left hand while he and Meaca began to stalk Offa. Slowly, and with great pain, Offa rose to his feet and took a deep breath. Meaca was first to strike, but Offa blocked it and struck a blow of his own, forcing Meaca to duck. *Stedefæst* sliced through the black bristles that adorned the top of Meaca's boar-crested helm. Offa saw each bristle as they showered the air and fell to the snow by his feet. Meaca gritted his teeth and charged at Offa, pushing him back with his shield, and brought his sword-arm around the shield to try and cut Offa in half. Remembering Wēland's training, Offa used Meaca's shield against him, placing his cold fingers around the hard, splintered edge and used his weight and strength to force Meaca backwards, before using *Stedefæst* to cut at the back of Meaca's left leg. Meaca roared in pain.

Before Offa could blink, Krampus was upon him and tried

slashing his throat open. Using his left hand, Offa grabbed Krampus by his wrist, raised his arm up above his head and thrust *Stedefæst* into his armpit, cutting deep into his soft flesh. Their eyes met and they stared at each other, two warriors, eye to eye, nose to nose. Offa stared into Krampus' soul and roared in his face with a deafening scream. Then silence. All became quiet, except for the sound of Krampus' heavy breathing. Offa took a deep breath, filling his lungs with cold air and retrieved his seax, listening as the air escaped Krampus' lungs and blood poured from his mouth. In one smooth motion, Offa spun around, screaming, and slashed his naked blade against Krampus' vulnerable throat. Krampus, chosen warrior of the Mire-Dwellers, never took his eyes from Offa as he dropped to his knees and clutched his throat. He looked up at Offa and tried to speak, but his blue eyes rolled into the back of his head and he fell face first into the cold snow, in a pool of his own blood.

Offa was shaking and gasping for breath, while a cold silence befell the Saxons and the Valkyrie looked on showing no emotion. Offa felt under his wolf coat, down the right-hand-side of his ribs and looked at the crimson gore that dripped from his fingertips. He was tired and hurting. Parts of his Wolf-Coat were torn, revealing his upper body that was painted entirely black with wolfsangle runes. Meaca looked unnerved. As the winter cold bit into his flesh, chilling him to his bones, Offa looked into the predatory eyes of the Saxon Prince and could smell his sweat and taste his foul breath on the air. They both knew only one of them would be leaving the island with their life, yet neither life mattered, only honour.

Snowflakes continued falling from the heavens, Niht began her long journey across the solemn sky, the moonlight disappeared behind the gathering clouds and darkness began to consume the land. With his greatest warrior lying dead by Offa's feet, Meaca stepped forward and smashed Offa hard in the face with his shield, once again knocking him to the flattened snow. The Saxons cheered and were banging their spear-shafts against wooden shields to the sound of war-drums. Whilst lying in the pink snow, Offa glanced across the river to see the Valkyrie had vanished, taking Krampus' soul to Valhalla, for he had died a warrior's death, sword in hand.

Offa struggled back to his feet and was breathing heavily. He gripped *Stedefæst* so tightly his knuckles turned white. Meaca spat into the snow and began cursing Offa, but Offa never spoke a word in return. Instead, Offa yelled a battle-cry and charged forward, feeling the battle-fury that he had heard about so many times before; all the while forgetting his training. Offa was young and clumsy. He believed Wōden was protecting him and that made him hopelessly reckless. Offa was well-trained by Wēland, who had worked night and day with him, but his youth and inexperience proved almost deadly on that cold winter night.

The bitter winds howled between the frozen trees, while Offa charged at Meaca, trying to cut him down before the two armies, but his recklessness caused him to trip and stumble over the tree roots that lay hidden under a thick layer of snow. Offa hit the ground hard. His ribs and right arm were sore, his heart was hammering and his hands and feet were numb from the freezing winter gales. Fearing for his life, Offa turned around to witness Meaca standing above him. Offa tried getting back to his feet, but he was too slow. Meaca kicked him in the ribs, again and again. Offa couldn't breathe. Meaca was yelling at him, kicking him in the mouth, loosening several teeth, again and again, over and over. Countless ravens circled high above, waiting to feast on Offa's rotting flesh.

Offa's face had swollen. He opened both eyes and tried to wipe away the blood, but his vision was blurry in one eye and could now only see out of his right eye. A part of him wanted to give up and surrender to death. Lying on the ground, bloodied, sore and half blind, Offa had the desire to end it all there and then. He closed his eyes and wished for it to stop, wanting the pain to leave his mortal flesh; to unburden himself. He wanted to die. He no longer cared about Valhalla or hell. At that moment, he didn't care about anything and just wanted it to stop. A part of him gave up. A part of Offa died that night. All went black. That's when the mist came. Offa was lying in the cold blood and ice, covered in his own gore, looking up as snowflakes gently fell from the heavens. Then he saw her approach, the Valkyrie with the long white hair. She stood over him and saw the seax in his hand. To Offa's surprise, she spoke to him in a gentle, ghostly whisper:

'*Wyrd oft neroð unfægne eorl þonne his ellen dēah*,' she said.

It was the same words the wolf-man had used and what his father had said to him before being escorted to the bridge.

Offa laid on the cold ground, struggling to breathe, snow-flakes melting as they fell upon his warm cheeks, his life flashing before his eyes; when he felt something burning deep within his soul. He was caught somewhere between waking and sleeping, between life and death. The Valkyrie had gone and the mist had disappeared. Wēland was right, Offa had never left the forest and his soul was still trapped between the realm of the living and the realm of the dead. But it was now the Winter Solstice, when the veil between the living and the dead was thinnest and Offa was ready to cross the boundary and return to the living.

Offa could hear his own heart beating inside his chest and heard the cries of Leofrīc, Grendel, Haakon and Bardawulf being eaten alive. He saw the lights in Wulfnoth's eyes fade and could taste his blood as it dripped into his mouth. He remembered Athils being blood-eagled and saw Fenris as a cub, running for his life, fleeing the pursuing pack of dogs. He was overwhelmed by Osgār's terror as he struggled against the fangs of the vengeful Fenris. He could feel Tor's anguish as Offa's seax bit into his soft flesh. And he saw Brogan's eyes whilst taking his last breath from beneath him. Offa felt the rage of the Rottweiler as he fought for his life against Bæda. He felt the sorrow of the mad feral as he fell to the ground, clutching his throat, spraying the air with blood. And he saw the savagery in Golden-Mane's eyes when he stood face to face with Fenris.

With the storm raging above, Offa laid in the cold blood and ice, while Meaca continued boasting to the crowd. Offa opened his good eye, gripped *Stedefæst* with his right hand and slowly rose to his feet. Once again, he pulled the wolf hood over his head and looked through the eyes of Fenris, seeing the enemy as he saw. He charged at Meaca like a wild animal, slashing *Stedefæst* through the air, slicing snowflakes in two, but Meaca raised his shield and Offa scratched a deep line in the wood. Offa's back was momentarily turned, giving Meaca the opportunity to slash his sword down Offa's spine. The pain was excruciating, yet Offa turned around in time to parry a second blow. As Meaca stepped past him, striking nothing but cold air, Offa raised his arm and cut the back of Meaca's neck. The Saxon Prince stumbled forward, before turning around, when Offa struck a second time, slashing across Meaca's face and spraying the air with blood.

Offa wiped the blood from his eyes and leapt forward, thrusting *Stedefæst* again and again, trying to rip Meaca's stomach open, but Meaca used his shield to block his every attack. Offa tried to strike between Meaca's bulging eyes, but Meaca tripped him with his foot and Offa crashed to the ground, face first. With Offa lying in the snow, Meaca stood over him and struck with his sword, forcing Offa to tuck his elbows in and roll away. Meaca's blows came fast and hard, sending shards of ice into the air. Meaca was limping and paused a moment to take a breath, giving Offa chance to regain his footing.

The two warriors stood opposite each other, both with wide eyes and heaving chests. Meaca roared and wielded his sword towards Offa's unprotected skull. Offa's vision was blurred, yet he parried the blow and knocked Meaca backwards, causing him to drop his shield. Offa stepped forward and tried thrusting *Stedefæst* into Meaca's stomach, but Meaca took hold of Offa's wrist and their foreheads smashed together like two raging deer locking horns. They were nose to nose, eye to eye, both brave and determined.

While Offa struggled against his opponent, Meaca hit him hard in the face with his elbow, hurting Offa's bad eye. The pain was horrific and Offa could just make out Meaca's blurred image as he stepped forward, using all of his strength to slice Offa's face with his sword. Blood sprayed across the island, splattering up the lifeless tree and startled the raven. Offa's skin burned. He had no time to think, only react. He ignored the pain and stepped forward, trying to bite Meaca's neck. Offa would have used his teeth to tear Meaca's throat out if he could. Meaca knocked Offa backwards and struck, but Offa raised his arm to protect his face, allowing the blade to bite his soft flesh. Offa heard the steel scraping his bone. The pain was intense. Offa instinctively tried protecting his injured arm, but the experienced warrior took advantage, sweeping Offa's leg and knocked him to one knee.

'Time to die,' spoke Meaca with a scowl, the snowstorm spiralling above his head. 'Hold your seax tightly. I want to make sure you go to Valhalla, so Krampus can take you before the Gods and make you his whore.'

Meaca stood over Offa and used the pommel of his sword to try and crack his skull, but Offa raised *Stedefœst* and slashed at his hands. As Meaca roared in pain, Offa used every ounce of strength he had left to strike at the back of Meaca's ankle, cutting through the tendon and bone. Meaca roared with a sickening cry and stumbled backwards on one leg, before falling over the sleeping corpse of his greatest warrior. Meaca turned his head and stared into the expressionless face of Krampus. He looked into his eyes, his dead, empty eyes. A snowflake fell from the heavens and rested peacefully on Krampus' pale white face. Krampus wore his death-mask well.

Slowly, and with great effort, Offa stood upon his shaking legs. Blood dripped down his entire body and the hairs on his arms pricked from the blistering cold. He took a moment to catch his breath and allowed Meaca to pull himself up, using the dead tree in the centre of the island. The raven was watching with a keen eye. Meaca roared in agony whilst struggling to keep upright, stumbling and jumping up and down on one leg, using the tree to steady himself. He stared at Offa, wondering what dark thoughts had entered his mind. The Angelcynn looked on with bated breath, watching from their boats and from on top of the riverbanks. Offa turned to the crippled Saxon, who stood there shaking like a leaf in the early days of winter. Offa stepped closer, confident in victory, but Meaca shocked everyone by drawing his seax and once again slashed across Offa's face, before falling to the ground, dropping his weapon onto the soiled snow and ice.

Blood flowed down Offa's cheeks, but he ignored the pain. He was beyond pain. Offa took a moment to gather himself and take a breath. He looked over at King Ēadgils sitting high upon his throne, watching in horror while his last remaining son laid helpless in the bloodied snow. Offa then continued to approach Meaca. Offa saw Meaca's seax resting on the ground and reached down in order to pass it to him, for he wouldn't kill an unarmed man and lose his grace, his hæl. But there was no grace in Meaca's actions. Offa was reaching for Meaca's seax, when he felt a deep sharp pain in the pit of his stomach. Meaca had stabbed him in his guts, using a small knife he had concealed inside his boots. The pain burned like fire. Offa dropped to his knees, blood poured from his stomach and mouth and he screamed loud enough to awaken the monsters that laid sleeping at the bottom of the river. He tried stopping the flow of blood that poured from his gaping wound, but it leaked between his fingers and he began to feel dizzy and sick.

Still on his knees, Offa's mind wandered to the Gods, to his father and his people. He knew he would die, as all living things must, but Offa's life didn't matter to him; the future of his people was all he cared about. He looked up at the supernatural storm that had formed high above his head and saw the shadow of Wōden leading the Wild Hunt upon the clouds. Life was draining from Offa's open wound and he began to scream with rage and his blood began to boil under his skin. Offa saw Fenris standing by his side, snarling at him; his blue eye glowing. Offa could smell his hot stinking breath upon him, but he wasn't frightened. Fenris' mane bristled with rage and saliva dripped from his knife-like fangs, lathering the ground, but Offa wasn't afraid. Fenris pointed his nose into the dark sky above, towards the moon that had reappeared from behind the grey clouds, enveloping the entire sky, and sang the song, the oldest song, the first song; the song of the forest. And Offa understood.

Offa was overcome with anger and rage. His senses heightened and his fear melted away, as did his humanity. The squawk of the circling ravens and the sound of the wolf pack howling in the forest was deafening. He heard Meaca's heart beating inside his chest and could taste blood on the air. He heard the echoes of Valhalla and the Wild Hunt raging from beyond the clouds, led by Wōden and his army of the dead. He could smell Ælfwynn's scent all over him, intoxicating him. The wolfsangle runes on his skin had taken effect, changing Offa's mental state, from a flawed, inexperienced Cniht, to becoming something better; something otherworldly. He screamed and screamed as blood poured down his cheeks and out of his mouth, working himself up into a frenzied state. One of his eyes turned milky white, the other blue. For úrum þéode wé weorðaþ wulfas. For our clan we become wolves. Offa had become a werewolf! Fenris had entered his soul and they both hungered for Saxon blood.

Meaca was still lying on the ground, unable to get back to his feet. He saw Offa on his knees, silhouetted against the silver-crested moon. The forest trees blew against the western winds and giant snowflakes fell from the heavens. Ignoring his bloody wounds, Offa snapped his head towards Meaca with wild eyes and teeth revealed. He began to crawl towards him on his hands and knees, growling and snarling, with *Stedefæst* in hand. Meaca's eyes betrayed his fear. Meaca tried to crawl away, but Offa was quickly upon him. Offa saw the knife still gripped in Meaca's hand and so he slashed at his wrist, forcing him to release his weapon into the snow.

'Please!' Meaca begged. '*Please! My sword. Allow me my sword.*'

Meaca was begging for a warrior's death, wanting to die with sword in hand, but Offa was beyond all reason; beyond all human consciousness. Meaca looked into his eyes and knew Offa was no longer there. Something else had taken over him. Something old. The primordial beast raged within and it was about to be unleashed. Offa placed his weight over Meaca's chest, roared in his face and squeezed his hands into fists. Mercy didn't exist to the primordial being, it was master or be mastered; the law of the forest. Offa punched and punched, again and again, until his knuckles bled, yet he couldn't stop. He was relentless and could taste Meaca's blood in his mouth.

Offa wanted more. He wanted to glut and gorge on Meaca's pain and suffering.

Meaca's eyes remained open and he was breathing heavily. Offa screamed, punching him harder and harder. He punched with his right hand, then his left, then his right, again and again. Blood shot from Meaca's mouth and into the snow, his nose splattered across his bloodied face and Offa felt Meaca's skull breaking beneath his heavy fists. The wolves in the sky were devouring the moon, turning him crimson red, and the snowflakes falling from the heavens turned to blood as Meaca's eyes rolled into the back of his head. Countless ravens took to the night sky, chasing Wōden on his Wild Hunt. Offa punched until his knuckles broke. He punched until he couldn't punch any longer. Offa was screaming the entire time, screaming into the snowstorm, to Wōden; screaming loud enough to shake the hall of Valhalla. Meaca, son of King Ēadgils, was dead.

Offa was breathing heavily and struggled to get back to his feet, whilst trying to hold his stomach wound together. He looked down at Meaca. His face was unrecognisable. He then looked over at Krampus. The giant's face had turned blue from the winter cold. With a great deal of pain and effort, Offa picked *Stedefæst* from off the blood-splattered snow. Despite his injuries, Offa stood tall, with Fenris draped down his back, and raised *Stedefæst* high above his head to the Gods in Valhalla. The snow spiralled above him as he screamed a primal scream, his voice echoing throughout the snow-clad forest of Ængla land.

'Wōden!!!!!!!!' Offa roared. Hundreds of proud Angles from across the riverbanks were banging their spears against shields and waving white dragon banners with pride and bouts of chanting. Many drew their seaxes and held them high above their heads like a pack of wolves raising their muzzles to the moon. Offa saw Meaca's sword lying in the snow and bent over to pick it up. He knelt by Meaca's side and wrapped the Saxon's cold fingers around the pommel, securing his place in Valhalla. Though his vision was blurred, Offa saw King Ēadgils and his daughter, Princess Mōdthryth, nod their heads in a show of respect. The ship that had brought Offa to Monster's Gate began to make its way towards him. The dragon-headed prow proudly nodded as it rode the silver water, its red eyes watching Offa the entire time. Offa looked towards the bridge, for his father, hoping he had honoured him and made him proud. Offa couldn't see clearly with his bad eye and the falling snow, but it looked like his father was standing on the edge of the bridge, sword in hand.

'All hæl the Gods!' the King yelled over the chants of the people. 'All hæl King Offa!'

King Wǣrmund threw himself from the bridge and into the freezing river below. His broken body was quickly snatched by the river serpents that took him to the bottom of the Eider and devoured him; flesh, blood and bone. Offa's heart felt as if it had fallen from his chest. He cried out in horror, but it was too late. There was nothing he could do. His father was dead.

Offa's body was broken, beaten and sore, blood poured from his open wounds and he had just witnessed his father plunge to his death. He looked into the crowd of onlookers and noticed Ælfwynn standing amongst them. He felt faint and turned to spew up gouts of blood, before collapsing to the ground. He laid flat on his back, bleeding into the snow and ice. He was breathing heavily, watching snowflakes as they danced through the cold air and made their way towards the ground to rest upon the fallen. For a moment, he was some-place else, at peace, but then suddenly everything became real, for Offa had indeed returned to the realm of the living.

Offa felt every cut and bruise on his body, every broken bone in his shaking hands, the swelling of his eye, the slashes on his face, the cut on his ribs and right arm, the knife-wound to his stomach; and the cut down his spine. Even the previous wounds from Fenris and the troll burned like fire. A mist began to form around him and he could feel his life-force slowly ebbing away. Offa heard his name being called by a thousand men in a faraway hall. Taking deep breaths, he looked up and saw the Valkyrie standing over him, waiting to take his soul to Valhalla, but Offa wasn't ready to leave this life, not yet. With great effort, he struggled back to his feet, took a deep breath and looked the Valkyrie in her pale white eyes.

'*Not... this... night*!' spoke Offa. '*Not... this... night*!'

The Valkyrie stared into Offa's soul before turning away, where she disappeared into the haze of the falling snow. Offa was in a great deal of pain and didn't know if he would live, but nothing could remove the smile from his bloody and bruised face, for he had given the Englisc back their honour, gave them reason to raise their chins, swell with pride, and reminded them of their God-given grace.

Epilogue

400 A. D.
One Year Later
Angeln

It was the twelfth night of Yule, the Winter Solstice, the Night of the Dead. Offa was bathing, being careful of the tender scars that now decorated his flesh. Once dry, he dressed himself in his finest war-splendour. His boots were made from a wolf pelt and his breeches were brown from ochre and wrapped in strips of leather. *Stedefæst* hung from his rune-decorated leather belt. Attached to the front of the belt was a golden purse, decorated with predatory birds and hungry wolves devouring young warriors. His long brown hair was plaited and fastened with leather wrappings. Down his back was the coat of Fenris.

In a separate dwelling, Princess Mōdthryth, accompanied by three fair maidens, bathed inside a small room; the steam rising from her naked flesh. Once cleaned of blood from sacrificed horses, the maidens dressed Mōdthryth in her finest gown, while her mother, the Queen, crowned her with a feather-crested swan-helm.

'Look at you,' spoke the Queen with tears rolling down her flushed cheeks. 'Look how beautiful and splendid you are. You honour us, daughter. This is your destiny. You are a great warrior and have done your family proud. You have taken many lives, but war with the Englisc is now over and a new battle will begin. Your greatest challenge lies before you, in marriage and motherhood. The Gods have blessed you with breasts and a womb. The greatest gift you can give to your people is to bring new life into this world. You are sacrificing your own happiness and marrying someone you do not love, as is your duty as a frithuwebbe - a weaver of the peace. Many women marry boys, Mōdthryth. It is your task to nurture him into becoming the man he needs to be, as it is his task to love you and be there for you and the children you may bare. You must replace the hate inside you and learn to fill your heart with love. I know you loved your brother and feel the need to avenge him, but the greatest way to honour Meaca is to make sure he didn't die in vain. It is your role as Queen of Angeln to weave our two clans together and bring peace to the land, so your children will not need to fight.'

King Offa mounted one of his father's finest black war-steeds. It was draped with white dragon flags upon red backgrounds and its nose was decorated with the rune of Tīw. Offa placed his glittering war-helm over his long brown locks and took a deep breath. The helmet was fashioned by Wēland and was made of iron and tinned copper alloy, complete with crest, cheek-pieces, neck-guard and mask. The mask was decorated with two elongated dragons, both with heads and eyes made of red jewels. One of the dragons formed the crest that ran along the top of the helm and down the face in a straight line, where it met a second dragon. The second dragon had a body and tail that made up the mask's nose and moustache. It also had two long wings that gave the impression of eyebrows, both ending with a boar's head and were lined with red garnets. The entire helmet, including the cheek-pieces, were decorated with warriors in combat and beautiful interlaced-serpents.

Offa looked like a god of war sitting upon his great steed, holding the Englisc banner of the white dragon, whilst making his way towards the gathered crowd. All the while Ælfwynn stood by her brother's and father's side, looking on with glazed eyes.

Accompanying Princess Mōdthryth to the Kingdom of

Angeln was a host of warriors, each decked in battle-gear and adorned with boar-crested helms; some holding the banner of the raven. With them was Mōdthryth's father, King Ēadgils, riding a great war-steed. Hundreds of Saxons, most carrying flaming torches, entered Angeln to the sound of drums and singing. Offa awaited in the courtyard, alongside his kith and kin. King Ēadgils helped Mōdthryth up the small wooden platform where Offa and Osthryth anxiously awaited. Osthryth, her face painted with sacrificial blood, formerly greeted the King and Princess. The King then turned to face Offa.

'My lord, you fought with great honour,' spoke King Ēadgils. 'You gave my son a glorious death. I know the Gods were with you, as they are now with my son in Valhalla.' King Ēadgils held out a hand and looked Offa in the eye. Offa took a deep breath, reached out and shook the King's hand. There was a distant rumble of thunder.

Osthryth turned to the heavens and addressed Frīge, the fairest of the Gods.

'Hæl to thee, Frīge, wife of Wōden, Goddess of love, peace, marriage and fertility,' spoke Osthryth. 'We have gathered here today to ask that you bless the marriage between the peace-weaver, Princess Mōdthryth, daughter to King Ēadgils, and King Offa, son of King Wærmund. We ask that you witness their vows and bless them with long life and many healthy children. And we ask that you help balm the wounds between the Angles and the Saxons, by binding these two young folk in holy marriage.' Osthryth turned to the bride and groom. 'You will now exchange the gifts you have sworn to share.'

After the traditional exchange of gifts, Offa drew *Stedefæst* and presented it to Mōdthryth.

'I give you my ancestral sword,' spoke Offa, 'to save for our sons to have and to use.'

King Ēadgils then presented his daughter with a sword, which she then presented to Offa.

'To keep us safe,' spoke Mōdthryth, 'you must bear a blade. With this sword, keep safe our home and hearth and any children we may be blessed with.'

'This sword,' spoke Osthryth, 'symbolises the father's protection of his daughter being passed to her new husband.' Rings were exchanged and oaths given. 'With the Gods as witness, I now pronounce you husband and wife. You may kiss the bride.'

Reluctantly, and with great discomfort, Offa and Mōdthryth leaned towards each other and kissed on the lips. King Offa and Queen Mōdthryth then turned to face the gathered armies, who raised their swords and spears in celebration of the union they now shared; all but Ælfwynn who stood and watched in silence, a single tear rolling down her cheek.

'All hæl the King and Queen!' the crowd chanted. 'All hæl the King and Queen!'

With hundreds of men and women chanting, Offa pulled a rope that was attached to a pole and raised the banner of the white dragon high above his head. In the distance, standing by the trees, Offa saw Wōden looking on. By his side stood Fenris and upon his shoulder there was a raven. Wōden removed his large grey hat and nodded his head in a show of respect.

Historical Note

Offa: Rise of the Englisc Warrior tells the true story of a young boy's courage over great odds. The English identity wouldn't have survived without him. The story of Offa being a mute, to his ancestry, to the story of Ket and Wīg avenging their father's death, to Offa's challenge against two men at Monster's Gate, and his ultimate victory, is all based on a true story. Offa's bravery was first recorded in the Old English poem, *Wīdsīth*:

'Offa ruled over the Angles,
Alewih over the Danes;
he was the bravest of all these men,
yet they did not outdo Offa in heroic feats.
For Offa, earlier than any of these,
while he was just a boy of thirteen,
won by warfare the greatest of Kingdoms.
No one of such a young age has ever

achieved a greater heroic feat in battle.
With his lone sword, Offa fixed the border
against the Mire-Dwellers,
at Monster's Gate.
Ever since, the Englisc and the Swæfe
have kept it as Offa won it.'

Other historical characters include Ket and Wīg, Earl Frēa-
wine, King Ēadgils, Mōdthryth, Meaca, Wīdsīth, Fólki,
Hemming, King Wærmund, King Bēow, Halfdan, Heorogār,
Hrōthgār and Halga. I've also added the troll from the Old
English epic, *Bēowulf.* Wēland the Smith and Wudga are taken
from various Germanic and Norse legends. It is possible
Wudga may have been a historical character and is also
mentioned in the *Wīdsīth* poem.

In the 13th Century, Danish writer, Saxo Grammaticus,
wrote *The Gesta Danorum* - The Deeds of the Danes,
immortalising Offa and adopting him as a common ancestor to
both the English and the Danes. The story of Offa's time in the
forest is fictional, however, the story of Germanic children
living wild, in the hope of becoming Wolf-Coats and returning
on the eleventh night of Yule, the day before the Winter
Solstice, the traditional Night of the Dead, is based on a real
Anglo-Saxon custom. Offa would have almost certainly gone
through this rite-of-passage.

Along with the Jutes, Saxons, Franks and Frīsians, the
Angles settled Britain in the Fifth and Sixth Centuries and
gave their name to Ængla land, Land of the Angles. Much of
what we know today of native English culture comes from
Roman writings on the tribes of Germania, the ancestors to the
later Anglo-Saxons. But nothing has more education value
than the Old English warrior-poem, *Bēowulf,* the oldest written
story in the English language. Interestingly, *Bēowulf* mentions
Offa by name. The passage is as follows:

'The great Queen Mōdthryth had done many wrongdoings. If
any mortal being dared look her in the face, if an eye not her
lord's stared at her directly, the outcome was sealed: he was

kept bound by shackles and tortured until his soul was forced to flee its skin-shield - death by sword-edge, slash of blade, blood-gush, a dark display of power. Even a Queen of other-worldly beauty must control her greed for blood-lust. A Queen must be a weaver of peace and not punish the innocent with loss of life for imagined insults. But Hemming's kinsman put an end to her ways, and men around the tables spoke of another tale; she was less of a burden to men's lives, less cruel minded, after her tying to the brave Offa, a bride arrayed in her gold finery, given away by a caring father, taken to the young Prince over rolling seas. In days to come, she would grace the gift-stool and grow famous for her good deeds and value of life, her great love of the hero king, who was the best king, it has been said, between the two seas, or anywhere else upon the lands of Middle-earth. Offa was honoured far and wide for his generous ways, his fighting spirit, his far-seeing defence of his homeland, for the wisdom he held.'

Offa and Mōdthryth had a son together named Ængeltheow. Their descendants include King Icel, the last Angle King to rule in Angeln. In the year 510, King Icel led his people to Britain and settled there. Other descendants include Penda, King of Mercia, a great heathen King at a time when Christianity had taken a firm hold over the minds and souls of the English in Britain. And, of course, Offa the Second, despite being a Christian, proudly claimed descent from Offa of Angeln.

Giwis, son of Wīg, was also a real historical character. After Offa's victory over the Saxons at Monster's Gate, it seems likely his kinsman, Giwis, took control of a Saxon clan and gave his name to them. The Gewisse later settled Britain and gave their name to the Kingdom of the Gewisse. Later, to distinguish themselves from other Saxons who had also settled Britain, they called themselves the West Saxons and later changed the name of their Kingdom to Westseaxna Rīce - The Kingdom of Wessex.

The most famous King of Wessex was, of course, Ælfred the Great. In the year 937, Ælfred's grandsons, King Æthelstān and Ēadmund, led the English to victory over the combined armies of the Welsh, Scots, Irish and Vikings, forcing Constantine II, King of Scots, to surrender at the Battle of Brunanburh, finally achieving their grandfather's vision by uniting the Anglo-Saxon Kingdoms as one nation, England, the world's first nation state.

Also available by S. A. Swaffington:

Siegfried the Dragon Slayer

Set in the world of Bēowulf and based upon the 12th Century epic, The Nibelungenlied, and real historical events, comes the legendary story of Siegfried the Dragon Slayer.

436 A. D.

Siegfried is young, handsome, arrogant, brave and ambitious, but after an encounter with a fierce, man-eating dragon, Siegfried becomes invincible - or so he thinks - and longs to become the greatest of heroes. Tired of hunting in the forest and having beautiful maidens throwing themselves at his feet, Siegfried hears of a Princess so beautiful no man is allowed to marry her except for one equal to her brother, King Gunther. Determined to prove himself superior to Gunther, Siegfried challenges the King to a duel, winner takes all. What follows is a series of events that would change the course of European history, leading to the rise of Attila the Hun.

Siegfried the Dragon Slayer is a powerful coming-of-age tale, a story of love, betrayal, murder and revenge; of war and death, but also the struggles of life and the triumph of the human spirit. In a world occupied by Roman armies, powerful women, Orcs, Dwarves, Giants and Dragons, Siegfried only need fear the monsters closest to him.

***

Ket and Wīg: A Song of Vengeance

394 A. D.

Based upon the epic true story, teenage brothers, Ket and Wīg of the Angle Clan, return home to discover their father has been killed by Danish raiders (the Shieldings). After travelling to Daneland, the two of them give false identities and swear oaths to the Danish King, whilst secretly seeking the man who killed their father, in order to take his life.

But before they can bring an end to the blood-feud, they must free their mother from the clutches of the Danes without revealing their true identities, in what may be the greatest tale of vengeance and courage in Anglo-Saxon history. All the while they are caught up in a murderous plot to kill the Danish King, King Bēow Shielding.

***

The Supernatural World of the Anglo-Saxons:
Gods, Folklore and the Pagan Roots of Christmas and
Halloween

The Supernatural World of the Anglo-Saxons is illustrated and unique, covering all aspects of Anglo-Saxon Paganism and folklore, including the Anglo-Saxon calendar. It is written with great knowledge and passion, exploring the Pagan Roots of Christmas and Halloween, of Wōden, the Wild Hunt and all the ancient Yule traditions. The Anglo-Saxons gave their name to England. Learn who they were, what they believed, who their Gods and Goddesses were. Discover the mythological beings found in Bēowulf and all across England's ancient landscape, and learn about the Pagan roots of Morris Dancing, along with other dances and Pagan traditions.

It also includes German folklore such as Holda, Perchta and Krampus.

Printed in Great Britain
by Amazon